Advance Praise for *Breath of Earth*

"Beth Cato's *Breath of Earth* takes the reader to a San Francisco filled with magic, danger, and tragedy. A rare woman with a geomancer's gift, Ingrid Carmichael must fight to retain control of her powers within the city's shifting landscape of political intrigue. And she desperately needs to find a way out of the city if she's going to get to the bottom of a murderous plot, but has no way to know who's friend or foe in a situation where allegiance isn't as straightforward as she's always been taught. All in all, a suspenseful and rousing start to a new series. I look forward to reading the next one."

—J. Kathleen Cheney, author of the Tales of the Golden City

"Beth Cato gives steampunk a magical, global twist in an action-packed adventure that keeps the pages turning in anticipation. And if you don't fall in love with Ingrid Carmichael after reading this, you have no soul."

—Michael J. Martinez, author of *MJ-12: Inception* and *The Daedalus Incident*

"*Breath of Earth* is that rare gem, a thought-provoking, imaginative adventure of the highest order, chock-full of wonder as well as heart-wrenching what-ifs. It's reminiscent of Jules Verne at his best, with brilliant characters who linger in the mind and heart. Bravo!"

—Julie E. Czerneda, author of the Clan Chronicles

"Cato cleverly brings her colorful Barbary Coast–era San Francisco to life, highlighting the neglected perspectives of the outsiders and the dispossessed who made up the majority of its populace."

—*Publishers Weekly*

BREATH OF EARTH

ALSO BY BETH CATO

THE CLOCKWORK DAGGER SERIES

The Clockwork Dagger

The Clockwork Crown

The Deepest Poison: A Short Story

Wings of Sorrow and Bone: A Novella

Final Flight: A Short Story

BREATH OF EARTH

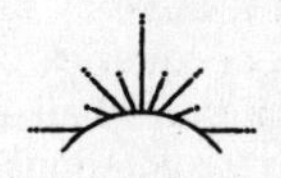

BETH CATO

This book is a work of fiction. The characters, incidents, and dialogue are drawn from the author's imagination and are not to be construed as real. Any resemblance to actual events or persons, living or dead, is entirely coincidental.

 For information address HarperCollins Publishers, 195 Broadway, New York, NY 10007.

HarperCollins books may be purchased for educational, business, or sales promotional use. For information please e-mail the Special Markets Department at SPsales@harpercollins.com.

FIRST EDITION

Harper Voyager and design is a trademark of HarperCollins Publishers L.L.C.

Map and interior book design by Paula Russell Szafranski

Library of Congress Cataloging-in-Publication Data has been applied for.

ISBN 978-0-06-242206-4

16 17 18 19 20 OV/RRD 10 9 8 7 6 5 4 3 2 1

To my agent, Rebecca Strauss

. . . Drop down, fleecy Fog! and hide

Her sceptic sneer, and all her pride.

Wrap her, Fog, in gown and hood

Of her Franciscan Brotherhood.

Hide me her faults, her sin and blame;

With thy gray mantle cloak her shame!

So shall she, cowlèd, sit and pray

Till morning bears her sins away.

Then rise, O fleecy Fog, and raise

The glory of her coming days . . .

—Bret Harte, "San Francisco"

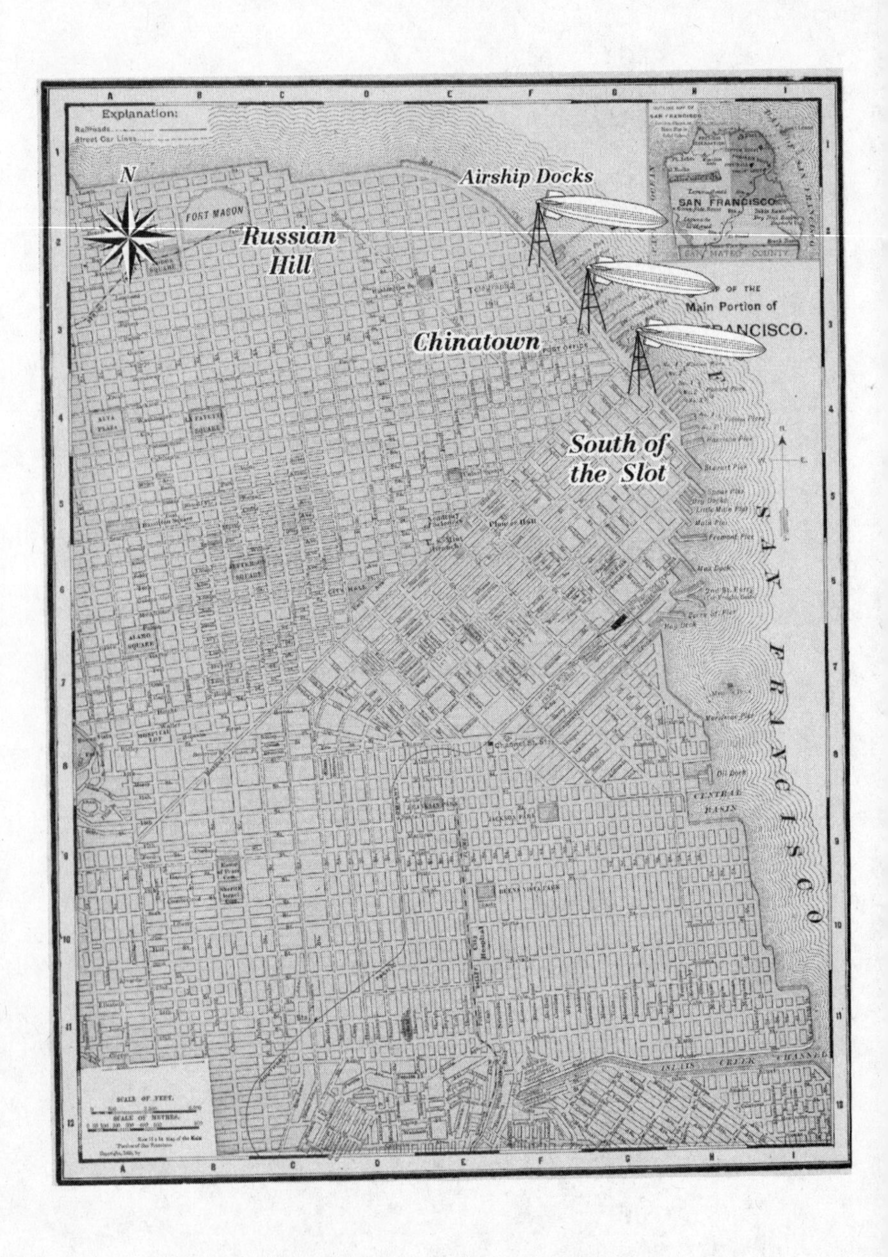

Explanation:
N
Airship Docks
FORT MASON
Russian Hill
Chinatown
South of the Slot
SAN FRANCISCO
SAN MATEO COUNTY
Main Portion of
RANCISCO.
CITY HALL
CENTRAL BASIN
ISLAIS CREEK CHANNEL

CHAPTER 1

APRIL 15, 1906

Ingrid hated her shoes with the same unholy passion she hated corsets, chewing tobacco, and men who clipped their fingernails in public. It wasn't that her shoes were ugly or didn't fit; no, it was the fact she had to wear them at all.

In the meeting chambers of the Earth Wardens Cordilleran Auxiliary, she was the only woman, and the only one in shoes.

The men seated at the table wore fine black suits, most tailored to precision, and a few downright natty. If she glanced beneath the table, though, she would see two rows of white-socked feet.

Cloth fibers conducted the earth's currents best; thick leather or rubberized soles dampened the effect. The wood floor was also an excellent conductor, though plain ground was the best of all. Nearby double doors opened to the back garden. In the event of an earthquake, it would take a mere fifteen seconds for the mob of middle-aged and elderly men to bound outside for direct contact with the soil. Ingrid knew. She had timed the exercise more than once. As personal secretary to Warden Sakaguchi, she performed many vital functions for all five wardens—four in attendance today. A dozen senior adepts occupied the rest of the table.

"Would you like more coffee, Mr. Kealoha?" she whispered as she bent over his shoulder.

The silver-haired Hawaiian warden nodded, his thick fingers already twitching on the mug. In private at Mr. Sakaguchi's house, he would smile at her and call her *hanai* niece, which meant foster niece in Hawaiian. He liked to joke that she could pass as a family member, but it was a dangerous jest. The Japanese overlords of the Hawaiian Islands had forbidden any use of his native language. Even on American soil, as a warden, he could lose his tongue for the offense—especially with a Japanese man as witness.

Mr. Sakaguchi, however, was not like most Japanese.

In any case, a Hawaiian would still be afforded more leniency than anyone from China. To speak any Chinese dialect was sedition and a quick path to a noose.

Around the table, the members' argument on Vesuvius continued as it had for the previous three hours. The ancient volcano's eruptions began on April 6, deluging Naples with hot boulders and toxic plumes of smoke. Mr. Sakaguchi had argued that they should send delegates to assist their European colleagues in quelling the eruption. "They report it's worse than the eruption in year 79 that took Pompeii and Herculaneum," he had said in his quiet way.

Others agreed that the Cordilleran auxiliary should dispatch wardens to Italy. "We have bountiful reserves of kermanite. This is a fine opportunity to harvest energy and fill our crystals. California has been extremely quiet of late," said an adept.

It had gone back and forth from there, how geomancers from all over the world would converge on Naples for the same reason, how those numbers would likely stop the eruption before representatives from San Francisco could even arrive, and on and on. Their words growled and tumbled together like fighting tomcats, and nothing would likely come of it. If Ingrid hazarded a guess at an outcome, a majority would resolve that California should remain their priority, and they'd send along a signed sympathy note to the suffering in Italy.

An ornate shield on the far wall was emblazoned with the Latin motto to guide all geomancers: *PRO POPULO,* "for the people," a reminder that auxiliaries acted as businesses but that their ultimate goal was to use their magic for the welfare of the public.

Magic itself was common throughout San Francisco. Advertisements for Reiki doctors spanned the exposed bricks of skyscrapers, while the wealthy of Nob Hill journeyed to Sunday picnics in wagons teamed by iron-shackled pookas.

Geomancy, however, was a rare skill among people and relied upon kermanite, an even rarer crystal that acted as a supreme electrical capacitor. Wardens absorbed the earth's energy from earthquakes and then channeled their power into kermanite, which was then installed in all varieties of machine. No other battery could keep airships aloft.

Kermanite had stimulated the Roman Empire two millennia past; now it was the manifest destiny of the Unified Pacific to govern the world, thanks in no small part to geomancers.

Ingrid poured coffee into Warden Kealoha's cup. He grunted his gratitude.

A few seats down, Warden Thornton twirled his teacup in his hands, his lips frowning along with his imperial mustache. She caught his eye, but he jerked his head in a negative. He had been brooding for the past few days, probably due to more dire news from India.

She refilled an adept's mug just as he bellowed, "Airship fares will be lower to that part of Europe! No one will want to fly near an eruption! We can charter a flight—"

"And for that very reason, any sensible pilot would charge more," said Senior Warden Antonelli with a blatant eye roll.

The earth shifted. It was the tiniest twitch, like the tickle of a gnat landing on her skin—not even enough to coax a blue sheen to rise from the ground. The men, unshod as they were, showed no response. These were supposed to be the most gifted wardens west of the Rockies. In nearby classrooms, they cultivated the next generation of geomancers, but no barefoot boys trampled onto the lawn to absorb energy either.

Women weren't supposed to be geomancers, but Ingrid was, and a damn better one than any of these men.

Earth magic was considered a hereditary trait among men, like baldness or an affinity for foul-smelling cigars. But then, women weren't supposed to do anything as well as men. No, Ingrid shouldn't be interested in reading, or learning, or anything that—heaven forbid—involved thinking. It was the dawn of the twentieth century, and given her skirts and complexion, she should be content to carry laundry for the rest of her life.

She carried something else instead: power.

The night before, Ingrid had fallen asleep in the first-floor library—Mr. Sakaguchi would launch into a tirade if he knew—and early in the morning an earthquake occurred. The energy coursed through her, hot and heady, like the time one of the adepts kissed her in a broom closet.

Hours later, power continued to course beneath her skin. Here she was, more sensitive to the earth than any warden, even with her feet stuffed in shoes. Shoes!

She squeezed the handle of her pitcher. Beneath the pressure of her anger, the ceramic cracked with a delicate *tink*. A foot nudged her below the table. She knew without looking that it was Mr. Sakaguchi. He would notice, as closely as he watched her.

Ingrid pasted on a smile. Not a very pretty smile, judging by the quick jerk of his head. She tried to dampen her constipated grimace as she softened her grip on the pitcher.

If Ingrid had to be a clandestine geomancer for the rest of her life, she'd probably explode—and to Mr. Sakaguchi's chagrin, that might be literal, and at the cost of several windows or dishware sets. Ingrid ached for the earth's vibrations to break out her skin in goose bumps and create eddies of heat along the length of her legs. She wanted—

"Da-drat," she muttered, almost cursing aloud. She was around old men too often, picking up their language and other bad habits. Heaven forbid she start growing a mustache.

She pulled a rag from her waist to mop up spilled coffee. Mr. Antonelli shot her a frown as he paused while clipping his fingernails. She wished she could stick her tongue out at him, like when she was little, even if the action caused Mama to wallop her upside the head. It had been worth it.

The coffee pitcher was empty; time to resupply. She scooted backward. The men paid her no heed.

Ingrid slipped out into the hallway where her father always stared her down.

"Papa," Ingrid whispered, offering his portrait a nod.

From the time she was very young, her greeting had become part of her daily ritual in the auxiliary. Mama always brought her along for a day of cooking and cleaning; the employment had been the least the auxiliary could do for a widow of their own. Abram Carmichael's aptitude had earned him the title of warden by age thirty and killed him by thirty-five.

Like the other dead men memorialized in portraiture, Papa's gaze was rendered as cold and haughty. Thick black hair had a slight kink to it and spiked out over his ears. His skin had the perfect hue of caramel, his eyes narrowed and bold as if lined by kohl. Broad lips smiled as if he barely contained a secret.

Ingrid's face mirrored Papa's but with long hair, while her body took after Mama's curvaceous form. No matter how Ingrid pinned or lacquered her hair, it defied any attempt at containment. It wasn't at all like Mama's hair had been—as bright and straight as stalks of wheat. Ingrid had always envied that hair.

"Girl!"

She turned toward the voice. One of the older adepts leaned from a classroom. White streaked his mustache, though his hair remained as black as slate.

"We need more kermanite. The classroom safe is out."

"I'll tend to it, sir," she said. She set down the pitcher. The adept granted her an abrupt nod and ducked back inside.

Girl. As if she was permanently a child, not twenty-five years old. "Heaven forbid you take care of anything yourself, or call me by my name after you've known me for a decade," she muttered.

Still, she knew which lesson the class was engaged in, and she hurried down the hall for the students' sake. She rounded the corner and stopped cold.

A stack of desks blocked the entrance to the basement. She huffed in annoyance. Someone chose a fine time to clean out storage. She could go outside and come in through the back of the building, but it would take twice as long, and likely three more adepts would stop her with other urgent requests.

"It's supposed to be blocked for a while yet, Ingrid." A deep baritone voice rang out behind her. An adept hobbled out of a side room. "Thornton is having the basement fumigated. Rats, again. What do you need?"

"The junior classroom ran out of kermanite."

The older man clicked his teeth. "Again? Those quantities should have been checked before the end of day yesterday. Come along. There are some smaller crystals in the senior room. No point in letting those young'uns suffer."

She followed him back up the hall and into an empty classroom. The seniors were sequestered in the library just up the hall as they prepared for the end of term; with tests so soon, all of the students were required to work half days on Sundays through the month. The fact that it was Easter didn't grant them any reprieve.

Ingrid feigned patience as he opened the safe and pulled out a small leather bag. He poured the contents into his palm, counting beneath his breath, and then trickled the crystals back into the pouch.

"Here. I hope no one else comes up short in the next while. Everything else is downstairs." He stooped over as he scribbled the transaction in a ledger.

"Thank you, sir."

He whisked her away with a motion of his hand. "Run along, girl."

She did. Her presence in the meeting would be missed by now, and Mr. Antonelli was sure to give her a gimlet eye as he gestured to an empty mug.

Whimpers and moans welcomed her to the junior classroom. Nearest to the door, a dozen boys half sprawled over their desks. A blue mist overlay their skin, and beneath that mist were the sure signs of power sickness—skin flushed by high fever, thick sweat, dull eyes. The rest of the class stared, their expressions ranging from curiosity to horror. Some of them still showed signs of very recent recovery in their bloodshot eyes. None of these boys was older than ten; the youngest was a pudgy-faced eight.

"There you are!" The teacher scowled, as if it were Ingrid's fault he'd been so inept with his accounting. Biting her lip, she held out the bag. He snatched it from her fingertips.

The chalkboard laid out the terminology of the lesson, one Ingrid had seen taught dozens of times: hyperthermia, hypothermia, and the quick timeline to a geomancer's death. These young boys experienced the hard lesson of hyperthermia. The last earthquake noticeable by the wardens had taken place three days before. These students had been directly exposed to the current and hadn't been allowed access to any kermanite. As a result, they spent the past few days bed-bound in misery as though gripped by influenza.

Thank God none of them were as sensitive as Ingrid. Another direct tremor would cause their temperatures to spike even more, and could even lead to death.

The teacher adept pressed a piece of kermanite to a boy's skin. He gasped at the contact. Blue mist eddied over his body, the color evaporating as it was pulled inside the rock.

If she could see the kermanite in the adept's hand, the clear crystal would be filling with a permanent smoky swirl. It took a trained mechanic to rig an electrical current to tap the trapped magic as a battery. When the energy within was exhausted, a crystal turned dull and dark. Once that happened, kermanite became a useless rock.

The young boy sat up straighter. "Thank you, sir," he whispered, voice still ragged. It would take him hours to fully recover.

Ingrid looked away, that familiar anger heavy in her chest. Wardens and boys in training carried kermanite openly from watch fobs and cuff links, or most any other accessory where stones could be easily switched out once they were full.

She had to be far more subtle. Her kermanite chunks clinked together in her dress pocket. She had to take care not to touch them today, or the energy she held would be siphoned away.

Ingrid loved this slight flush of power, because that's what it was—power. It sizzled just beneath her skin, intoxicated her with how it prickled at her nerves. Certainly, if she absorbed any more energy, she'd use the kermanite. She didn't want to feel sick, though she could hold much more power than these boys, or even the wardens. Mr. Sakaguchi said she took after Papa—that she stored power like a bank vault, while most everyone else had the capacity of a private safe.

When it came to her natural skill, Ingrid often regarded herself as a rare fantastic or yokai—not like garden ornamentals such as the kappas or naiads sold to the stuffed shirts on Market Street—but like the geomantic Hidden Ones Mr. Sakaguchi so loved to research. She was a creature relegated to idle fancy and obscure mythology, and aggravating shoes.

As she neared the meeting room, she heard the sound of chairs scuffing against the wood slat floor. The door opened and voices rose in volume. Warden Thornton exited first, one hand pressed to his gut while the other held a folded newspaper to his chest.

"My pardon," he said, moaning. "I think—I do believe I'm getting ill. Maybe the same thing as Mr. Calhoun."

"Oh dear," Ingrid said. Warden Calhoun had come down sick quite suddenly the day before, which had been quite a surprise considering he was hale and active in the way of Theodore Roosevelt. "Here, Mr. Thornton. I'll help you to the door and fetch a cab."

"Thank you, child." He moaned again. Mr. Thornton wasn't deathly pale as Mr. Calhoun had been, but his red eyes and shaky hands weren't normal. He was an experienced warden, so this certainly wasn't power sickness.

They passed the open door to the library. Inside, the seniors—teenagers—muttered as they stared at open texts on a table. Auxiliaries functioned like boarding schools for those gifted with geomancy, with the Cordilleran the largest in the country. Boys from age six through twenty resided in dormitories just above. During the day, they attended classes for their general education, and supplemented that with the basics of geomancy. Ingrid had absorbed their lessons as she ferried coal or scrubbed floors. Mr. Sakaguchi taught her more during evening tutorial sessions.

Mr. Thornton released a shaky breath. He stepped alongside her and fumbled open his watch. His fingers could barely manage the case. "Time. Such a peculiar thing. Passes so slowly, and then so fast." His British accent lightened the words as he looked out the windows overlooking the street.

Ingrid nodded, all the more certain the man was coming down with a genuine fever.

Mr. Thornton, like his ill comrade Mr. Calhoun, was from Britannia and had spent many years in India. The Cordilleran Auxiliary took pride in the acquisition of both experienced wardens—two priceless jewels thieved from the Unified Pacific's greatest rival. The Chinese had once held that distinction.

Ingrid followed Mr. Thornton's gaze and frowned. A laundry truck idled at the curb. Its canvas cover advertised a laundry company in Chinatown. "Odd. Laundry day is tomorrow."

"Oh, is it?" He sat on a bench in the genkan and handed off the newspaper to her. The small side room was modeled on Japanese households and featured cubbies where men and boys stored their shoes. The space served a practical purpose in the auxiliary, but like many other Japanese customs, had become quite commonplace in San Francisco and the rest of the country. Ingrid retrieved his shoes from the wardens' getabako and set them by his feet. She quickly replaced her house shoes with a thicker-soled set to go outside.

As he tied his laces, she donned a hat and headed out to the street. The laundry truck had departed, but plenty of other vehicles had taken its place. The auxiliary's stately brick building faced Battery Street. "This is a city built by geomancers, as surely as if we carried every brick," Mr. Sakaguchi had commented more than once. Tony buildings stretched ten to twenty stories high—such height would have been foolhardy without the presence of the wardens and adepts to siphon from the earth. It created a fine cycle of business. Even Mayor Butterfield had once proclaimed that San Francisco prospered due to the grace of God, the Gold Rush, and geomancy.

The thoroughfare was busy for a late Sunday morning, but by the finery of passersby, it seemed nearby churches had just finished their Easter services. Out of sight, a cable car chimed as it traveled along Clay Street. The stench of manure, autocar exhaust, and oil mingled like a rancid soup. A messenger bicyclist squealed to a stop at the steps, and leaning his transport against the stone railing, bounded toward the door.

Ingrid skimmed the northbound traffic. Mr. Thornton joined her.

"Nothing yet?" he wheezed.

"No." She glanced at the newspaper in her hand. "I should give this back to you. Is there news about India, sir?"

He straightened as if he was suddenly well, his eyes narrowing. "Here? Americans caring about that sort of news?" He almost shoved the paper in her face. "Page thirteen. About a half inch of a column. Another twenty thousand estimated dead in hellfire bombardments in Calcutta over the past two months."

"I'm sorry, sir," she said softly. News of Japan and China dominated the headlines. The rebellion in India was Britannia's concern, and most in America didn't really care how many died on either side there so long as it kept Britain busy. Only horrific killings by the modern incarnation of Thuggees seemed to get special attention. Ingrid often heard young boys in the auxiliary excitedly discussing the gruesome executions said to be committed in the name of Kali.

"Sorry. Yes, well." He stopped himself, shaking his head. He glanced at his watch again and pressed a fist to his stomach.

Since Mrs. Thornton's passing, it seemed Mr. Thornton took all happenings in India as a personal affront. He'd called the place home for much of his life, and now its cities and jungles were being rendered to ash as the rebellion continued.

Ingrid spied a red flag on a car and waved. The cab puttered their way.

She held the door wide as Mr. Thornton stepped inside. The light vehicle lurched and squawked as he settled in. As she swung the door closed, he held out a hand to halt her.

"I'm sorry, Miss Carmichael," he said, his voice tremulous. She gawked at him. Mr. Thornton had never regarded her with as much arrogance as other men, nor had he ever been friendly. "You—you and your mother—have always been so kind to me. I still remember well how you tended to my wife at the end."

Mrs. Thornton had always been a pleasant soul, her dark cheeks rosy and her saris bright against the gloom of fog. Influenza took her quite quickly not long before Mama died.

"It was only right, sir," Ingrid said.

Mr. Thornton flinched, his fist again curling against his gut.

"I'm sure Mr. Sakaguchi will ring you later to check in. I hope you feel better quickly, sir!"

She shut the door with a hollow metal click. The cab pulled away from the curb. The foulness of manure slapped her nostrils as the wheels rolled through fresh nuggets. Several men shoved past her, one granting her enough warning to snap, "Move, girl."

She hopped up the stairs, that familiar annoyance prickling at her chest. The messenger boy exited the front door and almost cleared the whole staircase in a leap.

"Miss! Pardon me, miss?"

Ingrid turned. A man stood on the first step, his body lean beneath a draped brown leather coat. He wasn't slender in a fragile way, not like some men who could be bowled over by a stiff bay wind. Chestnut hair with a slight wave was cropped to a few inches in length, and framed a face with a rather angular nose. He stared back at her through a pair of pince-nez glasses and smiled. Not a leer, not the stiff smile of someone exercising their dominion over her. No, he looked on her with genuine pleasantness.

She cleared her throat. "Yes, sir? Can I help you?"

"You work for the auxiliary, miss?" He doffed a brown derby hat that looked like it had been sat on more than once. Despite being popped back into place, little ridges marred the top of the dome.

"I do, sir. I'm a secretary for Warden Sakaguchi, but I help the entire board."

"The name's Cypress Jennings, miss, and Mr. Thornton expected me to call on him today about the private sale of some kermanite. He said he'd be in meetings and wasn't sure about a particularly good time?" A southern accent, luscious as sorghum, flavored his words.

"Oh. Yes. I'm sorry, sir. The board just adjourned for a break, but Mr. Thornton's come down ill. He left not a moment ago."

The brightness in his face dimmed. Ingrid wished she could tell him to buy from Mr. Sakaguchi or Mr. Kealoha, but he'd already initiated business with Mr. Thornton. It'd be rude to poach away a customer.

"You might try calling on him at home later," she said. "Maybe he'll feel better. I can write his address for you—"

"Don't fuss over it, miss. I can look him up. I do hope I can buy that kermanite today, though, before my business partner goes apoplectic."

"I hope you can make the purchase, too."

They stared at each other, the silence suddenly drawn out and awkward. He scratched at his chin, his lips working like he wanted to say something more.

"I had best get back to work, sir," Ingrid said, lowering her eyes as she knew was proper.

"Certainly, miss. Thank you kindly for your time."

What a nice man! She slipped back inside the auxiliary and shut the big door behind her, then paused to lean on it. She felt the sudden melodramatic need to fan herself, and almost giggled out loud. Good grief, but that man's accent alone could sweeten a pitcher of tea. She set her hat on its hook and switched shoes.

Wardens and adepts cluttered the hall, hunkered down in their cliques. She passed by, mostly ignored. One man spat a juicy wad of tobacco into an ornate copper spittoon. Mr. Sakaguchi was nowhere in sight, so she crossed the hallway and knocked on a wooden door. At the sound of his voice, she entered the office.

He stood in front of a furnace along the back wall. Dark cherry paneling and overloaded bookshelves created a claustrophobic cave. As she walked toward him, he shut the small iron door of the furnace. Odd; he used to always burn the notes he received from Theodore Roosevelt in that exact manner, but their friendship had been fractured for several months now. More likely, he needed to stoke the fire. Ingrid certainly hadn't been in there to tend it.

Instead, she contained lingering warmth from both the earth's power and her brief yet pleasant interaction with that man on the steps.

She fought the urge to smile too broadly, which would only invite nosiness. Mr. Sakaguchi had prodded her a bit too much of late. *You need more friends your own age. You are too dependent on Lee. You need a life outside the auxiliary.*

A life, where? Ingrid loved Mr. Sakaguchi dearly, but sometimes her ojisan seemed to exist in a world of delightful ignorance where he had achieved enlightenment and expected everyone else to be on the cusp of it as well.

He tended to ignore the fact that, at a glance, most people assumed Ingrid to be an immigrant and likely illiterate or ignorant of English and Japanese. She didn't fit in anywhere. Too educated to mingle with house staff in the off hours, too low in class to blend with the elite society with whom Mr. Sakaguchi often did business. Her age classified her as doomed to spinsterhood. Not to mention the complication of her magic.

As for her dependence on Lee, well, that wasn't about to change. She loved him like a little brother. It didn't matter a whit to her that he was Chinese and regarded with contempt by much of society.

Ingrid stopped in the middle of the room. To her surprise, Mr. Sakaguchi's brows were drawn together, his expression sober.

"Is there bad news?" she asked, again thinking of Mr. Roosevelt.

"Perhaps." He stood by his desk with his hands clasped at his back. "We may have company soon." By his expression, these guests were about as welcome as a kraken at a ship's christening.

"Should I send a note along to the house, ask Jiao to prepare dinner or rooms?"

"No. I don't think that will be necessary." Mr. Sakaguchi sighed and looked to the clock on his desk. "At least this matter of Vesuvius will conclude soon, my efforts as ineffectual as ever."

Ingrid frowned. It wasn't like him to be this grim. What sort of horrid company were they expecting? She pivoted to lock the door, then walked to the Victor Graphophone on the cramped bookshelf. She thumbed through the sleeved record albums stacked to one side.

"Ingrid, the meeting will commence in minutes—"

She set the record on the spindle and fastened it into place. A tug of the lever and the black disc began to spin. She set the needle on the outer edge of the album. Static screeched through the horn and then the twanged notes of the shamisen rang through. The three-stringed instrument resembled an American banjo, and here it played a short, simple melody in repetition for some thirty minutes. Not that she would need to play the album for that long.

"Then we have enough time for this. Here," she said, motioning to the rug.

He didn't look enthusiastic, but he still walked over and lowered himself to the floor.

She knelt to face him and tilted an ear toward the Graphophone, her hands poised in midair. Simultaneously, she and Mr. Sakaguchi clapped hands to a beat of three. She quickly moved her hands to make two Vs atop her head—fox ears—while at the same time Mr. Sakaguchi briefly rested his hands on his lap.

Ingrid cackled. She won that round—a kitsune's magic could bewitch a chief. Mr. Sakaguchi's face twitched as they began the clapping again. This time, she positioned her hands as if on a rifle, with her right hand on a trigger and her left extended like the barrel of a gun. Mr. Sakaguchi made fox ears. The hunter's gun could kill the kitsune. She won again.

"At least try," she teased.

He did—the next round, he laid his hands on his lap again to symbolize the role of the chief, outranking Ingrid's hand motion of the hunter with a gun.

The twanged music played on as they continued. A regular game of kitsune-ken ended after a player won thrice, but Ingrid didn't care about the numbers. They found the rhythm. Ingrid made fox ears and stuck out her tongue. Mr. Sakaguchi burst out laughing.

His next motion of the rifle turned into wiggling fingers as if he threatened to tickle her like when she was a little girl—an act that used to make her screech and roll with giggles without a hand being laid on her.

Kitsune-ken had been played for centuries in Japan along with a number of other hand-gesture games. This one was their favorite, though, because it was about a fantastic. Kitsune were powerful fox spirits known for their wiles and shapeshifting. Something about the game—about play-acting a being of power—inspired Ingrid to puff her cheeks, blow raspberries, and turn her pointy fox ears into arm-long ears like a donkey.

Happy tears streamed down Mr. Sakaguchi's cheeks. He gasped for breath as he doubled over in deep laughter. Cozy warmth filled Ingrid's chest as she looked on him. This was how Mr. Sakaguchi should be—his spirit buoyant, eyes bright, a smile branded on his lips, even if it was to her aggravation.

A bell chimed in the hallway; time for the meeting to resume. She turned off the Graphophone.

Mr. Sakaguchi wiped his cheeks with his sleeve. A few final laughs wheezed from him as he stood. "Well. I believe you won, Ingrid."

"I wasn't keeping score."

"I wasn't either, but you still won."

They entered the hallway as some adepts rushed by. She glanced back at him. "If you need another reason to cheer up, remember that *Lincoln* premieres the day after tomorrow."

She was puzzled when his smile diminished. "I do hope I can still attend."

"Of course you can attend! There's no reason for you to be called away. You'll even have protesters lined up outside the Damcyan Theatre." At that reminder, he grinned.

Mr. Sakaguchi was a fiend for opera, and had been delighted that a company dared to perform *Lincoln* in San Francisco. It had outraged critics for a decade with the parallels it drew between Lincoln's Emancipation Proclamation and his late-life work on behalf of the Chinese in America. The fact that Mr. Sakaguchi would attend such a pro-Chinese—and therefore anti-Japanese—work might raise a few eyebrows, but he had a reputation for attending every operatic performance in the city. He was also known to bring his secretary in tow so she could hold calling cards on his behalf.

Ingrid greatly enjoyed the outings. She could never dress like the other women in their furs, pearls, and masterful hats, but there was still something electric about the place. Plus, it was a delight to share in something that Mr. Sakaguchi adored.

Mr. Sakaguchi paused at the table outside the boardroom and picked up Ingrid's white pitcher.

"At least it's a small crack this time," he said in a conspiratorial whisper. "Not like that Wedgwood you shattered. Your warfare on dishware continues."

"Maybe I should do something more rewarding than handle dishes all day."

"You shouldn't hold power like that. You'll make yourself sick."

"I doubt I'm even running a fever." A lie. A small one. But her fever was under a hundred.

"Don't you have kermanite?"

"I'm fine. I haven't held this power for long, just since this morning." She noted the brief widening of his eyes as he took in that information. He hadn't felt the tremor at dawn, then. "And of course I have kermanite. I've been extra careful not to touch it."

Mr. Sakaguchi pursed his lips in disapproval. Here came the lecture. "Now, Ingrid, you know better—"

She felt the sudden shift of matter beneath her. Pressure. Raw power. Surging upward. Heat. In that space of two seconds, she threw herself over Mr. Sakaguchi, catching the briefest glimpse of shock on his face as the hallway shattered around them.

CHAPTER 2

The world exploded. Bricks, wood, and heat—searing pain that unfurled from her heart and roared through her extremities. Death. Fire. Agony evoked the worst descriptions of the hellfire of Atlanta or Charleston, but in the space of a gasp, the pain was gone. The sudden cacophony silenced, darkness falling over them in a suffocating quilt. Ingrid's ragged breaths echoed. The solidness of Mr. Sakaguchi's shoulder pressed against her chest. That's when she noticed her arm lifted above, her palm braced against something. She wiggled her fingers, just a tiny bit. The surface felt like glass heated by afternoon sunshine.

Heat. The tingle of power had evaporated from her skin. That's what she had felt—she had used her reserves to do this. It had never poured from her before, not like this, but then it never had cause to.

"Are you hurt?" Mr. Sakaguchi's voice was muffled in their tight confines.

"No. I don't think so." Her voice sounded raw and strange to her own ears. "You?"

"I'm unharmed."

"What happened?"

"Pardon me while I reach into my pocket." He shifted beneath her. Leave it to Mr. Sakaguchi to employ fine manners even in these circumstances.

Something clicked and a beam of soft blue light sliced the darkness and burned her eyes. He'd pulled out his pocket-sized kermanite lantern. The light angled upward to reveal sand of all shades pressed against a translucent bowl, along with larger debris—bricks, splintered boards, nails. An adult hand. Fingers limp and curled, as if reaching for a pencil. At the wrist a cuff link of kermanite glinted, still brilliant in its clarity, but there was only a scant inch of sleeve cloth. Where the forearm should be, white bone jabbed against a knob of brick. Ingrid stared, blinking, wondering if she could identify the hand's owner, and then realized anew that it was a hand. There. By itself.

"Oh God," she whispered.

Whatever just happened had been nothing like a full earthquake that rippled and rolled through soil. It should have felt like tugging on a taut string and knowing it stretched far beyond sight.

"This was too immediate, too abrupt," she said. "Like an explosion."

"An explosion. Yes."

The light aimed downward. The wooden floor was gone, replaced by gray tiles—the basement floor. They had fallen and she didn't even remember the sensation. Her only thought had been to grab Mr. Sakaguchi and keep him safe.

His knuckles rapped on the ground beneath them. It echoed and clinked like glass, not sounding at all like tile. Sweat dribbled from the end of her nose and created a dark splotch on his suit.

"You seem to have created a bubble around us. Very nice work."

"I try." The tremble in her voice ruined the attempt at flippancy.

"I never even saw your father do anything like this."

"I decided that if I'm going to do the impossible, I should make it unique. No copying." She took in a rattling breath. Her lungs felt strained, tight. "The air . . . ?"

"We're trapped in here with a limited supply, it seems. I don't think it will last us long."

"Oh." A pause. "I suppose I should remedy that next time. Make a bigger bubble."

"Yes." He craned his head to look up, frowning all the while. "It's always good to plan ahead for the next time we're buried like this."

Ingrid took in a shallower breath to calm herself. A hundred questions raced through her mind. How had she done this? What had exploded? Her power had always been such a fickle thing—as if its existence wasn't baffling enough. Very few geomancers could see the blue aura of the earth's power on the ground or in people, and no other geomancer could expel energy the way she could; not now, not in the histories. Everyone else took in the magic of the earth, could contain it for a time, and then poured it into kermanite.

Ingrid connected with the earth. That was the simplest way to state it. Now that connection had saved their lives, or at least extended them for a few minutes.

"You're going to have to open this bubble soon," Mr. Sakaguchi said. His voice was mild as always. In all her life, Ingrid had seen his veneer completely break only once, when Mama died. Apparently, exploding buildings and disembodied hands weren't of that caliber. "And don't look at me that way, Ing-chan. You made this field around us. You can unmake it."

"I can't hear anyone or anything up there. We must have two floors' worth of debris over us. If that bubble's gone, we'll be crushed to death."

And that hand would drop directly on her shoulder. Somehow, that seemed far worse than blades of wood and heavy bricks.

"Death by oxygen deprivation might be gentler, true, but sometimes you must take a risk. Sometimes you must fight."

Ingrid stared up at her hand where it was braced against the top of the bubble. If they were huddled on the basement floor, how would anyone find them?

Condensation beads formed across the top of the shield. Closing her eyes, she drew inward, searching for any remnants of energy. Heat fluttered through her chest, like the last swirl of water as it drained from a bathtub. Would that power be adequate? Sweat coursed along her arm.

Mr. Sakaguchi was right. They couldn't go out without a fight.

"I'm going to try something," she said.

"You'll succeed."

"Ojisan, no. Not the optimism like that, not now." Not like when Mama was dying, when he insisted everything would be fine.

"You prefer I be a pessimist? Very well. We may die in the next few minutes, but since we should already be dead, I'm grateful for these extra minutes we've had together."

"You're a lousy pessimist."

"I've been accused of worse," he said, then paused. "Ingrid, I know I'm not forthright with my emotions. Your mother's passing . . . I was never as open with her as I should have been. I regret that now. I regret many things."

"Ojisan . . ."

"I love you, Ingrid. I never expected to have children or a family, not with my wandering life as a warden, but I've watched you grow from a young child to a beautiful young woman. You are, in all ways but blood, my daughter."

Tears burned in her eyes. "I love you, too, Mr. Sakaguchi. I never knew Papa. I never needed to. I always had you."

She heard the hitch in his breath, that rare sound that showed how close he was to losing all composure. "I fear I've been selfish in keeping you here with me. I should have sent you away."

"Away? Where? I don't understand."

"How is your skin feeling?"

"Mr. Sakaguchi! You can't change the subject like that! Why would you send me away?"

"Answer me, Ingrid. How much energy do you hold?"

Mr. Sakaguchi couldn't see the auras of geomancers who held magic. Very few had that knack—no others in the Cordilleran Auxiliary, thank God. When any such wardens came to town, she had been housebound as a precaution.

She swallowed down her frustration. "I'm still holding some power, but it's dwindling."

She felt his body move as he nodded slightly. "If we wait much longer, you'll succumb to hypothermia."

The opposite extreme of what the students had endured earlier. Most geomancers only expelled the earth's energy into kermanite. A rare few—usually those who saw auras—poured out their very life force if they stayed in contact with large kermanite for too long. The consequences of that were the same as standard hypothermia, as if someone succumbed to snow or cold water: confusion, a drop in heart rate and body temperature, and death.

"Our options are suffocation, hypothermia, or to be crushed? Can we get a fourth, better choice?" she asked.

"If an earthquake strikes us down here, we won't have any means to disrupt contact, so we could both die of hyperthermia."

Ingrid half choked on a laugh. Her lungs felt tight in the swampy air. "And then be crushed."

"I think our need for oxygen is the most dire. Act now, Ingrid. You can do this."

Whether she could or not, by God, she had to try. Taking a shallow but long breath, Ingrid stood with her hand still straight up. Heat flowed up her arm and burned through her fingertips. An airy sensation filled her skull as a sudden chill quaked through her. She ground her teeth together to prevent them from chattering.

Above, debris rattled and roared as it shifted. The shape of the bubble had changed with the contour of her body, creating a tall cone. Mr. Sakaguchi scrambled to his feet. They were of almost equal height. Tears burned in her eyes as he hugged her. She wrapped her free arm around him and squeezed.

"We're not dead yet," she whispered.

"Maybe today is our lucky day." He craned up his head. "Light."

A pencil-thin beam of honest-to-goodness sunlight pierced the mound of debris over them. Seeing a sunbeam on a foggy spring day often felt as precious as encountering a unicorn, but at this moment it was like God ripped a hole through the clouds, just to shine down on them.

But they were still heavily buried by boards and pipes and what looked to be slats of the roof. The hand was gone, fallen to one side. Blood stained the glasslike sheen.

"Anyone there?" A male voice boomed from somewhere close.

She opened her mouth to yell back. Mr. Sakaguchi squeezed her forearm.

"You have to open the bubble now, before they find us."

"What would really happen if they knew what I could do?"

"You don't want to know." He said this with a strange tremble in his voice, as if he knew the answer all too well.

"If I drop this bubble, we could still be crushed or killed."

"Yes, but we can stand now, and we're that much closer to the top. Ingrid . . ." He hesitated. "I don't want you to be hurt."

"Mr. Sakaguchi, you and Mama have always fussed over me too much. I know you say I can't handle pain, but I can deal with—"

She screeched in shock as Mr. Sakaguchi grabbed her around the waist and heaved her toward the light. Her upheld arm shoved through more debris until her focus slipped. Everything slid inward with a horrible rumble. Her gasp cut short as dust and fibers clogged her throat. Pressure crushed her. Not the comforting waves that arose from the earth, but painful weight squeezing and stabbing her entire body.

"Help!" Her cry bounced and echoed back at her. "Help! Ojisan, are you okay?" She didn't care if anyone heard the familial term, not now.

She couldn't hear a reply, but his hand squeezed her leg.

"Help! Help!" Ingrid screamed with renewed vigor. Her right arm was still above her head, and she clawed at the slats. Grit burned her eyes and dusted her tongue. Raw pain radiated from her lower back, her thigh, her ribs. She still felt strangely cold, but from those points of agony, she recognized the heat of blood. The hole above opened a wee bit more. "Help! Down here!"

A small earthquake shivered through the wreckage. Blue flared around her for a scant second. Debris rumbled. She took in the heat as dread twisted her stomach. God, don't let a major earthquake hit now, not with the two of them and every other warden and student trapped in rubble.

"Hey! Hey!" The crunch of footsteps. A shadow, blocking the light. "We got one over here, alive! A woman!"

"Two of us!" Ingrid shouted. She could only see through slits; her eyes felt like they contained ground glass. Maybe they did. "Warden Sakaguchi's here, too! Alive!"

"Sakaguchi! Sir! Sakaguchi's over here!" the man yelled.

"They're coming," she yelled down to him. "Hold on." Her voice sounded so strange, her throat tight with pain.

More male voices, along with more crunches and clatter. Light dawned over her. Everything became a chaotic blur. Her lungs sucked in full breaths. Iron-strong hands gripped her arm.

"Don't pull me out yet! Everything will fall in on Mr. Sakaguchi," she cried.

"Where is he?" someone asked.

"Down by my legs. We were standing together when—when everything happened. I . . . I managed to climb up."

"Lieutenant, you and the rest move this beam. Start a line to carry this debris to the street. We need this warden alive."

Ingrid waited, her shoulders exposed to the air. Reality seemed to waver around her like a heat mirage, and she wasn't quite sure of the passage of time. Bit by bit, the weight against her vanished. The bodies around her flashed like shadows behind a campfire, and then hands grabbed hold of her again, and this time they pulled her out. Reality clarified itself as a hot lance of pain seared her backside. Someone screamed. She lay atop the rubble, acutely aware of pebbles and chunks of bricks grinding into the softness of her palms.

The earth moved once more.

The pressure wave was small, almost gentle. She braced herself, wondering if the building would swallow her again. The ruins shifted, but not much. Maybe the debris had already compacted. She absorbed the lap of heat, the risk of hypothermia fully gone, and blinked the grit from her eyes.

"Get her to the doctor." The commanding voice came from directly above.

"Mr. Sakaguchi?" she asked.

"We can see him. He's alive and almost out."

"Thank you. Thank God," Ingrid said. She looked up to see a pant leg of dark blue with gold trim down the calf.

They'd been rescued by the Unified Pacific's American Army & Airship Corps.

Located a block away from the auxiliary, Dr. Hatsumi's Reiki practice had been familiar to Ingrid for as long as she could remember. "You can't handle pain well," Mama always said, and rushed Ingrid there for everything from sliced fingertips to digestive irregularities.

Never had a visit been as urgent as this, though, nor had soldiers ever stood guard outside the door. She lay on her belly, lip pinched between her teeth, as the doctor muttered in Japanese. He didn't seem to consider or care that she could understand his gripes about filthy American soldiers taking over his shop, but he always conducted his business with brusqueness.

An assistant poured fresh seeds into the bin. Mustiness fogged the air. Dr. Hatsumi began work on Ingrid.

Reiki magic was one of Japan's many contributions to everyday American life. Its culture had infused society since the Unified Pacific had formed some forty years before during the brief War Between the States. Back then, Japanese airship technology had granted Union forces a quick victory over the Confederacy. The partnership had only grown stronger in recent years. Over a million Japanese citizens—mostly engineers of unparalleled skill—had moved to America's shores, though their native isles still abounded with billions of people in need of land. Hence the need to clear China for settlement.

In truth, America's contributions were milder, but vital—California contained kermanite, and the nation offered bountiful young men to serve in the Unified Pacific's armed forces.

With sinuous motions, the Reiki doctor drew inherent life from the seeds and directed energy into Ingrid's ki. Seeing auras was a rare skill for geomancers, but all Reiki doctors were said to see colors as they tugged on strings of life.

Ingrid gripped the thin mat on the wooden platform. Little earthquakes had continued since she was pulled from the rubble. A gauzy blue fog drifted across the floor. Ingrid looked to the pendulum light overhead and noted a smidgen of sway. With so many geomancers nearby, it was rare for a trembler to cause a physical reaction.

Pain spiked in her back again, and she muffled a yelp.

She couldn't see the magic of Reiki, but she felt it like a dry electric spark in the air. No power existed in a vacuum. Reiki relied on the power of life to heal life, just as any geomancer relied on the roiling strength of the earth. Hatsumi was properly licensed, and used seeds and plants. Less reputable practitioners were more potent and bloody, and yanked life from chickens, dogs, cats, or even worse, other humans. Willing or otherwise.

"Still!" Dr. Hatsumi barked. His accent was thick, even in one word. Quite different from Mr. Sakaguchi, who had an almost aristocratic British lilt from his early years as a warden in Europe.

Ingrid pressed herself impossibly deeper into the mat. Cool tendrils radiated from the cut in her back. The wound smarted something fierce.

The sight of the auxiliary had hurt far more than her injury. Its three floors had dropped into the basement, creating a mound that seemed scarcely higher than the street. She knew that the ground beneath the building and much of downtown San Francisco was considered "made," filled in with old rubble and other dirt to stabilize it enough to build on. In an earthquake zone, that generally wasn't wise, as a severe tremor could liquefy the unstable ground. However, that also meant that the earth was a potent conductor—ideal for the wardens, and for the boys in training.

With wardens present, made ground was safe. The city existed as it did because of the auxiliary.

The doctor's grunt signaled that her time on the table was done. She pushed herself upright, a blanket pressed against her chest, but the two men had already filed out and shut the door behind them. Her movement sent a mild stab of pain through her back. Reiki by plants didn't heal wounds completely, but it quickened the process. Within a few days, she expected to feel normal. Normal as one could be, after being buried alive.

She shuddered at the memory. Whose hand had been there, draped above her bubble? Had it belonged to a warden or an adept? She shoved the terrible image from her mind.

The earth shivered again as her feet met the blue-fogged ground. Warmth flooded her feet, her legs, and whirled into a cozy knot in her torso. She welcomed the heat, her eyes closing briefly in bliss. Within seconds, the trembling stopped.

Her clothes were bloodied and torn, but decent enough for the trek home. She certainly had nothing to be ashamed of, surviving that. She had just finished dressing when a heavy knock shuddered through the door.

"Yes?" she called.

"Captain Sutcliff will talk to you." No request, no niceties about it.

Ingrid opened the door. Despite her having shaken out her dress, every rustle of fabric emitted a cloud of dust. The soldier in the hallway gawked, his gaze unable to surmount her chest.

Indignation caused absorbed energy to flare to her skin. The current fashion was Orientalist and less formfitting, but Ingrid's dress was weighted by plastered layers of muck. Not that the dress's cut did much to hide her form anyway. Her body had the sensuous curves of the California foothills, her waist naturally defined as if she wore an antiquated corset.

"If you're done leering, sir," she said coolly, "I can speak with the captain now."

Surprised anger furrowed his brows as he turned away. She could read his expression—*you're not supposed to talk back to me.* She stood straighter, chin lifted as she followed him into the front parlor.

Mr. Sakaguchi and several soldiers awaited her. The doctor and his staff had vanished. Shades covered the windows.

"Miss Carmichael." Mr. Sakaguchi's smile tugged at new scabs across his cheeks and jaw. His suit jacket was gone, the white shirt blotched in black, brown, and flares of red. His vest, always prim and perfectly ironed, was shredded in spots as though a kitten—no, a Sierran wyvern—had used it as a scratching post.

"How are you feeling?" Mr. Sakaguchi asked. He didn't glow blue. He must have already funneled energy from the recent quakes into his kermanite.

"Much better now, thank you, Mr. Sakaguchi," she murmured. "And you, sir?"

"Well enough." He nodded to the man beside him. "This is Captain Sutcliff, newly arrived in the city. Captain, this is my secretary whom I was just telling you about."

Captain Sutcliff could have worn sackcloth and she would have known him for a soldier. His posture was rigid, as if his spine were bolted to a metal pole. Measured calculation shone in his pale blue eyes. His vivid blond hair reminded her of the Valkyries depicted in Mr. Sakaguchi's beloved Wagner prints, though Sutcliff's hair was parted perfectly down the middle and cropped close to his ears.

Even more telling were his shoes. The captain's black boots gleamed like mirrors, though she knew he'd been climbing about in the rubble.

"Carmichael." Captain Sutcliff drew out her name. "You don't look like a Carmichael."

She'd been teased on the subject before, especially by the Irish sisters who did the auxiliary linens. "I look like my father, sir, and he was a Carmichael."

"And where was he from?"

"I don't know, sir."

"Maybe he was Black Irish." Captain Sutcliff snorted at his own joke. Ingrid grimaced. Mr. Sakaguchi's smile was of poised politeness. He'd been Abram Carmichael's friend and peer, but both he and Mama made it clear that Papa never spoke of his past. The man may as well have emerged from the wilderness at age ten, ready for formal training in geomancy.

"Maybe he was Cherokee, Mexican, or Hindu. I don't know, sir." She said it lightly out of practice.

"Hmm. You usually don't have geomancers of *that* ilk, and he was a warden at a young age, correct? He must have been good." The captain was not completely clueless after all, but a politician. Even more dangerous. "If you'll both sit down, I have questions."

"As do we." Mr. Sakaguchi lowered himself to a red velvet seat, wincing. Ingrid sat on a carved bench across from him.

"Is there no one else from the auxiliary, sir?" Ingrid asked.

"Not yet. Soon, I hope. We have other matters to address now." Captain Sutcliff clasped his hands at his back. "Our business is urgent. I was traveling with my men on our way to the Cordilleran Auxiliary when we heard the explosion and witnessed the plume of dust. I am glad that you're well, Mr. Sakaguchi, and I extend the wishes of the United States and Japan that your recovery is uncomplicated."

Pretty words, no sincerity. Ingrid rubbed the gritty fabric of her skirt.

Mr. Sakaguchi bowed his head, gracious as always. "Thank you, Captain."

"Now, this matter I address is of a sensitive nature." He inclined his head.

"My secretary is discreet. She's accustomed to the ways of the auxiliary."

"I bet she knows all sorts of things, doesn't she? Very generous of you to take on your housekeeper's daughter." Captain

Sutcliff's gaze raked over her. Ingrid clenched her jaw and stared back. She wouldn't quail. "The Cordilleran Auxiliary owns a stake in the Rex Kermanite Mine in Boron, California, does it not? How closely do your people monitor operations? Actually." He pivoted on a heel to face her. "Perhaps this is something your secretary would know."

Challenge accepted. "The auxiliary owns a thirty percent stake in the mine. The wardens don't directly inspect the facilities, but our offices receive reports on a quarterly basis. I understand the Unified Pacific directly owns a third."

Captain Sutcliff's nostrils flared like that of a winded horse. His long face was rather equine. "Yes, yes. And Augustinian owns the other third, though that company controls damn near everything in regard to weapons. At least they're American. Did your recent report say anything unusual?"

Mr. Sakaguchi cleared his throat, and not just to regain the captain's attention. "Not that I heard, no, but I don't personally inspect the quarterly reports, only the annual. Quarterly assessments go through our most senior wardens, Mr. Antonelli and Mr. Thornton."

"Well!" Another nostril flare. "Kermanite is, as you are well familiar, a fickle rock formation. By its very nature, it tends to shatter into small pieces."

Ingrid had read volumes on the structure and known uses of kermanite. The crystals always accompanied boron deposits, and those deposits were only currently known to be in the Ottoman Empire—in Turkey—and in the Southern California desert. The Roman Empire collapsed when their kermanite supplies were exhausted, crippling their mighty dirigible force and ushering in the Dark Ages. California's rush to statehood was based solely on a rumor of kermanite; the discovery of gold was an added bonus.

Most pieces of the crystal were finger-sized—enough to supplement a steam-powered autocar—or smaller. Larger chunks were used for airships, naval vessels, and ambulatory tanks like Durendals. Its cost—well, there was a reason Warden Antonelli resided on Nob Hill. Wardens were paid in kermanite and set their own rates from there.

"Get to the point, please, Captain Sutcliff," said Mr. Sakaguchi.

"An unusual specimen of kermanite was recovered recently, one as large as a horse. I don't simply mean the body. I mean a standing horse, from hooves to withers." He seemed pleased at their shocked gasps.

"How much does it weigh?" Mr. Sakaguchi leaned forward. "I've seen pieces about the size of a leg, but to be that wide and tall . . . ! How was it recovered?"

"The effort took weeks. It required multiple winches to pull it out, and a twenty-mule team to move it to the fort—"

"My God." Mr. Sakaguchi sounded like a delighted schoolboy. "Even if it took months for us to fill, to work with kermanite like that, I . . ." His eyes shone.

It might take months for the wardens to fill, but Ingrid could do it much faster, especially if she had her hands on it during a significant earthquake.

Not like she'd ever be allowed near kermanite as priceless as that, not unless the wardens needed more coffee or tea.

Captain Sutcliff's tanned skin turned ruddy. "Yes. Well.

But." He looked toward the window, unable to mask his scowl. "It was stolen."

"Stolen, sir?" Ingrid gaped. "How does someone steal something that big and heavy?"

The captain's icy gaze gouged her. "The matter is being fully investigated, which is the very purpose of my visit. Your auxiliary is the largest on the continent. The expertise of your wardens—"

"You are not suggesting that we had anything to do with this theft." Mr. Sakaguchi made it a statement, not a question.

"What we know suggests that it is coming northward. You must agree that your auxiliary has the manpower to fill such a crystal, and a geographical advantage."

"A stone of that size, it would make more sense to bring geomancers to it, not bring the kermanite to the city."

"Maybe, maybe not. This is a major port for sea and air. Your membership here is rather, shall we say, eclectic, and has strong connections abroad. Of your wardens, only Mr. Antonelli is American-born, and he's first generation."

"Geomancy in America has only been encouraged for forty years, so of course the older men are from elsewhere," said Ingrid.

Captain Sutcliff showed no reaction to her words. "National loyalties can shift when power and money are involved, or due to personal vendettas." Something in his voice caused Ingrid to shiver violently. It was as though he had already come to a dreadful conclusion.

Mr. Sakaguchi went very still. "I was born in Japan and trained in Europe, but I have resided in the United States these past thirty years. I would not live elsewhere. So yes, my loyalties have shifted. To America, Captain Sutcliff."

That seemed to take the officer aback. "I see." The men stared at each other for a long minute. "Have you been to China, Warden Sakaguchi?"

"I have not."

"I have done five tours to China, two to the Philippines. I will not go into details, due to the sensibilities of present company"—Ingrid emitted a soft snort—"but it's an ugly war. You're well aware of what can be done with kermanite big enough to power an airship." He motioned the size with his hands and forearms. "What could our enemies do with kermanite the size of a horse?"

Mr. Sakaguchi waved away the implication. "Very little, under current circumstances. When the war began over twenty years ago, China hosted some five hundred million people, scores of geomancers, and thriving industrialization. Now there are what—maybe a few hundred thousand survivors, scattered across the terrain?"

"God willing, fewer than that," said Captain Sutcliff.

"Chinatown here has the largest portion in the States," Ingrid murmured. Its eradication would come soon enough. Everyone said as much, even Lee, though he never lingered on the topic.

"There are more chankoro—pardon my language," Captain Sutcliff added with an apologetic dip of his head as Ingrid openly scowled at the foul epithet. "There are said to be more Chinese residing on the West Coast of America and Canada now than in their old land."

Mr. Sakaguchi inclined his head. "They have a presence, yes, but they have neither industry nor geomancers. To utilize kermanite like that would require more manpower, more factories, than can be hidden away like some opium den deep in Chinatown. You would need all the factories of Atlanta working in concert to create something to use such a crystal. That minimizes the threat of this theft."

"Yet we are prevented from using it as well," said Captain Sutcliff.

"True."

"You say you're loyal to America now, Warden Sakaguchi. Prove it. This kermanite may well be the key to ending the war and saving countless American lives. Help me toward this goal."

Mr. Sakaguchi looked sidelong at Ingrid. "I'm not sure what you're trying to imply or ask of me, Captain Sutcliff."

"Then I'll be blunt. I grant you this one opportunity to tell me what you know, and I will speak well of your cooperation. Otherwise . . ."

"I had not heard of this piece of kermanite before our conversation. That is the truth."

Ingrid looked between the men, brow furrowed.

Captain Sutcliff sighed. "So you say. Maybe in twenty years you'll tell a different tale, hmm?" He shook his head, and Ingrid wondered what on earth the man was talking about. "I had hoped, as a Japanese man, you'd be more reasonable. Not like the Chinese. They're incapable of reason."

"Are they really?" A rare flush of anger colored Mr. Sakaguchi's cheeks. "The Thuggees fight the British. The Chinese fight us. If the denizens of the crowded isles of Japan decided to settle America by force, would *you* behave reasonably? Should any people simply consent to their own demise?"

Ingrid sucked in a breath. Mr. Sakaguchi's sentiments were nothing new to her, but dear God, why was he saying such things to an officer of the Unified Pacific? Did he *want* to be arrested for sedition?

Captain Sutcliff stared, his face unreadable.

Mr. Sakaguchi stood. "I believe we're done for now, Captain. My secretary and I have already dealt with a terrible trauma today. I must attend my colleagues at the hospital."

"Attending your colleagues will be rather difficult, Mr. Sakaguchi, as you're the only people from the auxiliary we have recovered alive."

Ingrid had never seen Mr. Sakaguchi turn so pale. In two strides she was at his side, supporting him by an arm. His lips quivered and parted as if to speak, but no sound emerged.

"No one else?" she asked.

Some of Sutcliff's haughtiness faded. "If anyone had been found alive, news would have been brought here straightaway."

All of them dead? Surely not. Someone else had to survive. The wardens—and the children, the adepts.

"What about the staff?" she managed to croak out. She had seen some of their faces most every day of her life.

"The building was torn asunder, Miss Carmichael. The damage—the bodies will be difficult to identify, and there were casualties within the flanking buildings and in the street as well."

"We had a hundred people in the building." Mr. Sakaguchi's voice was scarcely audible.

She and Ojisan rocked together, mute in their grief for a long moment. No wonder so many small earthquakes had been occurring.

Ingrid sucked in a sharp breath. "But there's still—" Mr. Sakaguchi's sudden grip on her arm silenced her, but she was buoyed by the thought that Mr. Calhoun and Mr. Thornton were alive. Their illnesses had spared them.

"The mayor's office wishes to speak to you when you're well," said Captain Sutcliff. "A report must be issued on the welfare of the city."

Mr. Sakaguchi's lips thinned at the allusion to Mayor Butterfield, but he nodded.

"It's been a strangely active year for tremblers, hasn't it?" asked Captain Sutcliff. "The terrible waves that struck South America, the tremor in St. Lucia, and of course, there's Vesuvius."

"And Peking twice over," Ingrid murmured.

Captain Sutcliff dismissed the mention with a flick of his hand. "Proof of God's favor. Even the Chinese believe they have lost their 'Mandate of Heaven.' Those quakes saved a million American bullets and bombs. When was the last major earthquake in San Francisco? Eighteen-seventy? The city should get along just fine, then."

"Eighteen sixty-eight, but—" began Ingrid. Mr. Sakaguchi shot her a look that stopped her before she could tell Captain Sutcliff that there hadn't been a major event in the city *because* of the presence of the auxiliary.

"I must attend to my duties at home," said Mr. Sakaguchi. "I must . . . I must reach out to other auxiliaries for assistance. This cannot wait."

How long would it take for more geomancers to arrive? Ingrid gnawed on her lower lip. Was Sutcliff even going to let them go, after what Mr. Sakaguchi said?

Captain Sutcliff squinted at them. "You are the only warden accounted for at this time, so yes. Attend your business, but don't leave the city—of course, you're already aware of that." He gave Mr. Sakaguchi a pointed look. "I'll speak to you again soon." Speak, meaning an arrest would likely come once bureaucratic obstacles were surmounted and other geomancers arrived.

"Here's my calling card." With a deft flick of his wrist, Captain Sutcliff pulled out the card and extended it toward Mr. Sakaguchi. Ingrid plucked it from his fingertips, and the captain's eyes widened in surprise.

"I *am* his secretary," she said. Mr. Sakaguchi proceeded through the foyer to the entrance.

"Is that all you are, ma'am?"

Ingrid took in a deep breath to quell her annoyance. Captain Sutcliff wasn't the first to insinuate such—no, according to gossip, she had to be either a lover or a charity case, or both.

"Captain Sutcliff, you're here to investigate, so let me make your job a little easier. I've lived in Mr. Sakaguchi's household since I was barely school age. My mother was his cook and head housekeeper, and cooked at the auxiliary as well. Mr. Sakaguchi's the closest thing I've known to a father."

When Ingrid had scraped her knee as a child, Mama ordered her to stop crying and move along; Mr. Sakaguchi was the one who kissed his fingers then pressed them to her knee, and made the pain go away faster than any Reiki. In the evenings, when Mama headed to bed early, he used to prop Ingrid up on his lap and read to her his favorite tales of the geomantic Hidden Ones. He was the one who, on her birthday mornings, always left a small tin of her very favorite Ghirardelli chocolates on her nightstand.

"I see." Captain Sutcliff didn't believe her. Pompous twit.

She stepped toward the door, then hesitated. She didn't like this man, but something still needed to be said. "And thank you, Captain. You and your men. Thank you for pulling us out."

"It was quite lucky you both survived." He said it as if there was more than luck involved. "We fetched shoes for both of you. One of my men can summon a cab—"

"No, thank you," she said. She would accept nothing more from this man. "We usually walk. We can manage on our own." Ingrid shot him a glare and turned, her indecently loosened hair lashing against her cheeks.

She shoved her feet into the supplied footwear—men's boots, surprisingly correct in size. She bounced down the steps, but the stiffness in her back slowed her down as she rejoined Mr. Sakaguchi. He looked so odd standing there, his fine suit shredded and filthy, borrowed shoes on his feet, no hat on his head.

Emotion burned in her throat. The auxiliary was gone. The wardens, gone. Everything changed today. Everything.

"I told him we were walking," she said.

"Are you well enough for the trek?" He stared at the ground as he spoke.

"Yes."

He nodded and started along Battery toward home. She followed.

The din on the street was more pronounced than usual. Stalled traffic around the block had created a tangle of trucks and wagons; walking had been the faster choice by far. Horns blared and harnesses jingled, sounds echoing against the tall buildings that lined the avenue. Overhead, a dirigible purred like a happy cat.

Ingrid and Mr. Sakaguchi limped along the crowded sidewalk. People stared at them, wide-eyed. Ingrid self-consciously shook more dust from her skirt.

"Captain Sutcliff wonders at the timing of all of this." When Mr. Sakaguchi spoke, it was in a monotone. "I wonder as well. For such an unusual crystal to be stolen, then the explosion . . . it couldn't have been an accident. I hope that the captain will have success in his investigation, though I fear his fixation on me will distract him. He's an even worse guest than I feared."

His wording sent a jolt through her. "Guest. He—you knew he was coming?" The events just before the explosion suddenly flared in her memory. "A messenger came. You were sent—" She stopped herself and glanced around.

Mr. Roosevelt—or someone—had sent Mr. Sakaguchi a warning that investigators were on the way. Good grief! She had cheered up Mr. Sakaguchi with kitsune-ken, even as he knew soldiers were on the way to confront him. A different man would have fled. Instead, he playacted the part of a fantastic fox spirit and laughed himself to tears.

"Why did they suspect you from the start? Why make yourself sound more guilty and talk of China that way? That's all the man needed. He'll make the evidence fit. It might be harder to arrest you because you're Japanese, but—"

"I didn't tell him anything he did not already know."

"It's different to think it than to say it. It's almost like you want to be arrested."

"Maybe that would be safer," he said softly.

Perhaps debris had struck his head. He wasn't making sense. "What about Mr. Thornton and Mr. Calhoun? He's going to find out they're alive."

"Consider how he treated us, newly recovered from the wreckage. How would he interrogate them, addled by fever?" Mr. Sakaguchi shook his head in disgust. "No. I will call them. We need to meet, regardless of their illness. I . . . I should break the news." A tremor shook through Mr. Sakaguchi.

"What about the risk to the city?" she asked in a low voice. "You know very well that the protocol says that San Francisco requires at least three wardens and thirty students present at all times to ensure that the city doesn't feel any tremors, and we've always had far more than that. There've been several seisms in the past hour alone."

"A crisis can be averted," he whispered. Mr. Sakaguchi, always hopeful, even against terrible odds.

Ingrid shook her head in frustration. "If Mr. Thornton and Mr. Calhoun are ill and not in contact with the earth, it's just us. How long can we hold back a major earthquake? How . . . how are we supposed to survive it?"

Mr. Sakaguchi bowed his head and said nothing the rest of the walk home.

CHAPTER 3

After a quick bath and a change of clothes, Ingrid could almost pretend the events of the morning hadn't happened. Never mind that she and Mr. Sakaguchi were home far too early in the day, or that she had somehow kept both of them alive while everyone else died.

No, not simply died. Were murdered. The cooks, the cleaners, the homesick little boys, the senior students all abuzz with talk of world travel in the coming years. The maid who hummed old hymns as she scrubbed the stairs to combat the constant filth of so many growing boys and careless men. Senior Warden Antonelli, as aggravating as he was, would bring in cut flowers when his garden was in bloom, and took care to personally arrange vases in the hallway. Then there was the elderly librarian who so often fell asleep tipped back in his chair, a book splayed open over his chest. What of the cats who lived in the alley next door, by the empty photographer's studio? The calico was bound to have kittens any day now.

Mr. Sakaguchi was right. That large piece of kermanite stolen, the explosion, Captain Sutcliff's arrival . . . The timing of everything was too peculiar to be mere coincidence.

She sat curled in the front hallway, her head pressed against her knees. The knotted tassels of the rug were stones beneath her socked feet.

Something scuffed against the floor nearby. A wooden floor board creaked. Lee was not being particularly stealthy about his approach. She could hear his breath as he sneaked closer. She feigned ignorance up until the cotton scarf whispered over her nose.

"Lee!" she snapped, swatting it away. Her hand caught one side of the scarf and stole it from his grip. The corner, weighed by coins sewn into the fabric, struck the wood with a muted thud.

Lee Fong dropped beside her and sat so close their knees glanced. "I was trying to surprise you, Ingrid." His voice was still boyishly soft, though it had recently begun to squawk at random moments.

"Surprise me by mock-assassinating me like a Thuggee? Really? Mr. Sakaguchi would be livid if he knew you still had that thing."

Earlier, in the nineteenth century, the cult of Thuggees in India had gained infamy as assassins; their technique involved strangulation with their weighted scarves. Murder for the sake of money and the glory of Kali, the stories said. The Brits had exterminated the cult.

Rebels against Britannia now called themselves Thuggees, and tales about how true they were to their roots varied wildly. Even so, the romantic morbidity of the Thuggees and their scarves had become quite the sensation with American boys. Some youngsters at the auxiliary had learned to sew just to weigh down their own scarves for mock battles.

The Thuggees, nefarious as they were, were also distracting the Brits from turning their attention to the Unified Pacific. In a roundabout way, Thuggees were heroes.

But Lee was not some boy from the auxiliary. He was Chinese. Carrying a Thuggee scarf evoked different connotations altogether.

She gave him her best scowl. Lee's cropped black hair, shiny with oil, stuck out every which way. Ingrid was Mr. Sakaguchi's secretary, but Lee was a bit of everything—messenger boy, house servant, assistant cook, hostler. Mr. Sakaguchi had taken in Lee about five years before, and now it was impossible to imagine the household without him.

He toyed with the blue scarf. Once upon a time, it had been Mama's. "I was tickling your face, that's all," he said. The logic of teenage boys would forever confound Ingrid. "Mr. Sakaguchi asked me to fetch you."

"How . . . how is he?" Her throat still felt raw from screaming and breathing in powdered debris. It seemed as if she had downed a gallon of water when they first returned home, but nothing washed away the grit.

Lee cocked his head to one side. The gesture reminded her of a bird considering something just before it fluttered away. "About the same as you."

As always, Lee wore his patch pinned to his upper arm. The scrap of cloth was vivid yellow, the threadwork in tidy black depicting the two kanji for Shina—the Japanese term for China, one often spat as if clearing phlegm from a throat. His registration booklet bulged from his breast pocket. He couldn't leave Chinatown without his patch or papers, not that either guaranteed safe passage.

A pink smudge marred the starched whiteness of his button-up shirtsleeve. "What happened?" she asked, pointing to his arm.

"I was running errands and found a wall. Dangerous things, walls. They sneak up on you sometimes."

Meaning someone attacked him, or tried to. "You're not hurt?"

Lee shrugged.

She frowned. A few months prior, a tussle had left him with two bruised ribs, and he'd had the audacity to try to hide the injury. Succeeded for a few hours, too, until Ingrid overenthusiastically recommended a book by flinging it straight into his chest. He had hit the floor like a deflated gasbag.

Lee's face lit up in a grin. "That's better."

"What's better?"

"You, angry. Though that means I should probably . . ." He scooted back, his beige pants gliding on the waxed wood.

He meant well, but she flinched. Lee had been around her on a daily basis for years. He couldn't help but notice what she could do. Not that they had ever talked about it. It was something to shrug away, like his hidden injuries.

Now her power carried such strange potential. What had she done in the explosion—how had she done it?

"Ingrid?" His voice cracked halfway through her name.

"I'm sorry, Lee. It's just . . . today. Everyone . . ."

His face softened. "Yeah. Speaking of which, Mr. Sakaguchi is waiting."

"Of course." She touched her cheeks to make sure they were dry and then stood.

Mr. Sakaguchi's study radiated warmth in mahogany and plush blue velvet. Shelves banded in rainbows of leather stretched ten feet high to crown molding at the ceiling. A leather armchair, squat and dense, angled toward the unlit fireplace. While opulent, it was austere compared to the home offices of most of the other wardens, who regarded their masculine spaces as lavish trophy rooms for their world travels.

Mr. Sakaguchi was more practical than that. His artifacts related to earth sciences and magic. The Chinese-made earthquake weathercock consisted of a large vase with marbles set at the points of the compass; the marbles were supposed to drop to indicate the direction of a seism, though large trucks set off the device more often than actual quakes.

Ingrid's personal favorites in the room, though, were the colorful namazu-e prints on the walls. The propaganda posters from the 1850s presented a peculiar mix of Hidden One mythology and public safety message.

Shuttered double doors led to a catfish pond just outside, but even that was an instrument of geomancy. Many nonmagical animals were known to be restless before an earthquake. In Japan, normal catfish—namazu—had served as warning systems for centuries. Somehow they were bound to the very magical and monstrous namazu that was said to carry the large island of Honshu on its back.

Mythology had attempted to explain the relationship between magic, creatures, and mankind, but modern science had done little to elaborate on the subject. Hidden Ones often had been declared gods in old stories. Fantastics, common or rare, embodied pure magic.

As to what magic *was,* that question was one perennially posed to new students at the auxiliary—one they were expected to get wrong. The textbook answer was that magic was raw energy, and that some beings—animal or human—were more adept at drawing it in and utilizing it. Some were born into it, the way a fish is born into water. That answer never satisfied Ingrid. It never defined what *she* was. What had she inherited from Papa?

Sometimes, it seemed like a gigantic, mystic catfish supporting a landmass bearing billions of people made more sense to Ingrid than her own body and mind.

She faced Mr. Sakaguchi at his desk. "Ojisan. What's the news?"

He sat with his back stooped. The collar of his smoking jacket dipped low, revealing a tidy row of mother-of-pearl buttons in the shirt beneath. He leaned on one fist while in another he held a pen.

"I just called Charleston. They'll dispatch two men tomorrow night, but they did send a group to Vesuvius, so they're already shorthanded."

"What about everywhere else?" she asked.

"St. Louis is suffering a bout of influenza. New York, as

Italian-dominated as it is, sent half their available men to Vesuvius. Honolulu can spare five adepts and perhaps one warden, but it will take them over a week to arrive. No one in Seattle answered."

"But San Francisco . . . the risk. Has the mayor—"

"Mayor Butterfield." Mr. Sakaguchi's face twisted in distaste. "The man barely let me speak. He assured me that no earthquake will happen while he's mayor."

She snorted. "Maybe he's found a way to bribe the dirt." Since their walk home, the tremors had stopped. No blue shimmered over the ground, but that could change in an instant.

"He has higher priorities right now. That corruption case against him is set to start on Monday. I told him that if tremors continued, the most at-risk sections of the city should be evacuated." For Mr. Sakaguchi to admit to such a possibility said a great deal about the peril. "He argued that the natives here managed to survive for centuries without problems. As if the collapse of a native Ohlone hut made of tules is equal to the public harm caused by a falling brick skyscraper."

He glanced at the Bakelite telephone on the desk, as if he could will it to ring. "Mr. Thornton and Mr. Calhoun are not answering their phones. They are likely sleeping, but . . ."

"If they both recover quickly, they'll be able to channel energy." The words felt fake on her tongue, but she had to say something hopeful. More than that, she needed to do something. "Lee!"

He poked his head through the cracked door. "Yeah?"

"Jiao started some soup for us. Please ask her to fill two kettles. I'll take them to Mr. Thornton and Mr. Calhoun." Like many of the first wave of Chinese to come to San Francisco, Jiao was Cantonese. She was a fine cook, and her soups were akin to magic.

"Sure, Ing," Lee said, and ducked away.

"Ingrid, you should rest—"

"Ojisan. Leave it to me. You have too much to do here, and you know Lee can't go to Mr. Calhoun's." Mr. Calhoun despised "Chinamen and other primitives," and only tolerated Ingrid because he never looked at her face. "They're stubborn men on their own. They'd have to be at death's door before they sacrificed pride to summon a doctor. I'll call you from each of their homes."

Mr. Sakaguchi frowned. "I suppose that will suffice, but I do want you to utilize caution. Even more . . ." He opened a desk drawer and set a dark object on the mat. Mama's pistol.

Mama used to take Ingrid on day-trips out to Mount Diablo so they could practice shooting. She had taught Ingrid to do most everything a man could do. Ingrid could saddle and ride a horse, rig a harness, check oil and basic functions on a standard steam-kermanite autocar engine, and read and do her own figures. She never quite mastered the art of pissing while standing up, though.

Mr. Sakaguchi had never come along on their target-shooting trips. Kitsune-ken's hunter gesture was as violent as he got. "If you must defend yourself against the Army & Airship Corps or anyone else, I'd rather you shoot them than use earth energy. People understand bullets."

"Whereas my power is about as well understood as Jefferson Davis's ghost."

His smile was tender yet weary. "You're you, Ing-chan. Your mother brought you to the auxiliary when you were barely five, all red and swollen with fever. Near death, by the accounts of Pasteurians and Reiki physicians alike. Boys will manifest their geomancy at that age, certainly, but no one had considered such a possibility for you. No one but your mother. The instant I pressed kermanite to your skin, the fever was siphoned away. Right then, I knew."

"I only wish we knew what. Or how. Or why."

" 'Some mysteries must stay with God.' "

She nodded. It was one of his favorite sayings, one that he used most often when speaking of the Hidden Ones. His favorite tale involved the massive namazu, but similar stories were told everywhere. The Chumash and other aboriginal tribes up north to Cascadia spoke of two-headed serpents within the earth, whereas the Iroquois and Algonquin told of a giant turtle. On other continents, Hidden Ones bound through earth magic included buffalo, horses, crabs, hogs, and several types of frog—fantastics so massive, so incredible, that most people doubted their existence in the modern world.

Ingrid slipped the gun into her dress pocket where the pleats would hide it from view. It felt heavy against her thigh. She was the hunter; now she only hoped she had to deal with kitsune, not village chiefs.

"Speaking of mysteries, Mr. Sakaguchi," she said slowly. "Who would want to destroy the auxiliary? The Chinese?" She glanced at the doorway in case Lee was there. She couldn't help but feel a little guilty for thinking of them first.

"The Chinese have legitimate reasons to target us, though

the Unified Pacific has a stockpile of charged kermanite. Creating a bottleneck here wouldn't affect the military right away. Regular business on the West Coast, yes."

"Someone mad at the auxiliary, then? In novels, the villain always takes out insurance on the building or person they wish to destroy."

"A personal vendetta does seem more likely. Someone angry at us, or angry at the city itself."

Ingrid thought of Lee and his scarf. "We do have two British-born wardens, which is unusual. Maybe it was Thuggees."

"That does seem extreme. If they wanted to hurt the British, there are far better targets within the city or elsewhere. Besides, anyone with an education would realize an act against geomancers here, on such strategic fault lines, could have consequences for the whole city. San Francisco's population is diverse. The auxiliary reflects—reflected—that." His voice broke.

"Maybe they'll find others alive in the rubble," she said softly.

"Surely they will," he whispered.

The door cracked open again and Lee leaned into the room. "Ing? The soup's ready."

"Thanks, Lee. I'll be back soon," she said to Mr. Sakaguchi as she backed away. "I'll ring you."

He nodded and said nothing. Grief flowed over her in a wave. Most everyone they knew, dead.

Ingrid failed to hold back tears as she walked away. The simple melody of the shamisen returned to her mind as the gun, in perfect rhythm, bumped against her thigh with each stride.

Mr. Calhoun resided in a flat near Russian Hill. Ingrid's breath huffed as she crested a rise. The two pots of soup steamed in the nippy air, handles heavy in her grasp.

It had been a chilly winter, and so far April hadn't shed its cloak of gray. Ingrid loved it, and she loved San Francisco. She loved the flowing hills crowned by jeweled mansions, the varied chimes of cable cars, and how everyone here came from everywhere else. The French patisserie owner set up his clapboard sign advertising prices for day-old croissants, while a quick-tongued Italian woman berated her children as she clipped laundry to a clothesline draped above an alley. Two Chinese men toted handcarts, yellow patches vivid on their black suits, and walked with the wariness of prey in a meadow.

For everyone else, the day was utterly normal, and there was comfort in that.

Airships buzzed overhead, out of sight above the clouds. She breathed in brisk air, not minding the underlying taint of exhaust and sewage and whatever strange brew wafted from the factory upwind.

Up ahead, braced between a leaning telephone pole and a gas streetlamp, stood a familiar figure. The woman wore a dress of similar fashion to Ingrid's, a Western modification of a kimono. The fabric was so dark it almost obscured the floral pattern. The high belt revealed a figure still curvaceous enough to make most men look twice, but Ingrid's focus was on the camera. The black box rested atop a tripod with telescoping legs adjusted for the street's slope.

"Miss Rossi!" Ingrid called, eagerness quickening her steps.

The woman remained stooped as she peered through the camera lens.

Ingrid hadn't seen Victoria Rossi in months, ever since the portrait salon beside the auxiliary shut down. Miss Rossi had done photographs in studio and also sold commercial images of fantastics—pegasi, selkies in midchange, grotesque ghuls, soaring thunderbirds, that sort of thing. Ingrid still had some postcards of unicorns tucked away in a bureau drawer.

Miss Rossi had something of an obsession with wild fantastics. Sometimes she'd close shop for days as she gallivanted off to the beach or hills to attempt a sighting through her lens.

"Hello, Miss Rossi!" Ingrid panted from the climb. Soup sloshed in the kettles as she came to a stop.

"You. The girl from the auxiliary." Miss Rossi didn't lift her head. She wore a crown of soft ostrich feathers dyed to match her navy dress.

"Yes." Ingrid preened at the recognition. "I don't believe I've seen you do street photography before. Have you set up a new studio?"

Miss Rossi straightened as though the camera scalded her. "New studio? Ha!" The laugh was practically spat. "You think they let me own another studio here, in this city?"

Ingrid stepped back, shocked at her vehemence. Miss Rossi had always been a bit clipped in her mannerisms, but this rage was something new. "I'm sorry. I thought—the business seemed to do well. It was a good location—"

"Oh, location. Yes, location fine, too fine. Mayor Butterfield, he has business fees and permits, you see?" Miss Rossi rubbed her thumb and fingers together. "Fees for location, fees for sewer, though sewer always backs up, fees for my safety as a woman, fees to keep his people from telling lies. No fee paid—things vanish. Chemicals no delivered. Windows broken."

Ingrid wasn't surprised. The wardens paid their own fees to Mayor Butterfield. However, no one used graft like the Chinese. It was rumored that the late emperor's treasures were used to bribe the city and state to keep Chinatown intact. It was yet another reason why his memory was venerated by his people.

"I'm sorry," Ingrid said.

"Sorry does not get my business back. It gets nothing back." Miss Rossi's eyes narrowed. "You not in building today?"

"You heard about that, then." Ingrid's throat tightened. "Yes. Yes, I was. Me and Mr. Sakaguchi. We . . . survived. We might be the only ones. It was . . . a miracle, I suppose."

"A miracle. Mary, Mother of God! Maybe so." Miss Rossi snorted. "Well, enjoy life as it is now, eh? I have work to do." With that, she bent over to look through the camera again.

Ingrid couldn't help but glance downhill to follow the angle of the lens. The shot would show quintessential San Francisco: wagons and autocars parked and driving; seagulls plucking at gutter trash; a gang of dark-haired boys in knickerbockers chasing a blown-up bladder ball across the street. Fog softened the horizon. If the image could capture scent, it needed the stale reek of beer from the German rathskeller across the way.

"It may not mean much, but I am sorry." Ingrid stalked on past. Miss Rossi offered no reply.

With her mood subdued again, the next few blocks passed in a blur of physical exertion. Nearby magic tickled her skin, and she spied fairy lights glinting in the bushes; Ingrid didn't pause to look closely, but guessed them to be invasive European pixies, the equivalent of flying, pretty weeds. She had always had a keen awareness of magical creatures around her, sensing their power like prickles of heat. It was similar to the feel of the earth's hot energy, but distinct, like the difference in ambience, smell, and sound between a wood fire and wax candle.

The ability had nothing to do with geomancy either. Ingrid learned when she was quite young that Mama and Mr. Sakaguchi had no explanation for it, and that she needed to keep her awareness secret.

Ingrid released a frustrated huff. So many blasted secrets.

Russian Hill was a hard slog even when she felt well, but with her back healing and soup in hand, she felt like an A&A recruit after a full day of boot camp—exhausted to the bone. At least the pain was gone.

The steps to Mr. Calhoun's apartment building creaked beneath her weight. She managed the front door lever with her elbow. Electricity lighted the hallway. Any geomancer skilled enough to make warden earned adequate money for electricity and most other modern comforts.

Up one more flight of stairs, and she reached his flat. Setting down her kettles, Ingrid wrung out her hands, wincing, and quirked her neck from side to side. Reiki or not, she was bound to ache tomorrow. She knocked on the door. Mr. Calhoun usually answered rather quickly; he seemed to spend his evenings in his armchair, listening to music on his new Marconi.

"Mr. Calhoun?" she called. "It's Ingrid Carmichael from the auxiliary. Mr. Sakaguchi sent me. May I come in?"

She waited a few minutes, rocking in her shoes, before she knocked again. Was he unable to rise from bed? Should she fetch a doctor? Frowning, she tested the doorknob, and was surprised when it turned.

"Eh eh! What're you doin', young lady?" The barked-out brogue stopped Ingrid cold. She turned to see the landlady halfway up the steps. Her brilliant red hair was highlighted by thick streaks of white, as though a giant had dipped his hand in paint and then trailed his fingers up from her forehead.

"Hello, ma'am. I work for the wardens. I came to check on Mr. Calhoun, and no one's answering—"

"I seen you before. What, you people don't speak amongst each other? The city's been and gone! Someone shoulda gone to that auxiliary o' yours."

"The city's been here? What message did we miss?"

The landlady stopped at the top of the stairs. Despite being shorter than Ingrid, the stout woman seemed to look down on her.

"Why, tha' Mr. Calhoun's dead, o' course."

To Ingrid, it seemed that the world became very, very still. "Dead? How can he be dead?"

"God called him home, simple as that. Considering the ugliness of how he went, was a right mercy, the poor man!"

"Ugly? How? I know he was ill yesterday—"

"Ill! Pah! I'll tell you, his rent for this month'll be spent cleaning the place up, that's for sure." The landlady stepped closer and tapped her pointer finger to her lips. "He lost everything in 'is guts, every which way. I never seen anyone 'ave it so bad. His skin turned yellow, too, jaundiced like a newborn babe. Most peculiar thing!"

The information spun around in Ingrid's mind. What could have caused jaundice like that? He hadn't even seemed that sick! "How long ago did he die?"

"Don't rightly know. I checked on him at lunch, brought him some broth. That's when I found him."

Ingrid looked down at the soup kettles on the floor. This soup clearly wasn't needed here. She sucked in a sharp breath. Mr. Thornton! If he had the same illness, he might only have hours left. There was time yet to fetch doctors and keep him alive.

One more warden might make all the difference in safeguarding San Francisco in these next few days until help arrived.

"I have to go!" Ingrid said, hoisting up the kettles. She pushed past the landlady and practically flew down the stairs. The first apartment door was open, and through it she could hear the wavering notes of an orchestra playing over a Marconi.

At the sidewalk she paused for a moment, panting, as she glanced at the slope ahead and whimpered. Two blocks more. Not far as the crow flew, but damned crows had wings.

Her calves screamed for mercy as she trudged uphill. Broth splashed from beneath the lids and warmed her fingers. Sunlight began to fade and colored the clouds in murky pink, like weak watercolors muddled with pencil.

"Almost there, almost there," she muttered.

"Look out!" cried a small voice behind her.

Ingrid turned to see a brown ball flying directly at her. Heat flared to her skin. For an instant it was as though she could feel the very presence of the baseball in the air—an instant that brought the ball alarmingly close. She yelped and stumbled sideways. The kettles clattered as she dropped them with just enough time to catch herself. Her knees banged on the hard ground.

"Damn—darn it!" She propped herself up and immediately set a leaking kettle upright. Branches snapped as the ball smacked into the bushes behind her.

The tingle of heat lapped against her as a blue cloud arose from the ground. She froze. Another quake, already? So many in a cluster today, especially when she was hurting at the Reiki shop. None since then, either. She rubbed her knees through cloth.

"Gomen-nasai! Sorry!" A little white boy dashed up, panting. He wore a battered baseball player's cap. Several other boys trailed close behind.

"I think it landed over there," she said, jerking her head as she picked up the soup. "Be more careful."

"Hai. Sorry again!" He offered her a gap-toothed smile then hurried in pursuit of the ball.

She walked on, new warmth within her skin. She almost collapsed in happy relief at the sight of Mr. Thornton's narrow town house. Her calves felt the strain as she worked her way up the stairs to the porch, but her knees no longer hurt.

"Mr. Thornton! Mr. Thornton, are you there?" She stepped back to study the windows for any movement. Nothing, not so much as the sway of a curtain. She set down the kettles and knocked on the door as loudly as she could. "Mr. Thornton! If you can hear me, make a noise! This is Ingrid Carmichael!"

Still nothing. She grabbed the doorknob and rushed inside the dark home.

Ingrid had braced herself for the reek of illness, and was stunned at the normality of the air. She recalled the switch box was near the door, and fumbled to open the panel and flip the lever. Yellow light revealed a floor heaped with papers, books, and other debris. The china press had notable gaps where pieces once sat on display.

"Mr. Thornton?" Her voice was softer now, wary. She dried off her soupy hand and let the fingers rest near her pocket. The bedroom would be the most likely place to find a sick man, but with what she knew of Mr. Thornton, she thought to check the study first.

A file cabinet drawer dangled like a slack jaw, its contents vomited onto the floor. The bookshelves reminded her of a pugilist's mouth with many missing teeth. Even a safe behind the desk gaped open.

A large empty space on the wall denoted where a full-color map of India had been pinned. Mr. Thornton had overlaid vellum and colored it in layers to show the progress of the imperial conquest of the subcontinent. It had been the showpiece of the room and visible evidence of his obsession. He had daily marked the shifts in dominion.

Bookshelves had been emptied in a way that made it impossible to know what may have been taken. Ingrid nudged a haphazard stack on the floor. The books were about China, the Qing Dynasty, and Japan's agrarian colonization of mainland Asia. The nineteenth century had brought repeated devastation to China as part of the majority Han populace rebelled against the Manchu Dynasty that had ruled them for centuries, even as Britain, Russia, and the Unified Pacific manipulated the people and economy through opium and forced trade. The last Chinese emperor, Qixiang, almost died of an illness, and emerged as a changed man. He broke with his predecessors in a major way and declared that the Manchu and Han would be treated the same beneath the Qing Code, uniting the people as never before. His Restoration came woefully late to avert China's decline. By then, Japan had already taken Manchuria, dubbed it Manchukuo, and partnered with America with an eye to even greater prizes.

Ingrid and Lee knew more than most people about the history of China and other places—a different angle of history than what was printed in these books from publishers in Tokyo and New York City. Mr. Sakaguchi recounted tales of India, tales that told of how the original incarnation of the Thuggee cult had likely been a threat greatly exaggerated by the British, an excuse to demonize and massacre settlers in the interior subcontinent; he also told tales about how Lincoln's Emancipation Proclamation had not truly eliminated slavery, and that thralldom continued through unlivable wages for freedmen, Chinese, and American natives; and so many other things that people never discussed in public, if at all.

When she was younger, being party to such knowledge was rather titillating. Now the subjects made her uncomfortable. The meaning of patriotism and sedition had evolved as she grew up, as the war dragged on. She had seen too many newsreels where hooded traitors convulsed at the end of a noose. In light of Captain Sutcliff's interest, the danger now felt eerily personal and real.

She straightened the books, simply because she couldn't bear the idea of them toppling over.

Why oh why had Mr. Sakaguchi spoken so openly to Captain Sutcliff? Why had the captain even regarded him as a suspect in the first place? She hoped that among Mr. Sakaguchi's calls, he had also contacted a lawyer. It was a shame he and Mr. Roosevelt had ended their acquaintanceship. He couldn't have a more powerful ally than an Ambassador.

She looked around Mr. Thornton's chaotic office. She couldn't see this as the work of Captain Sutcliff. If a man was particular enough to have his shoes shined in the middle of the day, he'd ransack a place and leave it tidier than he found it. It looked more like a hasty job of packing—valuable objects like coins still sat on the shelf, yet personal mementos like the map of India were gone.

She slipped her fingers around the revolver in her pocket. The worn ivory handle perfectly fit against her small palm.

The stairs were quiet as she treaded upward. The bedroom was empty, a bureau left wide open. No sign of sickness or strangeness about the bathroom either. Had Mr. Thornton even made it home?

The feeling of terrible wrongness increased as she went

back downstairs to the study. If she summoned the police, then what? Captain Sutcliff was sure to find out that two wardens had been absent today, and if he knew she had been here, his suspicion of her and Mr. Sakaguchi would worsen. Actually, he was likely to blame them regardless. Belatedly, Ingrid set her hat on the desk and brushed a hand over her hair.

The floor creaked behind her. Ingrid whirled around, drawing the pistol.

A tall shadow of a man loomed in the doorway, and he moved as she did. With a flourish, he withdrew a metallic rod from beneath his jacket. At the twitch of his thumb it telescoped to the length of a walking stick. A blue orb topped the copper pipe. She immediately noted it wasn't kermanite but some other stone.

Heat rose to her skin. Gritting her teeth, she remembered Mr. Sakaguchi's warning and shoved her power down again. She straightened her arm, the revolver at the ready.

"You!" The stranger stepped into the light.

"You!" Ingrid echoed, her jaw dropping in surprise. It was the fine-looking man who had spoken to her on the auxiliary steps, the one asking after Mr. Thornton. His hat was off, his brown hair mussed in a way that begged to be smoothed.

She really hoped she didn't have to shoot him.

"What's that?" Ingrid asked, motioning her gun toward the device in his hand.

"A Tesla rod, miss. If the tip touches you, the reaction will be quite unpleasant."

"Tesla! That fellow who blew up half of Long Island a few years ago?" Ingrid hastily backtracked until she half sat on the desk. Papers splashed to the floor. She had already endured an explosion and been buried alive today, and had no desire to repeat the experience.

He sighed as if he'd gotten such a reaction before. "It's quite stable, miss. Nothing is going to blow up. Not unless I want it to."

"That's hardly comforting. What are you doing here, sir?"

"You suggested I drop by here, so that's exactly what I've done. No one answered the phone." He said this in as friendly a way as could be, as though they'd met in a café, no weapons involved.

She eyed the Tesla rod and considered the man again. He didn't strike her as a hooligan. He looked like a teacher or an accountant—and not a very well-off one, at that. His leather coat had a few years of wear to it, with the edges fuzzed to white. The condition of the jacket and tie beneath looked similar, being tidy yet shabby.

Peculiar, though, how he showed up at the auxiliary so soon before it exploded. Ingrid lowered the pistol but kept it in her grip. No reason to trust the man, even if she wanted to admire him like a Remington bronze.

"This morning, I do believe you mentioned you were a secretary at the auxiliary?"

"Yes, I am, sir. Ingrid Carmichael. I work for Warden Sakaguchi, specifically, and assist the board."

"Don't see many secretaries toting about pistols."

"Shooting is taught right along with coffee brewing, shorthand, and bookkeeping, though I haven't taken the course in knife throwing yet. That's next on the list."

Amusement glistened in his brown eyes. “Maybe I should look into this training as a secretary. Might come in handy.”

“Always good to have another trade.” She almost smiled, but resisted the urge; no need to appear vulnerable. But goodness, this man made her want to smile, and for him to smile back. “Why's your need for kermanite so urgent?”

“It's for an airship, miss. Newly built by myself and my partner. Just need the kermanite, and we'll have her airborne.” He frowned. With a twist of his wrist, the rod fell back in on itself. “What happened here?”

“I'm not sure. I came to check on Mr. Thornton and found the place like this.” She stepped forward a little as he tucked the rod back at his waist, but still kept her distance.

“I wondered about that fine-smelling soup at the door. Have you checked upstairs?”

“Yes. Most everywhere. He's not here. The whole house is like this. What was your name again, sir?”

“Mr. Cypress Jennings. Cy for short.” The smile faltered. “Shouldn't we . . . contact the authorities?”

She opened her lips to speak and then stopped. This Mr. Jennings sounded hesitant about calling the police. Did he have something to hide? Well, so did she, but at least she knew her reasons were valid.

More importantly, this crisis needed to stay among the wardens. The public knew the auxiliary had exploded, but they didn't know most everyone was presumed dead. If they did, there'd be a panic. Now, with this matter of Mr. Calhoun dead and Mr. Thornton missing, the situation had grown even more dire. Any evacuation needed to be handled in a proper manner, not spurred by gossip.

"I need to consult with Warden Sakaguchi." She looked past Mr. Jennings to the wooden phone box on the wall. The switchboard line meant there'd be no chance of privacy, but if she could ask Mr. Sakaguchi to meet them at Mr. Thornton's house, that'd be enough. "Pardon me, please."

Ingrid might have just happened to brush her body against his as she passed by. He felt as solid as he looked, though he quickly backstepped as a gentleman should.

Goodness, she just met the man and here she was, all ready to drag him into the broom closet to sneak a kiss. She was almost giddy. She pulled the mouthpiece down and pressed her ear to the Bakelite receiver.

"Hello? Hello? Central?" She stared at the mouthpiece in her hand. "There's no sound."

"Allow me, miss." Long, thick fingers plucked the mouthpiece away. Mr. Jennings inspected the box and then undid the latch to open the cabinet. "Here's the problem. The kermanite's gone. There's no transmission power."

Other devices around the house had kermanite the right size to work in the telephone box, but Ingrid had no desire to linger here while a stone was wired in. "That explains why none of Mr. Sakaguchi's calls got through. There are public telephones close by, but . . ."

"I can drive you home, miss. If you don't mind, that is. It's a two-seater." He ducked his head in a deferential way.

She gnawed at her inner lip. Accepting autocar rides from strange men wasn't a wise course of action, but she didn't fancy another long walk, even downhill. Her legs might give out and she'd roll down Chestnut Street like a snowball in skirts.

"If you don't mind." Caution edged her voice.

"Not at all, miss, though I do have one favor to ask."

"And that is?"

"Can you put the pistol away? Unless I really am your hostage, in which case we should probably get some rope to make it all official."

Amusement lit his eyes again, and it occurred to her that the obi of her dress could work quite well to bind someone. Hog-tying wasn't a skill taught by Mama, but maybe Ingrid needed to look it up. It might come in handy.

She slipped the pistol into her pocket, but made sure to hover her fingers just above the opening. She didn't need a gun to defend herself, but he didn't know that.

And while her body might not mind some broom closet time with this fellow, her brain knew better. He was a stranger and not to be trusted, and she'd take care of him if necessary.

CHAPTER 4

Ingrid hated leaving Mr. Thornton's house in such a state, but what did she know? It's not as if the place featured smears of blood or direct evidence of any crime. Things were missing, true, but Thornton could have removed them himself. Maybe he had hurriedly packed his valuables and traveled to a friend's home for his convalescence. The lack of communication about Mr. Calhoun's death made it clear that if a message had been sent to the auxiliary, no one would know.

A harsh chill shook her, and she clenched her hands together on her lap, the slight bulge of the gun close by. Everything was going so horribly wrong. She and Mr. Sakaguchi needed to leave the city. If they couldn't save everyone, they could at least save themselves.

She thought that, but she knew Mr. Sakaguchi would never abandon San Francisco. And she would never abandon him.

Mr. Jennings's autocar puttered along. The interior displayed the same tidy shabbiness as the man's clothes. He definitely didn't come from wealth, yet he somehow had the money to buy a sizable chunk of kermanite.

Ingrid sat in the back, as was proper, and leaned closer to him to speak. "You said you and your partner have an airship?"

"Oh. Yes, miss. All ready but for the engine installation. We run a machine shop located South of the Slot. We repair automobiles, airships, washers, dryers, most anything with an engine." His voice contained a lovely, rollicking rhythm.

"Do you hail from Atlanta?"

His head jerked to one side, showing his profile briefly. "Thereabouts." He focused on the narrow street again and braked as two children and a dog dashed across. The dog trailed a tattered scarf. Children playing at Thuggees.

Mr. Jennings's accent indicated southern roots, but most every mechanist she'd ever encountered could claim Atlanta as home at some point. After Reconstruction started in 1863, the heart of Dixie re-created itself as a capital of industry. Atlanta boasted a dozen technical universities and factories beyond count, and produced most of the Unified Pacific's dirigibles. Part and parcel of that, the city's Japanese population was quite high. Mr. Sakaguchi flew there on occasion to meet with officials from his native land. People joked that babies around Atlanta were born with a wrench in one hand, blueprints in the other, and a hankering for sushi with their milk.

"Mr. Sakaguchi might be able to help you. The wardens don't generally poach from each other's private sales, but these are special circumstances, and . . . oh."

Most of the western United States's stockpile of kermanite was kept in a vault at the auxiliary. Mr. Sakaguchi had some at the house and larger rocks at the bank, but not much. He'd mentioned the consequences of a lack of geomancers to fill kermanite, but what if the crystals had been destroyed as well? Good God, the shortage would create a panic in industries across the country.

"Are you all right back there?" asked Mr. Jennings.

"I have a lot to think about." She and Mr. Sakaguchi would tend to the catastrophe. They had to.

"At least it's a beautiful evening." At that exact moment, a drop of rain splattered against her hand, and one must have struck him as well. "Tommyrot," he muttered, and reached for the dashboard crank for the roof canvas.

Ingrid couldn't help but smile. Mr. Jennings made for a pleasant distraction. "How long have you been in the city?"

"Six months. We don't set down roots for long."

"I see." She paused. "What would convince you to stay?"

His head jerked to one side. "Pardon?"

"I said, what would convince you to stay?"

"World peace."

The answer took her aback. "Well, that sets the bar high, and doesn't sound good for your business. Most industry is spurred by the war these days."

"My father's a businessman. He always said a person ought to be flexible, know a variety of trades. He . . . he told me once that if he had his druthers, he'd have been a baker, settled out in the desert, where he could breathe easier." Mr. Jennings chuckled to himself. "Hard to imagine that."

"What's his business now?"

"He runs a company. Airships, motors, that sort of thing."

"Like father like son. Now I understand your comment back at Mr. Thornton's house. I think you'd be a fine secretary."

His rich laugh filled the car. "Thank you kindly for the endorsement. It'd be nice to stay in the city, if circumstances allow. You're going to set about creating world peace, then?" The autocar stopped as a small mob of ladies in gargantuan hats strolled across the street. He glanced back at her, grinning.

"Someone needs to." She tucked a strand of hair behind her ear.

"I do like the way you think, Miss Ingrid."

Happy heat bloomed in her stomach and went straight to her cheeks. The man was *flirting* with her, treating her with respect and equality, as if she looked more like Mama instead of . . . well, herself. She smoothed out her skirt and stared out the window, suddenly shy. "Ah. You'll want to take a left up here. We're almost there."

Mr. Jennings parked in front of the house. She demurred to his offer to take the kettles and hauled the cooled soup up the steps to her home.

Like many houses in the neighborhood, it melded several modern aesthetics. An asymmetrical Queen Anne facade and wraparound porch were topped off with a Japanese irimoya curved roof. For the second time that day, the mere sight of the place was enough to bring tears to her eyes.

Lee answered the door. His sharp gaze shifted from the kettles to the strange man behind Ingrid, then lowered in subservience.

"Things are complicated," she said, and stepped inside. "This is Mr. Jennings. I'd like to talk to Mr. Sakaguchi before they make their acquaintance."

"Please, enter," Lee said, bowing low. Upon straightening, he plucked the soup pots from her hands. "I'll tell Warden Sakaguchi that you have returned with a guest, Miss Carmichael." He dashed away as she set aside her hat.

"Well, he's fast!" Mr. Jennings hooked his battered hat on the hallway rack and shrugged off his coat. "I didn't even get to tell him thanks."

Ingrid looked at him in surprise. That small show of respect for Lee raised Mr. Jennings in her esteem even more.

She sat and quickly removed her boots. Mr. Jennings did the same. She reached into the shoe cupboard and set down a pair of house slippers designed for larger American feet.

"Thank you kindly, miss," he said. Ingrid pulled on her regular slippers. Together, they stepped up from the genkan.

"You're welcome. Here's the parlor." She motioned him into the next room. It displayed more Japanese influence with pale silk upholstery, bamboo, and a singular shelf of books. A taxidermied crane, an old gift from Mr. Roosevelt, stood in the corner with one leg curled. "We don't keep a large staff here, but I can certainly fetch you a drink, if you like. Lee should be back in just a few minutes."

His attention immediately focused on the bookshelf; her gaze traced his backside. His suit jacket fit a tad too wide at the shoulders, which were about the level of her head. Not a bad height difference, really. His hands would fit just perfectly atop her hips and her head could easily tilt back for a kiss.

Goodness. She'd survived the day and now it was like she'd gone into heat to celebrate.

"I'm fine for now, miss, thank you." His fingers caressed the book bindings.

"Do you read?" she asked.

"Fairly well." He grinned over his shoulder as she rolled her eyes. "I used to read a great deal, but the life of a nomad makes it a challenge to carry books."

"You like Mark Twain?" She nodded to where his hand rested on the shelf.

"Indeed. *Connecticut Yankee* is an old favorite of mine. My sister and I read it to tatters. Can't help but enjoy a book where a man engineers a kermanite engine using Guinevere's stolen brooch and a medieval blacksmith's shop."

"That's one of my favorite books, too!"

"My sister loved the book, to a point, and then she needed to dismantle it, like she did everything." He stared beyond the shelf. "Was like poison ivy on her brain that the science wasn't right. Kermanite of that size wouldn't be able to run such an engine, she argued, and found most every other technical flaw she could."

"But she was fine with the idea of a man slipping through time?"

"Oh no. Not after a while. Not even Merlin's magic was right—didn't fit into any proper schools of the art. As for Hank's engine, she drew up schematics of what he would have really needed, even what kind of metallurgy was available in Britain at the time."

"How old was she then?"

"Seven." At Ingrid's arched eyebrow, Mr. Jennings smiled. "My twin sister was the cleverest person I've ever known. Made me look like a bumbling fool in comparison."

Ingrid noted the past tense but didn't wish to pry. She also observed how his hand lingered on the book's binding. "Mr. Sakaguchi may be willing to let you borrow books, if you meet with his approval. He won't lend to just anyone, of course." It'd give Mr. Jennings a good excuse to visit more often, too.

A smile crinkled at the corners of his eyes. "I'm doubly honored, miss. You didn't shoot me, and now you want to lend me books."

"Mind you, if you treat the books poorly—" She made the motion of aiming a gun, as if she played kitsune-ken.

"You should manage more libraries, miss. Patrons would be sure to return books in good shape and promptly."

"Or they'd be terrified to borrow books at all."

"All the more books for loyal patrons to choose from." That smile of his warmed her like a furnace.

"Miss Carmichael!" called Lee.

She turned, mentally cursing the interruption. "I'll return shortly, Mr. Jennings."

"Much obliged." He dipped his head.

She followed Lee into the hallway. His poise dissolved. "What's going on, Ing?"

"Long story. I don't want to tell it too many times."

"Ah. Understood. I'll eavesdrop from the hallway."

She jabbed him with an elbow. "Watch our guest."

"I was watching how *you* watched him. I thought he might have ripped his pants, but I guess they're fine."

She scowled and aimed a kick his way, but he scampered ahead, agile as a hummingbird.

Lee opened the door to Mr. Sakaguchi's study. Mr. Sakaguchi stood in the double doorway across the room. One of his sleeves was drenched with water. Weak evening light cast the backyard in gray but for the colorful motes of pixies above the pond.

"Playing with your fish again?" She caught him like this about once a week.

His eyes were thoughtful. "The catfish are restless. Strangely so." He used a towel to dry his jacket.

Ingrid couldn't help but look at the namazu-e prints on the walls. The giant catfish hidden beneath Japan was said to warn his brethren when he was about to move. "Well, if I saw your hairy fist coming at me through the water, I'd be worried, too."

Normally, her humor could coax a smile, but now he shook his head. "I don't like it. We don't have enough geomancers here. If I see other animals becoming restless as well, I'll have to press Mayor Butterfield again. Have you felt or seen anything since we returned home?" He tossed the towel onto the bench outside and shut the doors. The shutters remained open to show the green backyard.

"Yes. A very minor seism on my walk, but otherwise nothing since the Reiki."

"Are you hurting since your walk?" he asked.

"A little stiff, that's all."

Mr. Sakaguchi crossed to his desk. "If you feel a major earthquake coming, what do you do?" His brisk tone caused her to straighten as if she feared the slap of a ruler.

"Transmit energy to the kermanite I have at hand, and when I feel the flush of a fever, break contact with the ground immediately."

"And how do you do that?"

"Jump onto furniture, with metal being the best. Go upstairs. Lift myself up. Keep my wits at all times, because it's chaotic during an earthquake. Oh yes. I may need to escape a building. Many people die as they flee from a house because of falling bricks or masonry, so I should use extra caution. Should I go down the full list? There are other things I really need to tell you."

Mr. Sakaguchi sighed. "You're arrogant, Ingrid."

She blinked, taken aback. "What?"

"You can carry power and use it. You're not limited by kermanite. You see colors overflow the earth. It's made you cocky. It scares me. It scared your mother. If something terrible does befall the city, you can't simply stand there and assume you can use the energy as it comes in. In a prolonged earthquake, the fever could take you in a matter of ten, twenty seconds. I saw it happen to my father in Edo, when I was just a boy. I only survived because I climbed a tree, but even so, it was a tree and I still took in too much."

"Yes, I know, and you were left delirious for several days as your body fought through sickness, but that may not happen here, Ojisan." Ingrid didn't fully believe her own denial.

"The catfish are restless," he murmured again. "Never have I seen them behave like this in San Francisco." He braced himself against his desk. "I've loved you as my own since you were a little girl. I loved your mother dearly." His voice softened. "I should have married her, Ingrid. I should have damned all the social constraints and . . . and . . . everything else in our way. Your mother didn't care about the scandal. I did." Mr. Sakaguchi blinked rapidly and stared downward. Through his thinning black-and-silver hair, she could see the slight sheen of his scalp.

"The baby," Ingrid whispered. Mama had died in childbirth. The baby had never drawn a breath.

"Yes, our child, and more. Things that, God help me, I hope you never know. You're all I have left, Ing-chan. That's why I must send you away."

"What?" she squawked.

Mr. Sakaguchi glanced toward the cracked door. "Start packing her trunk, Lee."

"Damn it!" The words were barely audible from the hall.

Mr. Sakaguchi continued. "It will just be for a week or so, I hope, until more wardens arrive and stabilize the city. It will also get you away from Captain Sutcliff. He's far too interested in you."

"But interested in you most of all. Why is that?" She stared him down. He shook his head, tight-lipped. "Despite everything you've said, you're probably only free because you're Japanese and he knows you need to be where you can conduct energy in case of a quake. Once more wardens arrive . . ."

"If I am arrested, so be it." He made it sound so simple, as though the Unified Pacific didn't speed offenders through the system and execute them within weeks. And yet earlier, he'd made the comment he might be safer in UP custody. Nothing made sense.

"Where am I supposed to go?" Power and frustration burbled within her chest. Her hands curved into hard fists.

"I purchased multiple tickets as a precaution, creating—to use an American idiom—a wild-goose chase, but your real train ticket will get you to Fresno."

"Fresno? What am I going to do, pick grapes?"

"Of course not. Grapes aren't in season."

"Ojisan! I can't believe this." She glared at Mr. Sakaguchi and was suddenly struck by how *old* he looked. His hair was more silver than black. Deep wrinkles furrowed his eyes.

"I can't go." Her voice softened. "You nearly died today. Everyone . . . almost everyone else did die." It would devastate him to know Mr. Calhoun was dead and Mr. Thornton was missing, but he had to know. He had to know it was even more important for her to stay to safeguard the city, and him.

Who else would pull him from his desk, remind him what it was to smile and laugh? Captain Sutcliff be damned. Mr. Sakaguchi needed her.

She continued, "When we were in that . . . bubble, you told me I had to fight, I couldn't give up. My power, whatever it is"—she waggled her fingers in the air—"is the only thing that saved us. I can't simply walk away from you, or from San Francisco. I need to stay here, and I need to fight!"

Ingrid struck downward with her fist.

At the same instant, a sharp snap pierced through the glass of the back door. Blood spewed in a fountain from Mr. Sakaguchi's shoulder. His head rolled back, jaw gaping as he flopped backward. He smacked against the floor in a horrible, fleshy crunch.

Ingrid had no chance to scream or gasp. One moment Mr. Sakaguchi stood there; the next, he was down. Spattered blood oozed down the wall.

CHAPTER 5

When the second bullet whizzed by her ear, Ingrid had the sense to drop to the floor. Her mind galloped—someone was shooting at them—what happened—who was doing this?! The shooter—was it Jennings?

But most of all—*Ojisan*.

Hunkered low against the floor, she crawled to him. Mr. Sakaguchi lay sprawled behind the desk. His hand was limp, fingers loosely curled, the palm faceup. His eyes studied her, brow furrowed as if in deep thought. His lips moved but no sound emerged.

"I'm here," she whispered. Her hand twined into his and squeezed. How strange. They rarely touched like this, and today it happened more than once.

"Who?" The single word was a breath.

"I don't know. They're out in the garden."

She peered around the desk. Nothing moved along the

patio. Mr. Sakaguchi moaned and shifted slightly. Blood poured from his shoulder and oozed an expanding puddle on the floor. She tugged the blanket from his reading chair and pressed it to his shoulder. His body arced in pain, sound escaping in a hiss.

"I'm sorry, I'm sorry," she whispered, and pressed down.

The wound was inches above his heart. Had the bullet passed through? Had it ricocheted inside him? She had to get him to a doctor.

"Them," he whispered. "Can't . . ."

She wanted to shush him, tell him not to exert himself, but she desperately clung to his every word.

Something scuffled in the hallway. She pivoted on a hip and fumbled inside her pocket.

Lee emerged from the shadows and into the doorway. "Damn! Where was he hit?" He crawled closer.

"Shoulder. Can you call the police? I—"

"Line's cut," Lee said. "First thing I tried when I heard the shot." Another bullet clinked through the glass. Splinters exploded in a small fountain not six inches from Lee's hand. He moved a little faster to reach the shelter of the desk.

She pulled out the pistol. "I must get him into the hall, maybe get him out the front. Shoot anything that moves out there."

If Captain Sutcliff needed a proper excuse to fit her for a noose, now he had one. Supplying a weapon to a Chinese boy probably broke a dozen laws. Not that she gave a damn at the moment, not with Mr. Sakaguchi bleeding out.

Lee accepted the gun with a grimace and checked the bullets in the chambers. With a jolt, she realized he knew what he was doing.

Lee had handled a gun before.

No time to mull over his sedition now. She crawled to Mr. Sakaguchi's feet and wedged herself between his calves. Hauling his feet up over each hip, she leaned forward. After a few seconds of strain, he slid forward. Ingrid thanked God for the slickness of the wooden floor. Mr. Sakaguchi made only the slightest whimper.

Shattering glass caused her to jump. She turned. Lee crouched to the side of the door and had knocked out the lower glass panel. He fired the gun once, twice.

A few more feet, and she had Mr. Sakaguchi in the claustrophobic shelter of the hallway. She crawled forward. The crown of her head butted against something warm. She fell against Mr. Sakaguchi's thighs with a squeal. A shadow stood over her.

"Get back!" she yelped. The faint tingle of energy welled up, and she shoved the intruder away.

The figure flew back five feet into a wall with a resounding thud and a rather high-pitched "Oof!" Lamplight illuminated the man's face and the rod in his hand.

"Mr. Jennings!"

The wall clock over his head tilted and slid straight down. *Stop!* she thought at the clock.

It did. Literally. It pinned itself to the wall, cock-eyed, not four inches over his cranium. She gaped. She had always had some extra awareness of things around her—like when that baseball almost struck her earlier—but hadn't manipulated something beyond her grasp before.

That sense of coldness crept into her veins again, and she shivered. At the motion, the clock resumed its slide, but at her gaze it again stopped. She was reminded of the bubble she created earlier, and how it popped when Mr. Sakaguchi surprised her by picking her up. She scurried forward and set the clock on the floor.

Mr. Jennings groaned. "How the . . . ?" He stared at her from beneath furrowed brows. He had donned his leather coat again.

"What are you doing?" she asked.

"Coming to check on you, miss. The boy told me to stay put, but I couldn't wait about while shooting's going on." He pivoted his hand to show the Tesla rod, still contracted.

"You only have the rod, no gun?"

"No, miss. I'm a pacifist."

"Bloody hell," she muttered. Fancy that. Middle of a gunfight and here's this big, strong man, and he's a pacifist! She retreated to check on Mr. Sakaguchi. Blood had soaked through the thick blanket.

"My car's out front, but that sidewalk doesn't give us any cover." Mr. Jennings scooped up his hat from the floor. She noted his shoes were on, too, the laces untied.

"I think the gunman's gone." Lee backed into the hallway.

"Lee. When your ribs were bruised, you went to a man in Chinatown who did powerful Reiki—*lingqi*." She hesitated to say the Chinese word for it, a word she shouldn't even utter. "Take Mr. Sakaguchi there."

Lee stared at her. "Take Mr. Sakaguchi into Chinatown?"

"He's *dying*."

Lee's face tightened as he nodded. "It's a risk, but . . . Jiao!" he yelled loud enough to be heard in the kitchen. "Run next door, tell the boys to drive the Suzukis' flatbed over! We have to get to Uncle Moon's, fast!"

Not two seconds later, the side door clattered. Ingrid hoped it was Jiao, not the gunman.

Don't die, don't die. Ingrid laid a hand against Mr. Sakaguchi's cheek. She willed the words through her touch, as if she could stop his soul from leaving his body as she stopped that clock. The short stubble on his jaw prickled her palm. She had no sense of power, no flow of energy. She almost wanted another earthquake to happen—just a small one—so she might be able to do something again. Anything.

"Miss, sending a Japanese man into Chinatown, and a warden at that—"

"What else can we do?" she snapped at Mr. Jennings. Anyone desperate enough to venture into Chinatown for healing needed results, the kind that couldn't unfurl from a bucket of benign seeds. "I know the risks. But this—this is business. I'll pay your uncle whatever he needs, Lee. Mr. Sakaguchi just—he just needs to get in and out of there safely."

Seventy thousand angry, despairing refugees in Chinatown, all of them there because of Japan. None dared to strike out directly against the Japanese, not even the Chinese *tongs,* but sending Mr. Sakaguchi into the heart of their district carried risks that Ingrid didn't want to contemplate right now.

She just needed her ojisan alive.

Lee defiantly tucked the gun into his waistband and stared at Mr. Jennings. "I've heard about you, Jennings. Everything you've seen here, keep quiet. You have a good reputation, and you better live up to it. I know where you live." Even with his soft prepubescent voice, the threat came across loud and clear.

Mr. Jennings nodded. The Tesla rod remained in his hand. "I carry no grudge against the Chinese. Don't intend to create any either."

The front door banged open. Both Lee and Mr. Jennings turned, weapons at the ready. Ingrid shielded Mr. Sakaguchi. The Chinese servants from across the street skittered to a halt in the hallway, took in the scene in an instant, and shared an expression of shock and revulsion.

"You want to take *him* to Chinatown?" one spat.

"Yes, and you're going to help me carry him, even if you have to use a whole bar of soap after." Lee's voice carried a gravitas that Ingrid had never heard before. "Come on!"

The men worked as a team to haul up Mr. Sakaguchi. Ingrid stumbled back, suddenly lost and useless. The police would be here soon. They would ask questions she couldn't answer, and then that captain was bound to nose around. This house might end up as ransacked as Mr. Thornton's.

Ingrid ran back to the study. She yanked Mr. Sakaguchi's safe-deposit keys from their hiding place on a shelf, and then grabbed his planner and notebook from the desk. She dropped everything into one of her abandoned hats and folded them up together.

As she dashed toward the door, her feet slid and she caught herself against the doorframe.

His blood. She slid in his blood. A violent tremor of awareness almost dropped her to the floor. Almost. Grinding her teeth, she pushed herself away from the room, the doorway, the house. The stench of iron clung to her.

The young night sky glowered with gray clouds. A truck idled at the curb as the men set Mr. Sakaguchi in the back. Utterly distracted as she was, her foot struck something. Ingrid tripped and staggered forward, her house slippers flying from her feet. Her knee bounced against the walkway with a painful jolt as her hands caught her in time to prevent face planting. An object rolled beside her hand—Mr. Sakaguchi's slipper. She stuffed it into her makeshift tote. Abandoning her own stained slippers, she scampered forward.

"Damn it!" snapped Lee.

"A Durendal." Mr. Jennings said it as a growl.

"What?" Ingrid looked up. Chinese men filled the appropriated truck. Mr. Jennings stood at the open door to his car, gaze focused up the street. Trees blocked her view.

The truck lurched from the curb with a sharp squeal.

"Wait! Come back!" Ingrid cried, even as she knew they couldn't afford to stay here, nor could Mr. Sakaguchi. The truck made a tight turn and bounced down a side street and out of sight.

"Miss Ingrid! Here!"

There was no time. A Durendal meant the Army & Airship Corps, and the A&A meant Captain Sutcliff and all his incriminations and innuendo.

She ran for the autocar as a blue sheen rose from the lawn. The pressure wave penetrated cotton and stroked her skin like a baby's breath. It was a tiny earthquake, the sort most people could dismiss as a passing large truck—or the grinding heaviness of a Durendal. Lukewarm heat looped in crazed circles around her ankles and anchored on her bone, traveling up her calves with a static-electric zap.

The seism ceased just as she reached the car. She flung the door open and threw herself inside. She slammed the door shut as Mr. Jennings lurched away from the curb. Something hard jostled against her feet—her shoes, she realized. He must have grabbed them on the way out.

She twisted around to glance up the block.

The ambulatory tank's sleek metal body gleamed beneath the streetlights. Its two mighty treads crunched against the basalt block thoroughfare. From a block away, she could feel the vibrations of its approach. The gun barrel aimed dead ahead, as though it would blast any obstacle to smithereens. Along the right and left sides, objects bobbed behind a shielding wall.

"It's a transport loaded with soldiers. I'm curious to know why the A-and-A was on the way here before the shooting even happened, but I'm not about to linger to ask *them* questions." He glanced at her, clearly expecting some answers.

Ingrid faced forward, gasping as they took a hard turn. A car horn blared. Gas lamps illuminated the residential street ahead. The truck bearing Mr. Sakaguchi had already vanished from sight. Grief twisted in her chest. What if he asked for her? What if he took a turn for the worse? She should be with him! Damn all the dangers of Chinatown, and damn Captain Sutcliff and his ridiculous suspicions!

Behind them, the kermanite-powered transport tank roared like a hungry lion, and she knew very well that it intended to gobble her up.

CHAPTER 6

"Hang on!" snapped Mr. Jennings. The little car buzzed as it zoomed down the street.

"Hanging!" The scant window frame didn't give her much to cling to.

Ingrid looked out the back window. The Durendal was close enough for her to discern the individual soldiers that lined the walled running boards on either side of the armored ambulatory. Who knew how many were inside?

Releasing her death grip on her door, she stuffed the hat and its contents behind her cloth belt. The hard corner of the planner gouged at her belly. The car took another sharp turn, and Ingrid squealed as she slid across the seat and right into Mr. Jennings.

"Some warning?" she snapped.

"I said to hold on!"

"To what?"

"Me, if nothing else!"

No time for that as he took another fast turn and sent her sliding the other way. She felt his leg kick out and brush her hip as he shifted as well.

He glanced at her. "Look at it this way—could be worse. Could be an Ambassador back there."

"How do you know there's not?"

"Ambassadors don't ride with common soldiers. They're too good for that. With the exception of Roosevelt, maybe." True, that. She'd personally seen Theodore Roosevelt talk horses with several black hostlers at a livery stable downtown, treating them with perfect decency. "I'd rather face that full Durendal, running hot, than any Ambassador."

She grunted agreement; she wouldn't want to be on the wrong side of Mr. Roosevelt either, and she knew him. Ambassadors oversaw the Japanese and American governments and their joint military operations. The sheer amount of power they wielded made Captain Sutcliff seem about as mighty as an ant biting a giant's big toe.

Grappling on to the leather seat, she pulled herself up to check the tank's progress. Mr. Jennings was zigzagging up Russian Hill, and this time the slope was to their advantage. The car's engine roared with exertion, but it easily outmatched the heavy Durendal that pursued them from a block away.

"Durendals have endurance but they can't take tight corners well." Mr. Jennings turned again, looping to drive down Hyde, but this time Ingrid gripped the seat with both arms. Her hip jutted to the side and bumped him. This was not the body contact she had imagined earlier.

"You've almost gone in a circle!" Her heart had revved like the car engine, but the lingering burble of power beneath her skin was a comfort.

"Yes, almost, but not quite. Standard procedure has it Durendals never travel alone to a location, so they may very well have left unfriendly folk back at your house, miss."

He sounded surprisingly cool considering how that evening she had threatened to shoot him, brought him home to endure a gunfight, embroiled him in a conspiracy with seditious Chinese, and then fled from a tank that carried enough firepower to level an entire city block. He'd even had the foresight to grab her shoes.

She liked the man more by the minute.

"Just so you know, Miss Ingrid, I'm not keen on attracting the military's attention. I'd like to know why a Durendal happened down your street."

Another swerve, followed by a chorus of honks from other drivers and the abrupt neigh of a horse. In the dimming light, electric signs had already flicked on, advertising booze, dancing halls, and French-style restaurants—all the sinful glories of the Barbary Coast neighborhood. She tried to avoid these blocks, particularly as night fell.

"A fellow by the name of Captain Sutcliff thinks that Mr. Sakaguchi and I are somehow involved in the explosion of the auxiliary this morning."

"Explosion?"

"It looks like we gave them the slip. Give me a moment to catch my breath."

Ingrid let her hips collapse onto the seat again as she faced forward. Ahead lay the naval dock with its masts and massive shipping containers; beyond that, the dark sheet of the bay. The canvas top of the car didn't filter out the briny air and the tang of a thousand things shipped from around the world.

Her heart began to climb back down from where it lodged in her throat. "The auxiliary blew up earlier, right after you left. I was with Mr. Sakaguchi when . . . we were the only survivors." She forced her dry throat to swallow. Had that really happened just this morning? "Captain Sutcliff showed up right afterward, saying he was on a mission . . ." She let her voice trail off. This stranger didn't need to know about a missing hunk of impossibly large kermanite. "He insinuated Mr. Sakaguchi or other wardens were involved."

"Hmm. You think this might've been handy for me to know a little earlier?" The lightness in his tone conveyed a slight edge.

"I met you in Mr. Thornton's house, which had quite clearly been ransacked, and you expect me to tell you personal details from the day? Almost everyone I know *died*." Tears threatened and she blinked them away.

"My apologies." His voice softened.

The autocar slowed as evening port traffic squeezed in on them. Surrounding cars glistened beneath the high electric lights along the dock. The grand spire of the ferry terminal loomed ahead, and past that trailed short and tall rows of airship masts. Each resembled a steel lighthouse with exposed staircases and girders. Elevators lifted pallets of goods.

Airships bobbed in a variety of colors and sizes, taut ropes tethering them to the top cones of many of the masts. Rigid

Behemoth-class freightliners were the largest today, their gasbags swollen with hydrogen and decks receded within their hulls.

Commercial passenger vessels were a bit smaller, identified by the presence of windows along the deck. These were nicknamed Portermans after the man who created the first east–west American airship network in the years soon after the California Gold Rush.

A smattering of small vessels moored at the lower masts: Sprite-class personal vessels that seated anywhere from four to twelve, as well as a number of Pegasus gunships. She wondered which one had brought Sutcliff to the city.

Flags of all nations emblazoned the rounded hulls—the majority being Japanese, American, or the split flag of the Unified Pacific—but British, Mexican, and Russian dirigibles freckled the rows. Ingrid knew that if she leaned out the window, she would hear dozens of languages in a brilliant cacophony, all of them belonging to men who were laughing and trading and ready for a night on the town. Women in furs with hats the size of Spartan shields ambled past Russian sailors in heavy furs of a different sort. Machinery clanked and propellers whirred from crafts too directly above to be visible.

"Beautiful airships, aren't they?" Mr. Jennings's voice was quiet, reverent. "My father used to say that an airship at sundown was colored silver and gold, and worth far more."

Ingrid looked down at her hands. Mr. Sakaguchi's blood had dried in the crevices of her palms and itched beneath her nails. Emotion caught in her throat. On any other night, she would have delighted in speaking with a kindred soul, someone who saw the beauty beyond the everyday bustle of the port.

She tugged the wadded hat from her obi. Mr. Sakaguchi's slipper plopped out onto her lap. Her pointer finger traced the gold embroidery along the top. Mama's work.

"I'm sorry, miss. He's like a father to you, isn't he? The fellow shot?"

"Yes."

A horn honked somewhere ahead. Pedestrian traffic shuffled along faster than they did.

"Hey, hey!" a very loud man spoke just outside. "Word's a Durendal's driving about downtown! Let's go have a look!"

"Holy hell, I'd like to see one a' dem!" A whole mob of sailors crossed in front of the autocar, headed into town.

Mr. Jennings said nothing for a few minutes. Their wheels rattled across the cable car tracks at Howard Street. "It is peculiar for a Durendal to be mobilized in an American city."

"It seems like overkill. They could have driven over in a caravan of trucks." Her voice sounded thick to her own ears.

"Durendals hold three set purposes. They're to kill, awe, and intimidate, and if you can do all three at once, all the better."

That sounded like Captain Sutcliff, all right. He probably had his shoes shined before interrogating her and Mr. Sakaguchi. He'd have driven a tank across the peninsula from the Presidio and parked it at their curb, too, if it showed who was in control.

"You seem to know a lot about Durendals."

"To my regret, yes."

She studied him in the intermittent gas-lamp light. He had

to be a few years older than her, probably not past thirty. Certainly old enough to have fulfilled his conscription time in the Philippines or China or some other Southeast Asian isle that earned brief mention in newsreels.

He turned them away from the docks and into the older blocks known as South of the Slot, as they were below the main cable car lines along Market Street. Leaning power lines and older factories flanked the quiet avenue. Haphazard metal sheeting and planks reinforced holey brick walls. A building up the street churned out plumes of steam so thick she imagined cupping a hand and scooping it from the sky like whipped cream.

He guided the car up a short gravel drive and behind a slatted fence. "Here we are." Mr. Jennings shut off the car and hopped out to close the gate behind them.

She was slow to move. Even with the fresh tingle of power in her veins, a terrible sense of exhaustion weighed on her. She should be with Mr. Sakaguchi, not here.

Lee's Uncle Moon had to save Mr. Sakaguchi. He just had to.

Ingrid groped beneath the seat for her shoes, and after a moment joined Mr. Jennings outside.

Heaps of machinery walled off the back of the warehouse. Piles of parts mounded taller than her five and a half feet, and as she stepped around the autocar and looked closer, she noted everything was organized. Wheels, axles, and other parts she couldn't even name, all together in distinct stacks.

"Miss, follow me if you will. All this metal around, it's not safe for anyone in the dark."

Mr. Jennings walked her to the back of the warehouse. A flickering light above caused the brim of his hat to shine like a halo. At the sound of that first gunshot, he must have grabbed his accessories from the hall. He was not as fastidiously attired as Captain Sutcliff, but he had his vanity, too—and a lot of common sense. She certainly couldn't have walked barefoot through a place like this, not without the risk of lockjaw.

"Thank you for thinking to grab my shoes," she said.

He shrugged. "Sometimes old habits come in handy. If you have to skedaddle, know what you need to survive."

Yes, he most definitely had been a soldier. She followed him inside. Scant lighting revealed a winding pathway through more machinery. Tables weren't set with dinner plates and napkins, but with dismantled engines, the chassis of an airship's stub wing, and the extended canopy of an autocar.

Mr. Jennings motioned around them. "My partner believes in the high art of disorderly organization. It makes sense to him."

"You two keep busy." No wonder they could afford a piece of kermanite large enough for a Sprite-class engine.

"We do try." Pride warmed his voice. "Fenris! Where are you, Fenris?" Mr. Jennings's yell echoed against the high ceiling and bounced through gnarled metallic canyons.

"Working on the *Bug*! About time you showed up with my kermanite, damn it." The high voice was muffled in its echo.

Chuckling, Mr. Jennings led the way through the labyrinth and to an airship. Well, parts of an airship. A pulley system hitched to the ceiling supported the massive copper-toned hunk of the orichalcum cockpit. Filled gasbags the color of vellum hovered just above. Sporadic ropes and weights held it down.

She couldn't help but gape in fascination. Sprite classes always looked small in contrast to other dirigibles, but she'd never been up close to any craft. If a Sprite made her feel this way, beside a massive Tiamat-class airship, she'd be like krill before a whale's maw.

She stooped to pick up a piece of orichalcum. The golden metal was the length of her arm, and about as light as a bouquet of flowers. She set it down again, amazed at how metal so strong could weigh so little.

Two oil-smeared legs stretched out from beneath a big piece of something. An engine, judging by the empty kermanite chamber.

Mr. Jennings planted his fists on his hips. "Pop out of there for a bit, Fenris."

"Bah. Okay. Give me a minute to connect this." Something rattled within the metal block, followed by indecipherable muttering, and then the body rolled out into the light.

The figure was slender and slathered in oil and God-knew-what, and reminded Ingrid of fairy photographs sold by Victoria Rossi. The body was shaped like a lowercase *l,* with no hips, cropped hair, bug-eye goggles, and a scowl that suggested they interrupted him in the midst of something very important. A black-gloved hand pried up the goggles. Clean skin around his eyes created a reverse raccoon effect.

"That's a woman, not kermanite." His voice was high and raspy; a smoker, she guessed.

"Congratulations," said Mr. Jennings. "You are correct."

"Cy. We already had a talk about you feeding half the stray cats in the neighborhood. Now you're bringing home women, too? Couldn't you fill a saucer of milk for her and leave it by the rubbish bin?"

Ingrid folded her arms across her chest, tucking her meager possessions near her heart. "If I'm not welcome here, I can go back home."

"No. You can't." Mr. Jennings's voice was gentle and warning all at once.

She rubbed at her face. She wanted home. She wanted her reading chair and a hot fire. She wanted to hear the whisper of Mr. Sakaguchi's slippers as he paced between his desk and shelves as he did his evening work. Instead, her household probably resembled a kicked-in anthill of soldiers in blue, and Mr. Sakaguchi—no, she wouldn't think of him, not right now.

"I need my kermanite, Cy," said Fenris. "I can't piece together the engine compartment until I can wire it in."

"We have more immediate concerns, Fenris. We just escaped from a Durendal full of soldiers."

There was a dramatic shift in Fenris's expression. "Oh. Are you okay?" He glanced back at the mechanical debris. "If we can get the kermanite, I can assemble the *Bug* and be ready to go by morning if you pack up—"

"Not that sort of trouble. Not yet anyway." Mr. Jennings sighed and looked to Ingrid.

"Wait a second. You mean you rescued her from soldiers? You put yourself at risk because of *her*?" Those strange raccoon eyes appraised Ingrid and obviously found her very, very wanting.

Ingrid stiffened. The very notion of weakness on her part brought a flare of power to her skin. "He didn't rescue me. He . . . well . . ."

"I was an avenue of escape, that's all." He said it in such a gentle way that she was placated. "Fenris, don't look at her like that. Here's what happened."

Mr. Jennings proceeded to summarize the day's events while strategically leaving out the matter of Ingrid threatening to shoot him, or the fact she'd flung him back into a wall and almost brained him with a clock.

That made her think. If Mr. Jennings had been concussed by his strike into the wall, it certainly didn't show in his driving or wits after the fact. He had seen what she did, but hadn't said a thing. Why? Did he intend to hold it over her as blackmail?

Fenris listened to everything, acknowledging points with the occasional nod. Once Mr. Jennings was done, he said, "So you've brought home the person who can get my kermanite."

"Rather myopic, aren't you?" Ingrid snapped.

He showed no reaction to her attitude. "When I'm in a project, I need to finish it."

"Well, just about everyone I know was killed today, and Mr. Sakaguchi might be dead now, as far as I know." Tears threatened again. She did not want to cry in front of these strange men.

"You've dealt with a terrible trauma today, Miss Ingrid. My apologies that you must endure my partner's acerbic nature atop that."

Mr. Jennings adjusted his glasses on the arch of his nose

and offered her a soft smile. He cared. The knowledge caused sudden warmth to bloom in her chest, and it felt so much like the tingle of an earthquake that she almost dropped to the ground to pull in energy—but the origin of this heat was entirely in the wrong place.

Damn it all. If he kept looking at her like that, she might not care a lick if he blackmailed her.

"I can get kermanite for you." She almost regretted the words as they slipped out, but she desperately needed allies, even if this Fenris acted like he sat on something spiny.

"You can? Tonight?" Fenris perked up, and then abruptly scowled. "Goddamnit! If the auxiliary's gone, the ready supply of kermanite is nil. Prices are going to go cirrus-high. What sort of rates are you charging?"

"Fenris," snapped Mr. Jennings. "If she asks market value, then we'll pay what we need to." He turned to her. "Miss, you've already been through quite enough today. There's no need to fuss over—"

"You helped me. You helped Mr. Sakaguchi. I won't inflate the price, but I do ask for a favor in return. I can't . . . I can't go home. I hate the idea of hiding from my own government's men, but . . ."

Mr. Jennings nodded. "Once the military's decided something, it can be as single-minded as Fenris here."

"Hey!"

"If you can get me to the Bank of Italy over on Davis, I can access Mr. Sakaguchi's stash of kermanite."

"The bank can't be open now?"

"No, but the manager lives next door, and I've often fetched parcels for Mr. Sakaguchi at this time of evening, even on holidays." She and Mr. Sakaguchi had been visiting the bank often to fill up a particular piece of kermanite that was about head size, perfect for a Sprite. The heat currently brewing in her veins would be adequate to finish the crystal. "You've been especially kind, Mr. Jennings. This is the least I can do."

"We live as bachelors here, but providing you a refuge is the least *we* can do." Mr. Jennings turned to his partner and glared. "Right, Fenris?"

"Seems she's already dropped us waist-deep in manure." Fenris shrugged. Sweat and oil seemed to have lacquered his shirt to his shoulders. "If she can get my kermanite and avoid bringing any more gunfights or explosions here, then fine. I just want to get my work done."

"It's a deal, then." Ingrid looked to Mr. Jennings. "Let's go fetch that rock."

CHAPTER 7

April 16, 1906

"Hey." Something hard nudged Ingrid in the shoulder and shattered the blackness of sleep. She blinked. Ahead of her was a mottled metal wall with rusted bolts staring at her like albino eyes. She shifted on a mattress so thin that the bony knobs of the bed frame left imprints on her body. Unusual stiffness lingered in her back and down her legs. The events of the previous day flooded through her mind. The auxiliary. Mr. Sakaguchi. The soldiers. Mr. Jennings.

That's whose bed she occupied. Mr. Jennings hadn't shared the bed with her, of course. He had grabbed a few blankets and said he'd make do on a car seat down in the shop. His scent lingered, reminiscent of a spilled bottle of ink.

Awareness circled in her mind. She had slept in a strange man's bed. She was still in it. Her hand grazed the thin mattress and wondered how his body fit against it, tall as he was, and smiled at the thought.

Something cold jabbed into her shoulder. She lurched upright with a gasp. Her forehead collided with a wooden shelf. The audible thud ricocheted through her skull. She bounced backward onto the bed as it squawked in indignation.

"He warned you about that."

Rubbing her head, Ingrid rolled to find Fenris standing about five feet away, a long metal pole in his grip. The bedchamber was little more than a storage closet tucked away in the warehouse loft. Light poured through the window and caused her to wince.

"Did you just poke me?"

Fenris looked at the pole in his hand. "Yes, well, I didn't want to grab your shoulder." He nodded toward her. "You like him, don't you? Cy?"

She scowled as her cheeks flamed. Somehow, the observation sounded worse from him than it did from Lee. "And if I do?"

"Don't get your hopes up, that's all. We're hopeless wanderers. With his pretty little accent, Cy always has girls fawning over him. He leaves broken hearts wherever we go."

She masked a flinch. "I don't fawn over anyone." Cy's voice could probably calm a horse enough to walk through a fiery barn, but she didn't want to think of him with other girls. Or leaving.

Not like she'd made much progress on that goal of world peace yet.

Ingrid swung her legs around to the metal floor, taking care that her skirt behaved itself. The stiff pleats of her pseudo kimono had held up surprisingly well. She reached for her shoes.

"What time is it?" she asked, avoiding direct eye contact.

"Past nine."

Fenris wore the exact same clothes as the previous night, or maybe all of his clothes were in the same stained condition. His face, however, had been washed, revealing caramel skin lighter than Ingrid's. He could be mixed like her, or of Latin descent. His spindly arms crossed his chest as he watched her, making no effort to grant her modesty.

"You haven't been to sleep yet?" Ingrid asked.

"I'll sleep when I'm dead. In the meantime, there's coffee and work to do. Oh, and there's a Chinese boy downstairs waiting for you."

"What?!" Ingrid jumped upright, only at the last second leaning forward to avoid the shelf.

"Come on, then." Fenris left. Cursing, Ingrid shoved her feet into her shoes and hobbled after him, at the last second remembering to grab her hat from the floor. It was hopelessly creased and battered from its misuse the previous day, but she needed some sort of head cover.

Her feet pounded out a metallic drumbeat down the staircase as she looked around the sprawling warehouse. Mr. Jennings had taken her on a quick tour after they returned from their bank errand the night before. He had insisted on paying for the work outright, and she hadn't argued with him that much. Considering everything that had happened in the past day, possessing hundreds in ready cash seemed wise.

The open section of the warehouse was the men's personal playground. The airship, dubbed *Palmetto Bug,* had been made from scrap. How and where a person could find something as expensive as orichalcum as scrap, she hadn't a clue.

Fenris had the brisk pace of a man with a to-do list the length of his arm, but with her urgent stride, Ingrid quickly caught up. As they passed through the door to the front office where Lee awaited, she slowed down, suddenly overwhelmed with dread. Was Mr. Sakaguchi still alive?

She desperately read Lee's face for clues. He looked suitably blank, a proper errand boy.

"Miss Carmichael." Lee granted her a low bow.

She didn't care one whit for propriety. "Lee, how is he? Is he alive?"

Lee looked sidelong at Fenris, and Fenris flicked a dismissive wrist and showed no sign of leaving. Lee faced Ingrid again. "He's alive. But it was a grave wound. Uncle almost lost him a few times." His voice sounded even, but Ingrid detected the anxiety underneath.

"But right now, how is he?"

"He won't be walking out of there anytime soon. He's still on the edge. If infection sets in . . ."

Mr. Sakaguchi could still die.

She closed her eyes, wavering, as she remembered when Mama died. Ingrid had stayed at her bedside through hours of that long and awful labor. Dr. Hatsumi had visited and done what he could, all the while muttering about discordant energies. A Pasteurian had come and said much the same, but in regard to sepsis and bacterial infections. Mama hadn't helped matters as she insisted she'd be fine, even as her skin took on a white and waxy sheen, and she outright refused to go to the hospital.

Mr. Sakaguchi had been on a trip to Atlanta and was on the fastest Porterman home. "By the time I land, I'm sure the labor will be done and she'll scold me for returning early," he'd told Ingrid over the telephone before he boarded the airship. Mr. Sakaguchi, ever the optimist.

The next call Ingrid made was for an ambulance carriage. By the time it arrived, Mama had slipped away. The hand in Ingrid's grasp turned limp as a cut celery stalk left in the sun.

Mr. Sakaguchi returned home and made it to the doorway of Mama's empty room before sinking into a puddle of grief. Ingrid had grasped his hand then. It had also been limp, but still carried the quiver of his pulse.

She needed to hold his hand, know that heartbeat.

Ingrid took in a shaky breath and opened her eyes. "Take me to him, Lee. Please."

"Ingrid. No." Lee's gaze flicked to Fenris and back to her. "I'm just here to tell you how he is. I'm not sure when I'll be able to come back." A peculiar emotion flashed over his face. Fear?

"Then that's all the more reason for me to go. Mama—you were there when I lost Mama. You know she kept saying she was fine, and then she went to sleep, and . . ."

"Damn it, Ingrid. Don't put me in this position. Please."

"I've been to Chinatown to go shopping plenty of times along with you and Mama and Jiao."

"We'd have to go off Dupont for this." Lee's expression was hard. "You don't belong there."

Dupont Street acted as a neutral zone where different skin colors mingled for the sake of business. While Ingrid had surmised that Lee's uncle likely didn't practice in a certificate-adorned establishment, leaving Dupont meant discarding money, morals, and any remaining shreds of virtue. It meant entering the full domain of the *tongs* that had filled the power vacuum left by the fall of China's government.

When Ingrid was young, before Japan claimed Manchukuo, the Cantonese *tongs* had warred with each other in the narrow alleys of Chinatown. Assassinations by hatchet men dominated the daily headlines in *The Call,* sensationalized as anything the Thuggees did now. Since the influx of refugees, the *tongs* hadn't slaughtered their own, nor did they physically fight against Americans. That would have only invited obliteration. Instead, according to the complaints of men like Warden Calhoun, the Chinese *tongs* bled their host nation through vice—opium dens, gambling parlors, and prostitution—all evidence of the weak spirits and immorality of the Chinese race.

Mr. Sakaguchi had always taken care that Ingrid knew the counterpoint to the men's arguments. "True, the *tongs* manage these sordid shops off Dupont Gai," he murmured, "but the whites are the ones financing them. What does that say of their morals?"

"Mr. Sakaguchi!" she had whispered. "Don't use their words."

"You know very well that *gai* is another word for street."

"That doesn't mean I'm *supposed* to know," she mumbled, wary of the wardens close by.

A wave of sadness passed over his face. "When we kill a word, it's akin to killing off the dodo bird. Nothing can replace it, and it's impossible to know the scope of the loss."

The simile had made her roll her eyes at the time. Mr. Sakaguchi could make anything into a school lesson.

Now Ingrid would pay her weight in kermanite if she could hear him lecture again. He just needed to be healed and out of Chinatown before hatchet men became aware of his presence.

"Off of Dupont." Ingrid nodded. "Very well."

Lee shook his head, clearly exasperated. "Ingrid, this isn't a place for you to go. Ever."

"Take me there, just this once, Lee. Please. Let me have the chance to . . . to say good-bye. Just in case." She knew she had Lee when he groaned and trailed a hand over his face.

"I'm the first to admit that social conventions are a weakness of mine." Fenris shifted as he leaned on the wall. "But even I know that a woman needs a proper escort into Chinatown, and a Chinese boy doesn't qualify."

"Where's Mr. Jennings?" she asked.

"Making deliveries, and probably will be for a while yet. But I suppose I can go." Fenris straightened and sighed as if he took on an onerous burden.

The man was right, damn him. She and Lee couldn't go about on errands together; it wasn't proper, or safe. Lee took a risk every time he walked the city. Most American men in their majority had fought against the Chinese and had the scars, synthetic limbs, and grudges to prove it. Some regarded the death of any Chinese as a favor to the war effort abroad.

She grudgingly nodded. "Thank you. It's greatly appreciated."

"Anyone else you want to invite along?" Lee asked. "Maybe the grocer? A fishmonger?"

"No, but it would be nice if we could drop by the house for a change of clothes."

He shook his head, his unruly black hair draping over his eyes. "That, I definitely nix. There's a Durendal parked out front and several soldiers on watch. Jiao's too scared to even try to go inside. I can go elsewhere to get a lady's coat to cover your stained dress."

"That'll do," she said. Lee always had his ways. She looked at Fenris. "Mr. Jennings only called you Fenris. What's your full name?"

"Fenris."

Ingrid clenched her fists. It was a good thing she didn't hold any energy now, or Fenris might find himself blasted into the nearest wall, whether she intended it or not. "I can't call you that in public. We're not that familiar." And we're not going to be, she wanted to add.

He rolled his eyes as he stepped closer to the door. "Then call me Mr. Fenris."

The morning was crisp and cloudy, and the people of San Francisco bustled about their normal business. Ingrid, Lee, and Fenris melded with the crowd. Paper boys hawked the morning news. Rubber-lined and wooden wheels rattled and rolled by. On high, airships were blips against the gray canvas of sky.

Lee made a quick stop at a strange house and emerged with a tapestry-style overcoat that worked well to cover Ingrid's dress. Considering the circumstances, she wasn't about to ask questions. She tied the belt at her waist and walked on, afraid of what awaited her in Chinatown.

Afraid of what awaited the city, period.

"I haven't been out in a while." Mr. Fenris took in a deep breath, as though the air was pleasant. "And to be out walking with a lady!" He sounded surprisingly happy.

"Considering your personality, that must be a rarity," she snapped, then cringed.

Mr. Fenris looked away and sped his steps, but not before Ingrid saw the wounded look in his eyes.

Ingrid cursed beneath her breath, hating the meanness of her words and knowing it was far too late to take them back. He'd even called her a lady. Fenris was peculiar, but he was helping her, even if he was doing so only because she had fetched his precious kermanite. She tugged her hat tighter onto her head, as if that might inspire her wits to function.

With Mr. Fenris walking a short distance ahead, Lee fell into stride with her.

"What do you know about these men?" Ingrid asked in a low voice, and nodded toward Fenris.

"They've been here for a while. They have a reputation for high-quality work, but they're rather odd in that regard."

"How so?"

"They'll take any customer—Chinese, Mexican, Brit, anyone who drops into port—and they charge an honest rate, same that they'd charge a white. Plus, no abuse comes along with it. They probably get more business than they can handle now. Jennings is the front of the partnership. No one ever sees this Fenris Braun."

She noted the surname. "No mystery as to why." Ingrid toyed with the knot of her belt. "Thank you for escorting me to see Mr. Sakaguchi. I know it's asking a lot—"

"We're being killed off, Ing, and you demand entrance to

one of the few places left in the world we can call ours. Hell yes, it's asking a lot."

She flinched. "I'm sorry. I . . . I didn't think of it like that."

"No. Of course you didn't." He sighed. "I know what he means to you. I know what he's come to mean to me, and I'm Chinese. When we're off Dupont, you have to stay close to me, understand? Do whatever I tell you to do."

"I understand."

"In Chinatown right now . . . things are very strange." His voice lowered so much she could scarcely hear. "People are leaving. No one is saying why. Mr. Sakaguchi is leaving the city. I'm supposed to leave, too."

"Isn't it dangerous to move him in his condition?"

"Yes. But the *Chinese* are moving, Ing. If we're leaving, you know something bad is going to happen. For us to take that risk . . ."

"Good God. Is the A-and-A going to level the district?"

"I don't know." He sounded so frustrated, vulnerable.

"Where would you even go?"

"No one's told me yet. All I know is the Chee Kongs started to leave, then the Hop Sings. They are leaving in a trickle to avoid suspicion. Uncle is leaving within hours. This . . . this might be the last chance you have to see Mr. Sakaguchi, whether he lives or not." He shot her a frantic look, and in that second she knew.

"I'm a fool," she whispered. "A *lingqi* doctor that good wouldn't simply be a back-alley businessman. Your uncle works for a *tong,* takes care of their highbinders. Do they know who Mr. Sakaguchi is? Of course they do. Oh no."

Ingrid forced her leaden legs to move forward even as her stomach squeezed in a vise of terror. Mr. Sakaguchi had never promoted the politics of his homeland—quite the opposite—but the fact that he was Japanese was enough to make him a useful pawn. Then there were his skills as a warden . . .

"Which *tong* holds him?"

"Wui Seng Tong. It means Hall for the Restoration of Life."

She hadn't heard of that one. The name made it sound like some sort of *lingqi* fraternity, but it didn't mean they were a cluster of pacifists. There had to be at least a dozen different *tongs* in the city, and most all of them had names that boasted of protecting one virtue or another.

They crossed Market. A horse neighed shrilly, followed by a man's yell.

"Ingrid, they're not going to harm him."

"No. They'll wait until he's well to torture him so he'll fill kermanite. He won't cooperate. They'll realize that. They'll kill him."

Ingrid emitted a small moan. Mr. Fenris glanced back, and she forced her hands away from her mouth as she attempted to act normal. Mr. Thornton had always been the warden who worked in Chinatown because of his knowledge and experience in Asia. Mr. Sakaguchi never entered the ghetto.

"I wanted him to be kept alive. I knew there was a risk, but . . . oh, Lee. What have I done?"

"What have you done? I'm the one who took him there. What were the alternatives, Ing? Really? Mr. Sakaguchi would have died under the care of any other doctor, or he'd be in the custody of that captain. Would the Unified Pacific treat him any better?"

"I don't know anymore," she whispered. Mr. Sakaguchi had wondered if he would be safer in UP custody. Maybe he would have been, up until his execution.

Lee's elbow brushed hers, a subtle attempt at comfort. "Mr. Sakaguchi has worked with Wui Seng before. Not in person, but through me. Mr. Sakaguchi is respected. They won't *want* to kill him."

"Wait. He's worked with this *tong*? When? *Why?*"

Certainly, she knew Mr. Sakaguchi didn't agree with the Chinese genocide, but this? Mr. Sakaguchi wouldn't fill any kermanite that went directly to the war effort, not for either side. What else was he up to? Was Captain Sutcliff right in insinuating Mr. Sakaguchi had committed some act of treason—not simply speaking out—against the Unified Pacific?

And why hadn't she known about it?

Ingrid shook her head. She had no idea how to muddle through this mess. As for Lee, he hunched up his shoulders, making it clear he had nothing more to say on the subject.

A bell signaled the approach of the California Street cable car. Mr. Fenris rejoined them, his face impassive. Ingrid made sure to stay very close to Lee as they boarded the dummy car; his gaze stayed down, as was proper. He needed to appear meek.

To Ingrid's relief, the gripman was familiar to her—a freed slave she'd spoken with a time or two before. He'd never forced her off a cable car as other gripmen had when she traveled alone. However, the old man's face tightened in disgust as he looked back at Lee. Ingrid met his eye, making it clear that Lee was with her. The man ratcheted up the hook that snagged the cable underground. The back car consisted of bench seats facing outward, with poles and a sideboard for standing passengers; this side was almost empty. She understood from experience that it wasn't safe for any Chinese to hang from the poles on the outside. She motioned Lee to sit.

By the telltale grinding beneath the car, Ingrid knew to grab hold of the nearest pole as the six-ton car lurched forward. Mr. Fenris bowled into her and bounced off, fortunately landing beside Lee instead of in the street.

"First time?" she asked, surprised.

"Actually, yes." He looked away, obviously embarrassed.

From the front of the dummy car, a man advanced on them, clinging to poles as he walked. "I don't share no car with a goddamned chink," he snarled.

"Hey!" snapped Ingrid. "He's mine."

The man spat at Lee's face. Lee blinked as the spittle struck but otherwise sat immobile. "Yours? 'N who do you belong to?"

Cheeks flushed, Ingrid stepped between Lee and the stranger. "Do you want to explain to Warden Sakaguchi why we couldn't complete his shopping list?"

The name did the trick. The man scowled and retreated. He had only one hand. The other probably rotted somewhere overseas.

She stood over Lee, alert for anyone else's approach. In the shelter of her shadow, he wiped his cheek with a sleeve.

Fenris observed the whole exchange, his lips tightly compressed. Ingrid was irked that he hadn't spoken up, but pleased that she'd handled the incident on her own.

At the next stop, a woman and child boarded, the boy

about ten. The woman glared at Lee from down the bench and jerked the boy closer to her. The child never looked up—he was too engrossed in a dime novel. Ingrid caught a glimpse of the cover. It portrayed the iconic image of Theodore Roosevelt, a rifle held on high. Likely a propaganda piece about how Roosevelt's brilliance crushed the Spanish Empire.

The man could have easily won the election for United States president in 1900. Instead, he rose to become one of the twelve Ambassadors of the Unified Pacific—a more prestigious position, no question.

Few Ambassadors' names were known publicly. Roosevelt's tactical acumen, wealth, and his reputation as a social luminary made him the most prominent American. He occupied the vacancy left by the late Leland Stanford, whose mansion wasn't too far away on Nob Hill.

Ingrid genuinely liked Mr. Roosevelt and had always enjoyed his visits with Mr. Sakaguchi. She had been perplexed when their friendship so suddenly ended. Mr. Sakaguchi had refused to explain what happened, which made it even more peculiar.

Ingrid, Fenris, and Lee disembarked the cable car as St. Mary's tolled out the hour in resonant tones. An old Chinese man rattled by pulling a handcart brimming with three ladies in fur-trimmed smocks. The brilliant crimson gates of Chinatown flanked the entrance to Dupont Street. Brusque singsong calls of vendors rang out from within the district. The flow of pedestrians slowed at a bottleneck.

Just within the gate, Ingrid noted a soldier in deep navy blue. His full focus rested on what seemed to be an infinite line of Chinese men and women, each in diverse uniform attire.

All of them carried their paperwork in hand along with small parcels or metal lunchboxes.

"Is the line always that long these days?" she yelled to Lee. She barely heard her own voice in the din. It'd been months since she had visited Chinatown.

"For the registry checks? Yes." He tapped his chest pocket out of habit.

All the effort was on checking the Chinese as they left. Nothing impeded the returning Chinese, or the influx of whites. The avenue seemed busier than ever, so claustrophobic that Ingrid wanted to scrunch her shoulders to make herself fit. Brick and wood buildings extended a dozen stories high. From the rooftops, radio towers and bright red dirigible-warning beacons stabbed the heavy belly of the overcast sky.

When she was younger, she had talked with Mr. Sakaguchi about the odd nature of Chinatown. Many people openly hated the place and argued that it was a waste of prime real estate, sandwiched as it was between Nob Hill and the Financial District. But even as San Franciscans beat Chinese people to death for daring to walk down a street, or praised the butchery of thousands of chankoro across the Pacific, Americans and Japanese shopped in Chinatown and spent quiet Sunday afternoons pacing the length of Dupont.

The graft may have preserved it, but Chinatown had also become a destination. Mr. Sakaguchi had explained to Ingrid, grief in his eyes, "Native tribesmen of Africa, America, and Australia have been exhibited in fairs and zoos around the world as curiosities, as *things*. Now people visit Chinatown for a similar reason."

His words made her shudder back then; now, in light of Lee's concerns, the memory made her stomach twist in a hard knot.

Wooden balconies jutted over the narrow snake-tongue of the street below. Ingrid did a double take as she spotted a familiar figure. Victoria Rossi was on a balcony above, facing away to take a picture of the avenue. Ingrid had no desire to say hello, not after the way Miss Rossi had treated her before.

Someone jostled Ingrid and forced her attention to the street. Vendors lined the sidewalks. Some sold wares from open windows and Dutch doors, while others utilized wagons with rainbow-bright canopies.

"Tea! Buy tea! Hot-hot!"

"Silk! Silk for the lady!"

"Marconi, brand-new! Super fine! Opera at home!"

Lee stepped between her and Fenris, and Ingrid felt him grip the side of her coat. They waded through a sea of humanity. Smells assaulted her: the delectable odor of roast duck, the rankness of unwashed men, the saltiness of sea, a bludgeoning of jasmine perfume. She gagged.

Textures billowed from shops—satin in dozens of tints, many still reeking of dye. An embroidery shop featured old women on a balcony, their figures small and stooped like oversized porcelain dolls. Tailors advertised Western-style suits in their front windows, the creases ironed so finely they could cut like a blade. Signs boasted of the high fashion of Tokyo and Paris, all done for cheap.

No one here wore traditional Chinese clothes like mandarin collars, pajama-like suits, or broad basket-woven hats. Such fashion was taboo.

Lee jerked her to the left, toward an alley so narrow she did squeeze in her shoulders. Dented metal trash bins lined the way and seeped sweetness. Ingrid winced as her hips brushed the bins. The cacophony of Dupont faded, but the place was not quiet. Voices in broken English became more distinct as they neared the next avenue.

"Stay close to me. If anyone stops us, let me do the talking." Lee glanced between her and Mr. Fenris and then proceeded.

Light pierced her eyes. Autocars and handcarts moved along at steady clips. A donkey brayed somewhere out of sight. Most everyone was Chinese, adorned in drab, threadbare dungarees and striped cotton shirts, the sort she expected any poor white to wear. Few wore shoes. The glamorous scent of spices and food had been replaced by the dankness of rotting wood and the reek of chickens, along with ubiquitous autocar exhaust and manure.

A couple of white men walked along with low-pressed hats. Ingrid was keenly aware of how conspicuous she was, and couldn't help but walk closer to Mr. Fenris.

About a half block down, Lee guided them inside a building. They passed a window shielded by heavy curtains. Through the gap Ingrid saw a naked woman. No, not a woman—a girl, her chest flat and hips narrow, silken black hair falling to her waist. A man laughed, unseen, and the girl walked to one side with a practiced saunter to her hips and—

"Ingrid," Lee's voice was sharp as he yanked on her arm. "Walk."

She hadn't even realized she had stopped moving. Dry-mouthed, she followed.

After a series of quick turns, they pattered down a gray-walled staircase that stank of roasted peanuts. The smell invaded her nostrils as they walked on, down and down. She had heard rumors that Chinatown extended five stories underground, but had long dismissed them as ludicrous; anyone building that deeply underground into turf so readily liquefied in an earthquake, even with a school of wardens nearby, was foolish. Now she wondered if the rumors were true.

Slits in the brick walls cast slivers of light on the floor. She glanced at an opening and met a pair of eyes staring right back at her. Ingrid barely bit back a squeal. She jerked her gaze forward, to Lee, as the itchy feeling of being watched followed her all the way down the corridor.

"Boo how doy." Lee whispered the words so softly she almost missed them.

"What?" she whispered, discomforted to hear him speak Chinese.

"Hatchet men. Highbinders. Guards. Just walk, Ingrid. You're with me."

Assassins, the real thing—not a turbaned, dashing Thuggee on the cover of a dime novel. She walked. She walked quickly.

Finally, Lee led them upward. Ingrid sagged in relief at the presence of sunlight, and then they turned again, delving into the interior of some building. Not a ramshackle abode like the weary yet bright stores along Dupont either. Her boots clip-clopped across a parquet floor so reflective she could have paused to fix her hair. White wainscoting adorned the walls to waist level. It was what she'd expect of a staid office building off of Market.

A full-sized statue in jade guarded an alcove, and she knew it had to be of Emperor Qixiang.

The delicate drapery and pleats of his layered robes looked utterly lifelike. His hands were extended, one holding a scepter and the other seeds: symbols of royalty and his bond with commoners. The expression on his face was sorrowful and stern together, like a father disappointed with a child. A ponytail tugged back the hair on the top of his head, but the rest fell in green wavy locks to his shoulders.

Earlier Manchu rulers had ordered all Chinese men to adopt one particular hairstyle, the queue. To style their hair otherwise meant treason and death. Qixiang's Restoration made all haircuts permissible, and he had made an example of himself by altering his hair according to weekly whims. Not that he was a whimsical person in other ways. He famously defied Japan. If he had handed China over to Japanese rule, he and his family would have been allowed to live out their lives sequestered in the Summer Palace. Instead, he declared, "My Qing Code holds true. I will not live as a prince as my people die as rats."

He joined the last desperate wave of refugees from China and died of smallpox in San Francisco in the early 1890s.

"The image of Qixiang is illegal," Ingrid murmured. Everything about this place stood in glimmering defiance of the Unified Pacific—and the squalor of thousands of Chinese just beyond the door.

"Yes," said Lee, barely giving the priceless statue a glance. He walked down the hallway. Ingrid followed, casting the jade man a final look over her shoulder. The sadness in his eyes made her want to weep.

Other alcoves contained depictions of other men in both statues and paintings. It wasn't until they passed several that she realized they were of the same man—a robust figure in armor, his face flushed and eyebrows severe, a halberd hoisted in his left hand.

"Who's that?" she murmured.

"Guan Yu."

She blinked, recognizing the name from Mr. Sakaguchi's lessons. Guan Yu was revered as a god of war and a guardian, a figure to be granted offerings and prayers. To tell tales of Guan Yu, to evoke him, to read or perform *Romance of the Three Kingdoms:* the punishment for all was death.

"Ingrid." Lee stopped before a doorway. "Do you trust me? With your life, trust me?"

She didn't hesitate. "I wouldn't be here otherwise."

Lee gave a little nod and motioned her into the room. It was a pristine space to rival any of the fancier hospitals in the outer city. Chairs and laboratory equipment were spaced out every five feet. The sharp tang of antiseptic cleared her nose.

"This is downright Pasteurian," murmured Fenris.

Lee walked to one side and did something at a table, his back to them. "Fenris, I have to ask you to step back. I don't know you. I sure as hell shouldn't have either of you here, but this is just for Ingrid. If anyone here knew I did this . . . well, it wouldn't be approved."

Fenris frowned, brows drawn in, and stayed put.

"Lee . . . ?" asked Ingrid.

"Don't ask questions. Just trust me." He turned, holding a syringe. Clear liquid filled the barrel.

Fenris sucked in a sharp breath. "You sure about this?" he muttered to her. "Mysterious fluids being injected into your body?"

Ingrid didn't step back, even as her heart beat faster. At a motion from Lee, she rolled up her sleeve. He positioned the needle at her wrist.

"You've done this before," she murmured. She flinched as the needle entered her vein, but was surprised at the lack of pain. "It didn't—"

"I numbed the needle for you." A few seconds later, it was done. Lee discarded the syringe into a basin and met her eye. His expression was sincere, loving in a way that she had never seen before. "I've had in mind to do that for ages. That's one good thing to come of this trip."

"How much farther to Mr. Sakaguchi?" She noted the tiny red mark on her arm as she rolled down her sleeve again.

"We're almost there." Lee guided them onward. They rounded a corner and Lee opened a door.

Mr. Sakaguchi lay on a bed in yet another stark and sterile room. The bed frame was metal; good, as that meant it wouldn't conduct well in an earthquake. He was also at least one floor up, so if he was unconscious or unable to move, he'd draw very little power. Sheets snugly tucked him in all the way to the shoulders, reminding Ingrid of an exhibition of mummies she viewed when she was a child. His skin was blanched, as if it reflected the white of his surroundings.

His eyes met hers, and an expression of pure horror swept over his face.

"Miss Carmichael," he whispered. "You shouldn't be here."

The formality pained her. She bowed her head. "I had to come, Mr. Sakaguchi."

A chair scraped against the floor, and she noticed the old man as he stood upright. He was as wizened as a Fresno raisin left far too long in the sun. Fleshy folds buried his eyes in such deep crevices that she couldn't even see the whites. His clothes were cream satin in pure Chinese fashion. A Mandarin collar pressed against his neck, while a Manchu queue braided as tight and tiny as a rat's tail draped over his shoulder and to his waist. The entire front of his head was shaved.

She stared at his hair. Rebels were said to wear the bing as a tribute to Emperor Qixiang. She had heard of American soldiers who kept such Chinese scalps as trophies.

If this man dared to walk down any street outside of Chinatown, he'd be butchered within minutes. This man wasn't a lackey in some *tong*—he was a rebel to the very heart.

The old man's voice creaked out a long sentence in Chinese. Lee answered in turn.

Hearing Lee speak fluently unnerved her. She couldn't help but glance around, self-conscious, as if one of Sutcliff's soldiers lurked nearby.

"What are you two saying?" Ingrid asked, doing her utmost to keep her voice calm and level. Inside, she was ready to bolt for the familiar streets and smells of her San Francisco.

"You don't want to know," Mr. Sakaguchi murmured.

Did that mean Mr. Sakaguchi understood them? Ingrid sat in a chair at his bedside. Her fingers twitched with the need to hold his hand, and instead she tangled her fingers together.

"Thank you for taking care of him," she said in very loud English, making eye contact with the old man.

"This is Uncle Moon," said Lee.

Uncle Moon jabbed his hand in the air and rumbled out more Chinese. The more he spoke, the more anxious she became. Frustration tightened her throat. Damn it all, she wanted to know what he was saying! Was Mr. Sakaguchi going to die? Where were they taking him?

Lee bowed low. Taking the cue, Ingrid stood and offered Uncle Moon a gracious but shaky curtsy. The old man grunted acknowledgment and hobbled out.

She collapsed into the chair again. "What did he say?" *What did you say?* she also wanted to ask. She had always known Lee was born in America, but because speaking Chinese was forbidden, she had never asked how fluently he knew the tongue. Some part of her had just assumed he didn't, because he wasn't supposed to. Ignorance didn't feel like bliss. It felt like stupidity, and she hated it.

"That Mr. Sakaguchi needs his strength for the journey ahead. You only have a few minutes." Lee motioned to Mr. Fenris. "Come with me."

Fenris had struck a lazy pose, leaning against the doorway with his arms crossed, but his face was hard with tension. He nodded to Ingrid, and then followed Lee from the room. The door shut with a soft click.

"Oj—"

"No." His voice was sharp, and he jerked his head to the side to cough. "A shut door means nothing, not here." He motioned with his head, and she bent close to him. "You're unharmed?"

"I'm fine," she whispered back, though she self-consciously clutched the spot where Lee had injected her. "Lee said they are taking you away." She paused, and thought to change tactics. "Nihongo de hanashimashou ka?"

"No. Speaking in Japanese won't help. They know the tongues of their enemies, as well they should." He paused. His breath stroked her cheek, hot and stale. "You should never have come here, Ingrid. Something terrible is happening. The auxiliary. The attack at our house."

"Are the *tongs* behind it? I didn't know who Lee's uncle was—I mean, I knew sending you to Chinatown at all was a risk, but . . ."

"No. The Chinese do not want me dead, not yet."

"Can I trust Lee?" It was a bit late to second-guess that.

"Lee . . . Lee is important. A brilliant boy. That's why I took him in. So much depends on him, on his eyes being wide open, on his thorough education. You two need to take care of each other, and you must escape the city. The tickets. There can't be just three geomancers within the city. It's too few, too dangerous. You can't stop whatever comes. You can't . . ."

Oh God, she still hadn't told him about Mr. Calhoun and Mr. Thornton. "But—"

"There's a box hidden at home. The namazu . . . wall . . . the danger . . ." His voice trailed into a hoarse cough. He shuddered in pain as he wiggled an arm free of the constraining blanket. His strangely gnarled hand grasped hers. "Forgive me. Please." Another cough racked his body.

Ingrid reared back, blinking in confusion. "I don't understand."

"You will." The words were a hoarse whisper. "Sorry."

The door behind her burst open. "We have to go," Lee snapped. "Now."

Ingrid bent over Mr. Sakaguchi and planted a kiss on his cheek. "I love you," she whispered. He squeezed her hand with trembling ferocity, then let go.

She paused to form fox ears against her head, only for a split second, long enough to make him smile.

Mr. Fenris waited in the hall, and the two of them followed Lee at a half run as he took them opposite the way they came. "What is it?" she gasped.

"There are people you shouldn't meet," he said.

She opened her mouth to ask more, but thought better of it, and simply ran. The warmth of Mr. Sakaguchi's touch faded.

The grandeur and portraits and electric sconces blurred. What had Mr. Sakaguchi meant? The namazu—the wall of prints in his office? There had to be a hiding place there, some nook or cranny.

A staircase wound into the bowels of Chinatown, and through another corridor. The surroundings blended together as she ran. She focused on home—on a house guarded by an armored tank and soldiers already convinced of her guilt in something she didn't understand.

Blue fog rose through the floor, so thin and vaporous that she wanted to dismiss it as a trick of the low light. Momentum carried her forward for several more long strides. The sudden warmth of the energy teased at her awareness.

"Earthquake!" she cried, and only then did the tunnel begin to shift and rumble.

CHAPTER 8

Heat coiled up Ingrid's legs. She staggered at the sweet shock of it. She had only been underground during an earthquake a few times, and none of them had this much power.

Mr. Fenris and Lee gasped and stopped in their tracks.

Ingrid dipped to the ground to suck in the energy unimpeded. Power tingled up her fingers in happy whirls. She smiled, closing her eyes. God, it felt good. Like a heavy quilt ensconcing her body after being numbed by a bitter winter wind. When the energy flowed, she didn't feel frustrated at being a secretary, being a woman, being unable to help Mr. Sakaguchi, being ignorant, being so . . . so . . . powerless.

The warmth of a fever flushed her cheeks and sizzled on her neck, and still the energy poured into her.

That's when the sense of bliss stopped, and fear filled her along with everything else.

She was the only geomancer in contact with the ground. She was the only person here to take in this flood.

Ingrid's eyes snapped open and she lurched to her feet. For the first time, she was aware of rumbling and powder sifting from the ceiling. A metal sconce protruded from the wall not three feet away. Grimacing with sudden queasiness, she leaped for it. Her fingers wrapped around the coiled iron and her shoes kicked against the metal-paneled wall. Like a shut-off faucet, the flow of energy stopped, but pressure still burbled through her veins. Her head seemed to float, hot and buoyant, as her vision wavered and created a mirage of three dancing sconces not far from her face.

After several long seconds, the rumbling stopped. Ingrid let go. Her legs didn't quite work. Her buttocks smacked against the floor, followed by her back and skull. Pain exploded through her head as ceiling beams rotated like wagon spokes. Another small quake lapped against her skin, the additional heat addling her brain even more.

"Ingrid? Ingrid!" Lee's voice was far too loud. She shook her head to try to make it go away.

"What the hell was that?" said another voice. Mr. Fenris.

As the world continued to swim, her brain managed to latch on to one fact. Lee knew what she could do. He had for ages. He was just too integrated into the household. Had he told his uncle's people about her? No. No, he couldn't have. When Japan invaded mainland Asia, the first thing they'd done was target any magic users. Wui Seng Tong would want to use a geomancer—especially a woman, whom no one would suspect of possessing talent. If they knew about her, she wouldn't have been allowed to leave.

She squeezed her eyes shut to make the hallway stop shimmying about like a burlesque dancer. The pain was gone, but the weirdness of fever remained.

The highbinders would use Mr. Sakaguchi. Whether they had worked with him before or not, circumstances had changed. He was vulnerable and in their control. With him, they could fill kermanite. They could power airships at a cheaper, faster rate. They could fight back against the Unified Pacific, even strike here, in America. Under these circumstances, with the likes of Captain Sutcliff already suspecting the worst, America would think Mr. Sakaguchi was a willing collaborator.

Maybe he was. Maybe he had been for years.

"Ingrid?"

"Give me a moment. Please." She inhaled long and deep, and opened her eyes. The ceiling beams no longer spun. She propped herself up on her elbows. The two men crouched beside her.

"I get these strange spells sometimes," she said to Mr. Fenris, knowing the explanation was inadequate.

"That coincide with earthquakes?" Skepticism edged his voice.

"Can you walk, Ingrid? By yourself?" Lee asked.

She nodded. She'd make sure she could. Grinding her teeth, she worked herself upright. A blue sheen rippled against the floor like the ocean at low tide.

"Do you need me to, ah, help you walk?" Mr. Fenris asked. He made it sound as repulsive as probing a manure mound.

"No." Ingrid took a few unsteady steps. The others flanked her as an unsaid precaution. The end of the tunnel was in sight. She fumbled one hand beneath the coat and into her dress pocket. There, beneath Mr. Sakaguchi's keys, she found a cold chip of kermanite. Her fingertips tingled at the contact, and energy trickled out. Sweat beaded on her forehead and dribbled down her jaw. She searched out the second piece and found it tucked between keys. Her skin cooled, but only slightly. She still held too much within, and had no more empty kermanite.

Ingrid remembered the terminology on the classroom chalkboard when the auxiliary was ripped asunder. Hyperthermia, hypothermia. The quick countdown to death.

She needed to find more empty kermanite or vent power through brute force—that, or feel as though she should be bed bound with an intense bout of influenza.

The street had been busy before, but now it teemed with people who wailed and pointed to buildings around them. Words in English boiled together, but a word in Chinese stood out to Ingrid as it repeated all around.

"Dilong . . . Dilong . . ."

"What are they saying?" asked Fenris.

"That's one Chinese word the teachers were allowed to say at the auxiliary. *Dilong!* Earth dragon," Ingrid said. "A geomantic Hidden One of China." Images from lectures flashed through her mind—the yellow dragon, his talons digging massive fissures in the dirt.

Elbows and shoulders pounded against Ingrid as the throng squeezed in. A flailing parasol caught her hat and sent it spiraling into the stampede.

A frenzied neigh cut the air. A horse lay impaled against a wooden cart, the wagon behind it tipped on its side. Tiger-striped melons sprawled across the street like shattered skulls. Other horses whinnied, hooves tapping a rapid staccato beat.

Ireland's Hidden One was a horse, and nonmagical cousins always reacted most strongly to the shifting earth.

The catfish would be upset again, too, but then they probably had been restless for hours. Maybe this impending quake was why they had been upset last night.

A small cluster of men in navy blue flowed across the street. They wore fine uniforms with trim black belts and stripes down the outside leg. Soldiers.

"Damn them to hell! Why are they here?" growled Lee.

"They can't be here for her!" said Mr. Fenris. "How would they know?"

"Come on!" snapped Lee. "They won't last long here." He made a sharp motion with his arm.

Last long? Whatever did he mean? Reality was a fog as she staggered after him. The alley to Dupont seemed to squeeze her even more than before, the darks darker and the distant light aching in its brightness. Something bobbed ahead, like a buoy at sea, and it took her a moment to realize the objects were approaching people.

"Clear out, pigtail," snarled the leader. There were three men—white, broad, swarthy. Sailors, dockworkers, some occupation that involved heavy labor and ill temperaments.

In her dazed state, she almost corrected him, saying that Lee had no pigtails at all. The crude term made no sense with Manchu queues banned.

"Apologies, Master!" Lee offered a placating bow.

"Bah." The man shoved Lee onto the trash cans, and his eyes widened. "What's a pretty thing like you doing down here, eh?" Australian accent, maybe. British Empire for certain. *"Yo hablo español."* And he assumed she spoke Spanish. How typical.

"Stop! Miss, miss! Are you Miss Carmichael! I order you to halt!"

The brash voice caused her to spin around, her shoulder knocking against a brick wall. The soldiers. She immediately cursed her own addled brain—by responding to her name, she'd damned herself.

"Miss Carmichael!" The soldier stood tall and thick, a handlebar mustache stretched across his face like the spread wings of a bird. "We've had men searching the city for you. We're to take you in for questioning."

"Damn Yanks." That was spat by the sailor. "Can't even leave a pretty girl well alone, can you? Questioning, my arse."

"This is none of your concern!" barked the soldier. Behind him, his two companions reached for their belts.

The world wavered through her feverish eyes, but Ingrid had the sense to crouch down in case gunfire erupted on either side. She glanced back at Lee as he raised his hands overhead, as if to surrender, and clapped three times.

That's when the men leaped from the heavens. Or from a balcony. That seemed more likely.

Dark blurs dropped onto soldiers and sailors alike. Yells echoed on either side of the narrow passage. Knife blades flashed in the dim light. Mr. Fenris fell against a metal bin, and with a sweep of his arm a Tesla rod extended. It smacked against the nearest soldier with an audible crackle. A figure in black, only his eyes visible, brandished a white cloth and pressed it to a soldier's face. The man immediately fell slack. Ingrid stared in dreamy fascination.

"Bloody hell!" A heavy hand grasped her shoulder. "Come on, girl! S'no place for you in this mess! *Vámonos!*"

Ingrid did not like being called girl.

She also did not like strange men grabbing hold of her.

She shrugged his hand off of her, willing him away. It worked a bit better than she expected. He flew backward with a guttural yelp and the mad clatter of bins. Fumes of rotting garbage rolled over her.

Lee yelled out something in Chinese—spoken in front of soldiers this time. More evidence against her, against Mr. Sakaguchi. Now Captain Sutcliff would be certain they were working with a *tong*.

Using up power cleared some of her mental fog. Ingrid struggled to find Lee in the tight melee, then spotted him crouched atop a large bin, knees jutted out like a frog.

Mr. Fenris, panting heavily and clutching his coat, squeezed beside her. "Are you well?"

She nodded, unable to find the words to speak.

Lee conversed in Chinese with the masked men. They bowed and began to drag limp bodies across the pavement. Lee turned toward Ingrid. "Fenris, get her out of Chinatown. There's a scarf vendor immediately to the right as you leave this alley. Tell the shopkeeper, 'The thousand-*li* horse is always hungry,' and grab a scarf to cover Ingrid's head. She stands out too much."

She stared at Lee. Who was this? Where was the boy, the servant, she had known for years? He spoke and acted like he led a *tong*. Maybe he did.

"The thousand-*li* horse is always hungry," Fenris repeated, licking his lips.

Ingrid spied the sailor who had grabbed her. He lay unconscious, sprawled out like a sunning walrus.

"Lee, what will happen to the Brits?"

"Ingrid. Go." Lee stood a little taller. The men around him shuffled; she couldn't see their faces, but she knew they looked askance at her.

"They were in the wrong place at the wrong time. Don't kill them."

The coldness on Lee's face wavered, and she took comfort in that. "None of them will die, not even the soldiers. Even if they deserve it. Now go."

"Miss Carmichael." Mr. Fenris's voice was a hoarse whisper. His arm brushed hers as he pushed past. With one final, frantic look at Lee, she followed the mechanic.

Dupont Street was a sea of heads and hats, the air thickened by the cries of babies and the scents of perfumes and coffee. She noted bricks half crushing several swags and canopies. A woman screamed, shrill and high. Voices mingled like a panicked congregation in the Tower of Babel.

"We're not supposed to have earthquakes here!" snapped a man.

"Well, d'you hear what happened to the geomancers' auxiliary yesterday?"

"Bollocks! That's just a building. There's more of them wardens about, they . . ."

The reality of the situation left her dry-mouthed. This was a minor earthquake. One from which Ingrid had siphoned a great deal of power, yet it had still done this. If she hadn't been nearby, whole buildings could have come down. And if she hadn't broken contact when she did, she could have died.

The woman at the scarf stand was hurriedly packing her wares into wooden crates.

"The thousand-*li* horse is always hungry," said Mr. Fenris as he leaned to grab a green scarf threaded in gold and white. The vendor nodded, tight-lipped, and resumed her work. Mr. Fenris shoved the scarf at Ingrid, and she caught a glimpse of his face—too blanched, too drawn.

Ingrid snaked through the crowd to grab his elbow. She felt the hard knob of bone through the cloth. "What's wrong?" she yelled, and barely heard herself. Mr. Fenris shook his head.

Sheer numbers of people overwhelmed the guard station. Whistles split the air as more soldiers and policemen neared. The tide of humanity swept them out the gate and to the outer city. She guided him to a niche pasted with ads for the Barbary Coast. Mr. Fenris began to stumble, and she caught him by the back of the coat. He turned.

The knife wound arced across his chest, starting at the armpit, sweeping over his heart, and dipping almost down to the sternum. Between the darkness of his coat and the blackness of the alley, it just wasn't visible until she was up close.

"I don't think it's that bad," he croaked out.

"Bad!" She snorted. "Men! Always trying to be too brave for their own good."

Mr. Fenris laughed at that, light and airy through the pain, and Ingrid realized it was the first time she'd heard such a sound from him.

"Get the scarf on," he whispered. "We need to get home. There are other soldiers in the crowd. I can see them from here."

Biting back a frustrated snarl, she fumbled the scarf over her head and knotted it in place. It covered her wavy, tumultuous hair and the dark skin of her neck. “We have to get you to a doctor, and not one in Chinatown. There’s a Reiki—”

“No!” A note of panic elevated his voice. “We have to go home. Cy. I need Cy. He should be back by now. Please.” The intense vulnerability in Mr. Fenris’s eyes made Ingrid uncomfortable, and she looked away, nodding. She preferred his caustic wit to this.

“If I could bind the wound—”

“No. Not here. Home.”

“I’ll help you walk,” she said. The man flinched as she wrapped an arm around his waist, and she wondered if it was her touch as much as the injury that caused him to do so.

“You shouldn’t walk with me like this,” Mr. Fenris mumbled. “People will see—”

“To hell with what people see. I’m sick to death of propriety.” Tears smarted her eyes. She couldn’t help but think of Mr. Sakaguchi and his regrets about not marrying Mama.

“I care very much what people see.” The words were so low Ingrid almost missed them.

Crowds thinned as they hobbled along the next block. Normal city noises—wheels, engines, that constant backward clatter of dogs and chickens—seemed quiet compared to the intensity of Chinatown. It took her a moment to realize that the silence wasn’t simply because of the decrease in people.

Damage hadn’t occurred here to the same extent as in Chinatown. It’s not that the buildings were constructed that much better; this ground was still made, and would liquefy as it would under much of downtown.

It was as though the earth twitched just beneath Chinatown, even with her there to siphon much of its intensity. By everything she ever learned in the auxiliary, that just plain didn't make sense. What would cause such a localized explosion of earth energy?

Heat roiled beneath her skin. Her body was a reservoir still perilously close to overflowing, but now she did more than break dishes. Now someone needed her. She partially carried Mr. Fenris. She was huskier than he, but it was still a surprise how little exertion it took to hoist his weight.

A cab rattled by, and she waved it down.

"No," Fenris whispered. "He'll see, ask questions—"

"More people will ask questions if I'm carrying you across town," she whispered back. "Hello, sir!"

The cab consisted of a black buckboard wagon with a chestnut horse in the shafts. The skittish stallion danced in his jingling harness, restless hooves clopping on the basalt. His eyes rolled back to show whites.

"Hey, hey!" The driver tightened his grip on the reins. He spat out a wad of tobacco on the far side. "Eh. Wassup wit him?"

"My boss was injured in the earthquake in Chinatown just now, sir." She felt Fenris stiffen at the subterfuge; she gave him a reassuring pat on the back. Ingrid knew how to play this game.

"Earthquake. Bah. Shoulda brought t' whole section down. Want the nuns?"

The Catholic hospital was certainly the closest. As though reading her thoughts, Mr. Fenris leaned into her. She sighed. "No, sir. He wants to go home. I'll call a doctor."

"Eh. Suit yerrself. Hay-up!"

Using Mr. Fenris's body to shield her incredible strength, she boosted him up into the cab. He dragged his body into the seat. She hopped up after him, bounding up like a kangaroo, and almost squealed in surprise at her own athleticism.

The horse started to bolt when the driver clicked his teeth, but he kept the beast in check. Mr. Fenris moaned deep in his throat, and continued to bite back sounds the entire ride back to the workshop.

Ingrid assisted Mr. Fenris down to the sidewalk. His knees buckled, but she didn't let him fall.

"You're as strong as Cy," he whispered.

She didn't even know how to reply to that. Empowered as she was, she almost snapped off the doorknob when she leaned her weight on the front door to Jennings and Braun's shop. It was as though she had reached some fantastic middle ground between the delicious tingle of power she was used to and the state of being deathly ill.

"My cot," Mr. Fenris whispered. "Beneath Cy's room."

The room was spare and Spartan in a way that suggested an impersonal hotel rather than a daily living space. Ingrid set him down gently on the edge of the bed and pried off his shoes. Mr. Fenris's body quivered and seemed to deflate as he lay down. Ingrid turned on bedside lamps for better light.

Mama had taught her how to bandage a wound and do basic stitches, but from the sheer amount of blood, this was far beyond what Ingrid could handle with a needle and thread. Still, she had to do something.

"I can try to clean you up," she said, the doubt clear in her voice.

Mr. Fenris shook his head again, and Ingrid felt the profound urge to grab him by the lapels and shake sense into him. Didn't the man know how serious his wound was, how quickly infection could set in? Mama's labor was supposed to be easy, after all; Mama always said baking her first cake was a lot harder, and took longer, than Ingrid's birth. When everything went wrong with the new baby, it went wrong fast. So terribly fast.

Ingrid tried to block out her last sight of Mr. Sakaguchi, so fragile in that strange and sterile room.

A door banged, the sound echoing across the vastness of the workshop. Ingrid tensed. Had soldiers followed them?

"It's Cy." A smile wobbled on Mr. Fenris's lips. "I know his footsteps."

Ingrid stood and met Mr. Jennings near the now-completed airship. He sucked in a sharp breath. "You're bloodied. Were you attacked again?" His long strides covered the distance between them in seconds.

"It's not me. It's Fenris."

His expression shifted, hardening, and he stepped past her and stopped in the doorway. "God have mercy."

"Hello to you, too," whispered Mr. Fenris.

"Miss Carmichael?" Mr. Jennings turned to her.

"He needs the hospital, but he won't go. He insisted we come here, to you. It's hard to see now, but the cut goes all the way across, from armpit to sternum. I don't know how deep."

Mr. Jennings's jaw worked from side to side. "That settles it, then. Miss, this'll be messy work, but I need your help to prepare him for a doctor."

She arched an eyebrow. "Prepare him? He's not a turkey!"

"There's no time to mess around here." The gravity of the situation shone in his eyes. "I'll put some water on to boil and run to the market to dial up a doctor. Can you strip him down? There's a trunk beneath the bed with clothes you can use."

Confused, she nodded. Mr. Jennings dashed off toward the kitchen.

"It's his time as a soldier," Mr. Fenris muttered. "He gets in these moods and starts spouting off orders. Doesn't bother asking me what I think."

"I'll ask you, then. Do you want to die?" Ingrid asked.

"No."

"Good. That's a start."

Why was she the one taking off the man's clothes? If she had trained as a nurse, doctor, or midwife, then it'd make sense, but Mr. Jennings knew she had no such expertise.

"I . . . I am . . ." Mr. Fenris's words slurred.

"I'm working your coat off," she said. "Can you sit up?"

To his credit, he tried, but the instant he did so, his eyes rolled back and his body fell utterly slack.

"Hell and damnation!"

Well, maybe his fainting was for the best. The current of power still in her veins, Ingrid readily propped up the man and eased off the leather jacket. The motion caused a fresh welling of blood. She scanned the room and grabbed an ivory-handled penknife from a shelf. Drying her hands on her borrowed and hopelessly stained coat, she opened the blade and sliced Mr. Fenris's shirt open. Buttons pinged off as she yanked the rest of it free.

To her surprise, another layer of bloodied cloth swathed the width of his chest.

She stared. Suddenly everything made sense.

Ingrid had listened to Graphophone recordings of the opera *Jasmine in Bloom* more times than she could count. It had been a dear favorite of Mama's, too, with its powerful portrayal of a woman dirigible sailor. Undeterred by social mores, Leticia binds her breasts and goes off to war, and saves her entire Roman legion even as she dies an excruciating death by poison.

Mr. Fenris wasn't dying, but he most definitely had bound breasts that suggested that *he* might actually be a *she*.

By the time Ingrid had Mr.—well, Fenris Braun changed into a night shift from the trunk, Mr. Jennings arrived with a doctor in tow. One look at the physician, with his pale skin and suit and tie, and she knew he was a Pasteurian.

"Out, girl!" the doctor barked. "I must sanitize the area. Sweet Mary, Mother of God, you changed her clothes? She's bleeding like a stuck pig! Are you trying to kill her? Meddlesome git!"

He shooed Ingrid away like a fly. Accustomed to such treatment from the wardens, she forced a look of shame onto her face while she inwardly seethed. Heat prickled her skin, and she made sure not to stand too close to the doctor. As Mr. Sakaguchi's dishware knew all too well, when she brimmed with power, things around her tended to break.

Ingrid and Mr. Jennings were shoved out the door, and it shut with a clang that shivered up the metal staircase above. Mr. Jennings's brows furrowed. Ingrid stared, unsure of what to say.

Fenris was a woman living as a man, living with another man. Were they lovers? They were certainly close, though Mr. Jennings had foisted the clothes-changing duties on Ingrid. Maybe he had done that for propriety's sake, but good grief, what did propriety mean in a situation like this?

The door burst open again. "Where's that boiling water?" asked the doctor.

"I'll get it," said Mr. Jennings. He rushed off with Ingrid two steps behind.

"I suppose you have some questions, miss," he said in a low voice, guiding her to a partition on the far side of the warehouse. Far, she noted, from the airship with its hydrogen gasbag. Other spark-creating materials were also on this side of the building.

"You may as well stop with the constant use of 'miss.' I know it's the proper southern tradition, but it makes me feel like I'm supposed to be a little girl dolled up in a kimono and pigtails. We're all deep in this together now."

Through a stack of boxes, she caught sight of a familiar autocar and paused.

He glanced back, his expression unreadable. Ingrid scurried to catch up. "I suppose so, miss. Er. Well, if we're less formal now, I suppose we should be on a first-name basis in private."

"I'm Ingrid. I know you're Cy. And I don't know what to call *Mister* Fenris now."

Cy sighed and nodded. He ducked behind a rubber curtain and into a makeshift kitchen that featured an archaic electric stove, an icebox, a table with oilskin tacked over the top, and chairs made of wooden orange crates. A kettle on the stove already belched steam, and he grabbed thick towels to grip the handle.

"I'll take this to the doctor. Don't go anywhere, please."

Ingrid lowered herself to a crate pasted with labels for citrus fruit from sunny Tulare, California. She tugged off the scarf and set it aside. A battered metal breadbox sat in the center of the rough-hewn table, and she couldn't help but roll back the lid. Pastries. The reminder of food made her stomach moan.

She helped herself to a yeast roll speckled with poppy seeds. Her normal breakfast would have included pickled salmon, sourdough bread with jam, and tea, but right now she was hungry enough to lick crumbs off a counter. She found some cold coffee in a carafe, and needed it; the rolls had reached an advanced stage of life where they were best suited for bread pudding or duck food. She washed down the bread before it dammed her throat.

Somewhat satiated, Ingrid took off her coat and tossed it over her crate chair. She appraised the condition of her dress. The cloth was black, standard and understated attire for a house worker her age. Red-tinged large patches spread across her sleeves and skirt. Mr. Sakaguchi's blood. It wouldn't be noticeable from far away, but close up, there was no denying what it was. If the doctor saw, at least he'd think it was from Fenris.

Ingrid shuddered. Why was everyone bleeding on her?

She'd also endured her own share of pain over the past day. She'd banged herself pretty well in the tunnel before that aftershock hit, not that it caused any lingering damage. She'd thumped herself on the walkway when she fled the house yesterday, too. A small seism had followed that as well.

There had been many shivers of earth when she'd had her Reiki session after the auxiliary explosion. They stopped after her treatment.

She stilled. Were the quakes all coincidences, or . . . ?

Ingrid leaned over and, taking a steadying breath, tapped her knuckle against the cooling stove burner. Horrendous heat made her jerk back a half second later, nursing the injured hand against her chest.

A few seconds later came the tingle of an earthquake. Small, easily ignored by anyone else. The blue tinge of the earth's power lapped her feet and faded along with the pain. Yesterday's Reiki would still help in that regard.

"Dear God," she whispered.

Her pain provoked the earth. How, why? Even more—Mama and Mr. Sakaguchi *knew,* and had known since she was little. She stared at the red mark on her hand. She'd had so many little injuries over the years and had never made this connection before, but there had always been other geomancers around to siphon the energy. Plus, Mama had bustled her off to Reiki or confined her to upstairs until she was well.

The thought of injury and sickness put her in mind of Mr. Thornton. She left the kitchen.

Mr. Thornton's distinctive autocar sat there in the shop. The glossy black hood was mottled by rust spots, the front bumper lopsided like a rogue's smile. She hadn't thought to look for the car at Mr. Thornton's house. How long had it been here? This old thing broke down with regularity. The warden made plenty of money but the car wasn't his priority. Mr. Thornton's three principal hobbies consisted of complaining of Britain's treatment of India, of San Francisco's obliviousness to India's plight, and his horrid autocar.

She cast a self-conscious glance over her shoulder as she popped open the door. The leather seat was covered by a tucked-in blanket. She frowned and looked around. No signs of sickness or blood. Maybe he left behind a note or a ticket that could tell her where he might have gone.

Her hands dug along the creases of the seat, then beneath it. After another quick look for Cy, she climbed over the front seat and into near blackness.

She was stunned when her feet found an open expanse of floor. The backseat was gone. The thin carpet underfoot had bunched up like a basset hound's furrowed forehead, as if heavy things had been pushed about and ruined the floor. Mr. Thornton's missing possessions, perhaps? Book boxes would be heavy enough. If so, where had he taken them—and himself?

She probed the floor again, and this time she encountered something smooth, something that tried to siphon the heat from her skin. Ingrid lurched back, not quite ready to surrender her power to the kermanite. She pulled back enough to grab a sun-yellowed city map from the dashboard and used that to roll the kermanite into plain sight.

It wasn't just one crystal, but many—about a dozen, the largest about the size of a child's marble. By their clarity, they didn't hold energy yet. She used the map to scoop up one into better light, and gasped. The kermanite had a slight blue cast.

"The March batch," she muttered.

Last month's delivery from Boron had included a burlap bag of kermanite, all shattered to the same rough size, all with an unusual blue cast. Some hint of coloration wasn't uncommon, but Mr. Sakaguchi and Mr. Antonelli said they hadn't seen such a large group with blue in many years.

As of last Friday, that bag sat in the Cordilleran Auxiliary's vault, not yet inventoried and weighed for sale.

Mr. Thornton possessed keys to the vault. She'd seen him abscond with butter mints, but to steal a wealth of kermanite? Maybe the theft happened under duress—a knife to his throat, that sort of thing. Mr. Thornton wouldn't be motivated by money. His wife was gone, so she couldn't be held hostage. The only thing Mr. Thornton really loved was India, and the Brits were razing that country with civilized efficiency.

This kermanite had to have been taken before the Vesuvius meeting . . . or during it. She suddenly recalled how the auxiliary's basement had been blockaded for fumigation—under Mr. Thornton's orders.

The basement, where the vault was. Where the explosion originated.

No. No. None of this made sense. It didn't explain *why*.

"Are you looking for something, Miss Ingrid?"

She screeched as she bolted upright. The kermanite, barely perched on the map, went airborne and plunked against metal in the darkness.

She spun around. Cy leaned in the open doorway. "You nearly frightened me out of my skin!"

"I advised you to make yourself at home, but I didn't think to exclude customers' property in that." His voice held an edge of warning.

A guilty flush heated Ingrid's cheeks. "Well—no—of course not, but this is Mr. Thornton's autocar—"

"Is it now?" His mood shifted. "The car was dropped off while I was out yesterday. I looked at the repair manifests this morning. It's not under his name. I would have noticed that."

"Yesterday? When?"

"I don't recall. I'll need to check Fenris's notes later, if I can read them. He writes worse than a doctor."

The mention of Fenris and doctors reminded her of the higher priorities at hand. She motioned Cy back and then climbed out of the car.

For a half second, she debated if she should pocket the kermanite then thought better of it. The evidence might come in handy later, found here inside the car. Better for Cy to be left ignorant, too.

Tucking a strand of hair behind her ear, she faced him. "I don't make a habit of rummaging in other people's property, just so you know. This was a special case."

His lips quirked in a tired smile. "I hope that staying in my room last night wasn't termed a special case, too."

"I—you can't think I would—"

"I'm giving you a little grief, Miss Ingrid. That's all. Come along to the kitchen. I could do with some coffee if we're going to talk."

She hunched her shoulders as they walked back to the kitchen. "Oh. I finished off the carafe. I can start the percolator on the stove."

"Don't fuss about it. Much more coffee, I'll probably fly like an airship, anyway."

"How is Fenris with the doctor?"

"He's unconscious," Cy said as he collapsed onto a crate that creaked ominously beneath his weight. He thrust his long legs out to one side, the toe of his boots almost brushing her skirt.

For a second, she feared he meant the doctor, then realized he referred to the patient. "Yes. He, she, passed out quickly when I started to change her clothes. I put the wig on as well, as I'm sure you noticed." The wig of black hair had been woven into a tight bun, complete with sparkling silver pins. Ingrid had discreetly clipped it to Fenris's short hair.

He nodded and rubbed the short bristles on his chin. "He. Fenris has never been anything but a he to me. He never had the chance to tell you anything?"

"No. But how can you look at her . . . him . . . like that and . . ." She stopped herself. Her mind was an absolute muddle. She absently touched the small burn on her knuckles and winced.

Cy pursed his lips. He had pleasant, broad, pink lips. She looked away. Damn it all. Why'd everything have to be so hellishly complicated?

"Well, Miss Ingrid, how do you look at the Japanese man who's like a father to you?"

She scowled at the comparison. "Very carefully, depending on where we are, and people still try to make something lurid out of it." Like that Captain Sutcliff. She hoped he found that massive chunk of kermanite and it landed on his foot.

"That's the way of people." He sighed. "I should start at the top, miss. I mean Ingrid. Pardon me."

Even when he stammered, there was something charming about it. "Before you go on, can that doctor be trusted in there alone with her? Him? While unconscious?"

"We can talk just outside Fenris's room. I said I'm his cousin, so I have every reason to hover nearby."

A quick check on Fenris found him still asleep and the doctor cleaning in preparation for stitches. With the door propped open to vent the smell of harsh antiseptics, they resumed their chat close by, beneath the shadow of the airship.

Cy folded his arms across his chest, his shoulders bowed. "I first met Fenris at academy. I was there because . . . family connections and all, but I proved myself worthy fairly fast, I like to think. Fenris had no connections. He showed up, told them he wanted a slot. Some profs tried to stump him, but he could fix anything. Gave him a metal clothes hanger as his only tool and he used that and a smattering of train parts to re-rig a kermanite engine."

"As handy as Hank in *Connecticut Yankee,*" she murmured.

Cy acknowledged this with a warm smile. "They set us up as roommates, being as we balanced one another. I work best on paper, he works best with machines. Strawberries and rhubarb, as my father liked to say."

Ingrid despised rhubarb. "And you didn't know he was . . . ?"

"Of course not. Any technical academy is men only. Girls aren't supposed to be interested in intelligent things." He spat the words. "Fenris worked damn hard. The academy—it was meant for folks with old money. Fenris didn't fit in, didn't try to. He learned. He played janitor every night to cover tuition till he started selling wares from the students' shop. The secret kept for two years."

"How did you find out?" Ingrid sat on a stepladder rung.

Cy averted his gaze, blushing. "Female business."

"Ah. The monthly, then." She said it aloud for the pleasure of seeing his ears turn a pretty shade of red. "How'd you react?"

He shrugged. "No pride in how I behaved that day. I was angry. Felt the fool. Vulnerable, I suppose. He'd seen me change more than once, even tagged along for skinny-dipping and never jumped in the water. We'd both talked about girls and that sort of thing. I told him I'd keep the secret, but inside, I burned like Union hellfire on Atlanta. It took me a few weeks to realize that Fenris had always been himself, the way he saw himself. He wasn't living a lie. He wasn't making an effort to deceive me or anyone else. He was a man. He was at his happiest elbows-deep in an engine. We had been like brothers for years, and that's what we were. Brothers. We stayed on as roommates for the rest of our time there. I was more particular about my privacy, but nothing else changed."

She listened as though it were some pulp novel read over the Marconi. The whole thing was peculiar, but it also made sense. Cy and Fenris did act like brothers. Ingrid recalled how Fenris had prodded her with a pole to wake her up that morning, and how sensitive he—she—had been about the whole subject of touch. Which was a sensitive issue for Ingrid as well. She would bet that Fenris knew all too well how men could be, taking liberties they ought not to, and was trying to be a better sort of man in his own gruff way.

"It's a lot to take in," she said. "It's just . . . odd. I shouldn't be one to judge, with how my own life has been."

Mama and Mr. Sakaguchi, Mama's baby, Ingrid's skin such a contrast to Mama's, Ingrid's own strange power. To step outside her bedroom door, she had to be constantly vigilant about snide comments and leers and earthquakes. She hated living like that. And Fenris—Fenris was being true to himself amid a different set of challenges. She winced, recalling some of her sharp remarks to him.

Cy adjusted his glasses and stood there, hands in his pockets, elbows sticking out. "We're like brothers. Like I said. Nothing more. In case you were wondering."

Ingrid arched an eyebrow. "Now, why would I wonder such a thing?"

He shrugged, and his thumb twitched. There was something alluring in his sudden shyness. "Making sure to clarify, that's all. Ah. Let's do a quick check on Fenris, see how it goes."

Neither of them made it into the room. "Out!" the doctor barked over his shoulder. "I'm halfway through, and will move a great deal faster without these interruptions."

"Is . . . she doing well?" asked Ingrid.

"I don't sew up dead people. Yes, she's alive, and well enough, despite your earlier intervention. Out!"

Cy tugged her by the sleeve and they backed out. "Now, I do believe you have a story to tell me. How'd this happen, Miss Ingrid? You said you went to Chinatown?"

She studied him, hoping for another hint of his interest in her. Because, by God, she wanted more of those little looks from him. They warmed her belly like kindling, and on top of the heat she already held . . . Ingrid shivered at the pleasantness of it all.

But the subject had shifted and so had his mood. Releasing a huffy breath of disappointment, she recounted a sanitized version of events. Cy listened and nodded.

"You're saying we need to get into your house, past soldiers and a Durendal." Through the cracked door, they watched the doctor pack away his implements. "This is no minor thing, Miss Ingrid. Are you so anxious to play the hero?"

"I'm sick of playing any roles at all. Besides, the noble hero always dies in the end."

"You've been listening to too many operas."

"You're the expert on Durendals. You tell me what our odds are against such a machine."

"Maybe the odds aren't so bad as you think. The soldiers will be more troublesome than the tank."

She snorted in disbelief. "Are you willing to place a bet on that?"

Cy's brown eyes sparkled with mischief. "A bet? Now, I'm not normally a betting man, but I'm curious about what wager you have in mind."

If he was going to hint at an interest in her, then by God, she'd bludgeon him to make her opinion clear.

"A kiss." Ingrid's arms crossed her chest.

She was quite aware of how the posture thrust out her bosom and how the pleats of her dress draped from one uplifted hip. She'd seen such poses on many of her dime-novel covers and had practiced it in the mirror a time or two.

"A kiss," he echoed, eyebrows raising in surprise. Not with displeasure, she noted.

The doctor approached. Ingrid fought the urge to scowl at the man for his timing, but she was too eager for news to be perturbed.

"Well! That one'll need to be particular about the cuts of her necklines from now on, but she'll live. The slice was shallow, mostly, but it was long. She'll need to stay still and not carry anything heavy or move her arms much for several weeks as things heal. I left ointment and laudanum beside the bed. Stitches must come out in four weeks." The doctor's eyes narrowed at Ingrid. "And if any infection sets in, it's not my fault. There's modesty and then there's stupidity, young woman. No point in ruining more than one smock and making her bleed all the more!"

Ingrid knew her place, and dipped her head in shame. Inside, she felt the profound urge to kick him—all her fault, indeed! Like she was the one who wielded the knife! But since one of her empowered kicks would likely punt the doctor some twenty feet into a tidy stack of pipes, she judged it an unwise move.

It'd take forever to restack those pipes.

"I'm much obliged, Doctor," said Cy. "Allow me to walk you to the door." The two men headed toward the front office. Ingrid went straight to Fenris.

As a woman, Fenris's form would have been termed petite. But no, Fenris Braun wasn't a woman. Not really. No more than Ingrid was a demure secretary.

She plopped down on the bedside chair. If anything could

be said for Pasteurians, they left things excessively clean. There wasn't a speck of blood to be found on the bed and floor; Fenris wore an unfamiliar cotton shift that the doctor must have brought along. He had even stripped the bed. A pile of bloodied laundry sat beside the door.

She could understand Fenris and Cy staying as academy roommates after Fenris's secret came out, but how did they end up in San Francisco? It was a wonder that Fenris hadn't been conscripted like most men of their age, but maybe that was a reason they had moved around so much.

"It's ruined, isn't it?" Fenris's whisper was a hoarse croak.

"Oh! You're awake!" Ingrid leaned over him. "What's ruined?"

"My coat. The leather coat."

Ingrid paused, then she burst out in laughter. "The coat? Yes. I'm sorry."

"Damn. That was my favorite." The words slurred.

"You can always buy a new coat."

Fenris looked at her through heavily lidded eyes. "You know, don't you?"

"Yes."

"You give Cy any grief about this, about me, I'll kill you." Sincerity resounded in the words, even as they sloshed together.

"You love him." She couldn't help but feel uncomfortable saying that.

"Yes. He's the only person who's ever accepted me as I am."

Ingrid opened and closed her lips without making a sound. She had Mr. Sakaguchi, but had he really accepted her? Oh, she knew there were valid reasons to be kept a secret. The wardens were a stodgy and conservative organization, a good ol' boys' club if ever there was one. She'd be a freak, a scientific and magical curiosity. Like a Hidden One in plain sight, to be scrutinized and analyzed . . . and some would think, to be neutralized.

She felt the need to say something, though. "I . . . I wanted to thank you for coming with me to Chinatown. I'm sorry you ended up hurt because of it."

Fenris managed a breathy snort. "Cy's always telling me to get out more, to live, see the city. Finally take his advice, and this happens."

"Next time, be sure to request the tour that doesn't include scraps between soldiers and highbinders."

"How long have you used geomancy?"

The blunt question caused her to recoil slightly. "Almost my whole life. How long have you felt the need to live as a man?"

"As long as I can remember." The pain in his voice didn't come from the injury. "Look at us with our deep, dark secrets. We're keeping them about as well as burlap holds water." He started to chuckle and stopped with a wince.

Ingrid braced a hand on his shoulder. The mention of burlap reminded her of the kermanite she found. "Fenris, I wanted to ask you. There's a rusty car out in the warehouse, one that came in yesterday when Cy was out. Do you remember who brought it?"

His face scrunched in thought. "Yesterday? Yes. I remember. Brits. Or Australians. I can't tell the difference. Don't have an ear for accents. They were white."

"Was one of them tall with a mustache? Balding?"

"That describes half the men in town, and these men as well. Not like you see many younger men around." No. British or American, they would be off to war. "They were upset. Wanted to have the engine repairs done immediately, even offered extra cash. As if I'd drop work on the *Bug* to fix some car."

"Yet they still left it here."

"Yes. I told them it would be finished today."

Ingrid shook her head, smiling. "You never intended to have the repair made that quickly, did you?"

A funny little smile turned his lips. "It might have happened. Once my airship was done."

Ingrid touched his shoulder again, gently, and Fenris didn't shy from the contact.

Maybe Mr. Thornton had been one of these men. Maybe not. But it did seem that someone had taken advantage of his access to the auxiliary vault, willingly or otherwise on Thornton's part. She gnawed on her lip, not liking where these thoughts led.

The two British members of the auxiliary had been absent during the explosion. One was dead. The other, ill and missing, his autocar here.

Something terrible had befallen Mr. Thornton. She was sure of it. If she tried to warn people that some conspiracy was afoot, would anyone believe her? She was a foreign-looking woman, by popular judgment, and one already under suspicion.

God, what had happened in the past day? At dawn yesterday, her biggest crisis had been deciding how to fix up her hair.

She looked at Fenris's wig. It matched well enough, but still looked so wrong on him. "Do you want me to take that off?"

"Yes, damn it. Feels like a dead animal is pinned to my scalp."

Ingrid laughed and worked it free. "It looks like human hair to me."

"That's not much of an improvement. That thing's probably older than I am. Ah!" He sighed as the wig came free. "Throw that in its casket again." He motioned to the storage box.

Voices and footsteps echoed in the warehouse. One voice was especially familiar. Ingrid turned toward the door to see Cy and Lee.

"Ing?" asked Lee with a slightly pubescent squawk. The top of his head just reached Cy's chest.

Lee's posture made him once again look like an unassuming Chinese kid. The servant, the friend. Who was Lee Fong, really? Who were any of them? It was as though Ingrid had found out they were all bit players in some incomprehensible play. Not an opera, she hoped. She sang like a cat in heat. And she didn't want anyone to die at the end.

"Lee. You took care of the . . . of the men?"

"They'll have the worst headaches of their lives, but yeah, they'll live." Anger smoldered in his eyes. "We all know Chinatown won't stand for much longer. Graft only goes so far. Killing soldiers would be the perfect excuse for the Unified Pacific to raze Chinatown, and we're not going to give in that easily."

Ingrid stared at him and again wondered about the boy she had loved and nurtured for the past five years. She always knew he was Chinese, of course, but that was an entirely different thing from understanding what it was to *be* Chinese.

Lee hadn't made any attempt at tact in front of Cy and Fenris either. They were all bound in this together, this tangle of sedition and secrets.

"Is Mr. Sakaguchi okay? He didn't absorb power during the earthquake, did he?" she asked.

"No. He was still in that metal bed upstairs. He's headed out of the city now, in an autocar."

"Good. A car won't conduct well. That's one less thing to worry about." Even if he was held by a *tong,* near death, and had left her as the only geomancer in the city.

"What's the plan?" Fenris whispered. Ingrid realized with a start that Fenris still wore a woman's cotton shift, but he had pulled his blanket to armpit level. It looked like he wore a white blouse.

"The plan's for you to stay in bed and sleep and recover." Cy scowled down at Fenris.

"That plan doesn't agree with me." Fenris winced. "Actually, being stabbed doesn't agree with me either."

"Ingrid, I'm sorry I sent you off like that before," said Lee. "I didn't realize Mr. Braun was injured, not until one of the men told me. I would have arranged help for you both."

Ingrid thanked God for Lee's obliviousness back in the alley; Fenris didn't need his secret revealed to everyone willy-nilly. "We managed. Speaking of plans, I do need your help in another way. Mr. Sakaguchi told me I need to fetch something important from the house before I leave."

"Leave?" echoed Cy.

She stared at the floor. "Mr. Sakaguchi encouraged me to leave. I . . . I think that's the right course of action."

"What changed your mind?" asked Lee.

She brushed the burn on her knuckle again. "If I'm the only geomancer here and a large quake strikes, I will die, very quickly." It felt strange to confess to possessing magic out loud. "More geomancers will arrive here in a few days. I won't need to be away for long."

Lee nodded. "Maybe I can go with you." Ingrid cast him a grateful smile. Mr. Sakaguchi had wanted them to stay together, after all. He continued: "It might be awfully hard to get inside the house, though. The tank and soldiers haven't shown the slightest sign of budging."

"You can't make people disappear again?" asked Fenris.

Lee's expression was cool. "That's Chinatown. But I might still have some resources. Speaking of which . . ." He reached into his pocket and handed Ingrid her mother's pistol. "It's loaded."

"Thanks," she said, and tucked it in her pocket again. She looked to Cy. "What about that Durendal?"

"My offer to help still stands, Miss Ingrid," said Cy. The warmth in his eyes told her that their bet was on.

"It's quite a risk you'd be taking. You, too, Lee." Emotion caught in her throat. "I've already almost lost Mr. Sakaguchi more than once in the past day. This is my errand, and—"

"If you think we're letting you do this by yourself, your head's stuffed with straw tick," said Cy.

"That's right," said Fenris, wincing. "I'll even go as a show of support."

"You'll do no such thing!" She gave Fenris her darkest

glare, but inside she felt a comforting buzz of heat.

"Actually, Ing, can I speak with you alone for a minute?" asked Lee.

"Of course." She followed him outside the bedchamber. He ambled toward the airship, his hands stuffed in his pockets, feet scuffing the cement floor like any kid his age. He stopped, still facing away.

"Stop looking at me like that," he said.

She recoiled. "Like what?"

"Like I've suddenly sprouted arms like a Hindu god."

"Oh. Lee, I'm sorry, I just . . ." She didn't even know what to say. "There's a lot I don't understand."

"Did you really think we wouldn't fight back? That we'd just wallow here until the Unified Pacific decided to kill us off?" His voice was soft, his words sending a chill through her.

No, she wanted to say, but the truth was, she had never really thought much about Chinese resistance before, even with Mr. Sakaguchi's frequent observations on the subject. After all, she wasn't one of the elite, one of the persecutors of the Chinese. She was a dark-skinned woman who didn't even know where her father came from, why she looked as she did.

Ingrid always felt that she and Lee were bound in friendship, and because of that, their differences didn't matter.

"I don't know," she said in a whisper, feeling like a fool. Like she'd been a fool for years. She touched the spot where he had injected her again and wondered what she had allowed him to do, but she couldn't voice that doubt in him.

"You're my friend, Ingrid. No matter what happens, that hasn't changed. But you're not Chinese. There's a line there, between us." His head bowed as his shoes toed a crack in the floor.

"I never realized how big that line was."

"You've changed today, too. It's not just about me."

Ingrid wanted to argue with him but stopped at the realization he was right.

"I just want to know who you really are," she said.

"When I figure that out, I'll let you know," said Lee, pivoting on his heel to meet her gaze. Sadness lingered in his eyes, and she wasn't sure why. "You do the same for me."

CHAPTER 9

"A bored soldier's worse than a starved dog," said Cy. He squinted as he looked through the wall of bushes along the Suzukis' front yard.

"Boredom can be useful," said Lee. He crouched, knees jutted out. "They might be more eager for a distraction."

Cy glanced over, a skeptical eyebrow raised. "These fellows are in San Francisco, a port famed for its debauchery, and they're stuck here."

Here being the quiet, Japanese-dominated residential street Ingrid called home. Now it was quieter than ever. Vehicle and foot traffic had dwindled to almost nothing as the Durendal blocked half the thoroughfare. Defiant neighborhood boys, one with a baseball bat in hand, dashed over to touch the backside of a tread. They scampered away as though they were on fire.

"You said there are five soldiers total?" Ingrid asked. From their vantage point just across the street, she could see only two on the front porch.

Lee nodded. "Two on the porch, two on the sidewalk, and one inside the Durendal."

Still sounded like awful odds, even without the tank. "You're sure there aren't any inside the house?"

"That's not how they typically handle these affairs," Cy said. "That captain knows there's a shortage of geomancers here, so he likely intended to keep Mr. Sakaguchi under house arrest until more wardens arrive. To a passerby right now, it looks like these men are here to protect Mr. Sakaguchi after the explosion. The soldiers will have already searched the house, and I imagine there's a surprise or two inside, in case."

Ingrid snorted. "A surprise, like a cat bringing a dead mouse to the doorstep as a gift."

She leaned on one hand to keep her balance in a low squat, even as the narrow skirt she was wearing hobbled her knees like a roped calf at a rodeo. Lee had acquired clothing to replace her soiled dress—a simple work smock in periwinkle blue, paired with a coarse cotton apron. To complete the look, she had coiled her hair into a tight bun. She looked like most other working women of the city, but probably most other women weren't about ready to cut slits in their skirts so they'd maneuver better in order to break into houses.

The costume didn't allow her to conceal Mama's pistol either. Cy hadn't wanted the weapon, so she left it with her things at the workshop.

"These surprises wouldn't be fatal, likely," said Cy.

"Likely. There's a comforting adverb."

"My people have had an eye out," Lee said. "There are just the five. They do a loop of the house and yard every five, ten minutes. It varies. There's no way to sneak in, front or back."

His people. Why did that distinction make her feel so sad and frustrated now?

"This lot's young, too, all of them likely daydreaming of being the next Roosevelt," Cy said with a particular grimness. "Bet they're talking up plans to paint the town red once they're finally cut free."

"As long as they don't plan on painting Chinatown red, fine," said Lee.

"The Durendal would make that easy," Ingrid said.

A strange darkness glinted in Lee's eyes. "That time will come soon enough."

"You could steal the tank," she said.

"If it were at all possible," Lee murmured.

Cy gave Lee a look of disgust that said more than words, and all three of them focused on the Durendal again.

The Durendal's body contained gentle swells like calm ocean waves. A turret mounded at the top. The metal skin lacked obvious seams; seams meant points of vulnerability. So did individual wheels. The Durendal rolled on two treads, each as wide as a man.

Technological marvel that it was, in her eyes it was an ugly, intrusive metal box, a machine of war that didn't belong on this stately street with its glorious shade trees and shingle-sided homes.

The long gun barrel tilted to one side and aimed at her bedroom window. From her singular encounter with Captain

Sutcliff, she doubted that angle was an accident.

"Why even bring the tank down?" she asked. "They could park any A-and-A vehicle here and wait around for us to return home."

"It's all for show, Miss Ingrid. This Captain Sutcliff may have his suspicions, but after the auxiliary explosion and the gunfire here, other people will have put two and two together to realize something's afoot with the wardens."

Lee nodded. "Even if they suspect Mr. Sakaguchi of something, he *is* Japanese and a warden. They'd probably need an Ambassador here to take care of things, not some captain."

An Ambassador. She doubted they'd send Roosevelt either. A hard chill shook through her. If the Unified Pacific knew that a *tong* held Mr. Sakaguchi, they'd assassinate him just to prevent him from being used as a weapons manufacturer.

"The A-and-A wouldn't need to show restraint with me. I'm just a secretary." She couldn't hold back her bitterness.

"There's also power in being underestimated," said Cy, his gravelly voice soft.

Lee looked at Cy. "You know, I'd like to see how you plan on stopping a Durendal."

"I imagine you would," Cy replied in a long, even drawl. The man and boy stared at each other until Lee broke eye contact with a laugh.

"No point waiting around. Time to play the diversion."

"Please be careful, Lee."

He shrugged away her concern. "Just one piece of advice—when I say '*fan kwei,*' shut your eyes tight and look away." He crawled about five feet away and glanced back at Ingrid, his expression softening. "Don't come after me. You be careful, okay?"

"As careful as I can be while sneaking past five armed, bored soldiers and a Durendal," she said. If she was injured, he'd know. Everyone on the peninsula might know.

Lee crept off and Ingrid scooted closer to Cy. Even with her nose near the boxwoods, Cy still carried his particular scent of turpentine and ink. From somewhere down the block, a female voice sang in Japanese, the words high and tinny as they drifted from a Graphophone or Marconi at full volume.

Cy tilted an ear. "Is this whole street Japanese?"

"Yes. The whole neighborhood is, really."

"My father used to wonder, sometimes. China's being cleared of the Chinese so that the Japanese can settle there, but it seems they've done the same here, without any threat of violence. In Atlanta and Seattle, you can wander whole sections and see nary a word of English."

Cy certainly spoke a lot of his father. It was obvious he held tremendous respect for the man.

"Mr. Sakaguchi's made the same observation. He and Mr. Roosevelt would discuss the matter over scotch late at night, when I wasn't supposed to hear. 'A sly invasion,' Mr. Roosevelt called it."

Japanese dominated the upper class. They received preferred treatment under the law. The entire economy of the United States depended on their technological might. Ingrid had grown up with the social order—and in a Japanese household—so it was difficult to imagine things any other way.

"Pardon. Roosevelt the Ambassador?"

"The same. They used to be friends, until last year. They just plain stopped talking."

Cy made a thoughtful grunt. "He's the one Ambassador I'd want to meet, but only under pleasant circumstances."

Yes. Not in an interrogation. Much as she liked Mr. Roosevelt, there was a grim toughness to the man. There had to be, for him to be one of the Twelve. She wouldn't want to be on his bad side.

Cy stared at the Durendal, the expression on his face making him look like he'd tripped over a full chamber pot. She looked back and forth between him and the tank for a moment before she spoke.

"Was it your time in the A-and-A that made you a pacifist?" she whispered, making the question as casual as could be.

His leather coat rustled as he moved. "Yes."

"Where'd you serve?"

"Everywhere." His eyes stared somewhere beyond the Durendal. His voice lowered. "Lee shouldn't even have weapons like that, not here. Chinatown must be stockpiling, fortifying. The war's set to come stateside all too soon."

"Weapons like what? I didn't see anything."

"It was all in his warning. Be ready."

He stopped talking as Lee ambled toward them along the sidewalk, bold as a strolling tomcat. A strange leather bag swung from his shoulder. He stopped about ten feet from the tank.

"Hey—" one of the soldiers started to say.

Lee screeched out something in Chinese—not the words he'd warned them about—as he reached into his bag and threw something at the soldiers. Red exploded across the street. It took Ingrid a half second to recognize he was pelting them with tomatoes.

"Damn chankoro!"

The soldiers scrambled. The two men bounded from the porch. More tomatoes flew their way. Lee sprinted, tomatoes in hand. The soldiers yelled. Two set off after him, one with a gun brandished. The top of the Durendal popped open and a soldier emerged, in near hysterics.

"You said you wanted to lose your cherry tonight," the soldier said, gasping through belly laughs. He pointed down at one of the men. "Instead, you got a tomato!"

Ingrid couldn't see the two soldiers on the other side, but quite loudly heard their eloquent profanity. Beside her, Cy cringed.

"I work in a building full of men," she said. "I've heard worse." That didn't mollify him.

As the exchange continued, she looked both ways up the street, trying to see anyone else. She wiggled, her hip brushing Cy as she almost lost her balance again. He rested a hand on her knee to steady her.

"You're flushed. Do you have a fever?" He reached toward her and then froze, fingertips inches from her forehead.

"Probably," she said, and leaned into him.

His fingertips were soft and callused all at once. Strong. Cy had hands designed to grip something and hold on. She recollected a novel she once purchased that turned out not to be quite so appropriate for young ladies; it described in alluring detail how a man's broad hands could hold on to a woman by her curves and press their bodies together. She had an abundance of hip that could be quite useful in that regard.

She still had that book tucked beneath a floorboard in her room. Maybe. Sutcliff might read it at bedtime now.

"Yes, you are feverish." His hand left her skin, gently brushing a kinky strand of hair from her eyes. "I work with kermanite plenty, Miss Ingrid. I know how geomancers work. I'm especially curious about how *you* work."

She swallowed down dryness in her throat. "So am I. I fear that I'm figuring this out as I go along. I—"

Cy's full attention shifted to the street. "There."

Lee ran from the opposite direction, obscured behind the Durendal, and crossed the street. The man in the turret looked his way.

"Fan kwei!"

Ingrid threw herself down, squeezing her eyes shut. Cy flung himself over her, his chest heavy across her shoulders. Even so, through the veil of her eyelids a brilliant white flash of light illuminated the world. The soldiers' taunts turned to screams and moans.

"My eyes!"

"Goddamn chink!"

"Time to go," Cy said, pushing himself off her. "Head to the alley behind your house and wait there for me."

"Cy!" she gasped, but before she could stop him, he had dashed around the bushes. Dear God, there was still a soldier in the Durendal! What if he hadn't been blinded by that flash grenade?

Flash grenades—a weapon used in China. Ingrid shivered

as Cy's comments suddenly made sense. Chinatown was so close. She was so close to the Chinese, to Lee and Jiao.

So close, and so oblivious.

Despite his order, she crawled on all fours to stare through the thick branches in horrid fascination. Cy's long, lean body hopped to the running board, then to the railing, and up the turret. She waited for the soldiers to yell, climb the turret again, do something. She could see only one soldier from here, and he was curled up in a fetal position on the sidewalk, blubbering.

Cy slipped inside the turret. Ingrid stopped breathing, even as her heart roared like a kermanite engine at full throttle.

Silence. Nothing beyond the sobs of the soldiers. Not so much as a yell or thud from within the insulated metal hulk. What if he was attacked, what if he needed her help?

"Damn it, Cy!" Ingrid hiked up her skirts to knee level and skedaddled. She wound through the cover in the neighbors' yards and down to the next street, where she cut over to the alley. No sign of the soldiers Lee had led away. No sign of anyone at all. Even the birds had been rendered mute, as if in suspense.

The narrow band of the alley looked the same as always. Wooden fences lined the way while trees cast patchwork shade. If not for her heavy breaths and anxious heart, she could almost pretend everything was normal. She reached the fence at the backyard and crouched down into a ball, as if she could make herself small as a gnome. Her skirt restrained her at the knees and bowed her backward. She hit the dirt with a small grunt and pushed herself up to a crouch again.

God, please let Lee get away from the soldiers, please let Cy escape the Durendal. Ingrid pressed her face to her knees and was surprised at how the cloth was suddenly moist.

She had all this power—what could she really do?

Heavy feet pounded on the hard dirt. As low as she was, she couldn't see beyond the rubbish bins, and then a dense body leaped down beside her.

Energy accumulated against her skin and flickered outward just as she recognized Cy. Alarmed, she physically recoiled as she willed her body to stop. The heat dissipated. She sagged in relief.

"Don't do that!" she gasped. "I almost made you . . ." Fly like a sack of meat, but she didn't. Focus seemed to be the key, even when her power was triggered by an instantaneous reaction. "Were you seen?"

"Those boys won't be seeing anything for a good twenty minutes. I just so happened to truss them up and drop them all in the Durendal." He was sweat-soaked and panting from the effort. "Here's hoping Lee led the other two on a merry chase, and that any neighbors peering through the curtains are just as blind."

"Is the Durendal disabled?"

"Yes, miss."

"Is it really that easy to do?"

"Certainly is."

"Then other than the difficulties of getting inside one, why aren't more tanks being sabotaged?"

"Only the designer of the Durendal knows the flaw. Created the flaw."

"Oh." She looked at him, eyes widening. *"Oh."*

Who was this man? The Durendal was made by the Augustinian Company out of Atlanta. If Cy created it over a dozen years ago, he must have been little more than a kid at the time. Lee's age. Some pieces started to come together in her mind, jagged as they were.

He'd served in the military. He was a pacifist. He'd likely deserted. If he was caught by those soldiers, it could very well mean a firing squad.

"If you built a flaw into Durendals, then . . ." Her voice trailed away. Cy made it clear he didn't want Lee to know how it was done, but the very existence of the weakness meant that Cy planned to exploit it someday, or for someone else to. Interesting.

She jerked her head toward the fence and her house. "This will provide the best access to Mr. Sakaguchi's office. Will there be any surprises in the backyard?"

He peered over the fence. "No, not where birds or weather could set them off. Here, I'll help you over the top."

Mama used to say that whoever decided women should wear skirts should be forced to do constant jigs for the devil in hell, and this was one of those moments when Ingrid agreed.

The coarse wood of the fence grabbed hold of her skirt. Instead of heaving over the top and landing with finesse worthy of those *boo how doy* in Chinatown, she ended up upside down, the goddamned skirt tangled and half upended for all of three seconds before gravity did its job and brought her down with a mortifying rip of cloth. It took everything she had to not screech at the hard impact on her hands, her forearms, and then her knees. Blue mist flared again.

"Are you all right?" hissed Cy.

She choked down some blasphemy that would have made the southern man turn vermilion, and managed to crawl a few feet to hide behind a bush and assess her injured skirt and dignity. The cheap cotton had shredded from the knee on down to a ninety-degree angle at her other leg. The apron didn't fall quite far enough to cover it. The rip exposed her lacy bloomers up to the thigh.

Cy had seen that, and a whole lot more. Good Lord, of all people. Now she was feverishly red for a different reason.

Cy landed with lean grace that befitted the fantastic coyote. "I'm so sorry. Your skirt—"

"I'll make do." She grabbed the two ripped ends and tied them together in a knot. It bulged out and showed her knickers. "Pretend you don't see that."

He utterly failed to choke back a laugh. She glared him into muteness.

In naughty books, if a lady's bloomers were exposed, there tended to be kisses and other pleasantness involved, not to mention some semblance of privacy. Now she and Cy risked getting shot, captured, or worse. In the best-case scenario, she'd have to walk blocks through San Francisco looking like this. Dandy.

"I reckon they set alarm devices at all major entrances to the house and inside the house, too."

"Like . . . a trip wire? The sort they use over in China and the Philippines?"

"Worse. In a set environment like a house, they have automata that use a beam of light instead of a wire. If something interferes with the light, it triggers the blast." His brow furrowed, causing his pince-nez to rise on his nose crinkles. "The question is, what did they use here, and where? Could even be something akin to a flash grenade. They'd want to question, not kill, any interlopers."

"Ah, yes, because being maimed is so much more pleasant." Ingrid frowned toward the house she had loved all of her life. It looked different since the shooting. Ominous. Even the fairy motes had fully retreated from the garden; the distinct prickling sensation of their magic was gone. She leaned on a small statue of a kirin. The fabled creature was a chimerical mix of dragon, goat, and unicorn, and the fantastic's arrival was supposed to portend the coming of a wise ruler. As a statue, it was intended to bring good luck. She couldn't help but give the ceramic snout a quick rub; they could use any luck they could get.

"Where do we need to go within the house?" asked Cy.

"Mr. Sakaguchi said to go to the namazu wall. He has namazu-e prints in his study, over bookshelves. See those double doors?" The soldiers had nailed boards over the broken glass. Under other circumstances, that might be regarded as considerate.

He pursed his lips. The faint trace of a mustache colored his upper lip, the tint a deeper red than his wavy brown hair. "Almost too easy, having such direct access there."

"Easy?" she snapped. "After what you did, and then Lee . . ."

"Easy for them to rig something, miss," he amended, gently. "Let's go closer."

They snaked their way through the paradise of Mr. Sakaguchi's backyard. The gravel of the Zen garden crunched underfoot. The soft, almost rubbery leaves of the vivid Japanese maples stroked her arms and attempted to snare her skirt.

As they rounded the catfish pond, she couldn't help but glance within the rock-lined basin.

"Dear God," she whispered.

Dead catfish blanketed the top of the water, their white bellies exposed to cloud-strained sunlight. Wide mouths gaped open in the rictus of death. Some fish still lived, barely. Their sleek black bodies twitched and writhed as though starved for air. A day without food couldn't have done this.

"Poison?" Cy asked.

"No." The straightforward, scientific explanation was that they died because of the dearth of geomancers in the region, but she couldn't help but think of Mr. Sakaguchi's stories. Of a geomancy-bound Hidden One's agitation causing totem creatures to go crazed or die because of the looming energy of a major earthquake. Were the double-headed snakes within the San Andreas fault about to writhe and resettle their coils? Was that *because* of the lack of geomancers?

Cy waited at the door for her, frowning in concern. Ingrid shook her head. "Later," she whispered.

It was impossible to see inside the house with the door partially boarded over and the intact glass covered by shutters.

"Do you have any electronics on you? Are there any within the room, within about ten feet?" Cy asked.

"Me? No. Inside there's a Marconi, a Graphophone, a couple of other little things. Why?"

"I'm about to kill them. Until some components can be replaced, in any case. Here." He reached inside his coat for the Tesla rod and handed it to her. The metal rod was warm with his body heat. From the depths of a pocket, he pulled out a wooden box about the size of his palm. The lid was inlaid with stained glass panels, and through a clear triangle she could see a piece of kermanite the size of a walnut. It took up almost the entire box. Wires and clamps occupied the rest of the space, like a miniature heart and pulmonary system.

"If you don't mind, Miss Ingrid, please head toward the fence with the rod so I don't neutralize it."

She obliged and retreated. Cy set the box on the porch welcome mat and opened the lid. He twiddled with the mechanism and went very still. She expected something intense. A bright flash, a boom, something to reveal the nature of the weapon in his possession, something that might bring the soldiers swooping in like Valkyries to a battlefield. Instead, he closed the box and returned it to his pocket. He beckoned her over.

"Thank you," he said, taking the Tesla rod and extending it with an elegant flick of his wrist.

"What was that? Another Tesla invention?"

"No. This one is all mine. I call it a radioflash. Invented it a few years back, and Fenris near strangled me when I neutralized most everything he was working on." He eyed the door. "I think you'll understand when I ask that you—"

"Don't tell anyone? Of course. And before you get any fancy ideas about that door, I should tell you I have the key."

"Kicking's not fancy, Miss Ingrid. It's practical, if a bit too loud for our needs." His broad grin made her smile in return. "Please unlock it. I'll be ready for any surprises."

With trembling fingers, she worked the key in the lock, even as her anxious heart all but galloped up her throat. The door clicked. Cy led the way. Ingrid's fingers twitched with want of a gun, but at least she had her power. Maybe now she could figure out how to control the damn thing.

The wood-paneled room was as dark as a cave. Glass crunched underfoot. Cy held out the Tesla rod and did something at the base. Brilliant blue light spilled forth, kermanite-powered and pure. At his nod, she shut the door behind her.

The familiar room spooked her in its wrongness. The army had clearly visited, and their imprint made her even more certain that Sutcliff's men hadn't ransacked Mr. Thornton's house. The azure beam revealed tidy disarray. Books had shifted. A mantel clock faced the wrong way. The desk chair sat upright.

Blood had dried in long streaks leading out to the hallway. Sweet Lord, there was a lot of it.

"Don't look at it." Cy's voice was soft. "He's alive. He's with a ki doc. Focus on that."

"Easier said than done." Her voice shook.

His hand reached for hers, and she met him halfway. She sucked in a breath. She had never held hands like this with a man before. Fenris and Mr. Sakaguchi, that'd been different. Cy's fingers were long enough to encircle her wrist like a bracelet. His solidness anchored her in the present.

"We dare not dally too long, Ingrid." It jolted her, to hear him say her name without a title. "Think on where he'd hide important papers for you."

"Right."

Ingrid faced the wall with the namazu-e. The framed propaganda posters from Japan showed the massive catfish in many forms—in his native environment of the sea, as a monster being flailed for killing so many with his movement, and so on. Mr. Sakaguchi had said something about a box. Could there be a hidden vault in the wall?

Releasing her hold on Cy, she ran her fingers down the panels, exploring every crevice and knothole. Cy followed her example. The two went up and down every panel over a five-foot span, but nothing happened. She crouched down at the low shelves built into the wall. There were several netsuke of carved ivory, bone, or wood, most depicting earthbound Hidden Ones from around the world: the buffalo from Bulgaria, the turtle of Algonquin mythology, the frog of Mongolia. Cy pulled out books and flipped through pages, checking to see if they were actual books, and then tapped the wall behind them. It thudded as solid, not hollow.

More of Ingrid's hair slipped loose from its bun and dangled before her eyes. She blew the strands to the side with a frustrated huff.

"I don't know where else to look!" She scanned the entire room, desperate for any possibilities. Mr. Sakaguchi said to look for the namazu wall.

The namazu. She almost smacked herself in the forehead.

Ingrid headed toward the door. "When he said to look for the catfish, I assumed he meant the box had to be here, indoors, in the library. But that's where anyone searching would look first, so of course he wouldn't put anything here. I wasn't being literal enough."

"Then where's it hidden?"

"In the pond with all those dead fish."

CHAPTER 10

Ingrid stared into water littered with fishy corpses. She had no issues with preparing or eating dead fish, but the idea of sticking her hand in there turned her stomach. It wasn't so much what the fish were; it was what their dead bodies *meant*.

"Mr. Sakaguchi came out here often. I always teased him about playing with his catfish. He'd be wet to the elbow." Emotion caught in her throat again.

Leather fell to the stony patio with a heavy ripple. Cy had shed his coat and undid the buttons on his white shirt to roll back the cuffs. "That says a good deal. It means he wasn't wading to the middle of the pond."

"True." Light gleamed through the slatted patio cover and cast white spears against the dimpled surface.

Ingrid was relieved as Cy took the initiative and reached into the pond. He tugged at the rocks that lined the sides and bottom. Dead fish bobbed and rode on miniature waves.

"Loose rock here," he said after a minute. He hefted a sizable piece of quartz speckled with algae. He reached into the hole just beneath the waterline and pulled out a parcel wrapped in oil cloth. He passed it to her as he pulled on his coat again.

Ingrid stroked the slick black surface. She guessed there to be a wooden box inside. It was about the size of a Bible, but these contents were more personally relevant than any holy book. This was supposed to convince her to leave the city, to take care with her power—something that Mr. Sakaguchi had apologized for with immense regret. Did it contain some secret tract of the wardens? Maybe women like her had existed all along.

"Ingrid." The sharpness in Cy's voice caused her to jerk up her head.

Across the garden, another head stared at them—one topped with a navy cap with a black brim.

Ingrid dashed for the side yard with the box tucked into her armpit. Branches yanked at her skirts and pried at her hair. Cy loped past her with his long strides and grappled with the latch, swinging back the gate as she reached it.

"Waterfront," he barked out as she passed.

Waterfront. Four long blocks away, a downhill slope. The area would teem with people at this time of evening, the perfect place to lose their pursuers.

They just had to make it there.

She ran across the yard and bounded through the gaping front gate not five feet from the Durendal. An autocar was parked behind it, a cluster of soldiers piled atop the Durendal. The hatch was open, one soldier halfway down the ladder.

They turned in unison. One man shifted to unholster his gun, but Ingrid turned the corner and away.

A shrill whistle sliced through the air.

Oh God, oh God. She pounded out the words with every footstep. Her feet screamed in agony, her calves afire. Cy ran at her side, breath huffing, coat rippling. Gravity propelled them down the slope. Behind them, the car squealed as it pulled away from the curb.

Cy grabbed her arm, directing her toward a building—a factory, the doors open wide. She dodged tables and surprised women in white smocks, Cy leading the way on through. His holstered Tesla rod bounced against his hip and thwacked her. Through a courtyard, and into another business—a kite store. Rainbows of color blurred together as they burst through and onto the next block.

She couldn't hear the car anymore but whistles split the air and seemed to multiply.

Breath escaped her in massive wheezing gasps. Her lungs seared and seized and fought for every breath. Her strides slowed, even as she grimaced and forced them to keep going. Pedestrian traffic thickened as they passed card shops and dentists and delis. A bicyclist grazed her and sent her spinning but she ran on. Ingrid knew that if she stopped, if she had to walk, she couldn't run again. Her leg muscles were like rubber bands in a child's hands, stretched and stretched and unable to return to their previous shape.

A hundred masts pricked the cloudless sky. Beyond them sprawled the cool blue of the bay. Stevedores and deliverymen and trucks crowded the way.

Traffic forced Ingrid and Cy to a walk. Ingrid's agonized legs made to keep going, but Cy caught her against him. Her hand clutched at his lapel, her head at his chest. His hands cupped her waist and he all but dragged her across the street. Ingrid was aware of the blur of curious onlookers. She made her legs work, wobbly as they were. She ducked around a workman with a dolly.

Whistles. High, piercing. Close.

"Hide," she gasped.

Cy nodded, glancing back. His face was ruddy with exertion, his glasses halfway down his nose. Brown hair clung to his scalp in perfect curls.

There were buildings, warehouses, trucks. Men everywhere, ants swarming for their crumbs of work. Very few women. Ingrid stuck out.

"Split up," she gasped.

"No." His hand encircled her elbow. "This way. Hurry."

Cy guided her into a building. The heady scent of garlic reeled through her nostrils. Workers at their boxes looked up, eyebrows raised. She and Cy wound their way through, seeking any sort of privacy, any sort of refuge in the darkness. Nothing. They passed through a bright doorway and into daylight again.

"Stop! Stop them! Stop the dark woman!"

A boardwalk skirted the building. Seagulls squawked annoyance and fluttered away as Ingrid forced her legs to a pathetic run. Cy should leave her. He could outrun them, blend in. Fury at her slowness, at her lack of fitness, flushed heat through her already drenched skin.

"Stop them!"

An unloader turned, his mouth gaping in surprise, and reached for her. She swatted him back without touching him. Maybe that's what she could do—knock all their pursuers down—but what about the crowds around them, and the autocars and boxes? No, she couldn't risk hurting any bystanders.

But there was something she could do.

"Cy!" His name emerged sharp between breaths. "Hold on to me."

He didn't hesitate. He wrapped his arms around her from the back, pressing the oilskin-wrapped box even closer to her torso just as she leaped into the water and prayed it was deep.

Heat didn't tingle to the surface of her skin. It roared. It consumed. The ten-foot drop to the bay took only a matter of seconds, but in her mind, it was so much more. Mr. Sakaguchi had said that the next time she built a bubble, she needed to make it big. Very well. She pressed herself into Cy—no, she willed herself against Cy, even as they fell together. She focused on his height, his breadth of form. She thought on the danger of rocks below, and the need for the bubble to be heavy enough to sink and hide them beneath the waves despite the air it maintained.

Focus. She etched it like a blueprint in her mind, one she already knew by touch and texture within the scope of her imagination.

All this, in three seconds. Then, the water. Despite her preparations, she held her breath, ready for the bitter cold and the strength of the waves. The water came, but she didn't get wet. It splashed against the shield. Tiny bubbles danced past in streams, light and darkness mottled like a layer of ink spilled across a page. At her back, Cy strengthened his grip as their feet struck bottom, sort of. The seabed consisted of uneven sand and rotten pilings and God knew what else. The bubble settled. Plumes of sand rose and shifted around them and clouded the water even more.

They were underwater.

Panic drove a high, piglike squeal from her throat. Being buried beneath the ruins of a building was one thing, but this—this was worse. The bubble wavered, and she made herself focus.

"Miss Ingrid." Cy's voice was higher than its usual range. "What exactly just happened?"

"When I know, I'll tell you." She breathed in and out, quelling her terror, keenly aware of the heat still in her skin. She had enough power to do this for a little while. Whatever it was she was doing. She analyzed the nature of the bubble she'd created. Before, she and Mr. Sakaguchi had been crouched and low, and the bubble had been round. Now it was tall to fit Cy. She found the glassy sheen about six inches in front of her, the surface so cold it practically bit her hand. She jerked her fingers back.

They could have been in that frigid water. They were, in a way.

Ingrid thought of washing clothes, how a soap bubble would catch on the breeze. A bubble might look round, but it could bend and flex with the pressure of the wind. That's how this constructed bubble would work, too.

She stepped forward, gingerly. The bubble flowed with

them. Hesitating, Cy followed, his body indecently close. His lanky form fit against the curve of her backside. They were like dancers in a club, the sort she shouldn't spy on but couldn't help doing so if the opportunity arose. The heat of her body slid from her fingertips and deep into a well beneath her pelvis, where she could just imagine—

The bubble rippled. "Idiot!" Ingrid snapped at herself. Heat lurched up and out of her again.

"What . . . ?"

"Never mind." She tried to edge her hips forward a smidgen, but with every step he rocked against her again. She released a frustrated huff. She wanted to enjoy this close proximity, damn it all.

"I will mind, because in case you didn't notice, we're underwater and breathing." A straight line of bubbles rippled downward in front of them. "And that, I believe, was a bullet."

"Damn them all to hell! Do you think they can see us? Walk! Fast!"

"They can see something, evidently." His voice was still high with a slight trill. "I'd still like to know what you've done, miss. Miss Ingrid."

She had managed to confound and petrify the coolheaded Cypress Jennings. Wonderful.

They briskly walked as step-in-step as they could over the rough terrain, staying parallel to the land. The bottoms of boats swayed overhead.

"I made something similar yesterday when the auxiliary exploded. I grabbed Mr. Sakaguchi as the blast occurred. My only thought was to protect him. The bubble kept us safe in the rubble. There is one major deficiency. We'll need to surface soon, as the air in here will last for only so long."

"I see." The words were drawn out and measured. His fingers quivered at her waist as the box dug deeper into her side. She overlapped his hand and squeezed in reassurance.

"I'm sorry," she said, and meant it. "You said you were curious about my powers—well, this is what I can do, the full demonstration."

"Miss Ingrid, pardon my language, but this is a damn sight more impressive than directing energy into kermanite. I say that as a machinist with a fine appreciation of those rocks."

"Thank me when we're out of here."

How were they going to get out? It's not as though there were any stairs conveniently leading to the street. She had a strong feeling she would have to pop the bubble while they were still underwater, and worried about how Cy would react to that. Could he swim? If she asked him the question, would that only intensify his terror?

It's not as if she could swim either. She'd been to the beach with Mama a few times, but was never completely immersed in the water. That wouldn't have been *proper*.

Damn propriety to hell and back. She needed to get out of here, learn to swim, fly an airship, run up and downhill, and do whatever in God's creation she wanted to do.

Including Cy.

His hand fit against her waist. Every few steps, it seemed, they each shifted on the dense sand and couldn't help but press together. She made a concerted effort to focus on the bubble.

"Have you seen any other bullets?"

"No. But they likely are looking near that dock or where they expect the tide to take our . . . to take us."

Our bodies. Well, that thought was a bit of a damper.

A barnacle-crusted hull thrust out of the sand, and she led them around it. The shore was a smudgy shadow now. Less light filtered from above.

"Let them think we're dead, then. It should buy us more time. I hope no one recognized you."

"I don't do much business with naval ships. They tend to stay with machinists they've used for years." His voice trembled and he paused to swallow. "Airship industry has boomed with the war, brought in new folks who are also willing to employ new folks."

Ingrid was glad she couldn't see his face. Feeling the tension in his body was disconcerting enough. Seeing his terror, letting him see hers—no, that wouldn't be good.

They walked around the tall poles of a pier. No gentle slope led back to the shore. Instead, everything looked darker and deeper. Fewer boats swayed above, and if there were more, she couldn't see them. How far had they walked? How long until sunset? What were they going to do? She held the box and Cy's arm tighter against her side.

The slight fever was dissipating, her skin cooling. Sunset wasn't going to be an issue. She'd lose consciousness before then.

God, I'm not one for prayer, but we need help. Don't let Cy die because of me. Please, show us a way out of this. The intensity of the feeling radiated from her. *Help. We need help.*

"It's curious, Miss Ingrid, this matter of you being a geomancer. And a woman."

Terrified as Ingrid was, she couldn't help but smile at the change of subject. "Oh, so you noticed both."

"It seems a bit obvious. Being a geomancer. And being a woman." He shakily chuckled. "You're trying to get me in trouble, Miss Ingrid."

Such pleasant trouble, compared to the literal deep water they were in. "The magic manifested when I was five. My papa was a warden. Mama had been managing on her own since he died, but then I became very sick. Near death. No doctor could help. Mama had a hunch and took me to the auxiliary. Mr. Sakaguchi was the one she spoke with, and he found I could siphon power into kermanite. He hired Mama as his cook and housekeeper. I scarcely remember a thing before that time."

"Your mother . . . ?"

"She died two years ago."

"I'm sorry. I . . . my sister died last year. Hurt never really leaves, does it?" His voice softened. "I never heard of a geomancer doing these things you do."

"Neither have I. Well, Papa was supposed to be pretty powerful, but Mr. Sakaguchi says my knack is stronger."

"Your fever. The quake in Chinatown caused that? Gave you the power to do this?"

"Yes."

"It's my understanding that a geomancer isn't supposed to hold energy that long; it'll make him too sick to function."

Nor were they supposed to expend energy the way she was doing. She ground her teeth together to prevent them from chattering. They needed help, and fast. They were too far out in the bay now, and the pressure of the water kept nudging them along. If she lost consciousness, they were doomed for sure. Even if Cy could swim, he'd die trying to do so with her soggy carcass in tow.

"I can hold far more than most, but it still affects me. I was very sick in Chinatown right after the earthquake. Addled my brain for a few minutes, until I let some power go."

"We need to get you more kermanite. Maybe we can go to the bank again and—" A violent chill convulsed through her.

"Ingrid?" His fingers spanned against her ribs.

Through the murk, a gray ghost moved, sinuous and lean. Ingrid and Cy stopped. She practically hunkered over his arm at her waist. Sand clouded the water at their feet.

"Is that a seal?" asked Cy.

"A harbor seal, yes, but . . ." Pinpricks against her skin told her this was something more.

The creature's mottled gunmetal-gray fur blended in with the world beneath the waves. It tilted its head to the side, black pebble eyes unreadable. The seal wiggled. It was a slight motion, like a cat stretching as it stood up after a nap. The fur curled back. A human head emerged—a woman's head. Silver hair the same speckled color as the fur fanned out in the water. Her face was neither old nor young, beautiful with languid eyes. Her somewhat flat nose was reminiscent of a seal's snout, while her dark skin looked like that of a native tribe. A shade not that different from Ingrid's, really.

"A selkie. A fantastic in the wild." Ingrid's eyes brimmed with tears of joy. She had always loved it when she spied unicorns in the city, most often harnessed to sulkies driven by Nob Hill nabobs' wives or daughters—but she always felt guilty at that delight, too, at seeing a fantastic made domestic.

This selkie was old magic. Free, as it should be.

Oh, if only she had a camera as Victoria Rossi did, to be able to capture this moment! Not that it would matter in the long term. They would likely be dead soon, but this was a blessing, here at the end.

The woman's shoulders wiggled as the pelt continued to work downward. Ingrid stiffened in alarm. "Um, Cy, I do believe she's going to . . ."

"I'd say I won't look, but there's not much choice."

A slight giggle masked another violent shiver. "Well, I suppose this is more forgivable than you going to see some burlesque show down on the Barbary Coast."

"Forgivable?" Cy sounded amused. "Quite generous of you, Miss Ingrid."

Sure enough, a breast emerged, small and buoyant, and along with it a freed arm. Ingrid couldn't help but gawk at the selkie's chest. The only other bared breasts she'd seen were Fenris's, and they'd been painted in blood. She'd never even seen Mama unclothed.

The selkie reached out and touched the bubble.

"Oh." Ingrid gasped.

The motion rippled through her as a tiny pressure wave, the heat of it painful in contrast to the cold. It took everything Ingrid had not to lose focus and crumple to her knees. Sensing something, Cy tightened his grip, and he rooted her in place. Through pain-dazzled sight, she saw the selkie gesture up, then at the bubble, and back up. Behind Ingrid, Cy shifted to point up as well. The selkie nodded.

More ghostly bodies undulated through the darkness. They worked down their furs enough to expose full, human arms while keeping strong tails below the waist like merfolk.

Tales of fantastics always spoke of beings like selkies, djinn, and fairies as pretty ideals. These selkies were beautiful, but not in the willowy way of a Howard Pyle illustration. No, they were stocky and strong. Their arms rippled with both muscle and fat. One man's jowls bulged around his face and concealed his neck.

The selkies surrounded the bubble, their eyes on Ingrid. Oh God, they were all going to touch the shielding. What would her pain do to the earth? Was saving her worth the potential destruction?

But if she died, would that cause something far worse?

Ingrid didn't want to die. She gave them a curt nod. "Cy. Hold me up while—"

Even expecting the pain of their power, it burned. She screamed. The sound bounced back at her, foreign and strange.

Blackness swarmed her eyesight but she knew she couldn't let the cold consume her, couldn't let go of those last traces of heat. The magic of the sea felt so different from what she knew. It flashed a palpable taste on her tongue—sweet salt, overbearing, gagging. Cy's presence, physical, emotional, was the only thing that moored her to consciousness.

With everything so hazy, it took her a moment to realize they were being hoisted up. Bubbles of movement trickled past as a beam of sunlight glinted against the shielding around them.

She had prayed for help, and it was as though the selkies had come to rescue them. "Thank you," she whispered.

The selkie woman's eyes, so impenetrable and black, met hers then flared in alarm. Bubbles flooded by in a veil as the selkies wiggled frantically toward the surface.

That's when Ingrid sensed the earthquake.

It felt different when filtered through the water. The tremor rocked the bubble and brought heat in sharp contrast to the salty cold. She half closed her eyes and let bliss quiver through her. This was the power she knew and craved, even if it was tainted by the thickness of the sea.

The selkies wailed, and it wasn't a sound of joy. The earthquake pained them as if they'd been dropped into a fire. She *knew,* their powers of earth and sea twined as they were. Marine magic pierced the bubble and gouged her with a thousand prickles. She screamed, her own power rising in response.

Fierce cold smashed into her, and weight, and the full brine of the bay.

CHAPTER 11

Whatever power the tremor brought her, it hadn't been enough. The bubble was gone. So was oxygen, warmth, and Cy's secure presence at her back. Water welled in her throat, her chest. All she knew was blackness and pain. Then suddenly—light. Piercing.

Was this death?

Something slammed into her back. Again, again. She retched, her throat afire as if all of the bay was being expelled from her lungs and stomach and various other internal nooks and crannies. Her fingers dug into sand. Dry sand. Her face burned with grit. The weight of her dress dragged her down.

"Ingrid. Ingrid. Stay with me."

"Cy." His name emerged with another eruption of seawater. He was alive. A warm, broad hand girthed her waist, while another hand held up her right shoulder.

"It's all fine. We're on land. Get the water out."

She let her eyes close. The sunlight glowing through her lids didn't bother her. Sleep. Sleep would be mighty fine right now.

"No." Those strong hands shook her. "Stay awake, Ingrid. Christ Almighty, you're too cold."

The earth shivered. Power filtered into her as if the ground itself tried to warm her. Not with a deluge—she wasn't in excruciating pain anymore. Cold, soreness, and exhaustion rooted in her very bones. Somehow, the earth differentiated between them all, only responding to agony.

Her body shifted and she turned around and floated upward. An arm hooked beneath her buttocks while another had her back. The body next to hers was cold, the warm ground far away. All the world turned to ice.

"Help! Help!" Cy yelled. "Over here!" The next words puffed heat against her nose: "Stay with me, Ingrid. We didn't go through all that for you to die here. Come on, stubborn girl."

As though straining to lift a steel beam, she worked open her eyelids to see Cy looming and blurry above her.

"Not girl." The words slurred. "Woman."

"You . . . you . . ." His laugh was sharp. "I will never understand you."

"Good. Mys-tery. Lasts longer. Where . . . we?"

"Hey!" That was a different voice, distant and drawing closer.

"I think we're on Goat Island," said Cy.

Goat Island, located halfway between San Francisco and Oakland, smack-dab in the middle of the bay. Ingrid's awareness bobbed like the tide as she was carried inside a building. Another voice rang out, feminine and shrill. The heavy dress was peeled away. A fire crackled. Water boiled. Ingrid found herself wrapped in blankets, hot-water bottles heavy against her. Heat trickled into her skin. It wasn't the warmth of the earth's power, but the radiating force of life itself. A small spout was held to her lips as a hand tilted back her head. Molten lava poured into her sore throat. She choked and spat.

Close by, a man burst out in raspy laughter. "Aye, she'll make it. Whiskey's the stuff of Christ and Lazarus."

The drink created a cozy ball of warmth in her gut that seemed to fizzle out her ears. Ingrid blinked away the crustiness of salt and sand as she took in her surroundings. White walls, fairly austere. An askew print of an English country scene—a sheepdog, lambs, and a Porterman above.

"Ingrid?" Cy's voice was soft.

Her fingers probed the blanket. "Cy. The oilskin. Where—"

"Shush. Everything's fine." In other words, don't draw attention to the parcel. She had enough wits to recognize that.

She blinked at him as he came into focus. "Your glasses are gone."

He touched the bridge of his nose as if checking again himself. "Ocean waves are strong like that."

"Oh, I'm so sorry, Cy. Can you see at all?"

He bowed closer to her, so close he could have easily kissed her. "I have to be about this close to read something, and the rest of the world is a mite blurry, but it's nothing to fuss about. Here. Have another drink."

No argument there, though she was a bit disappointed that he didn't sit quite as close again.

She sipped more whiskey as Cy conversed with the lighthouse officer and his wife. It seemed she and Cy had washed up on the southeast corner of Goat Island, within sight of the peninsula.

"No surprise to me, that earthquake knockin' you outta a boat," said the man. "That wave was particularly high, 'twas."

"Haven't even seen any of our cats since it happened," added the woman.

A thin blue fog clung to the ground. The color was weak but contrasted with the white walls. Ingrid wormed a foot free of her swaddling blanket so she could dip it near the floor. No energy pull. Frowning, she tucked her leg closer again.

It's like the earth was tense with readiness of her pain, but wasn't provoked enough to vent power. Had her near death done this?

"We need to get back to the city," Ingrid said, voice raspy.

"You can't! You both still look like drowned rats, and with that wind off the water . . . !" The wife scowled. "You'll catch your death of pneumonia, dearie."

The city would catch a lot worse than that if Ingrid didn't figure out what was going on, but now one thing was absolutely clear: she had to assemble her meager belongings and leave with Lee as soon as possible.

"We really do need to get back," said Cy. "Our families must be all afright after seeing us go overboard."

The couple protested mightily, but Cy's smooth ways won them over. Ingrid had privacy to pull on her wrung-out dress and squeaking boots. Cold lingered in her skin, the sort that didn't just come from exposure to the bay.

A fisherman on a stopover to the island was kind enough to ferry them. Ingrid kept a wool blanket wrapped around her, but it didn't quite block the fierce wind off the water. The fishing boat bounced across the waves, its vivid red triangular sails rippling. The reek of fish drenched her senses.

The oilskin-wrapped box was tucked in the curve of her lap. How she had held on to the box in the water, she didn't know. She prayed the contents hadn't been destroyed by the harsh exposure.

They docked near the airship frontage South of the Slot. *"Grazie!"* Cy called to the fisherman as he scooped Ingrid up in his arms.

She pressed her forehead against the stripe of buttons down his shirt, not wanting to see the curiosity of onlookers. She couldn't miss that the trace of colored fog was here, too.

"I can walk," she growled. She had to say it, for the sake of her pride.

"You can fall, too."

"I'm not an invalid."

"Ingrid," he whispered, the word almost lost against the rumble of wheels. "You walked me underwater. You don't need to prove your strength to me."

She closed her eyes briefly, rocking against him, and smiled. Her strength. She'd been told she was strong as she hauled laundry, as she shifted dormitory mattresses—but this was different.

"What happened after the bubble burst?" she whispered. "The selkies . . ."

"The surge of water from the earthquake hit us and the bubble popped. Peculiar thing, that. That first wave warmed you like a light bulb, and then the heat snuffed out. The next water was like ice. We began to plummet, but then the seals—the selkies—were there, two grabbing each of us." He stopped, and traffic thrummed by for a moment before he walked on.

"They touched us?" Ingrid craned up her head, voice soft in awe. Cy's jaw was lined with reddish stubble. He dipped his chin so he could look her in the eye.

"Yes, but that wasn't a good thing, not for you." His Adam's apple bobbed as he swallowed. "You were still unconscious and didn't scream, but they held you up out of the water to breathe and you . . . you were hurting. From their touch. Your neck, your back, you were arched like a man in the thrall of lockjaw, like some circus contortionist. I thought . . ." He took in a shuddering breath. "They acted pained, too. You hurt each other, without even trying."

"Different magic. It hurt when they touched the bubble, too. I remember that." She shivered from memory as well as cold.

"Even unconscious, you never lost grip of that oilskin. I sure hope whatever's in there was worth all this."

"Me, too."

He tripped, falling forward. She yelped slightly as he caught himself against a pole. "Sorry, I missed that curb."

Why had the selkies come to their aid right after her prayer? It was strange, especially since earth and sea magic clashed in such a painful way. The selkies had been outright eager to get her and Cy out of the water. Maybe Ingrid's very presence in the ocean had pained them. Or maybe it was simple kindness on their part—selkies had been known to save drowning sailors, after all.

Whatever their motivation, Ingrid still had a sizable stash of money with her things in the workshop. Next opportunity, she was heading to the fishmonger to buy a wheelbarrow of fish to throw to seals along the piers.

Cy and Fenris's warehouse was quiet. Cy set Ingrid down just inside the office, and it took all her willpower not to collapse into a puddle on the floor. She hobbled a few steps and sat down on a wooden bench.

"I'll start up the heater," he said. "And get—"

"Cy. I can stoke the fire."

"—coffee going and grab some food. I know how hungry geomancers get after working kermanite, so you must be about ready to eat a roc trussed up like Thanksgiving turkey. And. Um. Miss. You have to get out of those clothes so you don't catch ill, and nothing of Fenris's stash will fit your, um, body type. I . . . I do have some long shirts that might work, if you don't mind."

Ingrid paused in the midst of prying off her boots to look at him in exasperation. "Do I seem like the sort of woman who'd prefer to freeze to death rather than wear a man's clothes? Food and coffee sound like manna from heaven, and anything dry will do."

He tucked his chin, cheeks flushed, and scurried away.

Ingrid let the wet blanket fall to the floor. Despite being shaky, she had plenty of practice in starting a fire, and soon enough she had the kindling ablaze in the little iron stove behind the desk. The thing looked like an artifact from Gold Rush days.

After locking the front door, she set about removing her damp dress again. Shedding that dank weight made her gasp in relief. Like a snake working out of its old skin, she shimmied her legs from her ruined stockings. The water had made a snarled bird's nest of her hair and stolen half the pins, so she undid the rest, wincing as she pried out the remaining bobbies. It'd be torture to brush it out later.

There she sat, indecent in her bloomers and camisole. The white fabric certainly didn't leave much to the imagination. She picked up the damp blanket again and draped it over her shoulders, and scooting close as she dared to the stove, she reached for the oilskin.

Thank God that Mr. Sakaguchi had stored it in a pond. She pulled away the final layer of oilskin to find a familiar wooden box. More than once, she'd seen it on Mr. Sakaguchi's desk over the years, but never paid it any heed, or wondered where it went. It was about as basic as a box could be. Polished golden pine, no ornamentation. It didn't even require a key to open. With trembling fingers, she lifted the lid.

There were two stacks of letters, each bound in twine. The top postmark read *Hawaii-Vassal Territory*. She worked the top envelope free and unfolded the sheets within.

The top sheet was gibberish. A made-up alphabet colored in red, blue, and black covered the page, with very few gaps between words. Some kind of code? Frowning, she went to the second sheet. Mr. Sakaguchi's handwriting was usually quite easy to read, but here he wrote in cramped, miniature script as he deciphered the message.

Dear Old Friend, read the salutation. Impatient, she

skipped over the two scant paragraphs to the bottom.

As always, thanks for tending to the child. With sincerity, A. Carm.

Ingrid froze. Abram Carmichael? Her father? She moved her thumb to find the date.

June 16, 1905. Ten months ago.

The box and letters tumbled onto the pile of oilskins on the blue-hazed floor. The cloth deadened the impact, but a thud still echoed throughout the room.

"Ingrid!" Cy burst inside, but she didn't look at him. She could only stare at the letter on the floor. The page and its words curled inward as if hiding in shame. "What is it?"

"I . . ." She pressed both hands to her mouth.

"Bad news?"

"I don't know." She continued to stare at the floor. "The letter . . . It doesn't make sense. My father. He's supposed to be dead. This . . . he wrote it last year, in some code, and Mr. Sakaguchi . . ."

Mama. She couldn't have known. It's not that she ever spoke fondly of Papa. In her brusque way, she accepted that he was dead and gone and she had a life to live. Ingrid didn't even know what he was like; from what she gathered, Papa had essentially abandoned her and her mother before he died. All she knew was that he was a warden, well traveled, and how he looked as depicted in that portrait in the auxiliary. A portrait utterly destroyed as of yesterday.

Mr. Sakaguchi never proposed marriage to Mama because he knew the truth. All this time, Papa was alive.

"I set everything down when I heard that racket. I'll be right back," said Cy.

He returned with a filled coffee carafe and the entire breadbox. His eyes politely averted, he set the box on the desk and the carafe on a woven mat. He opened a drawer and pulled out two coffee mugs, their interiors stained muddy with use. He filled them with steaming brew.

"Drink. Eat."

Numb, she followed his orders, not even caring how the blanket shifted as she moved her arms to chew and drink. She absorbed the welcome heat of the mug in her hands and solidness of food in her stomach, but took no pleasure from taste.

Cy came and went from the room. He set a tidy stack of clothes on the desk. "Something's bound to fit," he said. "I'll wait just outside. Fenris fell asleep, wrench in hand, so I'm leaving him be."

Ingrid nodded. Fenris had been grousing around his pet airship before they left for her house. Cy hadn't even tried to talk him out of it. Ingrid expressed her opinion to Fenris with a pointed glare, to which he responded in typical male fashion by being a damned fool and ignoring her concern.

As soon as Cy left the room, she changed clothes. Cy being so tall and her body so curvy, his shirt fit like an indecently short dress. She'd need to take care when she sat down. She layered on two shirts for warmth and found a pair of baggy cotton drawers, complete with a hatch in the back, that hugged her hips if she drew the waist really tight.

All the while she stared at the letters on the floor as if they were a big spider.

A soft knock sounded at the door.

"You can come in," she said.

Cy joined her near the stove. He had changed clothes as

well. The leather coat was gone—actually, she didn't recall seeing it since they entered the bay. Brown suspender straps held up tan pants that fit his long and lanky form in a delicious way; her brain might be addled, but she'd have to be dead to miss that. A black shirt was tucked in at his waist, where the Tesla rod dangled from his hip.

"You have glasses again," she said.

He adjusted the pince-nez. "I always keep a few spare pairs around. Working with machines as I do, damage to glasses is an occupational hazard. I wear goggles as often as I can." His black boots nudged the oilskin mound. "Forgive my prying, but I'd like to know what's going on."

"So would I." She sucked in a steadying breath and reached for the top bundle of letters. Paper crinkled as she worked the twine free. She skimmed over postmarks first. They had arrived twice a year, roughly. Quite a few traveled from Portland, Oregon; Papa must have lived there for an extended time. The more recent ones came from Hawaii. The man had gumption; both places had heavy Japanese populations and seismic activity.

Cy reached into the box. "There's one more letter in here. It's addressed to you and dated yesterday."

She set it on her lap. The handwriting was Mr. Sakaguchi's. Cy passed her more coffee. She took a long draft and, clearing her throat, read aloud for Cy's benefit.

"Dearest Ingrid,

"I write with the sincerest hope you will never read this letter or the contents of this box. Today, we survived the explosion of the Cordilleran Auxiliary. I do not believe this to be a

mere boiler explosion but sabotage, and an act we certainly were not intended to survive.

"Who the culprit is, I know not. As much as I disagree with the Unified Pacific, I do not believe they would willingly endanger an American city in such a way.

"I am far more suspicious of Japan acting of its own volition, but I cannot persuade myself of their guilt. The city would not concern them, but the loss of so many geomancers, adepts, and kermanite is a blow they cannot afford at this critical juncture of the war."

She wondered what he would think of Mr. Thornton's disappearance and the kermanite theft. She couldn't see the British conducting such an attack on San Francisco either. The brutal battle against the Thuggees should have their full focus—and why invite the wrath of the Unified Pacific? The British victory against the Thuggees looked as certain as the UP's against China. It only took time.

"Of one thing I am certain, and that is that you must understand more of your power and from where it comes.

"Twenty years ago, I assisted your father in faking his death. At the time, I knew he had a wife whom he rarely visited in Oklahoma Territory, but he said nothing of private matters. He was reserved in nature; a brooder, to put it plainly, and one who never behaved with the discretion of a married man. He could store earth energy with far more fortitude than his peers. His capabilities seemed to increase with age.

"In this, you surpass his skills by far; I have chided you often on this subject, but I should note, I am grateful for your rebellion this morning, as you saved both our lives.

"I digress. Two decades ago, I became keenly aware that your father's channeling skills had evolved in a manner that appalled even him.

"We were together on duty in Charleston, South Carolina, that balmy summer. New factories in the Lowcountry required massive quantities of kermanite, and as there are several local faults, we stayed there to harvest energy.

"Abram fell ill. His sickness and agony worsened over several days and culminated on the night of August 31, when he nearly died. You know well what happened."

"The Great Charleston Earthquake of 1886," interrupted Cy. "I remember it. I felt it clear in Alabama when I was just a boy."

Dry-mouthed, she continued: *"Every time he suffered a bout, an earthquake occurred. I realized this was no coincidence. It wasn't the fever that caused a reaction; we geomancers suffer fevers often, after all. It was the pain. The earth shared in his agony, as if in sympathy. As he recovered, it became clear that our adepts had also noted the correlation.*

"Abram was determined to flee. He was horrified that he had somehow caused so many deaths, even indirectly. At the time, Japan was beginning its full campaign against China, and the news abounded with stories related to the war. The factories we powered were to engineer weapons for these efforts. Abram could foresee, and I agreed, that he would be the ultimate weapon for use against our enemies abroad.

"Therefore, I became the sad witness to his death, while in truth he was smuggled out on a Porterman bound for the Azores."

Ingrid paused. "This is a lot to take in. Good God. He caused the Charleston earthquake."

She could cause a San Francisco earthquake. With the made ground and density of the population, it would be all the more devastating. Maybe she'd already hurt people because of her pained contact with the selkies.

"You know the tale of how your mother brought you to the auxiliary. I realized you channeled the earth's magic, and more. My academic interest in deviant geomancy became personal as you grew, as both you and your mother claimed my household and my heart.

"I have wondered about where Abram's skills arose—if perhaps his mother and father were both geomancers, enabling their progeny to be all the more strong. There must be some reason—in all my research, I can find no mention of a mortal woman such as you, born with earth magic; though certainly old tales do recall goddesses and other feminine fantastic beings of magical might. To my frustration, Abram has always refused to speak of his parents; all I know of his youth is that he came to California at age ten, was listed as an orphan, and enrolled at the Cordilleran.

"Raising you on the San Andreas has had risks, I will not deny, but you have also benefited from having so many geomancers and adepts in your proximity to balance the danger. That balance is no more.

"You have just returned home from your errand. I must bring this to conclusion.

"Ing-chan, you are your father's daughter. I can only imagine your grief, your legitimate sense of betrayal, if you have the misfortune to read these words, as you understand the full danger of your own potential. You must comprehend how

vital it is that you leave San Francisco. You must go to TR." She paused. "He means Theodore Roosevelt." Brow furrowed, she continued. *"He is aware of your skills—barring our new revelations—and will assist you. The schism of our friendship was a feint as it became necessary for me to make certain opinions public. I could not endanger his position as Ambassador. Too few of the Twelve hold true American loyalties. I worry what will come after China is conquered.*

"As you will find in the second set of letters, the Unified Pacific captured Abram sometime this past Christmas. His aptitude was not forgotten. He was transported to China, where I believe he was used as a weapon in Peking. This genocidal application of deviant geomancy is named the Gaia Project.

"Godspeed."

"He abruptly ends the letter there." Ingrid pressed her fingers to her lips.

"Those Peking earthquakes killed hundreds of thousands of dissidents, maybe millions," Cy murmured.

Papa did that. Ingrid's head felt as if it floated, and she set her shoulders against the wall to regain her bearings. The military had Papa. They used him. That meant . . .

"They tortured him. They made him hurt, to cause earthquakes like that."

"Ingrid," said Cy. "Think on what Mr. Sakaguchi said. You're your father's daughter, and more powerful than him at that. You could be a more potent weapon than any airship or Durendal. *You.*"

She raised her eyes to meet his, afraid of what she would find.

CHAPTER 12

Cy's expression was grim. Ingrid drily swallowed. Would he condemn her as a monster? She couldn't entirely blame him if he did.

"The earthquake in the ocean. You caused that," he said.

"It seems so." She tangled her fingers together. "In the past day, with all the other geomancers gone, I noticed the timing of some of the earthquakes. Not all of them. Not the big one in Chinatown. But the others . . . yes. That's why I wanted to get this box and leave. I don't want . . ." To be a weapon. To be like Papa. Tortured. *Used.* "I've always been told that I don't handle pain well. Mama and Mr. Sakaguchi coddled me over the slightest thing. Most of the other wardens regard the notion of geomantic Hidden Ones as ancient hogwash, but Mr. Sakaguchi is obsessed with the subject. All his research was because of me. Me and Papa."

"I don't know much about these sorts of Hidden Ones," Cy said. "They're monsters that live in fault lines, correct?"

She studied him, trying to gauge his mood. "Sometimes. Many ancient cultures describe giant creatures that hold up the land and toss and turn to cause earthquakes, but they might live in a fault or in the sea. Wherever they are, they're bound to earth's magic. Some tales are about the same fantastics, even though the storytellers are continents apart."

"Ingrid. You needn't look at me like that." Cy scooted closer, brown eyes thoughtful as he gazed over his glasses.

"Like what?"

"Like I'll turn on you like a rabid dog. This power isn't something you chose. I'm not judging you."

"I don't want to be a weapon." Her voice lowered to a whisper.

"You aren't going to be." He grabbed her hand and squeezed. A giddy spike of heat went straight to her chest. Here she was, completely improper, garbed in his cast-off clothes with her hair looking like it was styled by a cyclone.

"Just yesterday, Mr. Sakaguchi made a comment that he should have sent me away but he was selfish. I was angry when he said it. I didn't understand."

"There's not much there to misunderstand. He loves you."

"I know that, but . . ."

"There's no buts about it, Miss Ingrid. I wouldn't want to send you away either. Matter of fact, I plan to leave the city with you, soon as you're ready. We'll go to Mr. Roosevelt together." His hand felt so right in her grip. His expression was sincere, betraying not even the slightest hint of ungentlemanly behavior. Cy Jennings would always be proper to the core.

Ingrid was not so restrained.

"I'll be damned if I wait for you to make the first move," she said as she leaned into him. Her fingers gripped his neck to draw him closer. Their lips met, her eyes open wide to take in his reaction.

He gasped as their lips touched—oh, his lips! Wide and soft, a touch chapped. Hot. A current zapped from their lips and surged to her chest and belly, where it squirmed, all sizzling and cozy and demanding of more.

A kiss really did feel a bit like geomancy, but better. The softness of his skin, the sandpaper roughness around his mouth, the way his angular nose pressed against hers—those were all infinitely preferable to wiggling her toes into dirt. The very thought caused a giggle to vibrate through her lips. Something about that seemed to affect him, as that's when he decided to kiss back.

Oh.

His lips moved against hers, and it was like a lever was pulled and an engine roared to life. She moaned deep in her throat, the sound of her own body so strange she didn't recognize herself. His broad hand cupped the back of her neck and shifted their bodies closer together. With a jolt she realized that she didn't even have a camisole on beneath the baggy shirts she wore. He had to feel the full curve of her breasts, but she didn't stop kissing him. She didn't want to.

Not until she heard a throat clear rather loudly from the far side of the desk.

"Pardon me for interrupting. Or don't pardon me. Either way, good to see you're back and alive, though by the state of your clothing, I apparently missed out on more adventures. I suppose you'll need to update me on everything, once you've untangled your uvulas."

Fenris took care to slam the door as he left. Ingrid and Cy's lips parted but their faces remained close.

"Sometimes I wish I wasn't a pacifist," Cy said. His glasses looked the slightest bit askew, his breath rapid. "But whatever made you think you had the right to do that?"

In her belly, the giddy warmth turned lukewarm. "Oh."

His smile, however, stoked the sparks again. "I'm the one who won the wager. I got you past that tank, didn't I?"

"You did."

"Exactly." One eyebrow arched. "That kiss doesn't count."

"Well, don't expect me to apologize." Her hand slipped down to clench his again. Their fingers knotted together. The very look on his face was enough to make her want to shimmy free of her borrowed apparel and do things she should never have learned from any dime novel.

Cy's grin was crooked and more than a little silly. "I figure Fenris's lurking right outside the door. We erected these walls here, and the material is awful thin. Right, Fenris?"

"I chaperoned the lady down to Chinatown." The voice was muffled. "Does she need a chaperone in our building as well?"

Well, that was a right put-off. Blushing a bit, Ingrid scooted back, her hands brushing the letters in their bundles. "No, thank you, I think we'll manage. We're about to get back to work."

"While you do your kind of work, I suppose I'll get back to my *Palmetto Bug*."

Ingrid opened her mouth to scold Fenris, but Cy gave an

abrupt shake of his head. “It won’t do any good,” he said. “He could be in total traction and he’d still find a way to work a bolt and pliers. If he hurts too much, he’ll stop.”

Pain. Hurt. That brought her right back to the subject at hand. “There are a lot of letters here. There might be something we need to know before we leave. Do you want to take one bundle? If anything seems pertinent, we’ll tell each other?”

“Sounds like a plan,” he said. He picked up the letters Mr. Sakaguchi had referenced. Ingrid gnawed on the inside of her lip and hoped there was nothing too personal or embarrassing inside. She tugged another letter from her stack.

The blue fog on the floor had deepened a tad, flowing over the floor like a layer of delicate tulle. It eddied around her feet. There still was no heat to it, not even the electric spark she felt during the magic of Reiki. It was just there. Waiting.

She didn’t want to be here when the waiting came to fruition. Disconcerted, she began to skim the letters. Minutes passed.

“These aren’t written by your father,” said Cy. “These are about him.” He fanned the pages in his hand.

“What do you mean?”

“Abram Carmichael was arrested and they confronted your Mr. Sakaguchi about letting him escape years ago. Instead of fighting the charge or keeping quiet, Mr. Sakaguchi lobbied most everyone he could about Mr. Carmichael’s imprisonment. It’s not public record, but it’s by no means secret either.”

Papa fled twenty years ago. That’s what Captain Sutcliff had referred to when they spoke in the Reiki office. He knew what Mr. Sakaguchi had done.

"Papa was captured around the holidays. It was at the start of the year that Mr. Sakaguchi and Mr. Roosevelt ceased their friendship. Publicly, anyway. I'm guessing that Mr. Roosevelt fought for his sake behind the scenes or Mr. Sakaguchi wouldn't have stayed free at all." Mr. Roosevelt had sent a note warning of Captain Sutcliff's arrival as well, not that Mr. Sakaguchi had taken advantage of it.

"The UP's certainly killed men for less, and Japanese men at that. Possessing a powerful ally had to make all the difference. These papers say that Japan formally censured Mr. Sakaguchi, revoked his passport, and ordered him to remain in San Francisco."

He'd disobeyed that order now. Wui Seng Tong took care of that. Why had Mr. Sakaguchi been working with Wui Seng Tong at all? It had to be because of Lee, but why? With the suspicion Mr. Sakaguchi was under, no one in the Unified Pacific would think he was with the *tong* against his will. Not even Roosevelt could change how bad it looked.

A sob caught in her throat.

Cy drew her close. She tucked her head against his neck, breathing in the lingering sea salt from his skin, and let his fingers rest on her hair. There was such solid comfort in his mute presence. After a moment she pulled back, granting him a teary smile.

"Thanks," she said.

"I'm here."

She nodded, soothed, and returned to her own letters.

Papa wasn't much of a writer. His missives were curt, rather like a child checking in with a parent simply out of obligation. He spoke of good and bad beer, of the aggravation of frequently cloudy skies in Portland, of the boardinghouse where he resided. No questions about Ingrid or Mama. He made one brief comment on Mama's death—"good that Ingrid's grown up so that it doesn't matter to be an orphan." She had a hunch that Mr. Sakaguchi hadn't related the details behind Mama's death.

Ingrid wondered if she should feel more anger toward Mr. Sakaguchi for his web of lies. Instead, she felt perturbed, and more than anything . . . grateful. Everything she learned about Papa as a person made her all the more glad he was out of their lives. Mr. Sakaguchi and Mama had truly loved each other, and Ingrid couldn't have had a better father than her ojisan.

"Ingrid."

She looked up, realizing that she had been silent for a long stretch. "I'm sorry, Cy, this is all just—"

"The Gaia Project? My father's company, Augustinian, is somehow involved."

Her jaw dropped. "Augustinian? Your father? You're an *Augustus*?"

The Augustinian Company was the largest American manufacturer of airships, war machines, and most anything of orichalcum construction, including Durendals. Kermanite engines were its special expertise. No wonder Cy was a brilliant engineer. He'd been born into it.

"Bartholomew Cypress Augustus." He cringed. "You see why I go by Cypress."

"That's a mouthful of names so thick I could chew on it. You—your family—"

"My family." Cy stared down at his lap. "I haven't seen them in almost half my life. When I deserted the A-and-A, I had to leave everything behind."

"Except Fenris."

"That's right." He rubbed at the evening shadow thickening on his chin. "This Gaia Project. It's about kermanite, about how it stores and uses energy. My father's one of the most knowledgeable men in the world on the subject. It . . . it doesn't surprise me that he's involved, though I wonder . . ."

"You miss your family dreadfully, don't you?"

He nodded as he stared into his hands. "Yes. We were very close. Strangely so, I suppose. Mother tolerated society balls, but she was happiest painting calla lilies in the garden, or reading in her library. Father thought nothing of letting me build automatons as I played beneath his desk when I was young, and my sister . . ."

Ingrid recognized the grief in his eyes. "She died last year, you said?"

"Yes. Maggie—Magnolia—she was my twin, you see, and smarter than me by leagues. She could do anything. Make anything. Maggie was a mathematician in the league of Newton, Fermat, or Euler, though as a woman, she could never work outright. Everything was done through Father. She practically ran the company by age thirteen."

"Now I understand why you accepted me and Fenris as we are. You saw your sister deal with the same kind of thing."

He frowned and nodded. "A brain's a brain. The parts attached don't seem to matter as much. I beg your pardon. That's rather crude."

"I think you put it quite succinctly."

"I always felt like I was in Maggie's shadow, then I created the Durendal and felt like I'd proven myself at last. All the champagne toasts and claps on the back, everyone saying I was brilliant, that because of me the war'd be done in a year." He stared into the distance. "The A-and-A sent me to Asia. I saw what I'd really created: dead bodies. Mass graves. I ran."

"I don't understand, Cy. How can your father make machines that kill so many, and live with it?"

His gaze jerked to her, eyes blazing. "The kermanite that your auxiliary fills doesn't just power autocars and lanterns. You're just as much a part of this."

She flinched. He was right. She'd filled some larger crystals herself. "The wardens like to say it's all business."

"Yes, business. That's how Maggie looked at things. She didn't connect to people, really. She could rig a Tiamat-class airship to carry a massive payload of hellfire, and for her, the resulting deaths were numbers. I felt the same until I saw what I'd done. Until I smelled it." He took a deep breath. "My apologies for my outburst, Miss Ingrid."

"I deserved it."

"This kind of work, it does something to a person. My father battled the drink for years just so he could sleep. First a shot glass or two, then a whole damned bottle."

"At least you escaped, Cy."

"Yes, I escaped." Bitterness edged his voice. "I've lived in dozens of cities since I deserted. Finally got sick of remembering different first names, and risked plenty just to go by 'Cy.' My twin sister died and I couldn't be there. I had to find out in a newspaper. I always wonder, if I'd been there could I have done something?"

"I'm sorry," Ingrid whispered.

"Far as my folks know, I'm dead somewhere, or the A-and-A's got me chained down in some bunker drawing blueprints. I know I made the right choice, but there's a cost. There's a cost to everything." He frowned. "This Gaia Project may involve kermanite, Miss Ingrid, but I don't know how deeply Father is involved. There are different levels to these sorts of things, aspects that only the Japanese or American side may see. Now, don't you be giving me that look. I'm not placing all the blame on the Japanese. Americans aren't innocents. But what I am saying is that 'being involved' may mean my father's one of a few hundred who are providing some kind of input to the endeavor."

"That's fair." Ingrid kept her voice cool, though she inwardly winced at him calling her "Miss" again. "There's nothing there about deviant geomancy? About Papa?"

"No. Nothing directly about geomancers at all. Just that there's a Gaia Project, it needs kermanite, Augustinian had the contract, and that the result could end the war."

"Your father has to know more than that. Do you think he would help us?"

"Absolutely." Cy didn't hesitate. "The greater issue is how to talk with him. I can't exactly waltz into Atlanta. Even the family household over in Wedowee's bound to have spies. Government's got to know that eventually I'll cave in and go home. Only time Father ever leaves is for business and opera."

Ingrid perked up. "Opera? He loves opera?"

"Father practically joins the larger touring companies around the country."

She laughed. "I'll be damned."

Cy raised an eyebrow. "What?"

"*Lincoln* is opening here tomorrow night. I have Mr. Sakaguchi's planner up in your bedroom, the tickets right inside. Would your father attend a show like *Lincoln*?"

"Don't assume that because I'm from the South, we're all bound to be bigots in white sheets." Coldness cut with his words. "Remember that Lincoln was the one who rebuilt Atlanta, and he even lived in Savannah for a few years before he passed. Father met him more than once and thought highly of the man."

Chagrined, Ingrid looked down and rubbed the shirt buttons with her thumb. "If your father's a regular on the circuit, I imagine he and Mr. Sakaguchi have met. If not in the theater, then at Quist's afterward. I attend but—well, I'm just a secretary, of course. I don't directly interact with his companions."

"What do you do, then?"

"I quietly sit beside Mr. Sakaguchi during the opera and when he socializes later on, I wait at a table toward the back with his appointment book. If anyone gives him a calling card, he comes by and passes it to me. I can't stay with him."

A dark cloud passed over his face. "You're segregated with the manservants."

"Well, yes." She was surprised by his reaction. "Very pleasant men, for the most part. Likely the best company in the room."

"I can believe that. I'm not implying that their company is an insult; many'd be better businesspeople than the folks they work for, granted the opportunity. I do wonder why you attend at all if you can't truly be part of everything. You needn't do it for the money, not as they do."

"Who says I'm not doing it for the money? I'm a grown woman with a job to do." She paused, almost laughing at how much she sounded like Mama—Mama, who'd come home from her suffrage marches and returned to the business of minding house and was damn proud of the job she did. "True, I'm not an opera floozy. No one would ever mistake me for a high-society woman, but I *like* being there."

Sometimes she yearned for an especially pretty dress or the attention of a dashingly handsome man, sure, but her presence there was akin to peering through a portal into Fairy Land. That sparkle on the other side was never meant for her.

Being in the auxiliary, cradling the heat of her magic, wearing shoes—that bothered her much more. There, she knew she already *possessed* power, and yet couldn't admit it.

Ingrid shrugged. "Besides, I even dress up a tiny bit. Nothing showy, but something more than a cotton smock. There in the crowd, the lights dimmed, I blend in with everyone else to enjoy the show."

The door from the lab burst open. "Ah, the opera." Fenris reentered with a cocky sway even as he held his upper body rigid. He wore a slim pair of Levi's and a brown button-up shirt with red suspenders, all dappled in oils and muck like his previous clothes. "Diamonds and crystals and glitter. Like your old days, Cy."

Cy stood and frowned at Fenris. "Stayed at the door the whole time, did you?"

Ingrid stood as well. At the movement, her cotton trousers made an effort to slide south. She gasped, causing Cy to turn around just as she hoisted her pants up to the waist again. His lips quirked.

"I don't need a wrench in hand to be working. Some of my best handiwork is done up here." Fenris tapped his head.

"Did I just hear a hollow sound?" asked Ingrid.

"Yes. Ha ha. Good to see you're feeling better after . . . whatever happened."

"You're the one who's walking around after your chest was sliced open. You're supposed to take it easy."

"This *is* taking it easy!"

"It is," confirmed Cy. "Normally he'd be about knee-deep in machinery or using welders or some other incendiary material."

"Laudanum, I must say—and I'm sure the lady will forgive me—is one hell of a drug. I can see the appeal of lounging about in some Chinatown basement in a cloud of bliss. But I do prefer real clouds. Speaking of which . . ." He tapped Cy on the arm. "We have a ready airship."

"I reckoned you'd finish today. I booked your mooring tower already. It's the closest dock to our place, straight down Harrison. The crew's paid to man the tethers so you can take—"

"Wait, wait, wait." Ingrid held up a hand. "You're telling me that that you used my kermanite and completely reassembled the entire engine compartment and hull in a single day? That's ludicrous, even for a Sprite class."

"It's Fenris speed." She couldn't help but note the pride in Cy's voice.

Fenris shrugged without the slightest hint of modesty. "I did most of the work last night before that Chinatown escapade. It's a simple matter of knowing how the pieces fit together."

Ingrid shook her head in awe. "You two. No wonder the military wants you."

"They actually don't want me. Yet. I'd like to keep it that way." Fenris sniffed. "My real work isn't meant to roll off some assembly line."

A knock shuddered through the front door. The three of them froze, staring at it, then at each other.

"Expecting any clients?" Fenris asked Cy.

"No. Could be someone new, though the sign out front says we're shut." Cy stepped up to the peephole. Ingrid put a hand to her chest, keenly aware of her state of undress and ready to duck into the workshop. "It's Lee."

Cy unlocked the door. Lee hobbled inside and dropped onto the nearest seat with a sound between a groan and a whimper.

"Oh, Lee." Ingrid held her fingers to her mouth.

His face was mottled in shades of purple and green, interspersed with lumps. One eye was swollen shut and bulged like a frog's. He cradled his left arm close to his body and leaned on the right, and adjusted his position with little twitches. His yellow patch was gone, and part of the sleeve with it.

"Damn," said Fenris. "Speaking as a recent authority on pain, you look like hell."

"They called me a yellow man." The words emerged like he had a mouth stuffed with cotton. Lee paused, and the way his head tilted, Ingrid imagined he was trying to smile. "Now I'm a green-purple man."

Rage curdled inside her, hot and cold all at once. "Did the soldiers do this to you?"

"No. Other men did this, by the wharf."

"They could have killed you," she whispered. By God, if she could get ahold of the men who did this, she'd make them hurt.

Lee shrugged and met her eye, as well as he could. "Part of being Chinese."

"Can I get you anything?" asked Cy. "Water, coffee? I can run up the block and grab a pitcher of steam beer."

"I might even share my laudanum," added Fenris.

Ingrid couldn't think of anything sensible to say. She ached to hug Lee, but by the way he held his side, she feared that contact would only cause more pain.

"Believe it or not, I looked and felt worse earlier, but I made it to a plant *lingqi* doctor." Lee looked at her and sighed. "I'm not going to drop dead. This isn't your fault, I swear it on the Bible."

"You're not even Christian!" she blurted.

"And when did you last go to church?" He drooled and slurred. "I'll swear on any holy book you want. Swear it to your mother's spirit."

There was particular gravity to that. Ingrid knew how seriously he regarded his ancestors' spirits. She granted Lee a nod of grudging tolerance.

"You better have what you need from the house," Lee said.

She glanced at the papers still strewn on the floor. She loved Lee, but he couldn't know about what her father had done, or Cy's family, or that the Unified Pacific was directly at fault for the disastrous earthquakes in China. Cy caught her eye, and without a word he stacked the letters. She turned back to Lee, her arms folded over her chest to hide her bosom.

"Yes," she said, leaning against the wall. She resisted the sudden urge to yawn. "We think there may be some people at the opera tomorrow who can help us learn more about this mess with the Unified Pacific and Mr. Sakaguchi."

"I hope you're not wearing that outfit. The shirtwaist look is too New York."

"My evening dress is at the house." She put a hand to her hair. "I'm a mess."

"You have the tickets?" Lee asked. He swiped drool from his chin and winced.

"I grabbed Mr. Sakaguchi's personal books the first time we left. Cy, do you have a suit?"

He clamped the box shut and tucked it beneath his arm. "A suit, yes. A suit for opening night at the Damcyan? No. They wouldn't even let me clean washrooms in the suit I own, wearing it or using it to scrub."

"Why're you worrying about this, Ing?" Lee tilted his head back and closed both eyes. "Oh, right. Your duty's to worry about everything. I'll get you a dress. There's plenty of time. Damn, Cy, you're freakishly tall, but there must be something available."

Ingrid frowned. "What are you saying?"

"Who runs most laundries in San Francisco, in or out of Chinatown? I know people. I'll take care of it. You rest." Lee hobbled to the front door.

"Lee . . ." she said, and stopped. As if he needed to be told to be careful. He offered her a tiny nod and a grimace of a smile, then slipped away.

She eased herself into a chair. The excitement of the letters' revelations was fading away, and she was suddenly exhausted to the bone. Maintaining that bubble had taken a lot out of her, and then her and Cy's near drowning . . . She rubbed her cheeks with both hands. If she remained still for much longer, she'd probably fall asleep.

"Ingrid." Cy held the box up. "I'm going to have this and everything else of importance packed in the airship."

She nodded. "Good. We'll leave immediately after the show."

"And where exactly will we be going?" asked Fenris.

"Good question." Cy looked to Ingrid.

Where would Mr. Roosevelt be? He traveled so often between Japan and America. He had mostly attended operas as a courtesy to Mr. Sakaguchi—his pursuits tended to be more physical, more rugged. "North, I would guess. I think the papers said he was in Portland, Oregon, last week. He has an estate in Seattle, too." Better to try those cities first than go to his family stronghold all the way in New York.

"Guess that means I need to get the *Bug* to that mooring tower. Don't get shot while I'm away. Or do . . . other things again." Fenris cast them a strange look and then headed out as well. His thin body and scurrying grace reminded her of a rangy alley cat.

She yawned so widely her jaw popped. "Another full day here. Now I'll be in constant fear of injuring myself and harming the city."

"Don't fret too much. You can use my bed upstairs again, with all that metal keeping you off the ground. At the opera, I'll be there to watch your back."

"Watch my back. Yes. Because God knows, all we need is for Captain Sutcliff to waltz in."

"It's bad enough that he might arrest you, but think on what they did to your father." He leaned closer, his brow furrowed. "Think about what they'd do if they knew you can do the same, and so much more."

"Thank you, Cy. That will help my anxiety *immensely*."

His lips grazed her forehead. She closed her eyes to absorb the fleeting touch.

"Just remember that we're in this together. We'll talk to my father and be out of the city lickety-split. You won't hurt a soul."

Ingrid desperately hoped he was right.

CHAPTER 13

APRIL 17, 1906

Once the momentum of the day slowed, Ingrid had no energy to spare. She collapsed in Cy's bed and into a slumber so deep that a Durendal attack couldn't have awakened her. Sometime in the morning, she stayed awake long enough to inhale some onigiri, then collapsed in bed again. Fenris's voice at the door finally coaxed her to wakefulness. The opera started in three hours. It was time to get ready.

Lee arrived with an older Chinese woman with hair so tightly coiled it seemed to tug taut lines in her face. "She'll take care of your dress, Ing. She doesn't speak English, but she'll make herself clear," he said, then left again. He looked unusually strained, and not simply due to lingering bruises.

In the privacy of Fenris's chamber, the strange woman kicked Ingrid's feet to force them together and walked around her in a tight circle. She jerked up one of Ingrid's arms to full extension and placed her hands on Ingrid's hips to measure her waist. Ingrid shrieked when the stranger cupped a breast and hefted it in a hand, the way one judges a melon at a market stall. At that, the woman grunted and left.

With a fitting like that, Ingrid was left in dread of what she might be forced to wear. She might not be attending the opera with Mr. Sakaguchi, but she wasn't some society lady either. She didn't want to be shined up like a filly going to auction, and God help her, she did not want to wear pink. It made her feel like a large piece of fruit.

Cy dragged a washtub into Fenris's room. There wasn't sufficient time to heat the water, so Ingrid was forced to do a chilly birdbath reminiscent of her dip in the bay the previous day.

A short while later, the woman returned with a dress.

"I can't wear this." It broke Ingrid's heart to say that because she wanted to wear the garment, but more than that, she wanted to *belong* in such a gown. She never would. "Another dress. Please."

The woman scowled at her and pointed at the clock. Setting a cotton bag on the side table, she exited.

Ingrid drily swallowed. There was no time for another dress. This one would have to do.

The Dress. In her mind, Ingrid saw it as a proper name, as it was indeed a proper dress—blue silk, in a stylish kimono cut. The silk ended at the elbow, and from there bell sleeves flowed out in complementary navy-blue lace. The lace wasn't itchy to the touch, but soft as velvet. The same fabric was repeated in the obi at the waist and the hem at the ankle. The bodice was intricately sewn with beads that formed a tangle of vines and starry jasmine buds.

Inside the bag were slippers, jeweled hair clips and a silk hair band, a girdle, a vial of sweet floral perfume, a handbag in floral-pattern blue silk, and—miracle of miracles—a hairbrush and comb.

Ingrid perfumed her hair in an effort to eradicate the musty, salty smell, and then brushed out her locks with ginger strokes. She studied the floor in dread that her tangled hair might cause an earthquake, but nothing happened. Yet. The blue sheen was still there.

Maybe once a Hidden One was riled, it took it some time to calm down. That's all.

She kept an eye on the clock as she dressed and primped, and scampered out the door with a few minutes to spare.

"Well, well," said Fenris. He sat on a box just outside the room. His arms were folded across his chest, cuffs rolled back to the elbow.

Ingrid envied Fenris. He was comfortable in his skin, his clothes. He could walk down the street by himself right now, after dark, and just be a man out on the town. No worries about catcalls or abuse or lewd invitations. It didn't seem fair at all, that for a woman to get rights she had to fully assume the role of a man down to his swagger and blasphemy.

"Does it . . . does it look okay?" Ingrid blurted. A flush crept up her neck. Fenris being Fenris, his bedroom contained only a small stand mirror. Ingrid couldn't see how she looked, but she knew how she felt: strange, *guilty*. Like a little girl playing dress-up in her mother's best evening gown, and her backside would be swatted sore when she was caught in the act.

The dress fit as if it had been made for her. The beaded bodice hoisted up her breasts for all the world to see. As much as she hated the tight compression of corsets and girdles, by God, the garment did its job and defied gravity in a way that put an airship engine to shame. The skirt swished and rippled with Western-style pleats.

Fenris cocked his head to one side, lips pursed.

"Sorry. You don't have to answer."

"What, you think I'm not qualified to speak on the subject of dresses? I'm familiar with them, the way a dog knows a collar." Fenris's voice softened. "You. You can wear a dress."

Ingrid pressed her hand to the cleavage she'd never displayed before, suddenly shy rather than embarrassed. "It's not the sort of thing someone like me should wear."

"Someone like you. You use it like an excuse."

"What?"

"You're afraid people will talk when they see you? They will. People will always find something cruel to say, no matter what color your skin is, no matter how you're dressed." Fenris shrugged. "That's because most people are idiots."

"It's just—I never simply *go* to the opera. I didn't want this dress. I'm a secretary—"

"It was your job to be a secretary. That's it. Tonight, you're with Cy, not that warden. You might have been a damn good secretary every other time you've attended the opera, but that's not the issue tonight. A secretary is not what you *are*."

She flashed back to what Lee said earlier, about her need to find that out. "Then what do you think I am?"

Fenris looked away, expression wistful for a matter of seconds, then glanced back with a scowl. "Late, if you don't get in there." He jerked his head toward the front of the shop.

She walked onward. He didn't follow.

Cy stood by the office entrance. A white coat spanned his broad shoulders, with two tails draping over his buttocks. Black trousers, pleats perfect, led to shiny black shoes. He turned as she entered. His brown eyes widened behind the small round lenses.

"Oh," he said.

She stared back at Cy. "Oh."

Whoever had fitted Cy had done a masterful job. The jacket buttoned perfectly at the front, the taut drapery from the shoulders and armpits indicating fabric of the highest quality. A black silk tie adorned his chest. He had shaved, complete with a slight nick on his chin, and his wavy brown hair looked stiffer due to some sort of pomade.

The shoes, however, were definitely not him. They shone like mirrors. Cy belonged in shoes with soles lovingly worn thin.

But for now, he portrayed what they needed him to portray. He looked the very part of a young businessman. And Ingrid—she wasn't sure what she was supposed to portray. Certainly some people would recognize her from past visits with Mr. Sakaguchi, but tonight, she was Cy's companion. Definitely not a secretary.

She already could hear the snide whispers. That she was his mistress. That it was the only way someone like her would be *allowed* to dress like this. She'd seen other women endure the same treatment. Goodness, even going as Mr. Sakaguchi's secretary—even with people knowing about him and Mama—there was always gossip.

To have people assume that of her and Cy—was it really such a bad thing?

A throat cleared behind her. "The *Bug* is moored down the way. We can embark once your show's done," Fenris said.

"Good." Cy fidgeted with his tie.

"I barely had a chance to talk to Lee a bit ago. If he comes back, tell him he needs to rest," said Ingrid to Fenris. "And you should do the same."

Lines of exhaustion seemed to highlight the fierceness in Fenris's eyes. "Here I was, starting another pot of coffee just so I could stay up and wait for you. Or should I be collecting money for bail? No, that's right. If either of you is caught, you'll go straight to the military clink."

"We'll be careful," Cy said. He plucked up a black square-crown hat accented with a band of silk.

"Famous last words." With that, Fenris turned and stalked deeper into the warehouse.

Cy extended an elbow to her. "Shall we, miss?" His face crinkled in a smile.

A rush of heat zipped straight to her chest. Good God, that man's smile made her want to strip right down again. Unable to speak, she nodded and hooked her arm around his.

San Francisco glowed. At just shy of eight o'clock, the sun had barely dipped beyond the knife's edge of the Pacific, but Market Street sparkled more than it had in the daylight. Electric signs stacked over each other competed for attention as they peddled German beers and Spreckel's fine-grain white sugar and lubricators for high-powered kermanite engines. Autocars glimmered under thick lacquers of wax that reflected the riot of color above.

They debarked from the cable car, Cy offering Ingrid a hand as she hopped to the ground. Her slippers' thin soles allowed her to feel each pebble and crack in the sidewalk.

"So," said Ingrid, her heart in her throat. "Here we are." She clutched her handbag in a death grip.

Beautiful women laughed gaily as they strode past in their ermine opera cloaks and diamonds. The men wore hats like Cy's, brims crisp and lines smart. Despite having been here many times, Ingrid was dizzied by the cacophony outside the Damcyan Theatre. It took her a few seconds of disorientation to realize it wasn't merely her nerves.

Horses snorted and whinnied. Harnesses jangled. Carriage drivers yelled and more than one whip cracked. "Control your damn horse!" yelled a man from an autocar.

"Ingrid." Cy grabbed her arm with a gloved hand. "Are you okay?"

"Look at the horses, Cy." She flinched at the sound of hooves striking a car, followed by more trumpeting horns and profanity. "The geomantic Hidden One of Ireland is said to be a giant kelpie who sometimes tries to buck off her rider—the island."

"They're reacting like those fish in the pond earlier, aren't they?"

"Yes. I wish Mr. Sakaguchi were here. I listened to his tales so many times, but I don't *know* them, not like he does. I'm not saying I don't want to be here with you—"

"I understand." He squeezed her arm. Another horse balked. She wondered if they saw the blue fog as she did, if they felt the heat of the earth.

She almost smacked herself on the forehead. "Oh, I'm such a fool," she muttered.

"Why do you say that?"

"I slept the whole day through and I didn't think to grab any empty kermanite before we left."

Cy looked troubled. "I'm a fool right along with you. I busied myself with loading the *Bug* and scarcely thought beyond that."

She made a mental note to grab the kermanite from Mr. Thornton's car when they returned to the workshop. The sudden thought of the British warden caused her to bite her lip with worry. If he was a captive like Mr. Sakaguchi, God help him. San Francisco just needed to hold on for a few more hours. Then she'd be gone before she could make things even worse—make San Francisco into another Peking. She looked around herself, envisioning a landscape of bricks and dead bodies, and shuddered. The auxiliary—that disembodied hand—had been bad enough.

Oh, Papa. Alive out there. Tortured. Where would they use him next? At another rebel stronghold in China, or to crush the nascent rebellion in Manila? The papers printed rumors about the Chinese and Thuggees cooperating to access arms and supplies. Maybe the Unified Pacific would move to dominate India and strike a major blow against Britannia in the process. No one would even know a weapon had been used. It would be God's will, the whims of the earth.

Then there was Russia and the Ottomans, so powerful, so well established. They seemed content to let the children squabble, but how long would that be the case? Headlines fussed about the Russian settlements in the territory of Baranov a few thousand miles north and how that could be a launching place for an invasion of Canada or the American Northwest. The fault lines along the northern crest of the Pacific Ocean were naturally active, the geomancers few. A well-placed earthquake there could cause a tsunami to level enemies on the other side of the world.

Ingrid had yearned for years to be recognized as a geomancer, but she didn't want *this.* She wanted the power, but she didn't want to be a weapon, a tool.

Another horse reared in its shafts. Wheels cracked against a curb.

Men and woman mobbed the sidewalk in front of the theater. "Finish China! Save our jobs! Finish China . . ." they chanted.

Signs screamed out their messages beneath an electric glow.

YELLOW THREAT IS REAL!

THE ENEMY DOES YOUR LAUNDRY—SHAME ON YOU

GOLD-STAR MOTHERS SAY "DROP HELLFIRE" & SPARE OUR BOYS

Ingrid and Cy ducked into the doorway. She felt the weight of stares on her. Whispers. Scrutiny. Some admiring, some sharp as stilettos. She stood a little straighter and looked at Cy. He looked so handsome, so out of place beside her . . . and yet he glanced at her and smiled. It was the same warm smile he'd offered her when they'd first met on the auxiliary steps.

He didn't question being there with her. He wasn't ashamed.

Damn it all, she wouldn't be ashamed either.

Cy showed their tickets at the door. The steward looked from one to the other, a thick eyebrow aloft, and winked at Cy as he motioned them on. Ingrid didn't flush or scowl. She walked on by.

The noise of protesters was replaced by the more austere, excited buzz of high society.

Outwardly, the Damcyan looked like most any of the towering brick structures in downtown. It was older yet had gracefully aged. The interior, in contrast, was that of an alcazar, a Moorish-style castle: checkerboard marble floors and sandstone walls and inlaid mosaics. The lobby featured triple archways with swirling columns. Palm trees lined the concourse, many growing from pots almost as tall as Ingrid. The ceiling featured myriad gold inlaid stars that made the whole space glimmer. The scent of cloves and smoke drifted in the air.

"The opera in Atlanta is designed to look like a factory." Cy almost had to yell in her ear to be heard. "You even enter on a conveyor belt."

"That would be amazing!" she shouted back. Mr. Sakaguchi had told her tales of the place ages ago.

They waded through the mob. A man stepped on her foot and Ingrid froze in alarm, but it was minor enough that the earth didn't react. Even so, her heart raced and she hurried onward.

As a season ticket holder, she knew where to find their seats at the dead center of the second tier. Mr. Sakaguchi was comfortable in his wealth, but not extravagant enough to buy a private balcony.

"There." Cy motioned over his right shoulder as he sat. Yearning swept over his features and was promptly replaced by practiced stoicism.

Unfortunately for them, George Augustus ranked among the extravagant. He had a private balcony.

From their vantage point, Ingrid thought all of the white men looked alike in their white suits, with a few black jackets mixed in for variety. A black man served drinks.

"How can we access him?" she asked, her stomach twisting with worry.

"I don't know. As a boy, I confess, I didn't pay attention to such details. Miss Ingrid, please face forward or we'll draw the wrong sort of attention."

Back to formalities again. She sighed as she smoothed out her skirt.

"However," he added, "it might be nice if you acted like you enjoyed my company."

At the renewed softness in his voice, she couldn't help but smile. "Maybe I'm not a good actress."

"Or maybe I'm lousy company." He released a long breath. "I'm nervous to see him, and not simply because of the A-and-A and everything we found yesterday. I'm nervous to see him, period. It's been a long time."

She was nervous about this meeting for different reasons. Could George Augustus be trusted to hide his son's reappearance? If the man was a participant in the Gaia Project, what sort of scruples did he have? Not like the Cordilleran Auxiliary had been innocent. She knew there had been corruption among the wardens and graft to Mayor Butterfield, but the Augustinian Company was the single most powerful American company behind the Unified Pacific. Even Japan, technologically advanced as it was, clambered for their creations. That kind of power did something to a person.

"Pardon me." A man edged along the aisle toward them. He was middle-aged, a toothpick of a mustache stretching across his upper lip. "You're the girl who works for the wardens, yes? The Cordilleran?"

Ingrid sat a bit straighter. "Yes, I am. How can I help you, sir?" She would end up playing secretary after all, it seemed.

The man's attention shifted to Cy, there in Mr. Sakaguchi's seat. "Such a tragedy about the auxiliary. Terrible news." Pause. "I had a standing order for several pieces of kermanite, and I was wondering about the status of the stones."

A hundred dead, and this man fussed over his rocks?

"There's a lot to sort through right now, Mister . . . ?" Cy's voice was smooth and gentle.

"Campbell. Talladega Campbell."

"Well, Mr. Campbell, I assure you, the matter will be addressed very soon. Right now there are matters of grief to attend to, but I assure you, the wardens will take care of you and everyone else."

When Cy rolled out the southern charm, the man could lull a Porterman to a tower in the thick of a cyclone.

"Why yes, of course. My condolences. I'll hear from you soon, then?"

"Most assuredly." Cy smiled as the fellow backed off.

"Baka." Ingrid growled beneath her breath, talking to herself as much as the departing man, then looked sidelong at Cy. "If Mr. Sakaguchi is out of town, he lends these seats to someone from the auxiliary. Of course, everyone's going to assume you're a visiting warden, here to help. No one knows the dire straits the city's in."

That old anger flared in her chest. Cy didn't have to do anything but sit there, in that chair, and because he was a man, he gained the lofty status of a warden. And here she was—the secretary, the ornament, barely worthy of note.

She plastered on a smile for the next three men who approached with similar inquiries. Two were concerned about standing orders. The last heavily hinted that he detected an imminent kermanite crisis affecting the West Coast and that the wardens would financially benefit by diversifying their investments with orichalcum mines up in Baranov. Cy handled each man with such good-natured sincerity that Ingrid almost believed him.

"Hellfire," he growled at her after the last man left. "Do wardens deal with this every time they step out the door?"

"Yes. Mr. Antonelli and Mr. Kealoha would only discuss kermanite transactions by appointment, for that very reason. Mr. Sakaguchi is more flexible." It still felt so wrong to speak of the other wardens in the past tense.

A buxom uniformed girl worked her way down the aisle as she took drink orders. Ingrid pursed her lips in thought. "Cy, I could dress as a servant to gain access to the balcony."

"You've been reading dime novels, hmm?"

She blushed. "It's just an idea—"

"It's a fine idea, but the problem is that the men in those balconies tend to use their own servants for security's sake. See the black man up there? That's Reddy. He's been with Father since before I was born. The man's brilliant. Remembers anything anyone ever said, and as scrappy as a wyvern in a fight. You'd never get past the door."

She actually recognized Reddy. He'd come to the auxiliary before. He'd been quiet and pleasant, with a shrewd sparkle in his eye. She likely knew many of the most powerful men in the world, not by their names or faces, but by their servants.

The orchestra began to take their places. The mood of the place shifted. She glanced back at the balcony.

"The Cordilleran Auxiliary owns an interest in the mine down south. So does your father. There's common ground there, literally," she whispered. "He's bound to know what happened on Sunday and would be as concerned as anyone, probably more so."

Cy nodded. "Some eighty percent of large-chunk kermanite orders are for the military. You're right, we need to take the initiative and play this out."

The serving girl reached them as the lights dimmed. "Would you like to order a drink?" she asked, her accent French.

"Actually," Cy said, "I was wondering if you could get a message to George Augustus regarding a business deal. We have reservations afterward at—" He looked to Ingrid.

"Quist's," she said.

"Quist's, and I was hoping he'd be there as well."

She nodded with a coy smile. "And who should I say is inquiring?"

"The Cordilleran Auxiliary." He pulled something from his pocket and slipped it into her hand. She slowly drew her fingers across his.

"I will relay that and get back to you by intermission. No drinks now, sir? Madam?" They both shook their heads and she moved on, the curve of her hips brushing Cy's knees as she passed.

"You're not holding energy right now, are you?" Cy asked in a very low voice.

"No."

"Good. The woman's just trying to earn an extra tip. Try not to throw her into the orchestra pit when she comes back, or at least, let her speak first." His eyes sparkled with mirth.

"You!" She kicked his foot.

"That proves you're telling the truth. My foot didn't shatter."

She glared at him, but it was a fond sort of glare. Strings hummed from the pit below. Cymbals crashed, and trumpets burst out in triumphant fanfare. Young Lincoln strode onto the stage. Ingrid settled back in her seat.

It was strange, really, how the pleasure of the opera made all the terrible events of the past few days fade away. Mr. Sakaguchi had been so fond of *Lincoln* he practically wore out his Graphophone records, and arranged daily schedules around anticipated broadcasts of live shows over the Marconi. She knew every song and so much of the dialogue that she mouthed key lines with the actors.

Tears brimmed in her eyes, and not simply because of the fine performances onstage. Oh, how Mr. Sakaguchi would have loved this production.

It also comforted her that no blue fog haunted the Damcyan. Her thin slippers didn't even transmit any movement. She surmised there were multiple floors beneath her seat, and likely substantial metal supports.

Fully gripped by both joy and longing, she didn't feel any annoyance when the serving girl sauntered by during a quiet moment. The woman slipped a note into Cy's hand, and he returned the favor with a coin. Ingrid leaned over to read the folded paper.

Will talk at Quist's. Need status reports. —G. Aug.

"It's his handwriting," Cy whispered.

Ingrid slipped her hand against his and squeezed. Gossip be damned. This was a minor thing compared to their intimacy over the past day. He'd seen everything from her bloomers to her body soaking wet, not to mention the fact she'd worn his own clothes for a time.

Then there was that kiss—oh, that kiss. She felt all hot and shivery at the very thought of it. But being in public or not didn't matter. Right now he needed some support, and by God, she'd give it.

Cy's thumb rubbed the back of her knuckles in a slow circle, his coarse skin sending a tingle up her forearm. He didn't let go, not until the curtain dropped for intermission, and they joined the masses in the lavish corridors. Circumstances required they go their separate ways for a few minutes. As Ingrid returned from the powder room, she paused to look down at the orchestra.

The Damcyan was designed to awe, and it succeeded. Elegant sandstone columns stretched so high she had to crane her head to take in their full length. Realistic stars dappled the ceiling.

When she looked down at the stage again, she spied Victoria Rossi with her camera.

The woman had set up her gear on the far side. She wore a plush red gown that matched the rich shade of the upholstered seats. Her wavy black hair was coiled atop her head like a resting snake, perfect ringlets drifting by her ears. She looked like a model for a Pre-Raphaelite artist.

Miss Rossi angled her camera toward the magnificent pillars, then the drapery of the curtains, and then out to the seats as they began to fill again.

Strange, how that woman had been found over the past few days in so many places that seemed like quintessential San Francisco.

Despite Miss Rossi's rudeness the last time they spoke, Ingrid wouldn't mind talking to her now. The simple fact was, Miss Rossi was probably the most knowledgeable person she knew in regard to local fantastics in the wild, especially within the bay. She had even carried photographs of California selkies in her shop, though they hadn't sold that well. "Too native-looking," an adept from the auxiliary had commented as he browsed. Imported postcards of fair-skinned Scottish and Irish selkies sold better.

Ingrid retreated to her seat. Cy greeted her with a smile as he politely said farewell to yet another concerned customer of the auxiliary. It was as if word of their presence had spread.

That realization sent a cold chill through her.

"Cy," she murmured as she sat. "If these customers know to approach us here, what about Captain Sutcliff?"

He considered that for a moment. "There's no warrant out for your arrest—or no notice in the paper, at least. I checked today. A fellow a few minutes ago inquired about Mr. Sakaguchi, said he'd heard of a fuss at his house. I told him the warden was in protective custody and not to worry."

"Protective custody." She flinched. "I suppose that's true, in a way."

"Sorry." Sympathy warmed his eyes. He tugged at the outer seam of his pant leg, smoothing some invisible irritation. "My gut feeling is that word will spread quickly once the opera's done."

"We'll need to watch our shadows, then."

"Did we ever stop?"

The opera resumed with the mournful wail of clarinets. The performance reached an emotional crescendo at Lincoln's death as singers from the shadows sang "Sweet Freedom, Take Me Home."

Ingrid's lip quivered as she fought back emotion. Mr. Sakaguchi adored this aria. She had asked him once if it made him think of Japan, and he had shaken his head. "No," he said. "It makes me think of people, not places," and with fondness gazed across the room to the kitchen, where they could barely spy Mama through the door. She kneaded dough with the brutality of an Ambassador in an interrogation.

Ingrid started to bawl. She fumbled open her satin clutch, belatedly remembering that the Chinese woman hadn't included a handkerchief. Ingrid had, however, brought Mama's revolver. Priorities.

"Here," murmured Cy, pressing a red kerchief into her hand. Her fingers, wet with tears, squeezed his. He squeezed back. She dabbed the cloth at her eyes, and discreetly noticed

Cy's quiet little sniffles. Was he thinking of Atlanta or his childhood plantation in Alabama? Maybe some other place had captured his heart during his years of wandering.

Home. Ingrid thought of fog-shrouded hills and the low moan of foghorns and the cries of seagulls. No blue tint to the ground. Just dampness and drifting gray.

God, please don't let the city come to harm, not because of me, she thought.

As the audience dispersed, she and Cy hooked arms so they wouldn't lose each other in the crush. His body felt so warm and solid alongside hers. People jabbered and jostled around them, some still wiping tears from their cheeks.

The thickness of the crowd couldn't mask the tension of the earth, though. Ingrid felt it building with every step she took as they crossed the lobby, as they neared more solid ground. They exited onto Market Street. The night sky was clear for the first time in ages, vivid as if she could reach out and pluck diamonds from the heavens.

Ambient heat coiled around her foot. She stopped walking. Someone bumped into her from behind, cursing. Cy angled his body to partially shelter her from the mob.

"Another one?" he murmured.

"No, it's . . ." She hesitated. "Not a wave. You know when children blow up a pig's bladder to toss around, and if you fill it with too much air it gets that particular sheen to it?" He nodded. "That's how the ground *feels.* That's the only way I can think to describe it."

She walked on, but with every step tendrils of heat stroked and pulled at her as if she walked through a field of grass.

It wasn't as if the earth wanted to pull her in—more like it sought an outlet, like it would climb up her body. She shuddered. For ages she had craved thin-soled shoes so she could readily pull in energy. Now she had been granted her wish, eerie as it was.

The sign for Quist's gleamed with white and blue bulbs. Ingrid and Cy joined a queue. People pressed too close to allow any semblance of private conversation. Cy's lips were a tight line, his body taut as a bowstring. At last they reached the door.

The doorman appraised her at a glance and frowned. She recognized the man—he always looked at her this way, like she was a dark stain on a white marble floor. Ingrid ducked her head in a deferential manner. "I'm Ingrid Carmichael, secretary for the Cordilleran Auxiliary. I'm here on behalf of Mr. Sakaguchi," she murmured, as if she wore her usual, more muted attire.

"Ah, yes. I remember you. This man is . . . ?"

"Mr. Dennis," Cy replied smoothly. He'd given the same name to some of the customers who had approached during the opera. "Here after the unfortunate events on Sunday."

"Oh yes, of course. Our sympathies." His attention focused solely on Cy. "Mr. Sakaguchi's usual table is set."

"Thank you," Ingrid and Cy said in unison, and entered. "Follow me," Ingrid added.

The scent of pungent cloves mingled with the mouthwatering fragrance of seared steak and fried fish. The first room was decorated with the heavy, dark woods of a public house. People clustered around booths or stood at high tables.

The next room recalled the austerity of a different continent.

The people here were quieter, too, barring the occasional boisterous laugh. Guests sat on plush pillows around low tables, their shoes stashed in cubbies at their booths. Serving girls replicated geisha. Their kimonos weren't stylized like Ingrid's; they were true to Japan, with narrow skirts that caused the women to walk with small, precise steps. Rice-paper sliding doors blocked off private rooms along a balcony above.

"This is my usual table." Ingrid stopped in a back corner. No other servants lingered there; they had arrived too quickly after the show. "Mr. Sakaguchi sits over there."

"It's impossible to know if Fa—Mr. Augustus is even here yet," Cy said, glancing at the private rooms above. "I reckon there's only one way to find out. Pardon me." He stopped one of the waitresses, his smile warm enough to thaw an iceberg. "Could you inquire if . . ."

Ingrid slipped off her shoes and knelt on her usual cushion to survey the rest of the room. A moment later, Cy claimed the zabuton across from her.

"You really shouldn't sit here," she said.

"Neither should you."

"Cy, it's okay. I don't—we don't need to cause a fuss."

"I have no intention of causing a fuss, nor do I intend to let my companion for the evening sit alone. I sit here, or we're at that other table together."

The view from the other table was excellent. Ingrid felt out of place, rather naughty—and giddy at the act of rebellion. The waitress came around. They deferred ordering, to wait for Mr. Augustus, and she went on.

"The waitress may not say anything about my presence, but we are getting attention," she murmured. *She* was getting attention. "Is that wise?"

"No. But word is already out. People would have talked no matter what. Now I just pray to God that we're not kept waiting long." A grim current deepened his voice.

The strain of the earth resonated through the room, as it abounded in straw, bamboo, and other natural fibers. The conductivity of the place—and the excellent fare—were why wardens favored the restaurant when they were entertaining guests.

The blueness of the fog had deepened, too. Ingrid could feel that difference. Power trickled into her. Not the tidal wave of a tremor, but energy just the same. She breathed it in, eyes half shut, and basked in the buzz. The gun in her purse might be more reliable if she had to defend herself, more easily explained, but this power was hers. She needed whatever she could muster.

Cy was right. People might murmur about Ingrid's presence, *exotic*—oh, how she hated that empty term—as she was. But the attention would have arrived even if Cy had come alone and used Mr. Sakaguchi's seats. And Mr. Sakaguchi always visited Quist's after the opera.

Captain Sutcliff was no fool. If he got word of Ingrid's presence, he'd know where to search for her, for Cy. She casually looked around the room and noted doors to the front, to the kitchens, and to the lavatories. No uniformed soldiers in sight.

George Augustus could betray them, too. Cy's anxiety, though, stemmed from meeting his father at all. He drummed his fingers, his gaze scouring the room. A waitress asked again if he wanted something to drink. He shook his head.

A man in a white suit approached them and bowed. "Mr. Augustus will receive you now, sir, madam."

He carried their shoes and guided them up stairs that emitted cricket chirps with every step. No blue clouded the floor this high up. The man slid open a door to a small chamber.

A silver-headed man with a bold forehead sat at the end of the low table. Ingrid vaguely recognized him. Mr. Sakaguchi had definitely met him at Quist's before.

With his parchment-frail skin, he looked old enough to be Cy's grandfather, not his father, but the resemblance was certainly there. They shared long, angular faces and the same noble bump to the nose. The older man's blue eyes were surrounded by deep wrinkles, giving him the perpetually sad gaze of a basset hound.

"I know you, ma'am. You're from the Cordilleran Auxiliary?" Mr. Augustus asked. His voice was softer than Cy's, wispier. He stared at Cy a few seconds, frowning as though confused, and then looked at Ingrid.

Ingrid glanced at Cy. His Adam's apple bobbed and he seemed to have utterly lost the ability to speak.

"I am," she said.

"I don't believe we've been formally introduced, but Mr. Sakaguchi spoke highly of you, pointed you out to me." Mr. Augustus's forehead creased in thought. "Ah, yes. Miss Carmichael, is it?"

She was surprised but pleased. "Yes, sir." She motioned to the open door behind them. "Can the three of us speak in private, Mr. Augustus?"

At that, his eyes narrowed. "No, but four of us can, my dear." He tapped his pocket. Footsteps whispered down the hallway behind them. Dread brought a small flare of power to her skin.

Reddy entered the room. His close-cropped white hair was a stark contrast to his ebony skin. His gaze immediately snapped to Cy. With a deft move, he shut the door and shuffled to stand to Mr. Augustus's left, but his gaze didn't leave Cy. A rosy glow rounded out his cheeks as he smiled. "Sir?"

Mr. Augustus frowned, clearly puzzled. "The lady asked for privacy for us to speak. What are you smiling about, Reddy? Do you have a joke to share with the class?"

"I think the lady's right to ask for privacy, sir." Reddy granted Ingrid an abrupt nod. She smiled back and wondered if he remembered her. Regardless, she couldn't help but like a man who had such evident fondness for Cy.

Reddy pulled a small box from his pocket. The object was lacquered in black, the small lip of a hinge barely visible. He set it on the table and compressed the lid. A buzzing sound escalated in volume like record static.

"The walls are terribly thin here," said George Augustus. "This device prevents our conversation from being recorded. I'd also appreciate it if you set your weapons on the table. The purse and the rod, if you will." He said this sweetly as if he asked them inside for afternoon tea.

An observant man; like father, like son. Ingrid set her clutch on the table. With a slow movement, Cy flared open his jacket and removed the Tesla rod from its loop. He set it alongside her purse.

"Much obliged," said Mr. Augustus. "I'm not fool enough to expect anyone to walk around unarmed in this day and age, but it makes meetings go a mite smoother if the weapons are all out and open like a July window. That done, what can I do for y'all today?"

She glanced between Cy and his father. Well, tommyrot. He looked as tongue-tied as ever. "It seems as though introductions are in order. Mr. Augustus, here's your son."

"Father." The word emerged as a squeak from the tall man beside her.

Mr. Augustus's eyes went impossibly large. "No. It can't be. Here? All grown up? But you . . . you're . . ." He stood, shoving back the table as he did so. Reddy caught him and steadied him upright. "Barty? You're alive?"

CHAPTER 14

Father and son studied each other for a long moment and then rushed into an embrace. Reddy stepped out of the way, a brilliant smile lighting his face.

"I knew I shouldn't believe them. I knew it. Your mother said as much."

"You were told I was dead." The words were ragged.

"Yes. Porterman crash in Virginia. I had men look into it. We had all the proof but your body. Last autumn when you didn't come to Maggie's funeral, it seemed more certain that . . . that you were truly gone, my boy."

"Maggie." A wave of grief passed over Cy. "I didn't know she was dead until weeks later. But if you expected me to show up, they did, too."

"Yes, yes. *They.* The UP. My best customers." Anger replaced his grief even as tears streamed down the man's cheeks. Reddy flicked a handkerchief from his pocket and passed it over.

"How'd Maggie . . . how'd it happen?" Cy asked. "She was always either in the office or her laboratory—"

"It was the laboratory. An accident, fire. Her and five other engineers. Spontaneous combustion. Fast. Thank God for small mercies."

Cy didn't look comforted by that, but how was a person supposed to take the loss of their twin? "Figures it'd be in her lab. That's where she was most at home. I'd always tell her to be sure and remember to make something to save the world, not destroy it." His smile didn't reach his eyes.

"Losing her—losing both of you—scorched us like hellfire. Look at you, my boy! A dozen years have passed. Last I saw, you were all of fifteen, that caterpillar mustache on your lip. Oh, your mother! If only she were here!"

Cy touched his upper lip as if to reach for the past. "How is she, since . . . ?"

Emotion flickered over the older man's face and vanished in a blink. "She'd be so proud of you. Good God. Look at how tall you are. No wonder I didn't recognize you." He stared in awe at his son. "You went to school that last Christmas and you were a sapling with some baby fat to your cheeks. Your head only this high." He held a hand at midchest and glanced at Ingrid. "Your pardon, ma'am! Listening to this old fool going on."

"There's no need to apologize, sir." Her voice was thick with emotion. She couldn't help but think of Mr. Sakaguchi, and the kind of reunion she hoped to have with him.

Mr. Augustus clapped a hand on Cy's shoulder. "Sit! Please! Reddy, our security . . . ?"

"In place as always, sir."

Cy looked at Ingrid as he knelt on a cushion. "Augustinian invented all of the spy technology used by the Unified Pacific, which also means they know how to defend against it. That buzzer on the table is all most people will see, but knowing my father, there's a lot more in play."

Mr. Augustus nodded. "Reinforced walls in here, which Reddy checks for whirly-flies and whatnot. The rice paper looks thin, but there's orichalcum in there to slow a bullet or two. Of course, we can only do so much about spies in the dining rooms. That's the weakness."

Ingrid lowered herself to the zabuton across from Mr. Augustus and tucked in her skirt. Reddy was the only one to remain standing.

"So many defenses against your best customer," she said.

"I took on the family business, thinking I could save the world," said Mr. Augustus. "Older I get, the more I'm worried about saving my soul. I—I don't control much of the company now. The board's nearly booted me. I don't mind that much. War's never pleasant, but things have changed these past few years. Conquering a people is one matter, extermination is another." He studied Cy. "Then I have two brilliant children who inherited our family knack, to my grief. Bart—I knew Bart wanted out."

"Maggie never changed her mind?" asked Cy.

"No. But I knew she wasn't happy either, at the end. I . . . I was asking too much of her, wanting her to take on more of the business side. She wanted to invent, to meddle."

"Always," Cy whispered.

Ingrid looked to the clock on the wall. "I hate to hurry

things, I truly do, but we can't stay long. We need your help."

"I need your help, too, ma'am. What truly happened at the Cordilleran? No one at the UP is talking about it, and there're mumblings about an Ambassador being involved. Where's Mr. Sakaguchi?"

Ingrid and Cy shared a look. Where to begin? She rested her hands on her lap. "I . . . I don't know right now, Mr. Augustus. I wish I did." She took a deep breath. "What do you know about the Gaia Project?"

That clearly caught him off guard. "How did you ever hear about that? It's about as top secret as a project can be."

"We know it involves kermanite," said Cy.

"Well, yes, in a way. It was a project to create a kermanite-powered weapon to resolve the war in China, but it was scrapped in the early stages. Nothing ever came of it."

"The project is going on right now. My . . ." My father, she almost said, but couldn't manage the words. They felt too strange. "My understanding is that it caused those earthquakes in China earlier this year."

"The earthquakes? There aren't any Chinese geomancers left. Of course there'd be bad earthquakes."

"How long ago was the project scrapped?" asked Cy.

"Late last year. I was told I'd be consulting and to expect blueprints, but they never arrived. I reckoned the whole thing had been some general's fancy."

"Pardon me, sirs, ma'am, but can I get drinks or food for anyone?" asked Reddy.

"Tell Don we want the '39 La Fayette," said Mr. Augustus. "I've been wanting—"

"No." Cy's voice was so loud he seemed to surprise himself. "There's no time for that—that kind of celebrating."

The two men shared an unreadable look. Ingrid recalled what Cy had said about his father and the drink.

Reddy was quiet for a moment. "I'll see about some water, then." He exited the chamber. Ingrid heard the click of a lock. Despite Mr. Augustus's assurance, the walls still looked terribly thin. She wondered if the sliver of energy she held could tear apart a structure reinforced by orichalcum.

Orichalcum was likely to be used in this Gaia Project weapon, too. This whole thing was in the works before the Unified Pacific even had Papa in custody. Maybe he wasn't part of their original plan.

Tension lingered between the two men. Ingrid coughed politely. "Mr. Augustus, how big a piece of kermanite did this war-ender weapon need?"

"Well, that I do know, and that was why it seemed so fanciful. It required a massive piece. Solid. Nigh impossible, of course, with how it fragments."

Ingrid looked across the table to Cy. "I didn't tell you everything about Captain Sutcliff's arrival. Down in Boron, they retrieved a piece of kermanite as big as a horse. A standing horse, to the withers. And it vanished."

"Vanished?" Cy arched an eyebrow. "How does something like that vanish?"

"In Boron? We own a major stake in that mine. I have people there. How did we not know?" Father and son shared a perplexed expression.

"Captain Sutcliff said the kermanite was stolen and the

trail led him to San Francisco. He thought the auxiliary was somehow involved."

"That makes no sense at all," murmured Mr. Augustus. "Kermanite as big as a horse! How would you even move such a thing? It'd be so fragile! Why would he think the auxiliary was involved?"

She dismissed the question with a flick of her wrist. No need to bring up the drama with Captain Sutcliff, Papa, and Mr. Sakaguchi.

"My people aren't my people anymore. I'm too old for these games." Mr. Augustus rubbed his jaw. "Ten years ago, I had absolute control. I knew my agents. They knew me."

"You had Maggie with you then," said Cy.

"I also had you way back when, Barty. Don't sell yourself short. These days, victory in China looks inevitable. Britain's about ready to crush India, though the Thuggees will make them bleed. But using earthquakes as the weapon. How? Is this some perversion of geomancy?"

Ingrid masked a cringe at his choice of words. "Yes. We're not sure exactly how, though. We hoped you'd know."

"If only I'd seen the blueprints! If I knew more, I'd gladly tell you." Mr. Augustus's broad forehead furrowed into deep lines. "Lordy, Lordy. What about Vesuvius? Could a weapon have caused that?"

"I really don't know," Ingrid said, a pang striking her chest. The council had spent hours debating that matter of Vesuvius, and at the time it had felt like such a distant event, physically and emotionally.

If her pain could cause an earthquake, could rile Hidden

Ones in such a way, she might be capable of causing a volcanic eruption as well.

Reddy slipped inside the room again, locking the door behind him. "Mr. Augustus, sir, there are soldiers at the front door of Quist's. The attendants are delaying them."

Cy rushed straight to his father. The men stood together in an embrace so painful that Ingrid looked away. She edged toward the door and slipped on her shoes.

"Reddy," she asked, "what's the best exit from here?"

"The kitchen is fastest, ma'am. Goes straight to the back alley."

"Barty, I don't want us to part like this." Mr. Augustus wavered on his feet. "This is too fast. I need—I need to do more. Know more. In my room upstairs, there are things I can give you. Money. Jewels. I want to help you somehow."

"There's no time, Father." Cy took a step back but still didn't let go of him.

"Reddy, you can take him up the back way to my room, can't you? Quickly?" Mr. Augustus's voice quavered, and he paused for a deep, hacking cough. "I'm old, but I'm not entirely useless. I can distract these soldiers."

"Certainly, sir," said Reddy.

"Father—"

"Don't argue with me. Don't you dare. I wish I could go with you. I wish I had your spine. Whatever you're doing, whatever this fight is, let me help. Please. For you, for Maggie, for your mother."

"Cy, we should split up," said Ingrid. Maybe the soldiers had descriptions of both of them from the opera, but she knew for certain they'd look for her.

He nodded. "Right. Meet in front of the barbershop with the cigar-store Indian just a few blocks away."

"I know it." She wanted to kiss him right then, crush their lips together, absorb his heat and scent and everything else about him. Instead, she cast him a desperate look, grabbed her purse from the table, and she fled.

She flew down the stairs and made a sharp left toward the kitchen. The luscious scent of sizzling meat and peppers flavored the air, as if she could breathe and chew at the same time. She spun to dodge a laden waiter. Steaming trays lined an open counter, and she caught a glimpse of chefs in white hats, yellow bandannas tied to their sleeves. Voices muttered in heavily accented English.

The hallway turned. Ahead of her was a flash of brilliant red skirts. Ingrid stopped, recognition instantaneous.

Victoria Rossi.

Several signs marked the hallway ahead. Going straight led to the alley and escape, but Miss Rossi had gone right, toward an access to the flats above. Ingrid gnawed her lip and followed. Up ahead she saw a sinuous curl of black iron railing: a staircase.

"Damn it all, but you had me worried." A man's voice was faint. "Soldiers are trying to get in here."

"Oh, as if they'll know you, looking like that. A beard does suit you." That was Miss Rossi. "Business like this, with such hoity-toity people, they will keep the soldiers out. Besides, you're the one who wanted to come here a last time. The steak was tasty, yes?"

Whoever Miss Rossi was meeting, they'd probably try to

escape through the alley, too. Ingrid looked in the next open doorway—a broom closet. The harsh scent of ammonia stung her nostrils as she ducked inside. She pulled the cord for the light and shut the door behind her. In the back wall, water roared through pipes, a waterfall in an echo chamber.

"We can't afford to dally." The voice was so muffled that Ingrid had to focus to decipher what he said.

"I like it when you take risks." Miss Rossi's soft voice was even harder to understand. Ingrid scooted a stool closer to the shared wall and stepped up so that she could press her ear against a vent.

"Did you take enough of your pretty pictures?" the man asked, scarcely louder than before. He had an accent. British, perhaps.

"My pretty pictures. You say it like they're so . . . so minor. My photographs, they are important! I have spent these three days walking the entire damned city. I thought I was supposed to have months to do this!" Ingrid frowned as water continued to flush through the pipes, making it difficult for her to hear.

"I told you from the beginning that we may have to be flexible."

"Flexible. Feh."

"You'll make your money. You can buy new shoes to ease your sore feet."

"Money. It's never been just about money."

"No, hatred is a much better motivation."

It took Ingrid a moment to realize Miss Rossi was laughing. Only the highest pitch carried through the vent. "Oh yes. I will love to see this city fall into dust. I would love to see Butterfield's face when he wakes up in his soft feather bed and silk sheets and realizes what is happening. If he wakes up at all."

"Ah, familiar with Butterfield's bed, are you?"

"I should slap you for that."

"Hardly worth slapping someone over the truth, is it?"

"I just wanted my studio. To take my pretty pictures, as you say."

"Sometimes we don't get what we want."

"You have what you want now, don't you? That auxiliary is rubble. I like that my old studio collapsed in the explosion. Very nice touch. Oh, look at you. Sad-faced. Do you feel guilty? You shouldn't. This is war, yes?"

Ingrid gasped and covered her mouth even though she couldn't be heard from the closet. Miss Rossi's studio had been right next door to the Cordilleran Auxiliary. They were talking about her building. They caused the explosion. They murdered all the wardens and adepts and little boys and maids. Why? What could they gain from murdering the region's geomancers?

"Yes." The man's voice softened, and Ingrid strained to hear. "Sacrifice is necessary."

"Some Thuggee you are. What would Kali think, you with tears in your eyes?" Miss Rossi spoke of the Hindu goddess of time and change, a complex being often described as a Hidden One of old.

"Don't believe everything you read in the papers, that feculence. As if Hindus are the only ones fighting for the sake of India now. Christian, Muslim, Jain, Sikh—we are all in this together."

"A shame. I should like to take pictures of this Kali."

The man barked out a laugh. "You'd ask the devil himself to pose for a photograph, if you could. We should go get some sleep. We're due to meet the others at Mussel Rock at dawn. Tomorrow . . . tomorrow will be busy."

Ingrid knew Mussel Rock. The wardens would take students there on day picnics to pull in energy and fill kermanite, even as they played baseball and practiced sumo wrestling.

"Sleep? I can think of better things to do than sleep. Oh, not just that." There was another pause. "Let's hit the Barbary Coast! Go to Kelvin's or the Anastasia. This is our last chance. None of this will be here tomorrow."

"Are you sure you don't want to take more pictures?"

"I might take a few, but I am low on film, and I'll need it tomorrow, yes? Especially if we have a sighting."

"You and your damned monsters."

"Fantastics aren't monsters. Men. Men are better monsters. Maybe we go upstairs first? I bet there are empty rooms. I can pick a lock."

"Oh, can you? A woman of many talents."

"You don't even know."

Footsteps echoed in the chamber of the stairwell and faded as the two ascended. Ingrid braced herself, biding her time as the couple departed. She had to get to Cy and Fenris. The airship was ready. They had to make it to Mussel Rock to stop the assault, whatever it was.

Ingrid staggered from the broom closet and back to the main hallway. She ran to the exit, her shoes half sliding on the slick floor, and shoved open the door. Momentum carried her forward and directly into the double row of gold buttons lining a dark uniform.

"Well, hello," said a deep voice with a laugh. A hand clamped down on her narrow wrist, and twisted. The purse clattered onto the asphalt.

She looked up at Captain Sutcliff's rather equine face.

"Pick it up," he snapped.

Soldiers surrounded her. One stooped to pick up her purse.

"Thanks for grabbing that for me, sir," she said. "Now, if you'll pass it here, I'll move along—"

"Miss Carmichael, I've spent a great deal of time and fuss looking for you the past few days."

"Should I be flattered?"

"Sir!" It was the soldier with her purse. "There's a pistol here, sir."

Captain Sutcliff tilted his head to one side. "Anything else?"

"Stubs for *Lincoln,* sir, and a comb."

The captain returned his cool gaze to her. A light cast his face in bright yellow the same shade as his hair. "What did you have in mind for tonight, hmm?"

"Isn't it obvious? I planned to brush my hair."

Captain Sutcliff sighed. "Really, are we playing this game? Where's your *boss,* Miss Carmichael? Where's Mr. Sakaguchi?"

"I honestly don't know." She thought of him and felt an extra twist of anxiety. "I'm not the one you want. I just overheard a man, a Thuggee, speaking with Miss Victoria Rossi. They're plotting a new attack."

"Really. You think I'll be so easily distracted?"

"It's not a distraction!" snapped Ingrid. Heat curdled on her skin, and she gritted her teeth. "They are plotting some kind of attack on San Francisco. Please. If you search the upper-floor rooms—"

"Do you realize how many apartments are up here? Come now, Miss Carmichael. I'm not going to be led on any Sasquatch hunts. Who is your partner in this endeavor, the man with the glasses? Did he kill Mr. Sakaguchi?"

She gaped at him. "Of course not!"

"There was a lot of blood in your home. I'm surprised you didn't use poison again."

Ingrid shook her head. "Your gasbag's gone flat. I don't even know what you're talking about."

"I see. So we are going to play this game." Captain Sutcliff sighed. "Let's enjoy more comfortable surroundings, shall we?"

CHAPTER 15

Ingrid had passed the police precinct for years but rarely cast it a second glance. The structure was of tony red brick, quite stark and Federalist. A United States flag with its forty-five stars draped from a flagpole over the door, with a rising-sun flag slightly lower on the left side.

Across the street was a barbershop with a striped pole and a cigar-store Indian.

She made a special effort not to look directly at Cy. He slouched in the doorway of the shop, his posture reminiscent of Fenris. His head rose slightly, and with a glance at a nonexistent watch on his wrist, he casually walked down the street. Captain Sutcliff never looked his way.

It broke her heart to see Cy leave.

Not as if he could have done anything, of course. He was a pacifist, not an idiot. Ingrid was surrounded by five soldiers and Captain Sutcliff. The soldiers hadn't bound her hands or arms, but they walked in tight formation around her, firearms at the ready. If she tried to run, she had no doubt that they would shoot her. Probably someplace nonfatal, like the leg, though the ripple effects of that would be disastrous.

That fear prevented her from knocking them down with a pressure wave. Even if she did manage to topple the soldiers, they were bound to be crack shots. They were trained to roll off a downed horse and come up shooting, and did target practice from bobbing airships in windy weather. She wouldn't underestimate them.

She was suddenly put in mind of the game of kitsune-ken, as if she had made the motion for the hunter and lost to the higher-ranking village chief. Well, as far as Ingrid was concerned, the shamisen would play on. She refused to concede defeat.

They entered the building. A police officer in light blue stood behind a heavy counter, his salute crisp.

"Captain Sutcliff, sir, our captain has given you full use of our facilities, sir. We also have celled autocars available if you need transport to the Presidio or Fort Monroe, sir."

"I will question the young lady here for now, thank you, Lieutenant."

The captain guided her into a high-ceilinged chamber painted in ghastly sea-foam green. He motioned her to a wooden chair by a table. He sat in a cushioned seat across from her. The table legs were bolted to the marble floor. Two soldiers flanked the door, with another one behind her, and the others visible in the hallway.

If Ingrid hadn't been so frustrated and scared, she might

have been honored to be regarded as such a threat, but right now she had a more pressing concern.

Dawn. That would be about five o'clock. That's when the attack—whatever it was—would begin. She had to be at Mussel Rock by then. That gave her six or seven hours to get there. Hopefully Fenris's *Bug* was fully functional and fast.

"What have you found out about the missing kermanite?" Ingrid asked.

"I believe you're here to answer my questions, Miss Carmichael."

"What you believe and what will happen are very separate things. Please, have you learned anything?" Desperation edged her voice.

"It hasn't been recovered, I can tell you that much." He stood, smartly tugging his jacket down as he did. "But I have learned many things in the past few days that may be quite relevant to this case. First of all, on the subject of missing kermanite, I found it peculiar that the Cordilleran Auxiliary's vault was completely empty."

"Completely empty?" Had all of it been transported in Mr. Thornton's autocar? If so, it was a wonder the weight hadn't broken the axels of the rusty clunker. "I was in the vault last Friday when we fetched kermanite for an urgent shipment to the A-and-A. The bins were full."

"Not anymore. No point in losing kermanite during the explosion, correct?" He stared at her in clear expectation of a reaction, and when none came, he continued: "We already know that the blast wasn't from a boiler malfunction. Several high-powered explosives of Chinese make were set in such a way as to target both the meeting room and the classrooms."

She frowned as she followed Captain Sutcliff's logic. Mr. Sakaguchi was regarded as antagonistic to his own people and sympathetic to the Chinese. These Thuggees had clearly set up the Chinese to be the scapegoats for this attack. Mr. Sakaguchi hadn't died in the blast, so it was even easier to presume his guilt.

"Back at Quist's, I overheard that Thuggee talking with Miss Rossi. He admitted to the attack on the auxiliary."

"How convenient, to blame the Thuggees for the auxiliary and this attack to come. They make such romantic villains, don't they? Perfect for those wretched pulp novels. Was this fellow young, dark, and handsome in a heathen way? Did he wear his killing scarf at his waist so you would be sure to identify his affection for Kali?"

Ingrid shook with rage, heat buzzing on her skin. "Don't make a mockery of the explosion of the auxiliary or the man who caused it. That was my second home. I knew everyone there. I *loved* them." She took a deep breath, willing herself to stay in control. "I never saw the man. I could barely hear them from where I was. He had a British accent."

The captain shook his head in dismissal. "As if that narrows down the suspects. The woman with this Thuggee, you know her?"

"Yes. Miss Rossi. A photographer. She used to have a studio next to the auxiliary."

"A woman photographer? She *owned* this studio?"

"Yes. And was run out of business for not paying the city enough in graft." Ingrid couldn't help but feel a pang of anger on behalf of Miss Rossi, even as she wanted to slap her.

"More likely she couldn't balance the books." Despite his derisive comment, Sutcliff pulled a notepad and pencil from his pocket and scribbled notes. "The building beside the auxiliary, you said? That vacant shop?"

"Yes. She commented tonight at how happy she was that it had been destroyed."

Sutcliff grunted and tucked the paper away again. "Well. That many explosives, it was inevitable. Quite a miracle, however, that you and the Japanese warden survived. It's my belief that you knew exactly where to stand, that you had shelter of some sort."

"Knew where to stand? You were there! We were completely encased by debris, and injured as well!"

"Geomancy is a particular sort of magic. I don't pretend to understand its nuances, and I'm not sure anyone really does," he said. Ingrid's blood ran cold. Did he suspect her of possessing power as well, by association with her father? "All I know is that there were two survivors from the wreckage, and two wardens who were not present. Those two wardens are now classified as a murder victim and a missing person."

"A murder victim?"

"Yes, your Mr. Calhoun. Arsenic poisoning. Quite a heavy dose, I might add."

"Arsenic?" she whispered. The world spun slightly and she caught herself against the table.

"The problem with arsenic—for criminals, at least—is that it stays in the body a very long time and is quite easily detected by chemical analysis. Tell me about arsenic, Miss Carmichael."

"You're implying I had something to do with this?"

He turned his palms up. "I'm asking what you know about it. Poison is often considered a woman's method, but to be blunt, I don't know if it's yours."

There were so many insults woven into that single statement that she didn't even know how to begin her rebuttal. "What about Mr. Thornton? I hope you haven't focused on me so much that you haven't bothered looking for him. I'm afraid the Thuggees have him. He might be dead. All the other wardens are." Except Mr. Sakaguchi. She had to hold on to that hope.

"Of course we've looked for the man. His house was ransacked, as you know. Witnesses saw you arrive by foot and leave by car."

"Yes. I was there. I saw it was ransacked. The phone didn't work. I immediately returned home so I could ask Mr. Sakaguchi for advice."

"Ah. Your Mr. Sakaguchi, who you have conveniently misplaced."

"Soon after I arrived home, he was shot. That's why there's so much blood in his study. Someone was out in the garden. Then he was . . . he was kidnapped. I ran . . . escaped."

Captain Sutcliff sighed so heavily his shoulders slumped. "Yes, I witnessed your escape from the very troops who would have assisted you. Hardly the act of an innocent person."

As if Captain Sutcliff had ever presumed her and Mr. Sakaguchi to be innocent. "We're wasting time here. You have to get to Quist's and find Miss Rossi. She's in a bright red velvet dress. She'd be hard to miss. Please—"

"Miss Carmichael." Captain Sutcliff leaned forward. "What do you know about your father?"

Her fingers dug into the edge of the table. He'd been biding his time to bring this up. "Abram Carmichael was a warden and a geomancer, and he was killed when I was very young. I don't even remember him."

"And what would you say if I told you he was alive until recently?"

Until recently? She had expected Sutcliff to wield the truth against her like a knife—but this? "That can't be. You're mistaken."

"I read the report. He's gone, Miss Carmichael."

"Gone." The word resonated in her mouth. She stared into her trembling hands, willing herself to stay strong. Maybe this was for the best. Maybe her father was at peace now, no longer able to cause so much mayhem. But it would have been wonderful to meet him, just once. Say hello. But now, now . . . Hot tears streamed down her cheeks, but she resisted the urge to sniffle. Her chin stayed high.

Captain Sutcliff leaned back in the chair, arms crossed, clearly discomfited by her emotions. He motioned to one of his men. A soldier slipped out and returned, setting a glass of water on the table before her. She glanced up in gratitude and took a sip.

"Where?" she finally managed to choke out.

"He was in China, working with the rebellion to fill kermanite."

No, she wanted to say. He wasn't working for China. He was used as a weapon *against* the Chinese, more destructive than any hellfire, any Durendal.

"As for how he got there," Sutcliff continued, "Warden Sakaguchi smuggled him out of the country twenty years ago. The Japanese government has letters, evidence of them corresponding over the years. This past year, Japan censured Sakaguchi. He's forbidden to leave the Bay Area. I'll take a guess that he's violating that order right now."

"Then why didn't they arrest him? Put him before a tribunal?"

"The case was likely still being built against him." Sutcliff's mustache twitched. "With the evidence I've gathered, I'm sure judgment will be swift. But I need to find the man, Miss Carmichael."

"I think that's a wonderful idea." She stood, drying her cheeks with quick swipes. "Once you've found him, Captain, please let me know. I should head home. It's past my bedtime."

The two soldiers at the door sidestepped to block her.

"It's very late," said Sutcliff. "Not an hour for a proper lady to be wandering the streets alone. And where would you even go? You haven't been home in days. I do wonder what *tong* you're working with in Chinatown, but interrogation on that subject can wait. The matter of the auxiliary and the kermanite is enough for now."

"Are you arresting me?"

"The correct term is *protective custody*. One of my superiors is on a Wyvern set to arrive here at dawn." His nostrils flared. He didn't seem too pleased that he would soon no longer be the ranking officer. "They wish to question you. If you cooperate now, it'll make matters easier."

"It would also reflect much better on you."

"Miss Carmichael." Captain Sutcliff stood and looked at her levelly. Weary sincerity weighted his gaze. "This isn't about me. This is about the security of the United States. This is about a piece of kermanite that could be utilized as a very dangerous weapon against us. I don't want that to happen."

His loyalty was to America, not the Unified Pacific. A noteworthy distinction, and one Mr. Sakaguchi had made as well.

"I don't want it to happen either. That's why I want to stop this attack that's about to happen. I'm not trying to deceive you or distract you. They're meeting with others at Mussel Rock at dawn. Please. Send men there. Stop whatever they're trying to do."

He stared at her a long moment, frowning in thought. "Miss Carmichael, even if some attack is imminent, it's not going to be carried out with this piece of kermanite. It would take months, if not years, to engineer a machine able to tap that much power, and take countless hours for geomancers to fill it."

"I don't know how this could involve the kermanite either, but this Thuggee admitted to blowing up the auxiliary. Please—"

Captain Sutcliff raised a hand. "Don't demean yourself by begging," he said, but hesitated, frowning. Watching his face, Ingrid could almost see the cogs turn in his brain. She had to push him; she had to reveal the cards in her hand.

"I know about the Gaia Project," she whispered.

Captain Sutcliff's frown deepened. He motioned to the other soldiers and they filed from the room. The captain shut the door behind them.

"The Gaia Project," he echoed.

"It's something I only just found out about, but Mr. Sakaguchi wasn't part of it. He was trying to stop it."

"There have been rumors of it, but I heard it'd been scrapped . . ." He stopped, as if remembering who he spoke to.

"The weapon's already been used in China and killed hundreds of thousands. I know what you want to say, that those lives don't mean anything." She took a deep breath. "If you've been researching Mr. Sakaguchi, his beliefs, you know he's been central to any humanitarian effort the auxiliary's done. Mr. Sakaguchi isn't simply a Chinese sympathizer. He's a life sympathizer. He was even arguing we should send help to Italy for Vesuvius, right before the building . . ." She couldn't say it. "He wouldn't be a part of something destructive, and neither would I."

"All I know is that the project is run more by Japan than the UP, and it's supposed to end the war."

"If you have superior officers coming, maybe I *should* talk to them. Maybe they would know more . . ." Her voice trailed away as she pieced the scenario together.

This Thuggee was meeting his compatriots at a critical juncture of the local faults. He'd taken care to kill all of the other geomancers in the city, all the men who could absorb and stop a quake. What if these Thuggees had somehow infiltrated the Gaia Project and knew how to replicate the attacks on Peking, even without Papa? What if they had hold of the missing kermanite, or even another unusually large chunk?

They could simultaneously destroy the city and fill the crystal, if they had the skills of a geomancer. *Mr. Thornton.* Hurting him wouldn't provoke the earth, but if they had other means to do that, Mr. Thornton could certainly channel energy into kermanite. He wasn't of Ingrid or Papa's caliber, but he was a senior warden for a reason.

Ingrid didn't see any easy option here. She took several deep breaths and steeled herself. "Captain Sutcliff, if you won't send anyone after Miss Rossi and her companion, let me go. Let me try to stop them. I swear to you, I'll come back here afterward to meet these officers. Willingly."

"The odd thing is, I believe you." Captain Sutcliff frowned, perplexed at this change. She could have wept again in relief.

Someone rapped on the door. "Captain?"

Captain Sutcliff took a step back from her. "Yes?"

A subordinate opened the door and saluted. His face was eerily white. "Sir, there's an Ambassador here."

"An Ambassador?" Ingrid echoed. Could it be Mr. Roosevelt? Would that be a good or bad thing, to be interrogated by the very man she was supposed to flee to for sanctuary?

Sutcliff stiffened. "The name?"

"Blum, sir."

At that, Sutcliff paled. "Her? Of all of them?" He shot a glance at Ingrid. "God help you."

"There's a woman Ambassador?" Ingrid asked. Of the Twelve, only a few were known to the public, and she'd never heard of a woman named Blum. Perhaps she would be more sympathetic to Ingrid's plight.

"Move along, young man." A gnarled hand pushed the surprised soldier back. An old woman stood in the doorway. Her back was pole straight, posture regal, though her head likely only came to Ingrid's chest. Silver hair was pulled back into a bun so tight that the skin seemed strained at the cheekbones. Her pure ivory complexion contained fine wrinkles, but very few. There was no sagging, no ugliness. Dark almond-shaped eyes regarded Ingrid. A black dress hugged her stout form, ermine collar like a mane around her face. With her attire and demeanor, she could have easily mingled with the wealthy throngs at the Damcyan.

This was no mere Ambassador, though. Ingrid could taste the woman's presence like an electrical charge to the air. She *emanated* magic.

"I'm Ambassador Blum. You are Captain Sutcliff, I assume? And why were you alone with this young lady?"

The captain looked absolutely flummoxed. "Questioning her on sensitive matters, Ambassador. I didn't expect you to arrive until morning."

"Sensitive matters, hmm?" The woman eyed them up and down. Ingrid flushed at the scrutiny.

"Ambassador, due to your, er, fluctuating condition, I must verify your identity." Sutcliff unsheathed a knife from his belt. As he swung the blade, she extended her right arm as if to help.

His blade snapped against her wrist. Literally. The metal shattered without piercing the skin. Ambassador Blum didn't even recoil.

Ingrid did, curling back and half swallowing a scream. Metal shards pinged on the floor.

"Satisfied, Captain?" Ambassador Blum sounded bored. She flexed her wrist to show the jade ring on her finger.

Ingrid's eyes widened. The signet ring of an Ambassador.

An enchantment prevented any act of violence that would part the ring from the body. Only a quorum of seven Ambassadors could remove it.

Blum's heady magic didn't radiate from that, though—she was something more.

Captain Sutcliff dropped the broken knife. The hilt clattered on the floor. Tucked at his back, his fingers trembled, and he clenched them in a fist. "My pardon, Ambassador." He bowed.

Blum flicked her fingers. "I'm accustomed to such tests."

A soldier stooped to clean up the pieces of the broken blade.

With Sutcliff clearly rattled, Ingrid seized the opportunity. "Hello, Ambassador. I'm Ingrid Carmichael. I would like to—"

"I am not terribly concerned with what you'd like to do, Miss Carmichael. I represent the Unified Pacific and its interests, not yours. Though you are fortunate that I was already on the West Coast in anticipation of announcements from Baranov. I shudder to think of what fool things this captain would have done otherwise."

What kind of operation was going on in Baranov? That was Russia's chunk of wilderness attached to Canada.

Ingrid looked to Captain Sutcliff. His countenance hadn't improved much. His jaw was clenched, nostrils flaring as he breathed. What did he know about Blum that Ingrid did not?

Ambassador Blum followed Ingrid's gaze to the captain. "You're dismissed, for now. Leave your men to take shifts here during the night."

"My pardon, madam." He bowed with the stiffness of a clockwork toy soldier.

"We ladies require privacy." The Ambassador returned her piercing gaze to Ingrid, and like that, Sutcliff was dismissed. The door shut behind him with a sharp click.

"First things first. Did this Captain Sutcliff offend you or put his hands on you in an inappropriate way?" The heavy presence of sorcery felt almost as if the air itself cowered from touching Blum.

"Inappropriate way? He brought me here! That's inappropriate enough. I'm supposedly under protective custody."

"Well, yes, he would have to term it so for the paperwork. I'm not limited in that way. I can just take you." Ambassador Blum smiled brightly. "We should have grabbed Sakaguchi months ago and nipped this in the bud, but, well, politics and all. The man does have friends."

"Mr. Sakaguchi hasn't done anything wrong."

"Really? Hmm." Blum craned her neck up, eyes narrowing. "I don't know about this room. We have four floors above us and a basement below, but I need to completely survey the place. Excuse me, child, while I inspect the premises."

Ambassador Blum turned, black skirts rustling. The backside was gathered in a massive bustle that was a solid thirty years out of fashion. With spry steps, the old woman left.

Ingrid pushed herself away from the table. There had to be a way out of here. Being captured by soldiers was bad enough, but an Ambassador carrying some unidentifiable magic? Blum was one of the most powerful people in the world. *Here.* Wanting *her.*

The walls were solid brick, painted in that garish green. Ingrid pried off her slippers. Beneath the cool floor, tension lingered in the earth. Power was dampened here, without any blue visible; the Ambassador was right, there had to be a basement below, and likely substantial metal in the structure of the building. The place had only been built a few years before and probably had a steel frame. Better for surviving earthquakes, though less conductive for geomancers. She slid on her shoes.

No windows. The ceiling was high, maybe twenty feet, and the vents were also out of reach. She tested the door. Locked. She had just released the knob when it rattled and the door opened.

"Checking on the lock, yes?" asked Blum. She sounded far too perky for this late hour. A soldier stood behind her, his young face skewed in worry.

"Well, yes."

"I'm not surprised at all. Not in the least. You're not going to be meek, paralyzed like a kappa kept from water." Blum reached into a satchel she hadn't held before. "Child, look at me. You have something on your nose."

Ingrid looked up. The white cloth came at her face. She had a split second to gasp and try to lurch away, but Blum was far faster. A pungent, sweet odor slapped her nostrils.

The world went black.

CHAPTER 16

"Set her down there. Gently now. That's a good lad."

The voice sounded fuzzy and distant, as though it echoed down a long tunnel. Ingrid tried to move. The pull of gravity had quadrupled. It took concerted effort to open her eyelids. Ambassador Blum loomed over her, her visage blurred as if a dozen diverse faces overlapped.

"There! You're back with us already. You were only out for about two minutes. I know it feels like longer, but chloroform does that, even in tiny doses. I daresay, I'm rather proud of how I've adapted the formula. Mine is especially effective. Far superior to that *commercial* stuff. Tsk, tsk! Don't try to move around. It won't do you much good."

Ingrid immediately tried to move around. Her hands were secured behind her back, palms pressed together and heavy. She had a hazy sense of the earth's heat and something prickled her arms. It took her a moment to recognize it as grass. She forced her chin up, only to have her head loll to one side. Stars glimmered through a torn shroud of clouds.

"You're shackled right now so you can't escape or hurt yourself. That's why I took care to knock you out."

Ingrid blinked as the fuzz in her brain began to lift. Blum's face steadied, resuming its proper form. "What are you doing?" The words emerged as a drunken slur.

"Waiting a few minutes for you to be completely conscious. You're not feeling nauseous, are you?"

Ingrid shook her head. The motion made her mildly dizzy.

"Good."

A gag was stuffed in her mouth.

"I wanted to make sure you weren't going to be ill. Chloroform has that effect on some, and I don't want you to choke to death."

"Can I be of assistance, ma'am?" asked a male voice.

"No, Private, just stay close as a precaution. I need to set up my things."

Ingrid blinked some more and her vision clarified. She recognized the red brick of the police building, though she had never seen it from the back. A horse whinnied nearby. Three autocars gleamed in the dim light cast from the back porch. A high wooden fence was topped by barbed spirals. Blue vapor drifted over the ground as it had all day.

Something whined on the far side of the yard. Ingrid squinted, trying to identify the source. Sources, actually.

"There are dogs over there," Blum said. "I don't *like* dogs." She glanced over her shoulder and bared her teeth. The whining stopped with a soft squeak.

Ingrid had seen the station's dogs while passing by before—tosa inu, Japanese dogs bred to fight. God, what was this woman?

Ambassador Blum opened her large satchel and pulled out boxes. She hummed as she worked, opening lids and setting out items. A kermanite lantern illuminated the space. Ingrid winced at the glare, then did a double take.

One box contained a portable seismograph, an extraordinary one in brass, steel, and orichalcum. She had never seen one so small and delicate. The auxiliary's had been the size of a desk, with its roll of paper the length of her arm. Mr. Sakaguchi would be in ecstasy to see such a miniature model.

Blum set a scroll on the tiny spindle and fit a vial of ink into the pen brace. "Curious." She leaned over the device. "It's already picking up mild readings." She frowned over at Ingrid. "Well, I'll test it soon enough."

She unsheathed a tanto. A blade of six inches glimmered in the piercing beam of the lantern. Ingrid dug her slippered heels into the grass to try to stand. Instead, she flopped over like a sea lion. Her hair tumbled loose and shivered in a coarse black veil. Through strands of hair, she saw Ambassador Blum approach. She screamed into the gag and kicked out.

Blum glided around Ingrid's flailing feet with the finesse of a stalking animal. "I do apologize. I hate to stain a dress this beautiful."

The lightning-quick blade stabbed Ingrid's left calf. Pain knocked her flat on her back, a scream raging against the gag. Pain wavered and dappled her eyesight in black as heat poured down her leg.

The earthquake rumbled to the surface with a flare of cerulean. A wave of pressure caressed her skin with warmth, a far more welcome heat than the blood pouring down her leg. For a moment, it felt as if the earthquake lifted her up, rolling and tumbling her like a body in the surf. Her back arched. Pain was forgotten. The world tingled, cozy and comfortable, like Cy's arms wrapped around her and his lips pressed to hers. She moaned against the gag.

The wave faded. Pain bludgeoned her senses. Her moan turned into a pitiful sob.

"Oh my, oh my. I guess I should take care of this, and rather quickly."

A hand pressed against Ingrid's shoulder, the small fingers strong as orichalcum. Ingrid managed to turn her head. Blum had brought over one of her boxes—no, not a box. A cage. Through the wire thatch, the downy white fur of baby rabbits almost glowed in the darkness.

With her free hand, Blum reached into the cage, and with a deft move, snapped a kit's neck with a piercing pop. Her wrist sinuous, Blum coaxed the animal's invisible life energy as though coiling yarn around her fingers, and then brought her hand over to Ingrid.

The dark Reiki lapped against her skin. A strange, dank smell flashed in her nostrils. The pain faded so quickly that she gasped into the gag; Dr. Hatsumi's practice had never been so potent. She tried to move her legs. They tingled madly, as if the nerves had fallen asleep and didn't quite work.

"You see, Ingrid—may I call you Ingrid, as we'll become so well acquainted? I'm the only woman Ambassador of the Twelve. We're numbered like the apostles, or Charlemagne's paladins. I fancy myself as the Peter or Roland of the lot, simply because I'm a bit of a romantic." Another neck snapped, and that cool energy ebbed around Ingrid's leg. "The men, they know a lot, you see, but some don't know how to respect a woman. They think a woman in power is unnatural—as if they are any judge of that, short as they've lived. I'm underestimated all the time—which grants me the advantage in any fight. You're treated much the same, aren't you, my dear? A secretary of the Cordilleran Auxiliary! What a waste. I imagine they had you do their laundry and shine their shoes."

Ambassador Blum knelt on the grass beside Ingrid. "When your name came up, the men were ready to dismiss you as *just* a woman. I knew better. I was the one willing to ask, 'What if?' Your father was such a peculiar man in his gifts. Up close, you even smell like him."

Blum's nose lowered to almost touch Ingrid's cheek and she inhaled. The Ambassador's breath warmed her skin. "Strange. You both smell of hot rocks." She pulled back. "You deserve respect, Ingrid. Now, is the pain all gone?"

Ingrid nodded, one ear pressed to the grass.

Ambassador Blum twisted around. "The seismograph is still reading some activity in the earth below. The captain's initial telegraph said you were injured and healed after that blast on Sunday. Small wonder there've been a few earthquakes reported here, with all the other geomancers dead. Floral Reiki should be confined to children learning the craft. Oh, I almost forgot." She reached into the satchel. A lump of kermanite mounded from her palm. It was nearly the size of the rock Ingrid sold to Cy.

Ingrid made to roll away, but her skirt yanked her still. Blum had stepped on the cloth. The kermanite pressed against Ingrid's helpless hands, and like that, the heat siphoned away. She ground her teeth together. Damn this woman. Ingrid stared at the ground, willing another earthquake to happen, willing for the power to break free.

"Now, the private here will help you stand up. Take it easy with that leg. You'll be limping for a day or so yet—I didn't want to heal everything! However, the pain won't be an issue, not with the way I knit your ki together."

Blum's thought processes confounded Ingrid. The Ambassador had no restraint on her tongue and acted strangely *honest*. She seemed the opposite of a sly politician, the sort Ingrid would've expected in such a role.

The soldier grabbed Ingrid by an elbow and pulled her upright. "My pardon, Madam Ambassador, but will the gag remain in place?"

"For now. I'll come up in a few minutes and supervise her as she drinks and uses the facilities, but yes, I fear she'll need the gag. She'll cause a fuss if she can. The police should have a cell ready for her upstairs. The guard can show you where."

Blum cupped Ingrid's chin and forced their gazes to meet.

"Ah, pet, don't look so miserable. That captain was myopic in his treatment of you for entirely the wrong reasons. He operated with the information he had, poor as it was. Now I'm here to attend to you." Her lips pressed together. "So many distractions right now. Bothersome, when plans must be adjusted.

My rock *must* be swiftly recovered. Mr. Sakaguchi and his Chinese allies must be found as well. It would be helpful if the rock and men were all in the same place, but in my experience, humans are rarely *convenient*. Well! I'll parley with Mr. Sakaguchi soon enough. I imagine he has interesting tales to tell."

Ingrid breathed through her powerless anger, her mouth parched against the gag.

Blum sighed and smoothed her skirts. "Best to get you indoors before another seism. Being upstairs should mean very little energy conducts to you, Ingrid, and if it does? Do remember that there are apartments and businesses in the floors above. It'd be a shame if a pressure wave caused the building to collapse. A steel framework is better than mere brick, but it would still topple like twigs. Ah, yes, I know all about what you can do. I studied your father, and I have a hunch you're his superior in geomancy. It'll be our secret, yes? The men would never understand. In the morning, we'll breakfast together and chat. I'd like to learn more about you."

Ingrid almost wanted that talk. Almost. Blum was the nexus. Ingrid desperately wanted to know about Papa, and this Gaia Project, and why this woman thought of a horse-sized piece of kermanite as her property.

Ambassador Blum patted Ingrid on the cheek. "Let's go inside. You need your rest."

Ingrid closed her eyes and shuddered. As much as she wanted to know more, it wasn't likely to happen, not if the attack at Mussel Rock succeeded.

That might be a mercy for the world. The loss of San Francisco would be minor compared to the devastation Ingrid could cause if she lived in Blum's custody.

Once Ingrid was in a cell, Blum was generous enough to secure her arms in front of her body. "Restraining hands at the back is terribly taxing on the shoulders. I'd rather the life energy focus on mending your leg and other wounds."

Any efforts to talk while taking a drink had been instantly squelched. "Leave your arguments and rage until the morning. Try to say a word more and I'll gag you again, and you'll have to stay thirsty."

A few seconds later, Ingrid was gagged, this time with a scarf. She didn't miss that irony. Blum tied it so the knot pressed like a rock against Ingrid's jawbone.

Ingrid's anger festered beneath her skin just as it had every time she poured coffee for the wardens, or filed paperwork for mindless hours, or wore those damned house shoes while most everyone else wore socks.

She'd finally earned respect as a geomancer, only for this result.

No one else occupied the prison corridor. Her cell sat in a far back corner and looked like any generic jail shown on the cover of a dime novel. Red bricks lined two sides, while the others consisted of black iron bars dinged by use and abuse. A lone light bulb flickered like a weak heartbeat.

Blum released the hobbles from Ingrid's legs and secured the door. On the other side of the bars, she paused to tug at a chain at her neck. A pendant emerged and lay at the level of her breasts. It was a small white ball, shaped like an onion.

Blum fondled the orb while staring at Ingrid. Ingrid stared back. Blum's behavior was purposeful, and Ingrid had the sense she was supposed to realize something and react, but her brain and body were too overwhelmed to cooperate.

"Well, the game's no fun when the opponent's too tired to play. Do try to get some sleep." With a small sigh, Ambassador Blum tucked the pendant away. Her brisk steps echoed down the hallway.

Ingrid's attention turned to her cell. Chains attached an iron cot to the brick wall. She sat on the fingernail-thin mattress and pressed her bound hands to her face. The mattress seemed only slightly worse than Cy's bed.

She knew Cy, Fenris, and Lee wouldn't leave the city without her. Cy had vowed that they were in this together and he'd never leave her behind, even knowing the danger involved if she were injured.

They'd try to save her, and when the Thuggees attacked, they'd die.

That area South of the Slot was so prone to liquefaction that any significant seism would render dirt the consistency of soup. Fenris and Cy's workshop abounded with flammable materials, as did so many buildings around. Cooking fires alone caused so many blazes throughout the city. This—this would be so much worse.

Well, Ingrid wouldn't burn to death, not by fire. More likely, the power overload would cook her internal organs within her sack of skin and kill her within a minute.

The church down the block tolled out twelve times. Five hours to go.

Mr. Sakaguchi's advice stayed with her. She couldn't go out without a fight.

She brought her fingers to the gag. The scarf was tied so tightly she couldn't even fully wedge the tip of a thumb beneath it, and the mere effort tore at the corners of her mouth.

Growling deep in her throat, she wormed off her slippers and winced as the mending muscles in her calf contracted. She eyed the cell. The space was about ten feet by ten feet. Not huge, but it was something. She backed up to the bars and took a deep breath. The brick wall opposite looked nice and solid. Good. She sprang off of the bars, forcing her leg to work, forcing herself headfirst into the bricks.

Pain. Horrible pain. Dazzling white stars. The ceiling spun like a child's top, complete with flashes of color and vague animal shapes. Seconds later, the shiver of the earth arrived, as mild as a cold chill. No wave of energy. The structure of the building had absorbed it. She spat profanity against the gag.

Ingrid closed her eyes to make the world go still. She could keep hurting herself and accumulate power that way, but it'd be too slow, and carried too much risk for everyone else around.

Besides, Ambassador Blum would be on the alert. One earthquake she might dismiss, but too many of these tremors would cause her to return to Ingrid's place of imprisonment.

She scooted herself to sit, waited for the world to steady its spin again, and then used the brick wall to stand. Hot tears pooled in her eyelashes. She had to find a way out.

Ingrid paced. She examined. There were no guards here to bribe, even if she could speak. She kicked the bars and bricks.

She tested the chains at her wrists. Iron. A smart choice, since it deadened magic so efficiently. It would take an enormous swell of power to shatter those. Her tangled hair tormented her eyes as she looked for some weakness in the walls, some possibility of escape.

Nothing.

The clock struck one. She sat in the corner, her skirts hitched up so she could squeeze her arms between her knees. The room was cold. She was cold. Her leg ached. The city she loved was about to be destroyed and no one would listen to her. She thought of Cy, the sandpapery scrape of his lips and the gentle whiff of coffee on his breath, and smiled. No regrets.

Maybe next time she wouldn't be alone in his bed.

Darkness stole over her.

Several restless hours later, heat woke her.

CHAPTER 17

April 18, 1906

The heat didn't come in a slow, tingling caress. No, it seared as though she'd been dropped into Nebuchadnezzar's oven. She screamed as her eyes burst open, the sound muffled by the tightness of the scarf. That's when she heard the rumbling. Cliché as it was, the sound was like an approaching train, roaring and threatening to run her down. A hundred repetitive auxiliary lessons flared in her brain. Go. *Go.*

Ingrid launched herself at the iron bars, and as she struck them, remembered her hands were shackled at the wrist. She gripped the bars as best she could, inches apart as they were, and kicked her feet off the floor. It took only a second of extra effort to kick off the slippers, but it cost her. Despite being in a modern building, despite being on the second floor, she sucked in energy like a sponge. Her vision wavered in a feverish mirage, and then she realized it was no mirage. The room rocked and rolled like an ocean wave flowing northward.

Mussel Rock was south. This was the attack.

The flickering light in the corridor exploded, the sound muffled by the terrible roar, as if a geomantic Hidden One had reared up to devour the city itself. The throaty rumble of the earth didn't stop.

Ingrid pressed her forehead to the bars. Through the haze of energy sickness, she concentrated on a roughly welded seam of her iron handcuffs. The link exploded. The recoil knocked her back, but just in time she managed to grip the bars again, her hands spaced out. Her toes clung to a narrow crossbar.

Keenly aware of the heat of her breath, she focused on the scarf in her mouth. The fabric weakened beneath her exhalation, and when her tongue jabbed forward, the scarf shredded and fell away. She gasped in relief despite the rawness of her lips.

The roar continued, punctuated by nearby avalanches of bricks, cascades of breaking glass, and screams. So many screams.

If Ingrid could stay here, on the second floor, she might survive. She'd be ill, but she could manage.

Dust sifted from the ceiling. A magnificent crack resounded through her ears and reverberated through her body. In the darkness, it was nigh impossible to see, but she felt the floor give. It groaned like an arthritic old man standing upright. The bars in her grip leaned forward.

"Oh God," she whispered. The roar swallowed her blasphemy.

The whole building folded inward. With a mighty snap, the iron bars ripped from the floor in a long untidy row. A ceiling tile crashed down, followed by another. Dust thickened the air, and then she fell. She released her grip on the bars and let the heavier weight drop away as she drew on the terrible heat that roiled in her chest.

A protective bubble snapped into existence. Even filtered, the roar continued to reverberate through the shell, far worse than the auxiliary explosion. This was deeper, more prolonged. Blackness and dust squelched light from the world.

The bubble smashed into solidness, throwing her forward. She grunted as her hands caught most of the blow. A great weight pressed down on the back of the bubble. Her awareness of the debris felt different from the auxiliary blast. It took her a half second to realize why: she absorbed the energy-laden reverberations through shattered bricks and wood.

She fell forward again into nothing, that new source of energy cut off. A splash of water embraced the bubble and she rocked backward, momentarily floating.

Water? The ground might be liquefied, but how could it be that she was in actual water? She was nowhere near the bay. Bubbles streamed past. She shoved herself to stand upright. Her bubble rocked and rested. Water sloshed at chest level. Heat surged through her feet as she took in more energy. Ingrid screamed and caught herself against the pseudo glass before she could topple to her knees. Frothy water churned against her protective shell.

Thin illumination filtered from above. Something massive and dark blotted most of her view, but honest-to-God morning sunlight shone from on high. This was the basement Ambassador Blum had mentioned. The quake had burst the water main.

Ingrid quivered as her heart threatened to gallop from her breast. Nausea bubbled in her stomach. The quake wasn't stopping. She had to break contact with the ground. Cy wasn't here to help, nor would selkies come to her aid. She had to get out on her own.

Cy—she had pushed him away with her power before. Maybe she could push the floor away, too.

Ingrid breathed in. All she tasted, smelled, touched was heat. She angled her head to stare downward, and she shoved herself away.

With a brilliant gunfire-loud crack, the bubble soared. Light blinded her, a cloudy sky tilting into view. While she was airborne, the flow of power was squelched again, but she had already taken in so much. So very, very much. The bubble faded. The harshness of smoke and dust smacked her senses, and then she pounded into the ground shoulder first. She screamed. Within the haze of fever, the sound felt disconnected and foreign. Her body landed splayed on ground, still coursing with power. She convulsed.

"Get up! Move!" Mr. Sakaguchi yelled in her ear. "If you stay still in a massive earthquake, you'll die. You have to get off the ground."

"You're hurt!" snapped Mama. "You'll provoke another earthquake, perpetuate the cycle! Move!"

"Ingrid! Get up!" yelled Cy. "Come on!"

She lifted her head. Wind buffeted hair from her face and lapped coldness against her skin. She shivered, violently. She couldn't see. Her vision was blackness with white spots, but her ears recognized the low rumble of an airship engine.

"Vent it, Ingrid!" Cy yelled again.

Vent it. Get off the ground. Find metal, a tree, something.

She couldn't feel anything through her hands and feet. She flung out her right hand, blindly, and shoved out power.

The white specks faded from her vision. All she knew was the roar in her ears—the roar from above, the roar from below. It shook through her the way a terrier shakes a rat.

I'm dying.

Pressure seized her. The waves of power stopped, but stored energy still buzzed throughout her body.

"Ingrid!" Cy shouted into her ear. "I have you. You have to get some of the power out. There are people who need help. They're trapped in a building. I'm going to place your hand on something for you to push away. Do you understand?"

She tried to nod, but she wasn't sure if she had a head anymore, or a hand, or anything besides awful blackness and heat like hellfire.

But she felt the pressure of his broad hands around her wrist. She knew his touch. She trusted him. People needed help. She had to help.

"Now," he said.

Ingrid shoved power away. This time, she felt it go. The world lightened. The roar stopped, and there were other sounds. Not the common morning sounds of the city either. Screams. Thudding bricks. Sobs. The keen of a horse.

"Can you get out now?" Cy's voice was directed away from her. "There! Get out to the street, away from the building."

"Cy?" She could barely hear herself. Her throat felt raw and tight, as if squeezed between meaty fists.

"Ingrid. Thank God. You're burning up. Here. There's a car in the street. Push it away. Vent more."

She did. Blurry shapes took form, but they weren't buildings. The edges were too sharp, too strange. Acrid smoke stung her nostrils. A horse screamed again. A single gunshot rang out.

"Dios. Dios. El niño!" A woman half sobbed, half screeched.

"My husband, my husband, I can see his hand, I can—"

"God Almighty," Cy whispered.

"Buried?" Ingrid whispered. "I can help. Push."

"No. No. You can't help anyone in that building. Here. Is anyone alive in there?"

"Hai!" The man's voice was faint. "Under here. We're pinned."

This time, she felt the rough divots in a brick beneath her palm. She pushed it away with such intensity a hot wind sprung from her hand. There was an immediate rumble from above.

"Damn it!" Cy jumped backward, and she bounced in his arms.

"What? Did I—"

"No, no, it's not your fault, there was no other way to get him out. Christ!"

A wave of dust burned her eyes. She sneezed as his feet pounded backward. The movement speared agony through her shoulder. She screamed against his shirt.

"Ingrid?"

She pulled back and opened her eyes. A fog of brown and gray filled the air, but she could see Cy. A pair of thick aviator goggles covered his glasses. Her shoulder pulsed in pain, but it was an almost welcome sensation. She could feel something beyond the heat that relentlessly paced her body like a caged wyvern.

"I'm better," she whispered, then coughed. "The man . . . ?"

"Sir?" Cy called loudly as he walked forward. "Can you hear me?"

Ingrid clutched at Cy's lapel. Her handcuffs' chains dangled against his chest. He wore a tweed jacket powdered with gray. She could hear his rapid breaths, feel the racing thrum of his heart, but from the wreckage, nothing.

Islands of bricks and mortar rested in a sheen of blue. The miasma, turbulent as the ocean, lapped against the wreckage. Tall, elegant buildings had been rendered into architectural skeletons against a smoky sky. She could see flames only a block away. Their stench tainted the wind.

Figures staggered down the street. Men, naked but for blood and filth. Women and children in shredded nightgowns, a mother's hair up in a bonnet of rollers.

"It happened. It really happened." Ingrid had known it was real, had experienced the chaos for several minutes already, but seeing it—that was different. "The fires. The quake shattered the water lines, the fire department—"

"I know. We have to get out of here. What's left is a tinderbox." Cy cradled her closer in his arms and headed down the street. Part of her was indignant at being carried, but this was no time for pride.

Besides, the fog of power was so thick she wouldn't have been quite sure where to step with so much debris about. The last thing she needed was to hurt herself again while in direct contact with the ground.

That blue layer roiled in and out of a jagged crack that split the road. The miasma prevented her from seeing inside, but she had a terrible sense that it was deep. Where the fissure crossed beneath the cable car tracks, the metal rods curved through the air like a dead snake gone stiff in the sun.

"I thought I heard an airship," she said.

Cy coughed as they walked through a foul billow of smoke. "You did. The *Bug*. Our grand rescue attempt. Fenris got me low enough to jump out. We saw you fly out of the building. It was beautiful. And awful." His voice lowered to a whisper.

"You jumped out of an airship? Onto pavement?"

"What was I going to do, look for a mattress to land on? I had to. You were—you were dying. I've seen death. I know it. Grabbing hold of you felt like gripping a live coal with both arms. I don't know how you're still alive."

The Ambassador's Reiki. It used living animals. That's probably all that prevented her brain from boiling in her skull. "How long did the earthquake last? It felt like forever."

"A minute, I think, but it looked like forever. God as my witness, I never want to see anything like that again."

She shivered as heat lapped her skin again. His body created a gap between her and the earth, but he was still organic, and still conducted power.

"Cy, off the ground! Now!"

He didn't hesitate. In two mighty bounds he made it to the bumper of an autocar and from there onto a hood already peppered with broken bricks. The earth shuddered, followed by another roar. Ingrid slid down to stand. Her rubbery legs wobbled and she almost fell, but Cy grabbed hold of her.

His head jerked up. "Ingrid!"

From instinct, she formed the bubble around them, venting power even as more heat trickled in through her feet. She looked up as the full brick facade of a building smashed into them. Tons of material bounced and cascaded off the barrier. The dust didn't reach them, trapped inside as they were, but a cloud of brown blocked out the world. Cy pressed her head to his chest. His heart drummed a chaotic, fearful beat, even as he felt so strong and stalwart against her.

"Why won't this end?" she whispered.

"It's not . . . not because the earth feels your pain, is it?"

"I was hurt last night, but no, I can say this wasn't my fault. Thank God."

"You were hurt?" Rage rumbled in his words. The cloud around them began to dissipate.

"It wasn't the soldiers. They . . . It was an Ambassador. Ambassador Blum. She knew about Papa, she knew what they had done to him. She . . . she stabbed me to see what would happen."

"God Almighty." His breath drew in with a hiss. "Ambassador Blum. I'd call her a bitch, but that'd offend many fine dogs."

"You know her?"

"Know her? Yes, I know her." The bitterness in his tone surprised her. It didn't sound like Cy at all. "Blum oversaw the building of my prototype Durendal most every day for months.

She omitted the minor fact that she was an Ambassador, though, among other things."

"But the signet ring—"

"She always wore gloves, like some proper lady." His grip around Ingrid tightened, as did the hard line of his mouth. "Ambassador Blum. I wonder if she's incapable of lies. She'll tell you everything, yet nothing all at once. Most dangerous person I've ever known."

The dust settled enough that they could see again. Ingrid let the bubble collapse and immediately began to cough. Agony seared through her shoulder. Cy held her upright. She cringed into him, dreading another earthquake in response to her pain. She felt the slightest burble, but the solid metal of the car did its job.

The autocar had become an island in a sea of bricks set within a greater ocean of deep blue fog, like gradients of color around a Caribbean atoll. The building beside them was exposed at the front like a little girl's dollhouse. There was a parlor, and an office with fine cherrywood furniture, and a bathroom where black water spurted from a shower head. A bed looked perfectly made but for a single ceiling beam dropped into the middle. A pale arm draped outside of the sheets.

"Ingrid, look at me. Not the building." Cy's broad hands cupped both sides of her face and angled her head to look at him. Dust painted his cheeks in blotchy brown. His voice sounded softer again. "Where did Blum stab you?"

She blinked as she struggled to remember what they had been talking about. "My leg. She used dark Reiki right after so it didn't hurt for long. It's even helping my shoulder now."

"We've got to get to the docks to meet Fenris."

"He can't fly through here again? There's no rope ladder?"

Cy gave her a look as he scooped her up in his arms. "Miss Ingrid, that works dandy in books, but in reality, if you have a loose rope dangling beneath anything smaller than a Tiamat class, it'll get sucked up into a turbine and could very well cause an engine fire. That's why mooring is tricky business."

"Oh." Bricks slid and crumbled underfoot as he hopped to the street. It unnerved her that she couldn't see his feet through the cloud. Heat still fizzled through her, as present as the miasma. The bubble had helped, but it only offset so much damage.

"Thuggees are behind the attack. I overheard their plot last night as I left Quist's. The attack was set for dawn at Mussel Rock. Maybe they're still there."

Would San Francisco ever rise from this? Tears and filth burned her eyes. The city looked like a newsreel from Peking or Calcutta or Manila, the aftermath of hellfire and prolonged warfare. This was war. That was the attackers' intent. Why? Why strike here, not at a British holding?

Smoke lashed her face. People hobbled past, crying, muttering, some absolutely still. An older woman limped past in a long calico nightie, chin uplifted and a small straw hat on her head. In her hand she held a cage containing cooing lovebirds.

"How are they doing this? Do they . . . do they have your father?"

What a terrible thought. "Sutcliff and Blum both said Papa was dead. Killed in China. This . . . maybe there are others like me, like Papa. I don't know. But the man who did this killed everyone else in the auxiliary so the attack could proceed without interference."

"We'll find him. We'll interfere. But foremost, let's get to the airship and far away from Blum."

Ingrid could see the spire of the Port Authority still upright straight down Market Street. The shredded skyline revealed mooring towers and gasbags that should have been hidden behind skyscrapers.

"Look," she said, bobbing her head instead of pointing. Far down the pier, two Portermans were ablaze. Flames clawed the sky as the airships danced and quickly sagged, hydrogen depleted.

"The whole port may go up. If Fenris can't moor here, we'll have to catch a boat and get to Oakland." He put more hustle into his step, though he already breathed heavily from exertion.

Up ahead, a man sobbed and cried out as he dug through bricks. Ingrid squeezed Cy's arm. "We can work that way, but I'm still holding too much power. My fever must be around a hundred and two."

"Ingrid." He said her name in a way that warned her a lecture was coming. "You may not be able to do much. Your power's strong, but it's a bludgeon. These buildings—it'll take time and care to get people out, and God help us all, but they don't have time and neither do we."

A full five-story building was alight. One side of the structure had caved in. It slouched against its neighbor like they were sailors leaving a Barbary Coast saloon. Dark windows lit up with flashes of red. People stood in the street and dumbly stared.

A loud bell dinged behind them. Cy turned. A fire wagon made to turn and confronted debris. Swerving away with the bell still ringing, the wagon rumbled down a side street, taking with it a load of half-dressed helmeted men.

Tears coursed Ingrid's cheeks. Even if the firemen made it down the block to that particular building, there wouldn't be any water. The mains had likely snapped beneath all of downtown.

Blood-streaked women stumbled past. In the road, a milk wagon sat unblemished, its wooden sides ornate with swirls of color. On the far side, a dead horse slumped in the shafts. Bricks almost completely buried it from head to yoke. Tufts of mane emerged through dust like grass in a sand dune. The horse's haunches were still propped up as if it knelt to drink from the shifting blue fog.

"You got a light?" a man asked. He stood outside a wrecked building as if he waited at a cable car stop. A gigantic suit jacket draped over his bare torso and red flannel pants. An unlit cigarette waited between his lips.

"Don't light anything," snapped Cy. "The gas lines have been ruptured. The slightest spark will start more fires."

"Damn." The man lifted a hand to his cigarette. The large sleeve slid back to reveal half of his fingers in a mass of mangled, flattened flesh. Spears of bone pierced through the tips. His hand trembled violently and lowered again. "Can't think why, but I can't work my lighter."

Ingrid sucked in a sharp breath. "How does he not know?" she whispered.

Cy walked on. “He’s in shock. It happens in battle.” Rivulets of sweat trickled around his goggles and dribbled clean lines down his neck.

The tower of the Port Authority still had to be seven or eight blocks away. It was hard to gauge with other landmarks shattered. Several gunshots cracked the strange quiet of the morning. Something moved down the street. Several somethings. People screamed. Ingrid squinted to see.

Bulls. Just a few at first, then a full herd. They crowded the avenue. Even from blocks away, she could hear the mad clatter of cloven hooves on asphalt.

“God. The pens down at the port. Cy—”

He twirled in place as he looked to either side, back up the street, and then to the stampede again. “There’s nowhere to go!”

Down the way, a man was tossed up by a pair of horns. He flew upward, slack like a doll, and landed somewhere amid the pounding of hooves.

“Kneel down,” Ingrid ordered.

Cy immediately dropped down to one knee, Ingrid’s derriere supported by his bent leg. Her bare feet dangled; the ambient heat of the miasma stroked her skin and scalded her nerves. She drew in her breath with a sharp hiss.

Hoofbeats reverberated through the pavement and sent shudders through their bodies. Cy hugged her closer. A gun fired once, twice, followed by a bovine wail.

Ingrid shifted enough to face the onslaught, and instantly regretted it. Even after all the awful things she had just seen, she quailed to be at leg level to a mob of frenzied cattle. Their black eyes had rolled back to reveal glints of white. Froth flew from their lips. They were a churning wall of brown, their musky scent so thick it blocked the stink of smoke and dust.

Half closing her eyes in order to focus, Ingrid thrust out a hand as if to halt the bulls.

CHAPTER 18

Heat poured from her palm like water from a pitcher. The bulls didn't slow or swerve. Ingrid grimaced and ground her teeth as she braced for impact. Cy's grip on her strengthened. If he dug in any tighter, he'd rip through silk to her bare skin. The basalt underfoot shuddered and then the lead bulls smashed into her shield.

There was a blur of brown, a vision of flailing hooves, and a deafening cacophony of squeals and grunts. She poured out more heat as the bubble flexed and quivered. A bull reared up and bounced off the top. She felt it—the weight, the momentum, even the surreal scratchiness of the scabbed hide—as it slid off the far side. Then came the next crash. A bull crumpled headfirst, neck snapping. Its back end flipped up like another layer of shielding, followed by fleshy smacks and slices and squeals. Hot blood and gore splashed against the bubble. The hide tore apart like parchment. Entrails showered over them in glossy chunks. She flinched, blinking, anticipating the hot splatter. Instead, the bubble glazed over in red.

Nausea rose in Ingrid's throat and she clenched her eyes shut, but sounds left nothing to the imagination. Raw, juicy tearing of flesh. Animal screams. Hard hooves sloshing and sliding. Thuds and thunks of tons of bodies clashing against them. Cy's fingers pressed deeply into her thigh, almost painful, but she didn't want his hold to slacken. They clung to each other, breaths rapid in terror. Then, abruptly, the pounding faded and the shudders moved past.

She opened her eyes. The fever still flowed through her, but her mental clarity had increased. Perhaps too much.

Thin light filtered through a dome of red dye accentuated by black spatters of God-knew-what. The blue fog couldn't mask the slaughterhouse-sized piles of meat mounded around them. It was as though the bulls had been packed with explosives. Some remnants were recognizable as hooves or horns or scraps of hide, but the rest was red, mushy pulp.

The air already felt drained and swampy within the bubble. Her extended hand trembled, the weight of the chain dragging on her wrist. "I've got to . . . I've got to . . ."

Cy sucked in a quivering breath. "I'm ready."

Ingrid shut her eyes, cringing, and let the shield fall.

A slurry of hot blood and flesh rained over them. Ingrid had thought the meat market on a hot day was bad enough, but nothing compared to the fresh, raw, and rank odor that surrounded and coated them. The mush that had leaned against the barrier slid inward, sloshing against Cy's legs. Something slippery and warm pressed against her bare feet. She shuddered.

Cy cupped her body closer and stood. His arms trembled with exertion; strong as he was, he was wearing out. His feet slid as he gingerly stepped through the muck. He made it about ten feet to perch her on the tiny unburied bumper of a metal wagon. She clung to the iron caging as Cy turned away and retched.

"There," he said. He reached a hand to wipe the back of his mouth, then looked at his hand and thought better of it. Instead, he swept a thumb over the lenses of his goggles.

"Cy, you're strong, but you can't carry me all the way."

"I can throw you over my shoulder."

"I wouldn't be able to see what's coming to shield us!"

His eyes clenched shut within the goggles, and then he opened them again and looked past her. "Mother of God. Not them, not now."

Ingrid was barely able to shift on her precarious shelf to look down the street. Soldiers. "There are thousands of soldiers at the Presidio. These can't be Sutcliff's men."

"Blum'll have the full fort at her disposal. If you're alive, you'll be in this area. They'll be told to look for you."

"Good thing I decided to switch to a red dress."

A weary smile creased the bloody dapples on his face. "I have an idea."

He carried her down the next block, past more bodies and debris and a few bulls that'd been shot square in the head. He headed down a side street. Heavy smoke rolled over them and caused them both to hack and choke. Cinders whirled on the wind. This whole block was bound to go up in minutes.

"Oh, of course! There's a boarding stable over here." Ingrid could see the wooden storefront still intact. "But we can't trust any horses right now. They'll be as crazed as the cattle, probably more so."

"I'm sorry, Miss Ingrid, but any sort of noble conveyance will need to wait for another day." The wooden gate to the stables had already been busted down by an ax or hooves; whatever had done it had left the posts splintered. The sound of frenzied neighing rang out from the enclosure. Earthquakes, and now fire. The horses knew.

Cy headed straight to a wheelbarrow half filled with manure. Ingrid couldn't help but burst out laughing, even though it sparked more pain in her shoulder.

"Really, Cy?"

He kicked off the peak of the fecal mountain and looked around, as if for a place to set her down. With no options in sight, he plopped her onto the fetid pile. She winced at the prickling of straw, but by God, she was not going to complain. It couldn't make her look or smell worse than she already did.

Cy shook out his arms. "What? It's going to be a cushy ride—better than a wooden bench."

"It's a good thing I'm not some proper lady," she said.

"I thought you were quite proper last night."

"Well, yes, and this is the morning after."

"What's tonight going to be like, then? No. I don't even want to know." He grinned, shaking his head. "Now, if you'll pardon me for a moment."

He advanced into the stable. At the opening of the door, the desperation of the horses grew louder—squeals, kicks, panicked snorts. She heard the snap of a lock. A horse galloped past, then another, then a dozen. Sweat soaked their withers and left long salty lines down their crests, as though they had been hauling heavy wagons uphill all day long. Embers waltzed down from the heavens.

Cy emerged, and at that moment Ingrid realized she was utterly, incorrigibly in love with the man.

Something must have shown in her gaze; he gave a little dismissive shrug as he stepped behind her to grab the handles. "I have a deep and abiding affection for horses. Wasn't about to leave them to burn."

Yes. She loved him.

Ingrid gripped the metal sides of the wheelbarrow as he heaved it up. He wheeled her out to the street and deeper into the mishmash of businesses South of the Slot. The wooden wheel roared against the asphalt. A few reedy boys darted past, their arms loaded with burlap bags. Somewhere nearby, screams repeated to a strange rhythm. She hunched up her shoulders as if she could block out the sound. Cy jogged down a block, then two, dodging debris. Several buildings smoldered. A rancid stream of black water gushed from a sewer grate.

"Stop! Stop there!" a deep voice yelled behind them. Cy turned. Ingrid leaned to see around him. A portly man advanced on them, holding out a rod with a blue crystal on the tip.

"Sir?" asked Cy, as pleasant as always.

"I need that wheelbarrow. Fire's coming, and I must empty my vault." Ashes danced on a wind that was far too warm for a crisp April morning.

"I'm sorry, sir, but this woman is injured. We need to get to the dock. If you go to the stable a few blocks back—"

"No! You're here, my building's here!"

The blue fog churned, boiling. "Cy!" Ingrid gasped.

That slight distraction was all the stranger needed. With a wildness in his eyes reminiscent of the stampeding cattle, he dove forward, Tesla rod extended. Cy shifted to draw his own rod, but she knew he wouldn't be fast enough.

The thin structure of the wheelbarrow hardly filtered the heat that coursed upward and directly into her spine. Her vision speckled in black. She reached out blindly for Cy and found the backseat of his pants. Propriety damned, she planted her palm against his pocket. She pushed out power just as she heard the electric zap of the rod and a loud crackle as it made contact. Cy cried out.

No. She would not allow him to be hurt.

Ingrid couldn't see the electricity with her eyes, but she knew it. She knew power. Heat channeled through her palm and through Cy. She envisioned him like a lightning rod on a rooftop, the electricity passing straight on through. She sheathed his skin, creating a formfitting bubble, but the power still needed an outlet, as hers did. The blast from the Tesla rod coursed atop his skin but couldn't penetrate. She felt the spark against her palm like a question, a test, as it tried to enter her instead. She gritted her teeth and shoved it away.

Denied, it glanced back across Cy's body and straight into the rod, which promptly exploded. The recoil sent Cy lurching backward over the wheelbarrow handles. The wheelbarrow tipped. Ingrid screamed as she slid off her bed of manure.

She couldn't touch the ground. She wouldn't.

She made herself stop.

The boiling heat of the miasma licked and lapped at her skin. Ingrid opened her eyes. She hovered inches over the basalt, floating atop the blue fog like an Italian fishing boat on the bay. She vented energy in order to stay up, even as she absorbed more.

"Cy, if you don't mind, can you pick me up?" Her voice sounded unnaturally high to her own ears. Cy stood with a scrape of boots on basalt bricks. The wheelbarrow rattled as he set it upright.

"Woman, you amaze me. I don't know how you did that, how you do any of this." He bent beside her. His arms fit against her curves. At his touch, she undid her hold on gravity and sagged against him.

"I'm learning as I go." She nestled back into her bed of manure. The fever made her fuzzy-headed again. Her vision warped the cityscape like a mirage. Venting power didn't do enough, not as the quakes continued. She let her eyes close. "That was . . . almost flying."

"Don't tell Fenris. He may want to test that hypothesis."

"What happened, back there? The man, he—"

"He's gone, Ingrid. The metal shards, they . . . just take my word."

"Oh." A pause. "I killed him." She expected more guilt, more emotion, but instead she just felt tired. Her stomach roiled, and even with the world in black, everything bobbed and wavered.

"You didn't mean to."

"I bet Papa didn't mean to kill anyone in China either, but he did. What am I? What is this? For God's sake, geomancy is supposed to be a business venture, all about energy and rocks. Not this. Not this." Her words slurred.

"We're almost to the dock. Hold on."

She did. She clenched the curved metal lips of the wheelbarrow and shut her eyes against the world. The foulness of smoke increased. Buildings crackled as they burned. She licked her lips and tasted blood and soot.

The fresher scent of salt and fish carried on the wind. The fierce roar of kermanite engines on high, louder now with the lack of ground traffic, almost drowned out the madness along the Embarcadero.

"Come on, lads! Get aboard!"

"Should we grab the freight? We need to get paid! This lot's expected in San Diego—"

"Please, let us on! We don't have money but I swear—"

"Mama! Mama, it hurts, it hurts!"

Ingrid squinted. The world still wavered. "Damn it all, why won't you behave yourself?" she growled at the blue-fogged ground.

"What?" asked Cy, leaning closer.

"Nothing," she muttered.

"I don't see the *Bug* along this section," he said. The wooden wheel whirred beneath the cart as he pushed her along at a good clip.

"Hey! You, with the wheelbarrow! I'll pay you five hundred cash for that!"

The wheelbarrow rolled faster. "She's injured! I need it for now!" Cy yelled over his shoulder, then muttered, "I should probably carry you again. This many people, there could be a riot over this cart, but I would feel better if I could—there! I see it!"

"The airship?" she mumbled. Dirigibles often looked alike with their white or parchment-colored envelopes and golden orichalcum cockpits. They looked even more alike now, as airships danced in place like chorus girls, multiplying as she watched. She giggled to herself. At least airships didn't kick their heels in the air.

Blurry as everything was, she did recognize a larger craft farther down, the bold red circle of the rising sun on the side. She shivered at the thought of Ambassador Blum.

"Ingrid." Cy's hand rested on her forehead. "God Almighty. You're almost as hot as when I found you." His skin, sticky with matter, tugged at hers as he pulled away.

"Every time I vented, more quakes," she mumbled. "Couldn't . . . wear it down. If had kermanite . . ."

"There are empty crystals on board, I made sure of it. They're small, but better than nothing. Stay with me, Ingrid." His arms scooped around her waist and thighs again. Nuggets of manure plunked onto the ground as he lifted her.

Her head rocked against his chest. It was nice there. Cozy. "Like it how you say my name, even when you say 'Miss.' 'Mizz-ing-red.'"

"I like saying your name, Miss Ingrid." His low whisper sent a different kind of hot chill through her.

"We survive this . . . I want a bath. And . . . kiss you again. Not at the same time." Not that that was such a bad thought for later on, but during this particular bath? Absolutely not. The tub would need to be steeped in bleach afterward.

Cy smiled beneath his goggles. "Let's focus on surviving first."

Being so close to the airship brought a new spring to his step. They abandoned the wheelbarrow and he worked his way through the teeming mob. Men and women yelled up at the towers and airships, waving cash in hand. Men with shotguns guarded mooring towers. Children cried. Babies wailed. Caged chickens, in a frantic and fluttering mass, showered the ground with speckled feathers.

"That ship can fit my boys! We aim to take it, and no damn pigtail's going to stop us! You been beaten, but we can finish the job."

"This pigtail could notch your earlobe at a hundred yards, so you might want to think about what I could do at ten feet."

"Lee," Ingrid whispered.

Cy rounded a stack of crates and the black steel base of a mooring tower came into view. A gang of about six or eight men blocked the way. She recognized the shape and color of a baseball bat, but couldn't identify any other weapons right away. Not that it mattered. Even seeing them blurred, she could tell the men weren't saplings. They stood in a way that commanded respect and fear. Cy apparently agreed, as he quickly backstepped behind the crates again.

"Lee saw us," Cy whispered.

"I can . . . push them away."

"The tower is just on the other side, and so's Lee. You can't take the risk."

He was right. Even if she used a bubble to bowl them over, the pressure could strike those metal support legs. If she toppled one tower, the rest might collapse like dominoes, and the hydrogen—no, she wouldn't even think of that.

"I don't want to kill anyone. I didn't even want to kill those cows," she whispered.

"I know. Trust me, I know." He squeezed her against him. Yes, if anyone knew, he did.

A gunshot, very close, caused Cy to pivot his body around as he shielded Ingrid.

"Damn it!" a man screamed.

"Oh, come on, now. You didn't need that finger, anyway," said Lee. "It was naughty. It wanted to pull a trigger."

"Damn you to hell, you bastard chink."

"I am a bastard by quaint American standards! How did you know? Now, it's been really nice talking to you and your boys, but I hope you get the point. That airship up there? Not yours."

A siren blared farther down the dock, and voices rose in chorus. A woman screamed. Cy stood. Ingrid only had a view of more crates.

"God help us all," he muttered. "Cinders lit up an airship farther down. Behemoth class. We have to go. Now."

CHAPTER 19

Bold as a Durendal, Cy rounded the corner and confronted the gang directly. They had turned to face the sirens, some of them pointing. One man hunkered down on his knees, sobbing and rocking back and forth.

"Pardon me, gentlemen," said Cy, his voice as good-natured as if he passed them in a park. He weaved between the stunned men.

Lee stepped aside to let Cy through. His face was mottled in a camouflage pattern of purple and blue bruises. "About damn time. What did you do, take the cable car up to Nob Hill for a picnic? And is that *blood*?" His words hardly slurred now.

"Not ours," Cy said. "And the picnic's been postponed."

Ingrid wanted to say something, but she was just too tired. The weak morning light angled through the exposed diagonal support beams of the tower and draped a stripe of shadow over her face.

"Good to know. Now, boys, it's been nice chatting, but I believe we're ready to embark. Mister, you should really get that hand looked at. Thuggees get all the reputation for poisoning, but maybe chinks know a thing or two."

Cy headed up a narrow stairwell and took care to tuck in her head and feet at the turns. Lee's footsteps rattled behind them.

"Fenris should be pleased," Cy said over his shoulder. "Maiden flight and folks are already lined up to ride."

"Yeah, well, it's odd for me to say this, but I wish they were a higher-class sort."

"No, you don't. You'd have a lot harder time if it was a family with kids standing there and begging to board."

"Already dealt with that, and damn it, yes, it was worse. Sorry for the language, Ing. You can talk right? Ingrid?"

She opened and closed her lips but didn't manage more than a few limp jabs of her tongue.

Another flight up. "She's barely conscious. Her fever's too high. Every time she vented, another aftershock hit. The back-and-forth is wearing her out."

"I hear my friends coming up the stairs. I better play guard. Hey!" Lee yelled downward. "I hope nobody else has a naughty finger. Or head."

It was strange, being up this high. She could sense the distance from the ground. It made it easier to think, even if it didn't do anything to offset the energy already inside her. Shadows shifted, and then they were on the deck of the platform. Wind blasted her face. She caught a brief glimpse of the city sprawled below and sucked in a sharp breath.

Very quickly, Cy turned her face away to a view of the bay with Goat Island and the shore of Oakland beyond. Plumes of smoke drifted from that city, too. He hopped up a small wooden staircase, his body bowed over hers. She didn't have the strength to look around, but she sensed the claustrophobic interior of the *Palmetto Bug*.

"Could you have been any slower?" Fenris's voice carried down a short passageway.

"Yes," snapped Cy. "We could be dead. Ingrid, I'm going to set you down on the floor right here. Fenris, we've got to head toward Mussel Rock."

She slid out of his arms and caught herself on a palm to prop herself up, just barely. Her fingers rubbed at the tatami mat, taking in the slickness of the woven straw. Such a comfort to find a floor cool to the touch and in a color other than blue. She let her eyes close.

"Where's that?" yelled Fenris.

"South! Toward San Bruno Mountain! If you left the warehouse more often . . . !" Cy's words ended with a growl as his heavy boots pounded away.

"Damn. You have been to hell and back." Ingrid felt Fenris's presence over her. "Once we lift off, we'll get you cleaned up, okay? I loaded up on food and supplies. Hang in there." His voice softened to a surprisingly feminine timbre. Fingers glanced her cheek.

The engine revved with a soft purr. The floor vibrated. Half asleep, Ingrid started with panic as if another earthquake had struck. Her eyes opened. She had never been on an airship before. She had always been afraid of being aloft, of completely severing her connection with the earth. Now, if she had had the physical energy, she would have wept in relief. Male voices rumbled together and then Cy burst through the open hatch with Lee about two steps behind.

"Go! Go!" yelled Cy. He yanked on a tether and pulled up the hatch. The stairs attached to the door collapsed flat with a clang. The airship lurched upward, Ingrid's guts threatening to bounce higher than the rest of her body.

"Hey, Ing." Lee crouched beside her. "Sorry I couldn't linger before the shindig last night. I had a lot to do. Don't ask where I got these, okay?"

She felt his hand, icy cold against hers, and the hardness of stones pressed against her palm. She gasped. Her spine arched as the kermanite siphoned away energy. The wavering lines of the world didn't waver quite so much. Sweat dribbled down her temple.

"You brought kermanite?" Cy crouched on the other side. Together, they fully blocked the tight hallway. "I was just getting our stash."

Ingrid licked her lips. Blood still lingered in the creases. Cy scooted back, and seconds later he had a canteen to her lips. He placed gentle fingers beneath her jaw to assist in tilting back her head. His touch almost felt as good as the cold water on her raw throat. She was certainly giving the Reiki plenty to work on.

"Thank you," she whispered to Cy.

"No need to worry about that," he said. "Here. Fill these up, if you please."

Jagged kermanite the size of marbles rolled into her palm.

She curled her fingers to cover them as more power drained away. Some of the terrible tension in her chest eased, though her heart still raced as if it held as much power as the kermanite.

His hand brushed her brow. Funny, how his touch felt so distinct from Lee's. Cy's hands were large, the skin soft and rough at the same time, while Lee's fingers were fine and slender—more like Fenris's really. Ingrid snorted. The fever still had a firm grip on her. The city below was destroyed and here she was, waxing philosophic about her friends' hands.

The city had been destroyed.

She shoved herself off the floor, handcuffs rattling.

"Whoa! Take it slow!" said Cy. The man and boy had each gripped her by a shoulder as if to hold her down. Her injured shoulder now felt sore more than outright painful. "I can fold out the bunks—"

"I need to see," she said.

"Can you even walk?" asked Cy.

"I won't know unless I try, will I?"

Gritting her teeth, she took a tentative step. Lee backed off, but Cy didn't let go; he knew better. Ingrid leaned on the smooth orichalcum sheeting of the wall. Her legs wobbled, but they did work. Mostly. Her knees seemed to have a case of amnesia and couldn't quite recall to go rigid at times. She caught herself against the wall, and Cy's grip tightened enough to hold her up.

"I still want to know how you got bloodied like that," Lee said behind her. "Did you have to run through a slaughterhouse? And roll in manure?"

"The whole city's a slaughterhouse," said Cy.

"I didn't even expect you to be here, Lee," said Ingrid. She panted from exertion. "I thought you'd . . . go with the others." With his people, the people he somehow commanded.

"I have my reasons," said Lee.

"Lee, I'm really not feeling up to cagey responses."

"Why, I can't be here because I enjoy your company?" He scowled. Ingrid heard it in his voice.

She rested at the doorway to the cabin. The five-foot walk had drained her like a fifty-yard dash.

Three glass panels shielded the cockpit. There was enough space for two chairs side by side, and additional wooden seats flanked the doorway. Ingrid had expected artistry in Fenris's engine design, but the finery of the cockpit was far beyond her expectations. A waxed mahogany-and-copper dashboard held meters and monitors depicting numbers that she couldn't comprehend in the slightest. The whole thing shone as it emanated a sharp chemical scent. Vents in the floor and wall gushed excess heat circulated from the engine room. The two pilots' seats looked like fancy office chairs with their legs chopped off, the heavy wood and leather set upon pedestals.

And then there was the view beyond the window.

The *Bug* hovered near Alcatraz and looked south. The waters of the bay looked deep and peaceful compared to the smoking wreck of San Francisco. Exposed crosshatched lines demarcated block after block of charred and crumpled masonry. A few tall buildings still stood, but they looked small compared to the pillars of smoke that stretched to the clouds. Red and orange flickered from the debris.

With an audible blast, a Behemoth-class dirigible exploded with a spurt of brilliant white flame, setting off a cascade of pops as the two flanking crafts lit up. A string of tugboats sailed that way, water cannons already aimed at a warehouse as it caught the fluttering gasbags.

"Do you think your building is . . . ?" she asked.

"Oh, it's gone." Fenris shrugged. "The place was cheap and old. If the earthquake didn't do it, one of the fires from the dock will get there."

She swallowed a dry lump in her throat. Her house was in a better area, but that didn't mean anything. There were things that belonged to Mama she would have loved to have—a necklace brought over from Norway, the old family Bible with its genealogy, a few rings and things, an ivory knife that Papa gave Mama. There were possessions she would have grabbed for Mr. Sakaguchi, too, like his grandfather's katana set that had survived more than one earthquake on its native soil, and some old books that he particularly treasured.

Everything was gone. Even if the objects remained, she couldn't stay. Not with Ambassador Blum after her.

Even more, Blum was after Mr. Sakaguchi. Ingrid needed to find him first.

"Here, Ingrid, have a seat," said Cy, pointing behind him. It was a curt motion, with his arm so long and the space so cramped.

She let her body slide down the wall and onto the seat directly behind Fenris. A safety strap was a lump against her derriere. Cy climbed into the other crew seat, while Lee lowered himself onto the stool just across from her.

"Give me your hand," said Lee. She did. He pried a needle from his sleeve and began to pick at the lock of her handcuff.

"You're full of surprises," she whispered. He caught the handcuff as it unlatched and motioned for her other hand.

"You don't know the half of it, Ing. People are looking for me." Lee's voice was so quiet it almost blended with the soft purr of the turbines. He set aside the second cuff.

Ingrid rubbed her freed wrists. "What exactly are you saying, Lee?"

The boy sighed and glanced at the seats ahead of him. "It would really make it easier on all of you if I lied. Most people in Chinatown know me by association with Uncle Moon, and there's power enough in that. He's probably one of the best *lingqi* doctors of the past hundred years. Everyone fears him."

"So, you're saying that the people looking for you might kill us?" asked Fenris. "You do realize there's an existing queue for that, right?"

San Francisco was behind them. To the right sprawled the Pacific, and below rolled green hills wearing their spring finest.

"Yes, well, some people like to cut in line." Lee leaned against his knees and looked over at Ingrid. "Mr. Sakaguchi took me in. I was told, 'Go there. Be a servant and a student. Learn.' When a *tong* gives an order, you listen. I knew that, even if I didn't know what it meant to *be* Chinese through the first years of my life.

"I wanted to hate Mr. Sakaguchi. I did hate him, at the start. Somehow, that changed. He never treated me like a slave, or even a servant. He let me read books from his library, any book I wanted. I knew a boy in Chinatown whose hands were cut off because he touched one of his master's books. Mr. Sakaguchi wasn't like that."

Ingrid smiled softly. "No. We probably had the best education available."

"Probably." He smiled back, a lopsided and painful expression. "That was the whole point, that education. I'm expected to know everything American, Chinese, and Japanese."

"You do know everything," Ingrid added.

"I play the shadow well enough, I suppose, but it never seems like enough. Maybe if I'd known more . . ." He shook his head.

"You spied for your uncle." Cy looked over his shoulder as he pried the goggles over his head. The leather band, sticky with blood and muck, practically tore away from his hair. White circles of clean skin framed his eyes. He tweaked his glasses on the arch of his nose.

"Of course. Any Chinese in the city knows to pass along information. It's how we survive." Ingrid couldn't help but flinch, and Lee saw and sighed again. "Mr. Sakaguchi's smart. He knew what I needed to do. It doesn't mean I told them everything. It doesn't mean I told them about *you,* Ing."

"Does Mr. Sakaguchi know who you truly are?" she asked.

"Yes. And if you're going to play this game, you'll have to know, too." Lee Fong's gaze met hers, dark-eyed and fierce. "I'm the last living child of Emperor Qixiang, and I'm here as your volunteer hostage so you can get Mr. Sakaguchi back alive."

CHAPTER 20

"Emperor Qixiang."

"Yes," said Lee, clearing his throat.

Despite being with him on a daily basis for five years, Ingrid stared at Lee as if seeing him for the first time. His father, the model of that priceless statue in Chinatown? Lee Fong as the figurehead of the Chinese rebellion, the greatest enemy of America and Japan?

For God's sake, she'd engaged in tickle wars with him.

"But weren't your early years spent in a Catholic orphanage?" she blurted out. "How . . . ?"

"My mother was known to be one of Qixiang's concubines, the only one to stay with him through the end. But even more, the *qilin* acknowledges me."

Ingrid stared. A *qilin*. Known in Japanese as kirin, represented in the fawn-sized dragon statue Mr. Sakaguchi kept in the backyard. A fantastic so rare they were regarded as extinct or mythological. They were ancient and divine judges who only appeared to sages or rightful rulers.

"Didn't Qixiang die of smallpox here in California about fifteen years back?" asked Cy.

"Yes. I never knew him."

Cy leaned on a chair arm to frown back at Lee. "How does the heir to the Qing Dynasty end up with a Japanese warden?"

"This Sakaguchi seemed a bit overly involved," added Fenris.

Lee grimaced. "I wasn't allowed to ask."

"Not allowed?" Fenris's voice rose in pitch. "If you're the emperor's kid, who's to tell you what you can or can't do?"

"Emperor of what? Cities that look like *that*." Lee gestured sharply behind them. "Even in Chinatown, only a handful of people know."

It was bad enough that the UP thought Mr. Sakaguchi was somehow involved with the kermanite theft and the auxiliary explosion. If they knew he'd been hiding Qixiang's heir, approved by a *qilin,* on American soil . . .

"I don't understand why Mr. Sakaguchi kept you so close, Lee. He knew something bad was going to happen." She paused. "But he kept me here, too, even with the potential for other terrible things."

"A few months ago he called me in to talk." Lee stared away, frowning. "He said the Unified Pacific had targeted him. He said he could fire me. Accuse me of theft or something, give me a good excuse to keep my distance. The danger was, the timing could make me look even more suspicious. I told him I would stay, continue as normal. Uncle agreed."

"Mr. Sakaguchi knew who your uncle was?" asked Ingrid.

"Yes. I was carrying messages to Chinatown for him. I have for years. They were in code; I couldn't read them."

"You tried?" asked Cy, an eyebrow arched.

"Of course he tried," said Ingrid. "This is Lee. He's like a kitten, his nose into everything." She felt the urge to ruffle his hair, as she often did, but resisted touching him. The emperor's son and heir. "You . . . you think they will kill Mr. Sakaguchi, then. Eventually."

Lee sighed. "He's not going to cooperate. He doesn't want all us Chinese dead, but he's not going to help power rods or engines that'll be used against Americans either. Plus, he's Japanese. There are going to be some who'll want him dead from the start, just for that. With the earthquake, the *tongs* on the run . . . it's complicated, Ing."

Always. "How long do we have?"

"I don't know. Weeks, maybe."

Mr. Sakaguchi, working with a *tong*. Keeping Qixiang's heir in his own household. She wanted to grip her ojisan by the lapels and ask him, Why? Why work with such dangerous people, knowing that if the balance tipped, they would turn on him? Why fight for Papa, knowing the attention it would bring?

She knew the answers all too well. Because Mr. Sakaguchi was a fool. A darling, wonderful fool who wanted to save the world, no matter the danger it brought upon himself.

Wherever you are, Ojisan, I will find you. I will save you.

"Ambassador Blum and Captain Sutcliff were right," she whispered. "Mr. Sakaguchi was a traitor to the Unified Pacific. To Japan. But not to the United States."

Cy granted her a small smile. "He's not alone in those sentiments."

Cy was hiding for those same reasons. And then there was Mr. Roosevelt. He and Mr. Sakaguchi had plotted something for years. All their concerns about Japan, and what would happen after China was subjugated. Did Mr. Roosevelt know the truth about Lee? Mr. Sakaguchi had trusted Mr. Roosevelt enough to tell him about Ingrid's deviant geomancy, after all. Once Papa was captured overseas, Mr. Sakaguchi had made sure Mr. Roosevelt wouldn't take the fall with him.

She wanted to trust Mr. Roosevelt—for so many years, he and Mr. Kealoha had been Mr. Sakaguchi's dearest friends—but he was also an Ambassador like Blum. When Mr. Sakaguchi advised her and Lee to go to Mr. Roosevelt, he didn't know Ingrid's power would be revealed, that Ambassador Blum would join the hunt.

Good God, where were they supposed to go? What were they supposed to do? Who could they trust?

"Wait, wait." Fenris shifted around. The airship tilted slightly and he adjusted the steering without looking forward. "Blum? Did you say Blum?" He looked at Cy, one eyebrow raised.

"Don't tell me you had dealings with Ambassador Blum as well!" said Ingrid.

"An Ambassador—not Roosevelt—is involved? Damn," muttered Lee.

"Not personally, though, but I think Cy had dealings enough for both of us."

"Fenris," Cy growled.

Fenris responded with a flippant shrug as he tapped a panel above. A pair of binoculars attached to a brass arm dropped down, and he adjusted them to his eyes.

Ingrid blinked. "Maybe it's the fever, but is Fenris suggesting that you and Blum were . . . a couple? But she's . . ."

"An Ambassador, yes." Cy had flushed and stared at the floor between their seats. "I didn't know that at first, as I told you."

There were times for tact. This wasn't one of them. "Actually, my first reaction was that she's . . . old. She has to be in her sixties at least." She sat up straighter as if she could distance herself from him.

"What?" Cy looked genuinely confused. "She's near our age. That's why I never guessed she might be an Ambassador."

"Maybe Ingrid met her grandmother?" asked Lee. "What did she look like?"

"Long red hair, curly. Blue eyes. Freckles," said Cy.

Beautiful, in other words. The kind of pretty face that sold cigarettes at the Damcyan, that could sell pretty much anything. Had Cy *kissed* this younger Blum? Ingrid shifted her mouth in revulsion, as if he'd spread contamination to her lips. Had they done more than kiss?

"That's not who I met," Ingrid said, voice thick. "Like I said, she was much older, though gracefully aged. She looked Japanese, spoke English without an accent. Captain Sutcliff couldn't cut her hand off. She was definitely an Ambassador."

"That's about the most extreme way to verify an Ambassador." Cy's brow creased in a heavy frown, causing the red layer on his skin to crackle. "How peculiar."

"Captain Sutcliff. He acted terrified of her." Ingrid said the name again as thoughts slipped into place. "He knew who she was by name, but he didn't know her by her face. That's why he tried to cut off the ring."

"Like she had more than one face?" asked Lee.

The way that dogs reacted to Blum. Her keen senses. The way she manipulated Ingrid while always saying the absolute truth. The thickness of her dress at her derriere. That necklace she made sure to show off to Ingrid. "My God," Ingrid whispered. "She wore a hoshi no tama."

"A star ball?" said Cy. As soon as he said the words, he blanched. He was raised among the New Southern Nippon; he knew Japanese fables.

"Blum is a kitsune." Ingrid shivered, suddenly more terrified of the woman than she had been before. Fenris still looked blank, but Lee sucked in a loud breath. "A Japanese fox spirit, a shapeshifter that can look like a woman with fox tails. The more tails they have, the longer they've lived, the more powerful they are, the more forms they can take. Her dark Reiki was like nothing I've ever seen . . . I . . ."

Blum was a fantastic. A very old and very powerful one at that. How many tails did she hide beneath her skirt? That woman—that thing—had personally tortured Papa, and knew exactly how to torture Ingrid. That spirit would use Ingrid like hellfire to destroy an entire people.

She looked at Cy. Kitsune were tricksters and seductresses, but he hadn't seen Blum's tails or even the onion-shaped pendant at her neck that was said to contain part of her very soul. Ingrid felt an odd sense of relief.

"Forget Blum for a bit. We're nearing San Bruno Mountain and I see some curious activity down by the beach." Fenris made a sharp motion. Cy pulled down another pair of binoculars and began to scan. Ingrid stood to get a better look out of the window.

"Ingrid!" Lee yelped as he stood to help.

"I'm holding on to the seats," she snapped.

"Here." Fenris tugged on the hinged brass arm and brought the binoculars farther down. "Follow that dirt road toward the beach. No, not on the mountain's side, but on the Pacific."

As viewed from their elevation, water flanked both sides of the peninsula. San Bruno consisted of a long, green ridge that looked squat from so high up. Sinuous lines of smoke trailed into the sky. The earthquake's devastation extended far out into the hills, likely into the San Joaquin Valley.

Leaning on the seat, Ingrid pressed the binoculars to her eyes. A tree sprang into her vision in such stark detail that she pulled away in surprise.

"These things are powerful!"

"Military grade. Not technically for civilian use," noted Fenris.

"It's impressive how many things can fall off the back of a truck," said Lee.

"I found people down there," Cy said. "Took me a while. Fenris has eyes like a hawk."

Whereas Ingrid had bleary eyes that had been sporadically blinded over the past hour, and it didn't help that the miasma tinted everything in blue. She found the coast and followed it along until she spied a road and some large vehicles. "Is that a modified Durendal?"

"Yes," said Cy. "That model uses a hefty kermanite engine to haul logs or other heavy freight. There's a canvas over the back. If you look over to the right, there's a small airship."

It was a small passenger craft, about the same size as the *Palmetto Bug,* but designed for direct ground landings. Large, rubber-lined wheels skirted the sides of the gondola. Blue energy lapped the craft as if it rested in a wading pool.

"Direct landers aren't that good," muttered Fenris. "They crash easily. The tires often blow out on contact with anything sharp or hot and they're generally—"

"I'm not seeing anyone on the ground now," said Cy. "Engine on the truck just started up. Whatever's on there isn't simply large, but heavy." He glanced over at Ingrid. "That might be your missing kermanite."

"You're both machinists. How long would it take to build a weapon that could use kermanite of that size? Mr. Sakaguchi thought it would take a large effort, maybe all the factories in Atlanta."

"That's likely an exaggeration, but I reckon it depends on what you want to do with it. My question for you as a geomancer, Miss Ingrid, is how that kermanite could be filled so quickly."

She pursed her lips. "It couldn't be. Not yet. Even if a dozen average geomancers crowded around to touch it during the earthquake that just happened, it would barely pour anything into a crystal of that size. It would be wasteful to hook it up to anything before it was filled, too."

"Which means we're unanimous in that we have no idea what that is and how it works, but we know it or something near it just destroyed San Francisco. Dandy," said Fenris.

Ingrid's gaze panned back over to find the truck. The broad vehicle rattled down a narrow dirt road. Whatever it carried could definitely be the size of a horse, or larger. "It is leaving, which is good. Except . . ."

"Except what?" asked Lee.

"There's more involved here than the Thuggee weapon, than how animals have been acting for days, than Mr. Sakaguchi's namazu dying. I'd bet anything there's a Hidden One beneath the earth that's downright irritated. They don't calm down easily. There's one tale about a man climbing inside the shell of a Hidden One turtle and tickling it with a feather. The turtle convulsed later at the memory of the incident, causing more earthquakes."

"Doesn't sound like these Hidden Ones are very hidden," said Fenris.

"They usually are. Be on the lookout for any large fissures in the earth. We might actually be able to see something. Most sightings by natives along the Pacific Coast are from north of Sausalito and up as far as Vancouver."

Fenris adjusted some toggles. The noise of the engine changed as the airship entered a vertical climb. Turbulence rocked the dirigible as a layer of cotton draped over the cockpit. Ingrid could barely see snippets of blue-tinted green through shifting bands of moisture.

"There. We're hidden for a bit. We need to make a choice here," said Fenris. "What do we want to follow, the truck or the airship?"

"Airship."

"Truck."

Ingrid and Cy looked at each other.

"I don't know. Does this thing have guns or bombs we could use to stop them?" asked Lee as he stood.

Fenris scowled. "It's a Sprite class. It's not designed for heavy freight or weapons." Lee sat down again, disappointed. "Hurry, people."

"The man I overheard last night with Miss Rossi must have had an airship to get here this morning, and maybe he's still on board now," said Ingrid. "Follow them and maybe we can see what they have planned next."

"I'm guessing that the truck has the kermanite. If we have that, maybe we can prevent their next attack," said Cy.

"Oh, hell." Fenris scowled at them. "I'm breaking the tie. I say airship."

"You just want to chase another airship and prove yours is better," said Cy.

"I don't need to prove it. I know it." Fenris patted the mahogany dashboard. "So, Ingrid, what exactly do these not-so-Hidden-Ones look like?"

"The one in our area is said to be a massive double-headed snake," she said.

"A massive double-headed snake!" Lee brightened in that particular teenage-boy way, even through his bruises.

The truck drove out of sight. Anxiety twinged in her chest. Maybe they should have followed that instead, but she couldn't miss a chance to confront the man who had murdered so many in the auxiliary.

"Massive? How massive?" asked Cy.

"I don't know. It depends on how old the fantastic is, I suppose. In Japan, the magical sort of namazu is said to be so big that his head is under Hitachi and Honshu's on his back."

"The ship is lifting off!" Fenris practically cackled. In anticipation of movement, Ingrid grimaced and pressed a hand to her stomach. Cy stood, stooped, and squeezed past her.

"Which way are they going? I can't see!" cried Lee.

"North," said Fenris. "Probably want to check on their handiwork. There's plenty of cloud cover for us to trail them."

"Here, miss." Cy pushed a tin into her hand and slipped back into his seat. Ingrid opened the lid and found divided sections of ginger cookies and salted crackers. She knew from Mama's pregnancy that these were foods to quell an upset stomach. Cy and Fenris had taken care to pack this for her first airship flight.

"Thank you," she murmured, and sat back to eat.

"Are you sure they won't see us?" Lee leaned way over Fenris's shoulder to look out, and Fenris applied a quick jab to Lee's torso to force him back. Lee crumpled with a whimper. Ingrid stuffed the rest of a cracker in her mouth and dove to the floor, motioning Cy to stay seated.

"Oops. Sorry. Forgot about the ribs," said Fenris.

"Forgot? Forgot! Because I always look like this?" Lee moaned and returned to his bench seat. More turbulence rattled the craft.

"Buckle up," said Cy, reaching for his own harness. "The crosswinds here can be pretty strong, and the heat of those fires will affect the weather up here, too."

Ingrid slipped on the harness, wincing at the strain in her

shoulder. Lee cringed in a similar way. Clouds thickened as though they flew into a pillow. Jostled and exhausted as she was, the lack of a landscape made her nausea even worse. She shut her eyes and shoved cookies into her mouth. They were hard, store-bought, and not at all as good as the ones Mama used to make at Christmastime, but after all the foulness, they tasted divine.

"Damn," Cy whispered, the word almost lost against the soft purr of the engine and gushing vents.

She couldn't help but open her eyes. The clouds had cleared and afforded them a view of San Francisco from another angle. She hated looking, hated the sight of it, yet she couldn't look away. The patchwork blocks of the city she loved were slowly yet surely being eaten away by flames. Not even the fading blue fog could hide the devastation. The waterfront looked utterly gone, most of the dirigibles cast away or blending with the omnipresent blackness. Smoke suffocated the morning sun and cast a strange red glow.

"They're not turning to Oakland, not unless they're doing a wider pass to come back," said Fenris. Clouds whipped against the window and stole the view again. Ingrid couldn't even imagine how Fenris remained so cool and in control while flying blind.

"Are you sure they didn't see us?" she asked. Lee's hand snaked over to grab a fistful of crackers.

"Am I sure? Of course not. But it's unlikely. We're in their blind spot, and in clouds. And before you ask, we don't have a blind spot. I have mirrors, see?" Fenris pointed to disks located at various angles along the console and directly overhead where the glass met metal and showed a tinge of frost. Since she wasn't in his seat, Ingrid hadn't noticed that they were actually mirrors and not simply more dials. "Also, we're at about max elevation for an airship because of temperature regulation. No one is over us, and if they are, we have viewers at the back that I'm sure Cy will check on sporadically."

Cy took the hint and unbelted again. "Because Cy loves walking like a hunchback through these hallways," he said, deadpan, as he walked past.

"Our next airship will be a Tiamat with nice high ceilings, then, huh?" Fenris yelled back.

"As if you'd trust anyone other than me to be crew!" Cy called. Fenris grunted in reply.

The craft rumbled again. Ingrid rubbed the back of her hand against her forehead. It came away sticky with sweat and blood. Her body temperature, along with the necessary heat of the craft, made her feel swampy. A glint of light caused her to look out of the cockpit again. They had cleared the smoke and another patch of clouds. Below lay the fast oval of the smaller airship. Dark spots—cows, she guessed—moved through the blue miasma that coated the hills. A jagged line in the earth caught her eye.

"A fissure!" she cried. "That's far larger than the one in downtown."

"They're landing!" yelled Fenris.

With heavy steps, Cy returned to the doorway. "Maybe they're meeting compatriots out here? And, Fenris, some of the vents at the back weren't angled right, so the mirrors iced over."

Fenris dismissed this with a flick of his wrist. "It's her maiden voyage. There're bound to be some problems. What's our plan? Are we landing, following . . . ?"

"A ground confrontation isn't in our favor," said Cy. "What weapons do we have? One rod . . . ?"

Lee managed to flare back his jacket enough to show a pistol holstered by his armpit.

"And me," Ingrid added quietly.

Cy nodded. "And you."

"It'll be damn hard to find a mooring tower out here, anyway," said Fenris. "I don't think cattle can manage a tether line."

"What was it you were saying about ground landers before?" asked Cy.

Fenris gave him a quick gimlet eye. "They might crash and burn yet." He checked his mirrors. "However, we've lost our cloud cover, and no one else is in the sky here. If we're going to stand out, let's be extra nosy. Ingrid, can you see anything big and serpentine in that hole in the ground?"

She unsnapped her belt just as the craft made another lurch. She gripped a handle and willed her stomach to obedience as she looked over Fenris's shoulder. The *Bug* had dropped substantially. Trees looked alarmingly close. Fenris pointed straight ahead, and Ingrid forced her eyes that way.

Since she had grown up in the company of geomancers, her only experience with fissures had been in textbooks or moving-picture presentations at the auxiliary. By any scale, this crack in the earth was massive—a minimum of ten feet in width, as broad as twenty in spots. The energy flow here was so potent that blue poured out of the chasm like a waterfall in reverse.

She could well imagine Mr. Sakaguchi and other wardens being outright giddy about such a discovery, but if they had been here, this never could have happened.

"Looks like that's their destination," said Fenris.

She studied the figures that disembarked the craft. Thick magic eddied against their knees. The lead figure was a tall man in a brown suit. Next came a woman with a high coil of black hair, toting a tripod and several other satchels.

"That's Victoria Rossi!" Ingrid looked back and forth from Rossi to the crevice. "Oh! Of course. She wants to photograph the Hidden One."

"Are you saying that they just leveled San Francisco and now they're going to stop and take pictures?" asked Lee, incredulous.

"She already spent the past few days taking pictures all over the city, showing it as it was. As it should be." Emotion choked her voice. "The mayor's graft killed her photography business. She wanted revenge. If she can actually photograph a Hidden One—well, her career would be set for life."

Victoria Rossi had preserved all the beauty of San Francisco on film, and then willingly assisted in its utter destruction. Ingrid's hand curled into a fist as heat bloomed across her skin again.

"That man there might be the one you eavesdropped on at Quist's?" asked Cy.

"Maybe. I never saw him."

Airship turbines churned overhead as another man

debarked. As soon as he stepped onto the ground, a slight blue sheen overlapped his form.

"That's a geomancer!" Ingrid gasped. "It's Mr. Thornton!" Relief left her limp. He was alive and he looked well enough. He wasn't shackled—indeed, he looked dapper as ever. He turned, one hand holding his bowler hat in place, and scowled up at them.

Ingrid's relief was quickly replaced with dread. Mr. Thornton didn't look like a captive. He wasn't a captive.

The man she'd overheard at Quist's had a British accent, and Mr. Thornton . . . He had never fit her image of a Thuggee with his pasty complexion, groomed mustache, natty suit, and a red rose near his lapel. No weighted scarf. No cries of glory to Kali. But the modern Thuggee cause? The fight for his beloved India? Yes. It described him so well, and she had never allowed herself to see it.

Mr. Thornton had been the one who had closed down the basement for so-called fumigation. That's where the bombs had been planted. His car at the workshop had kermanite from the auxiliary vault. It was *him*.

He had boarded his taxi as he left the auxiliary knowing Ingrid would go back inside to die. That everyone he and she knew in the building would die.

And now he had destroyed the city. Destroyed her city.

"They see us!" Lee squealed.

The first man pointed at them with something clutched in his hand.

"And that's them shooting at us," said Fenris.

The airship turned sharply, the window shifting to a

blurred view of brilliant green trees and rounded hills. Ingrid clung to the seat's headrest with both arms. The floor vibrated so fiercely that the cracker tin danced across the floor. Ingrid's teeth rattled together.

"Don't expose the broad side of the ship!" snapped Cy. "It makes us a better target!"

"Thank you for stating the obvious, copilot," said Fenris. "I think you should start looking around for a mooring tower."

"I thought we weren't landing?" asked Ingrid.

"Yes, well, that was before the *Bug* was shot." Fenris remained eerily cool as he checked gauges and popped the binoculars back into their overhead box.

"Shot!" Images from matinee newsreels flashed through Ingrid's mind, of massive conflagrations that burned everyone to a crisp.

She could get them out alive, though. If she could walk Cy beneath the ocean, she could shelter them through a crash landing and fire. Ingrid was stunned at her own calmness. This seemed minor compared to everything else that had happened in the past day.

"We're not losing air." Cy leaned over the panel. "It clipped a horizontal stabilizer on the left side, meaning—"

"We're slightly less horizontal and stable while in flight," added Fenris.

The airship rocked again. From where she stood, Ingrid could see the tension in Fenris's slender arms. Lee emitted a small moan. He was doubled over at an odd angle, his lips moving as if he prayed.

"We could make it to Mill Valley, I think," said Fenris.

"You think?" Lee squeaked, vibrations dragging out the words.

"If we do that, we'll lose them!" cried Ingrid.

"That man hit us with one shot. He's good, a marksman," muttered Cy. His head jerked up. "There! A tower."

The black metal structure stood just across the lot from a domed Russian Orthodox church. It looked to be a converted windmill, rather skinny, but sufficient to dock a smaller-class dirigible. Ingrid guessed they had to be a half mile from the fissure. There were no other vehicles close by. Farms scattered across the hills. By the look of things, there were more cows than people.

"Here's where it gets tricky," said Fenris. "The tower's not staffed. I'll need to drop someone to moor us." The *Bug* hovered over a dirt road. Dust lapped against the trees.

"I can't let Mr. Thornton get away," said Ingrid. "He's not a captive. He did this. The auxiliary. The earthquake. *He can't get away.*"

Cy shook his head. "Ingrid, they already fired on us—"

"Fenris, please," said Ingrid.

"Oh, damn it, don't start with the 'please.' There was a field back there and some trees blocked the view from that crack in the ground. I can probably drop you there—"

"This is suicide!" snapped Cy.

"Mr. Thornton killed almost everyone I know!" Ingrid shouted. The betrayal caused a fierce ache in her chest as if she'd been stabbed again. Heat flickered from her arms. "Maybe this man with him is the one who shot Mr. Sakaguchi! I can make a shield, I can protect myself."

She could hurt these people, too. Out here in the middle of nowhere, she could fling a pressure wave that could knock them all flat and may even ignite the ground lander airship. She *knew* she had the power to do it.

She had always wanted to use her power. Truly use it. Mr. Thornton and Miss Rossi were not getting away.

"If you're going, you're not going alone," said Cy.

She glared. He'd try to stop her. "But—"

"If they're off on a gallant suicide mission, I can moor the ship," said Lee. He unholstered the gun and shoved it at Cy.

Cy's lips curled in disgust but he accepted the weapon and dropped it into a coat pocket.

"Meadow it is, then," said Fenris, bringing them out of a hover and back around. The ship hugged the ground, Fenris's arms rigid as steel as he fought to keep the *Bug* level. The treetops looked so close she could have sworn they'd brush the bottom of the gondola. "Cy, make sure everything's secure since the hatch will stay open."

Wordlessly, Cy stood. He grabbed the tin from the floor and went on down the hallway.

"Hey," said Lee, tapping Ingrid's shoulder. "Do me a favor. Don't die."

She looked at him and remembered who he was, really. "The emperor's son. All this time. I made you scrub the floors."

"You don't know what was funniest about that. Remember your mom's favorite brand of wax?"

It took her a second to recall, then she burst out laughing. "Imperial!" They giggled together.

Suddenly overcome with emotion, she flung her arms

around Lee, remembering at the last second not to squeeze him. "Everything is so strange now, but thank you. Thank you for saving Mr. Sakaguchi. Thank you for being . . . you."

"Don't thank me yet." His voice was muffled at her shoulder.

"He's still alive. He wouldn't be otherwise. The rest . . . we'll figure out." What the Wui Seng Tong would do with Mr. Sakaguchi, how this earthquake might change everything, how to conduct hostage negotiations. What Mr. Sakaguchi and Mr. Roosevelt truly intended.

"We're locked down!" yelled Cy.

"Very well." Fenris looked over his shoulder. "Been nice knowing you both. Don't die."

"It's not on the agenda," Ingrid said.

"Hey, Fenris, don't go up in a ball of flame either," said Lee, heading off down the passage. "Especially when I'm mooring you!"

Ingrid leaned closer to Fenris. "If we don't meet you at the church—"

"Don't even say it." He scowled and faced forward again. "Back at the warehouse, about Cy. I said we've moved around a lot, but that whole thing about him leaving behind a trail of broken hearts? I lied." His shoulders shifted in discomfort. "Now get the hell off my ship. First voyage and my beauty's already dinged up because of you. Go."

CHAPTER 21

Cy stood over the hatch. "Lee, close that door behind you, if you will." He did so. "Ingrid, we'll be about fifteen feet off the ground. I can duck and roll, but you two haven't trained for that. Do you think one of your bubbles would work here?"

"Yes." No hesitation.

"Lee, hold on to her tight, no matter what happens." Cy unfastened some latches on the floor, keeping the stairs secured flat, and came around to Ingrid's other side. "All of us sit down, right on the edge. I'll kick the door open and we'll drop."

Unable to manage words, Ingrid nodded as she sat, her knees tucked against her chest. Lee wedged in beside her, a thin arm clinging to her bloodied waist. Cy barely fit in. His grip on her was as strong as always.

"Go!" yelled Fenris.

Cy kicked the floor, hard, and it gave way beneath them.

The stairs rattled against their restraints. Grass rippled within a sea of turbulent blue fog, and then Cy was over the edge and dragging them with him. Panic spiked in Ingrid's chest as gravity seized her. She drew out power, but instead of focusing it on her feet, she pushed it below her soles. She imagined it like a mattress, something to catch them, cradle them. The ground zoomed closer and then they struck—not the grass, but the invisible cushion just above.

The impact shuddered through her feet as though she'd made a mere five-foot jump. As her skirts flew up and her bottom impacted, she felt a jolt again along the length of her spine. The fog stroked her like lukewarm water. Cy grunted, while Lee managed a somewhat piglike squeal. Neither let go, though Lee's hold was tenuous on her silk obi as he bounced alongside her and stilled.

She let the buffer fall away. Soft, tall grass embraced them, and the heat welcomed her. It curled up her calves in sinuous tendrils, like a hot version of the grass. She'd used enough energy in their fall that the new flow didn't completely addle her brain—not yet, anyway. It wouldn't take much for her to be overcome by energy sickness again.

"That was almost fun," Lee said, scrambling to stand. The grass came up past his knees.

"Good landing," Cy said to Ingrid as they both stood. Without cloud cover, sunlight shone directly down on them for the first time that day. His clothes were crackled with blood and soot. The blotchy red of his face looked strange next to the raccoon rings around his eyes.

Ingrid stepped forward, the heat whispering against her

bare feet. Her terrible sense of dread increased. "I think they may be preparing to attack again. There's so much power here."

Cy grimaced. "We're grounded for now, whatever happens. Lee—"

"Yes, yes. Good luck, be sure to tell Fenris that we might be swallowed up by another earthquake at any time, et cetera. I better see you two in a while. Don't make me come after you."

Lee's worried gaze raked over Ingrid. She offered him a soothing smile, though with the blood on her hair and face, she probably looked like a ghul. He set off across the field.

"What are you feeling from the earth?" Cy asked as they walked. "Should I carry you?"

"No. It's not that bad, not right now." She could see the stiffness in his movements now, the pain. It was a wonder he hadn't killed himself jumping out of the *Bug* back in San Francisco.

"I have a smidgen more kermanite. Let me know when you want it."

She granted him a curt nod. They entered the strip of woods, and from here, they could see the rigid hull of the airship on the far side.

She stopped to press a hand to the leafy duff. The fog of heat ebbed and flowed, as if the earth itself breathed. Her own breaths fell into sync with it. She couldn't even comprehend the majesty of a creature that could create such an outpouring of power.

"It's the Hidden One," she murmured. "The snake. It's really here. I can feel it *breathing* through the ground."

"Will they—it—attack us?"

"I don't know. Maybe there's a reason so few people have

sighted the Hidden Ones and told the tale." Heat increased with each step she took.

Despite the danger of this confrontation, she could imagine the delight on Mr. Sakaguchi's face when she told him that she'd seen a Hidden One in the flesh. She *would* tell him, too. God willing.

Voices rang out. Arguing, loud voices. The airship's engine had been shut off. Ingrid hunkered down low to pass beneath some branches. The miasma lapped against her with a slightly audible electric buzz. There was so much . . . *potential* to it, like a thoroughbred at the starting gate with its muscles bunched in anticipation of the bell. She joined Cy behind the bushes at the edge of the tree line.

"We have to bring him out! Completely out here!" That was Miss Rossi, her voice high and imperious.

"You're a fool. I poked him with a fork in Chinatown a few days ago, and the building almost fell in. You saw what the Hidden One's thrashing did to the city from thirty miles away just now. What do you think will happen with us standing *here*?"

Mr. Thornton stood by Miss Rossi about ten feet from the edge of the fissure, on the far side from Ingrid and Cy. His blue glow had intensified since she'd seen him from above. If he stood on the ground long he'd become ill as well.

"In *Chronicles of the Fantastics,* they say biggest cracks near fault zone mean nearest to head. These heads, they are what I want!"

"They may want you, too—for breakfast, you bloody ninny. Besides, I dosed him with enough chloroform to sedate a Clydesdale."

The third man was silent. He stood tall and pale, a brown tweed suit a bit too loose on his lanky form. He still held the pistol and eyed the sky, clearly their bodyguard. The airship sat behind them. The entrance door was on the side of the craft, with the stairs swung down over the landing tires.

"The cows are alive!" snapped Miss Rossi.

"The cows are a quarter mile away, and more. Even cows have more sense than you."

"Quite the affectionate relationship these two have," Cy murmured.

"He wasn't like that with his wife, but he changed after she died. Became angrier." A sense of sadness weighed on her. "He changed more than anyone realized."

"You two might make the creature rise with the way you go on!" The bodyguard spoke with a clipped British accent, not unlike Mr. Thornton's. "That airship could come back."

Mr. Thornton turned on him. "That airship was probably checking to see if we needed assistance, or wanted to look at the crevasse themselves. There was no call to shoot them and draw attention to us!"

While Mr. Thornton spoke, Miss Rossi whirled around with a flounce of her lush skirts and headed back inside the airship.

"Maybe, maybe not," said the man. "I'm not about to take the risk. They see us, they die."

Cy looked at Ingrid in warning, and she glared back. She wasn't turning back now.

"Except they didn't die, did they?" asked Mr. Thornton. "They flew away. Christ."

"The craft moved strangely fast, even for a Sprite."

Fenris would have preened at that.

"And if they had crashed here, we'd have a plume of smoke to attract everyone in Olema. I'm surrounded by bloody fools."

The man stiffened at that, his gun shifting in his grip.

Miss Rossi reappeared on the stairs of the airship with her arm wrapped around the waist of a tall, frail figure. Long silver hair trailed past his shoulders and blended with a scraggly beard that reached to midchest. He wore a robe red with blood. Ingrid could see fresh patches against fabric that had already been fully saturated. Fainter stripes crossed him horizontally from his shoulders to the blue fog at his knees, as if straps had held him down.

Miss Rossi certainly didn't care about his injuries. She all but dragged the figure down the stairs, treating him like a spoiled girl would treat a doll.

"No!" yelled Mr. Thornton. "Don't let him—"

As soon as the bloodied man's legs made contact with the ground, the earth shuddered.

Caught off guard, the two arguing men were bowled over. Bright blue power boiled up from the fissure and lapped against Ingrid's legs. The bloodied man stood upright as he looked across the divide and straight at her. Azure spirals encased his body.

"Another geomancer." The words were both a whisper and a scream. He pointed straight at her, as if he could see her hidden in the brush. A sharp crack shuddered through the air. Cy grabbed hold of Ingrid's shoulders and shoved down. She dropped. A succession of tree branches crunched to the earth, several larger than entire Christmas trees. Leaves rattled and stilled. The man had lopped off a tree's canopy with a motion of his hand.

"You fool!" screamed Mr. Thornton. "The energy shocked him awake! He's feeding off it!"

"Come out!" called the man drenched in crimson. He paid no heed to Thornton. "You're powerful, too powerful. You glow like the sun. Who *are* you?" He sounded more curious than angry, even as he waved his hand again. More branches crashed to the ground just a few feet away. Loosened leaves whirled across her bare feet.

Cy's hand rested on her shoulder. "Dear God," he whispered.

Ingrid kept staring at the man as she struggled to see through the blue sheen. His sunken eyes. The cheekbones. His dark skin, chalky, perhaps from loss of blood. The way he pulled and contained an abundance of energy from the earth—the way they saw each other, both aglow.

"Come out and say hello," said the man, waving her forward.

His hooks of power latched on to her legs and shoulders, not with pain, but with immense pressure. She jerked into the open, her feet scraping on the grass. Grinding her teeth, she called on her own magic. Her heels dug into ground and created small furrows as she dragged to a stop. She felt the man's sharp intake of surprise more than she heard it.

"Hello, Papa," she said.

CHAPTER 22

Papa.

Captain Sutcliff and Ambassador Blum had been wrong. He was alive. He was here. Papa was more extraordinary than any Hidden One, more mythical. Ingrid could sense Cy coming after her, but she gently propelled him away without a backward glance. Energy rolled from the crevasse and wavered in the air. She breathed in power as she walked into the meadow.

Across the gap, Abram Carmichael stood with his arms dangling slack like a marionette. His head tilted to one side. How alike they looked at that moment, both of them slathered in blood and gore and rippled in blue.

"Ingrid?" The word was a whisper, but somehow it caught in the fog of power and rang in her ears.

"I was told you were gone. Killed in China."

He grinned. It was an ugly thing of crackled blood and missing teeth. "I don't die easily."

Papa's presence, saturated in blood, made everything clear.

The attacks on San Francisco had indeed been caused by him. He was the weapon. His pain had devastated the city, and in turn created a harvest.

No other geomancer could channel energy like Ingrid—no one except her papa. He had at least partially filled the stolen kermanite. That's why the rock had been brought to the Bay Area. It wasn't powering a weapon—not yet.

"Ingrid Carmichael?" Mr. Thornton worked to his feet. The ground quivered. He looked at her in utter disbelief. "A geomancer?"

"Why? Why attack San Francisco?" she shouted at him. To her surprise, the words boomed as if shouted from a megaphone. "How could you kill everyone in the auxiliary? You walked away from the building. You left us there to die!"

Mr. Thornton and the others staggered backward and covered their ears—but not her father. He stood there with a grotesque grin, his teeth bared, dried blood cracked on his cheeks.

Mr. Thornton looked from Ingrid to her papa. Some twenty feet separated them, the ten-foot fissure in the middle. "You can't be a geomancer! You're a woman! I've known you since you were a child!"

Miss Rossi burst out laughing. "Men! Think they know so much."

Mr. Thornton glared at Miss Rossi and then back at Ingrid. "Why destroy the city? Miss Carmichael, have you seen what the Unified Pacific has really done to China? No, of course not. Newspapers and theater reels don't show reality—it's all waving flags and parades here. China is destroyed. Leveled. Ashes and debris for mile upon mile. Farmland is little better, with rivers dammed or contaminated, fields left to desiccation or rot. Britannia will do the same to India, and who will stop them? The Americans? No. Factories in Atlanta are churning out Durendals and dirigibles and painting Union Jacks on them now. Because if the Brits are fighting in India, they won't be fighting the Unified Pacific, and there's money to be made. Brilliant, eh?" Mr. Thornton's lips curled back in a snarl. "My beautiful India. They'd make it a wasteland."

"But why attack San Francisco?" Tears stung her eyes.

"By necessity. This was our first strike, our test. The auxiliary . . . that had to be done first. The wardens would have lessened the impact too much." His expression softened. Sweat made his skin shine as the blue energy thickened over him. "I hated having the others killed, Miss Carmichael. They were my friends, my colleagues. I knew Mr. Calhoun from the time we were boys."

"Yet you killed him first," Ingrid said with a nod. "Arsenic."

"Yes. I had to." Mr. Thornton stared at her, blinking, as though stunned to realize that she had added two plus two. "I thought his experience in India would bind him to our cause. He didn't agree."

"Enough of this!" snarled the bodyguard. He aimed his gun at Ingrid.

A gun fired from just behind her. Blood gushed from the bodyguard's shoulder. Almost simultaneously, he lifted up ten feet in the air, then twenty feet, and hovered there for the space of a breath. Cy's gun certainly didn't cause that.

In a blur, the man slammed into the ground—not dropped, but flung. His body sloshed at the force of the impact, bloody pulp wrapped in tweed. Miss Rossi screamed, high and shrill. Mr. Thornton, awash in spatter, fell backward.

Papa smiled at Ingrid. It was the guileless smile of a child expecting approval. Ingrid's stomach roiled. The cattle earlier had been bad enough. But that was—had been—a man.

Cy stepped alongside her. The earth quivered. "Ingrid, we—"

"Get away from her." Papa flicked a hand. Cy jerked away and landed in the bushes with a terrible crackle.

"Cy!" Ingrid yelled, then whirled to face Papa. "Don't hurt him! He's on our side."

"You can't trust anyone. You're just a little girl. He'll hurt you. They all hurt you." He glanced down at himself. "These people don't even know how to properly torture. The Unified Pacific—now, those people know their jobs. When they used me in China, I didn't even have bruises. Certainly not this *mess*."

Papa waved a hand toward Miss Rossi. She screeched and spun in midair, striking the ground with an audible crack of breaking bones. She moaned and lay still. Ingrid looked to where Cy had landed. She couldn't see or hear him, and if she approached him, Papa might attack again. Her heart galloped. Heat siphoned through her skin. She wavered on her feet.

"Lucas Thornton." Papa stood over the fallen man. "You always were a pompous bastard."

"How can you pull in such power while in so much pain?" Mr. Thornton squealed out the words. "Anyone else would be comatose or dead."

"Oh, Lucas. I'm worse than a cat."

Papa glowed with an intensity that made Ingrid's eyes ache. He opened a hand, fingers splayed like spider legs, and he drew power up in tendrils of blue. He wove the strands, like a Reiki doctor at work, though now she could see the very ki of the earth. At his feet, Mr. Thornton curled up, his hands tucked against his body.

Ingrid had thought she could confront Mr. Thornton. She thought she could kill him. She looked at the mush of bone and flesh, and back to Mr. Thornton.

"Papa, no!" she said. "We need to know what he has planned, what they're going to do with the kermanite. He needs to be alive. The government—we can hand him over." She thought of the worst possible fate. "Give him to Ambassador Blum. She can make him talk."

"Ambassador Blum!" Papa snarled the name. "What do you know about that *thing*?"

That distraction was all Mr. Thornton needed. He lashed upward. The knife caught Papa in the thigh. Arterial blood gushed out in vivid red. Papa crumpled over Mr. Thornton, the two men in a blue knot splashed in blood. With a sharp pop and a gurgle, Mr. Thornton's head flung back, far too flexible for a human being.

Blue dissipated from his body, as if the energy escaped along with Mr. Thornton's soul.

Simultaneously, the earth groaned and shuddered. Ingrid stumbled to her knees. A terrible roar filled the air along with a choking wave of dust. Trees snapped. Ingrid, doubled over, coughed and tried to breathe as a tidal wave of power swept over her. For about a half second, it felt good—deliriously, exquisitely good—and then the heat came, and the scorching fever. She didn't realize she lay facedown on the ground until she tasted grass on her tongue.

Something else roared, and it wasn't the earth.

Ingrid barely managed to raise her head. Through the brown-and-blue cloud rose an elongated shape the size of an autocar. Dust faded to show the ripple of brown scales, the pattern mottled along the spine, and black eyes the size of dinner plates. She *felt* its gaze on her. With a loud, air-shuddering hiss, the other head emerged. It was darker than its mate. The mouth parted and a tongue as long as Ingrid's body slithered out to taste the air.

She had no fondness for snakes, but this being was beautiful. Elegant. She could see why Hidden Ones had once been revered as gods. This felt like a god, with so much power, power that would kill her in steadily accelerating degrees.

"Ingrid." Cy's voice was close to her ear, his hand on her shoulder. "Use your power to throw me over the chasm so I can get the airship."

"What?" Her consciousness wavered.

"Throw me over the gap! Hurry!"

Airship. Escape. Survive. Yes.

Cy stood back. She forced herself up onto her knees. As she had seen Papa do, she drew up strands of blue and grabbed hold of Cy as with a fist. Feathery tendrils, like cirrus clouds, gripped him from shoulder to knee and hoisted him up. Unlike Papa, she didn't fling him. Power swirled through her like a whirlpool; there was no way she could vent it as it flowed in.

Cy was ten feet away, suspended in the air, but she could feel his entire body as if it fit in the hand, like a porcelain doll. His rapid heartbeat quivered beneath a mighty thumb. It would be so easy to *squeeze.*

The fact that she even thought such a thing frightened her. What was this power doing to her? She didn't want to be like Papa. She couldn't be like him. She refused.

Cy's gaze on her conveyed absolute trust. Even his posture conveyed trust. He was scared, yes; he'd be stupid to feel otherwise. Taking a steadying breath, Ingrid lifted him high over the pit and the sinuous snake heads, and to the far side. The snakes showed no interest in him at all. Another quake jolted through her with a slice of power. She gasped. Cy fell. Blackness swarmed her vision, the fever searing her brain.

"No," she whispered. *Don't let Cy be hurt. Don't let him be dead.*

The snake heads roiled, hissing like vents of steam. She couldn't see them anymore, but she knew their movements, just as she sensed waves eddying around her ankles as if she stood on the beach with her eyes shut. A few minutes more and she'd drown. If she truly shared in Papa's resilience against death, the past day must have exhausted all nine lives.

But Cy might be alive. He might get to the airship, get them out of there. She couldn't give up.

"Papa, I . . ." She knew he could hear her, but what could she say? That she missed him? She hadn't; she had Mr. Sakaguchi, her ojisan. But she did wish she had known him, if for no other reason than so she could understand herself, and this power.

"I've been thinking these past few minutes, Ingrid, about the best thing to do. You should kill yourself." Papa sounded so matter-of-fact. His voice echoed like a rattled, broken thing. "Your whole life will be spent running from them, or being tortured to the brink of death, again and again. They'll kill ten people through Reiki to revive you. If you jump into the crevasse, you'll die, and it will be fast."

She knew the shock waves as he stood, tottering like a tree in a tornado. She couldn't see with her eyes, but through the thick magic, she sensed him as if he stood inches away. Blood boiled down his thigh. The sheer heat of him was like a furnace. Frothy red bubbles popped and sizzled as they struck the ground.

"I can still hear them scream at night, the people in Peking. When I sleep. When they let me sleep. I hear the walls crashing down. I hear them dying." Papa sighed. "Nobuo Sakaguchi never wrote the truth about you, what you *really were*. Only that you looked like me. That you were bright.

"If I'd known, I would have come back to California. I would have smothered you in your sleep, back when you were small, innocent. You're too old to be innocent now. You're damned, same as me. The old stories always say gods and goddesses are so powerful. My mother always whispered of the old glory, how it used to be, but the truth is, Christianity is the closest to getting it right. When you're like us, every day is a Garden of Gethsemane. We can plead to God, to people, for mercy, but in the end we're still nailed to the cross."

Ripples of power slapped Ingrid as he walked forward.

"I don't want to die. I want to live," she yelled.

"Do we ever get what we want? Really?" He sounded so fatherly.

"That doesn't mean we stop trying. There has to be hope."

"Ah, Ingrid. You've been around Nobuo too long."

Tears stung her eyes at the thought of Mr. Sakaguchi. She ached for his reassuring presence. She pictured his smile of delight at the sight of the Hidden One. The twin heads wouldn't merely appeal to his academic side—no, he would love them the way a little boy loves his first puppy.

Through the cloud of magic, she sensed as the two massive maws opened wide. The snakes' forked tongues prodded the thick air. Liquid dripped from a fang as long as her arm. But for some reason, she wasn't frightened—not of them, in any case. Ingrid smiled at the snakes in Mr. Sakaguchi's stead, focusing on them as if she could transfer the impression of their might to him through sheer willpower.

The heads shifted. She jolted at the intensity of their four eyes. She couldn't truly see them, but she felt their focus like the heaviness of metal pipes. They stared at her, through her, as if they read her thoughts.

That was an idea.

Hello? she thought at them.

Words didn't pop into her mind, but images. Impressions: *hot rock. sunny day. skin warmed.* Happy thoughts, the things that would delight a snake. Happiness directed at her, because she had somehow initiated contact. Their joy mirrored hers at the thought of Mr. Sakaguchi—of that special bond with someone.

How long had it been since they had spoken with anyone?

She pictured the sun and moon, of trees in all seasons.

In reply, intrusive images pressed on her consciousness. Cold earth, warmed; slickness of rain on skin, and sounds—voices, in a foreign tongue. Natives, unseen, their drums and rollicking rhythms shuddering through the earth to caress the growing Hidden One in its burrow of the San Andreas fault.

She thought at them again, this time picturing Cy. Maybe, with their keen awareness, the snakes could tell her if he was okay. She imagined his kiss, his smile, the way he carried her through the heat and pain. The feel of gratitude and security in the face of agony.

At that, the snakes flinched. The heat against her flared: *pain.* Yes. They knew pain. They knew it, because Papa knew it.

Through them, she comprehended that Papa was dying.

As hot as the air was, his arms and legs were cooling, drained of blood. Papa's brain still boiled with power, even as his life force faded. His thready pulse was a baby's breath against hurricane winds. His spirit was far stronger than his frail, abused body. Mr. Thornton's knife had struck true. Whatever Papa's powers were, they didn't include self-healing. Nor could he communicate with the snakes.

Ingrid knew this by their delight in her presence, even through their empathetic pain with Papa. She didn't detect any malice. They simply *were,* in Zen simplicity.

She had called to the selkies, too, projected her prayer into the depths of the ocean. She could communicate with fantastics. A week ago, that knowledge would have caused her to erupt in delighted giggles and dance about the house. Now the thought of yet another mystery made her weary.

Papa stepped forward. Ripples brushed her skin.

"The killing will continue, Ingrid, despite your fancies. If that old fox Blum knows about you, if anyone knows about you, you'll never have peace. You'll kill and kill. Japanese, Thuggees, Americans. Who holds us doesn't really matter. The result is the same."

Sudden pressure clenched her neck. A final wheeze escaped her throat.

"The world isn't meant for gods like us anymore. Our power doesn't let us rule. It makes us slaves."

Adrenaline flooded through her veins. She grabbed at her neck, her fingers flailing at air. She drew on her own heat to push him away as she had before, but he blocked her throat from within. Her lungs seared in desperation.

The snake heads recoiled at her pain. Their distress penetrated her fading awareness.

A strange sense of sadness broke into her mind, with images:

animal attack. eggs breaking. nest mates dying. stop?

Ingrid replied, picturing Papa. Picturing him as the raccoon attacking the egg.

Silent and sinuous, the snake heads reached out of the fissure. Blood pounded in her ears, but she still heard a slight squawk, a juicy crunch.

The pressure on her released. Ingrid fell over, gasping. The heat around her whirled and flowed and withdrew, like water sucked into a drain. Papa's pain no longer provoked the snakes.

She didn't have the strength to raise her head, but she didn't need to see with her eyes.

The Hidden One was gone. Retreated into the deep recesses of the earth.

Papa was gone.

She was too weary for grief, if any existed at all. Something roared overhead and strangely cool air caressed her feverish skin, but the world was still too hot, and she was so very tired.

CHAPTER 23

Ice pressed against her palms. It burned through her, stark against the heat that sweltered in her veins. Ingrid gasped. She heard herself as if she echoed down a long tunnel, distant and tinny.

"Relax, Ingrid. I have you."

She knew the strength of those hands on her, the fingers large and long enough to encircle her wrists. Cold pressed against her palms again. She tried to orient herself. She faced down. Something dripped from her head and trickled down her nose. Everything was hot. She opened her lips. Liquid dribbled inside. Water, flavored by iron. She might have spit it out, but her parched tongue craved any moisture at all, and spitting took energy she didn't have.

Funny, really. So much energy inside, yet she couldn't muster the strength to spit.

Heat trickled down her hands. Ingrid cranked her eyelids open.

She stared into a chunk of kermanite. Not horse-sized, but like a bowling ball, big enough to power a Behemoth-class vessel. Her body curled around it as if to protect the stone. Cy's hand was inches from her face, holding her fingers secure on the surface. Smokiness whirled inside the clarity of the crystal; half full, perhaps. She could likely fill it.

"Cy?" Ingrid's voice creaked.

"Thank the Almighty. I have water here. Let me lift your head."

She was limp as overcooked udon in his hands. He draped her back onto his lap. Her head lolled to one side. Sleek silver and copper arched overhead—the spines and ridges of a dirigible cabin, one she had never seen before. An engine rumbled, louder than Fenris's ship. Cy cupped her jaw and tilted her head back enough for her to take a sip of water, then more.

"Need to stop meeting like this," she slurred. "You have to keep . . . carrying me around. Taking care of me like a baby."

"A baby who can make men fly and shatter buildings with the touch of a hand."

"Does only . . . so much if I'm too pathetic to even walk on my own."

"I should make a sling for you, like mothers use. Might be relaxing in the long run, like a portable hammock."

She tried to laugh and it came out as a small cough. He helped her take another drink. "Where are we?"

"Hovering over Olema Valley. I was afraid to land until you vented power. I almost sang the full 'Hallelujah' chorus when I saw they had a stockpile of empty kermanite on board."

The auxiliary's stolen kermanite. Everything flooded back

to her. Blum. The horrible earthquake. The Hidden One. Papa.

"The Hidden One, it . . . ate him," she whispered as she crouched over the kermanite again. Heat poured out of her.

"I didn't see it happen. From here in the cabin, though, I heard you and your father talking." He paused. His thumb idly stroked the back of her knuckles. It felt so good she wanted to lean into him, like a cat. "I saw an opera performed years ago, *Mount Sinai*. They had the voice of God boom from a megaphone offstage. That's what the two of you sounded like. Voices of God."

Papa and his talk of gods and goddesses. Ingrid shivered. Mama hadn't raised her to be a churchgoer, but Ingrid still knew blasphemy, and she didn't like to be deified that way. It felt topsy-turvy and wrong.

"When I was little, I always wondered what Papa was like," she whispered. "I rather imagined he was like Mr. Sakaguchi, only he looked like me. Silly, I know."

"You filled in the blanks, Ingrid."

"With a fantasy."

The reality: he would have smothered her in her cot.

That cruelty had always been there. He hadn't willingly slaughtered whole cities, but even so, there was poison in his blood. Was that same poison in her? She thought she could confront Mr. Thornton and make him talk. If Cy hadn't been there—if Papa hadn't bludgeoned him with his power—would she have gone through with it?

"Did you . . ." Cy hesitated.

"What?"

"The question is a mite personal."

She had enough strength to raise her head to look over her shoulder at him. His face had been scrubbed clean but for soft red swirls on his forehead. "Cy. You've seen me in a wide variety of inappropriate situations this week. Ask."

"Did you feel any urge to do . . . to do what he asked?"

Ingrid looked down at the smooth facets of the kermanite. She could see some of her reflection in its clarity—her skin smeared with red, as if with battle paint.

"No," she said softly. "Maybe I should have. Maybe it'd be better for the world if I killed myself. It's selfish to live, when so many people can suffer because of it."

"I've questioned the same thing myself." His fingers curled around hers. "Our minds are weapons, and so long as we have a choice—"

"That's the problem, isn't it? If someone like Ambassador Blum gets hold of us, we have no choice."

"Miss Ingrid, if it comes down to that, the best choice might be to jump." Cy's voice was level. "But until then, we live."

The way he said her name made her shiver in a whole different way. "I . . . I'd like to clean up a little more. If I could."

"Can you sit up?"

Ingrid did.

He moistened a towel at the tap. Ingrid scrubbed her face and hair as best she could. It wasn't a bath, but it felt wonderful to get that horrid stiffness off her skin.

"Do you need anything else?" he asked.

"A favor, if you could come down here."

Cy immediately dropped to his knees beside her. "Yes?"

Ingrid grabbed his head with both hands and kissed him.

There was nothing gentle about how their lips met. They pressed together, sloppy with passion. Off balance, she was suddenly reminded of how weak she was, and tipped forward. He caught her full body against his and cupped her waist with both hands.

Cy kissed back. Oh goodness, did he kiss back. His lips massaged hers, his bristled skin scraping hers in a way that set her nerves pleasantly alight. Ingrid moaned. She wanted this. She wanted him. She wanted to know she was alive and he was alive and people they loved were still alive and that, by God, there was hope in the world.

His hand worked up to cup her jaw and cheek. His callused fingers teased back an aggravating strand of hair. The heat deep in her pelvis had nothing to do with energy or earthquakes and everything to do with him.

Cy came up for air, his breath rattling. "Kisses like that will make a gentleman forget himself."

"Sometimes, maybe it's nice to forget," she whispered.

His lips quirked in a smile. "Maybe. But forgetting right now might be a bad thing, as we're hovering."

"I suppose an airship crash would disrupt the moment."

"There's also the fact you need time to recover. I wouldn't want you to think I'm taking advantage."

Ingrid arched an eyebrow. "I see. So that's how things will need to proceed."

"Pardon?"

"Chivalry is good and fine, but it's clear to me that when we're on the ground and we're not near death again, I need to take advantage of you." She pressed a hand to his chest. It kept her from flopping over, but she also just plain wanted to place a hand there.

His Adam's apple bobbed as he swallowed, and he adjusted his glasses.

"You were saying you need to pilot this craft before we crash and die?" she asked.

"Oh. Yes. I should." He eased himself back from her, slowly, giving her time to balance on the wall instead. The cockpit was about five feet away, just through a doorway. Sunlight reflected on the gauges. This airship was designed in a dark color scheme—cherrywood, steel, black matting on the floor—and stank of cigar smoke and blood. Ingrid crawled a few feet to see if she could get more water on her own, and through another doorway, she spied a hand draping to the floor.

It was Miss Rossi. She was unconscious, her jaw slack and face bloody. Cy had her strapped down in a bunk, and not straps like a harness; no, he'd found a coil of bloodied rope and had her trussed up like a calf. The rope had likely restrained Papa in a similar fashion.

"Ah. I see you found our other passenger." Cy stood over Miss Rossi and Ingrid.

"What are we going to do with her?" asked Ingrid. Dark possibilities danced through her mind and she forced them away.

"See about getting her a doctor. Find out what she'll say about these rebels and their plans. I imagine she'd rather talk to us than to an Ambassador."

"Maybe." Ingrid stared at Miss Rossi and shook her head.

"You know what's funny? She did all of this to get a photograph of the Hidden One, and then she never even got to see it."

The *Palmetto Bug* was not moored in the churchyard. Cy circled the vicinity, frowning, while Ingrid huddled in the copilot's seat. Miss Rossi was still unconscious. Ingrid had downed two imported digestive biscuits and more water, but she was still shaky. Her body had vacillated between healthy and deathly ill too much over the past day. After this, it was clear she couldn't bounce back again. She needed to recover for a week, just as she would from a bout of influenza.

They were on their fifth low pass over the church when Lee emerged from the trees. He motioned them to a field across the way, and Cy landed there. He did so gently, but the jolt still jarred through Ingrid's aching body.

"Stay here," Cy said, a hand glancing her shoulder. The airship's engines wound down with a piercingly high whine. She nodded. Pride was all well and good, but she had a strong hunch that any attempt to stand would end up with her drooling on the floor.

"I was panicked when I saw this ship circling overhead!" Lee's voice carried up through the open hatch. "I watched through the trees and finally saw you piloting. Where's Ingrid?"

"Here," she managed to call, voice hoarse. Lee bounded down the hallway and launched himself against her in a brief, tight hug. Painful as it was, she didn't rear back.

"Christ. You've wasted away in the past hour." Lee stepped away, frowning.

Ingrid rubbed her arms, suddenly self-conscious. She

looked at Cy, but his gaze escaped hers, slippery as a seal.

"And that," said Cy, "goes on the list of things you should never, ever say to a lady under any circumstances."

Lee looked abashed. "I was just surprised, that's all. But you're both alive, and less bloody. What happened? I was going to head to the chasm, but Fenris said it went against my role as a hostage."

"Where's our airship?" asked Cy.

"There's a mechanic down the road. Some farm boys came over and hauled the airship down there. Fenris is doing the repairs in their barn. It doesn't involve deflating, so he says we should be ready to go in an hour. Which is good because the mechanic isn't happy about how Fenris has taken over the place."

"No. Fenris doesn't readily make friends." Cy cringed. "Ingrid, what did you tell the officers at that police station about the attack plans you overheard?"

"That something was set to happen at dawn at Mussel Rock, caused by Thuggees. They didn't listen. They were all too eager to blame Mr. Sakaguchi."

"Maybe the A-and-A did listen. They could have done a flyover. Or they might follow up on leads on local Thuggees. They might know to look for this ship." He glanced around the control car. "We need to clean out the craft as best we can, squeeze their valuables into the *Bug*. We might find out more about their plot. There's additional empty kermanite, too. We can sell off some energized crystals in the next port."

"Like pirates," murmured Ingrid.

"Yes, like pirates." Cy didn't say that unkindly. "I'm sorry,

Miss Ingrid, but from now on, you're living beneath the law. Lee, does that mechanic have room to keep this airship under-cover?"

Lee nodded. Even with his face bruised, he looked so strangely normal in contrast to them; he looked like he did every day when he sauntered into Mr. Sakaguchi's study—his white button-up shirt partially untucked, his too-big beige trousers puffing out where they tucked into his boots. He even had a new yellow patch on his arm. "There's another empty barn I happened to see."

"Good. Maybe this local repairman'll be the sort who'll accept the donation of an almost new ground lander for scav-enging, and stay quiet about us for at least a few hours more. We've already drawn too much attention here, and that crack in the earth will get people talking, even if the Hidden One is hiding again."

"What about Mr. Thornton?" she asked.

"I took care of him."

Ingrid was rather in awe of how casual he was about all of this.

"Thornton." Lee shook his head in disbelief as he turned toward the hall. "Tell me all the details later. I'll run back and tell Fenris you're coming over and—"

"That's the last thing you'll do," said Cy.

He stopped in the doorway. "What?"

"Lee, I know you've been beaten and abused in San Francisco, where they're actually accustomed to the sight of your eyes and skin. You're the enemy, essentially enslaved, but you're *useful* there. That's not so elsewhere."

Cy frowned as his fingers tapped on the wooden chair arm.

"The Chinese were fleeing Chinatown," Ingrid whispered.

"What about them?" asked Lee.

"You said the big *tongs* were leaving a few days ago. Mr. Thornton worked in Chinatown. He used Chinese explosives in the auxiliary. I bet he hinted to the *tongs* that something was going to happen. If your smaller *tong* noticed others leaving, other people did, too."

Cy's mouth tightened. "He set them up to take the blame for the auxiliary explosion, and for the earthquake, too. They look guilty because they knew to leave."

"The bastard framed us." Lee's bruises flushed with anger. "But most of Chinatown didn't know. Most of them stayed. I saw when we flew over. It burned. All of it burned." He looked away, too overcome to speak.

San Francisco had wanted to be rid of Chinatown for years; wish granted. Ingrid blinked rapidly to hold back tears. It was likely that any remaining Chinese enclaves in America would be attacked in retribution.

"Lee," she whispered. "Where was your uncle going?"

"I was supposed to go with them, so I don't know exactly. They . . . don't like to tell me much. I worked with a Japanese warden, after all. North is my guess. Portland, Seattle, Vancouver."

All places that were seismically active, where Ingrid could siphon more energy and cause more damage, too. It was a risk they had to take.

Cy nodded to Ingrid. "Same way we'd head if we want to find Mr. Roosevelt."

"Wait. Mr. Roosevelt? But—he's an Ambassador, even if he was Mr. Sakaguchi's friend. Can we trust him?"

"Does he know who you are?" Ingrid asked.

"It's . . . been implied. He's seen me. Asked about me. But it's never been stated outright."

"Plausible deniability," muttered Cy.

Ingrid pressed a hand to her cheek. "Mr. Sakaguchi said to go to Mr. Roosevelt, but now . . . I don't know. I don't know anything anymore. If I was just risking myself, that'd be bad enough. Cy, Roosevelt thinks soldiering is the highest calling besides being an angel for God Almighty. If he knew you were a deserter—"

"All of us have chips down." His expression was resolute. "Our one certainty is we need to skedaddle from here. If you don't mind, Lee, kindly close up the hatch. We'll fly right to this machinist and get this craft undercover." Cy adjusted some toggles. Engine noise rumbled through the floor. Lee closed the door with a loud clang.

"After that?" Ingrid asked, softening her voice so she barely heard herself above the noise. She rested a hand on Cy's knuckles. He stared down at it, suddenly reluctant to meet her eyes. For a moment, she wasn't sure if he had heard her.

"Fenris'll fix up the *Bug* right as rain and we'll fly out. We need to stop in a sizable port, very soon, and get Miss Rossi to a doctor. After that . . ." Cy's brown eyes met hers. There was heat in his gaze, the sort of heat she wanted more of.

She nodded and stroked the soft skin of his hand. "We'll see what we find in the north?"

He nodded. "We'll see."

The airship lifted off with a lurch and a roar. The view panned over a valley still tinted in faint blue. Beyond that, horrible black smoke smothered the southern sky.

The craft rotated until it faced north, and away. Verdant hills rolled down to the pristine flatness of Tomales Bay. It looked so beautiful and perfect, and so wrong after everything else she'd seen that day. Ingrid breathed in the lingering stench of smoke and blood and closed her eyes.

For the first time in her life, she didn't crave a connection with the earth below.

Author's Note

The world of *Breath of Earth,* grim as it is, has basis in historical truth.

Japan's actions in World War II are well documented, and their motivations for those atrocities stretch back well over a century. Sato Nobuhiro, who died in 1850, called for Japan to form a "world empire." "The ignorant masses of this corrupt age, having been informed of the vastness of China and India on the one hand, while seeing on the other the smallness of their heavenly land [Japan] and the weakness of its power, have been convulsed with laughter when they heard my arguments for unification of the world, telling me that I lack a sense of proportion. They have no awareness that heaven has ordained our country to command all nations."

As a native Californian, I knew that Chinese immigrants were treated poorly, but it was a subject largely ignored in school textbooks and in local histories. My research for this series has forced me to confront the racist history of my state—even my hometown of Hanford—in a direct way.

Chinese laborers, who first ventured to California as part of the Gold Rush, came to be regarded as heathen pests who stole Americans jobs. In the 1890s, Chinese really were forced to carry photo identification cards as part of the Geary Act. The Chinese fought against it in the courts, calling it the "Dog Tag Law." Throughout the western United States, they were subject to harassment, abuse, and outright murder. Justice was not served. The epithets used in *Breath of Earth* are genuine and horrid.

I incorporated many details of the actual San Francisco earthquake on April 18, 1906. Enrico Caruso famously sang in the opera *Carmen* the night before the disaster. Cattle really did rampage through the streets in the aftermath of the quake. Mussel Rock is near the epicenter and Olema is where an incredible chasm opened in the earth. The true number of dead from the earthquake and fire will never be known, as the authorities who released the figures after the fact severely downplayed the scope of the disaster.

Other historical elements are altered significantly. Emperor Qixiang may be better known as the Tongzhi Emperor, the name given to him after his death in 1875. There was no declaration of equality between the Manchu and Han peoples. The Qing Dynasty is remembered as ruthless, corrupt, and extravagant. During the nineteenth century alone, *tens of millions* of people were estimated to have died as a result of rebellions within China.

One of the signature elements of Manchu rule is the queue

style of haircut, also called the bing, which is presented in *Breath of Earth* as a sign of rebellion. In reality, it was a mandatory sign of loyalty to the Manchu Dynasty, and a man's failure to wear a bing was cause for execution.

Some historical and cultural changes in *Breath of Earth* are deliberate. Others are the result of ignorance; I humbly beg your apology for any inaccuracies and omissions.

Research for this series is an ongoing process. I have used many online resources, as well as these books:

San Francisco Around 1906

Disaster! The Great San Francisco Earthquake and Fire of 1906 by Dan Kurzman

1906: A Novel by James Dalessandro

McTeague: A Story of San Francisco by Frank Norris

The Barbary Plague: The Black Death in Victorian San Francisco by Marilyn Chase

Early Twentieth-Century America (General)

Sears Roebuck and Co. Fall 1900 Catalog (reproduction)

How to Shoot a Revolver: A Simple and Easy Method for Becoming an Expert Revolver Shot by Colonel William Preble Hall (with thanks to Walter P. and Donna for the gift!)

Earthquakes and Things That Go Boom

Krakatoa: The Day the World Exploded: August 27, 1883 by Simon Winchester

A Crack in the Edge of the World: America and the Great California Earthquake of 1906 by Simon Winchester

Legends of the Earth: Their Geologic Origins by Dorothy B. Vitaliano

China, Its Mythology, and Chinese in America

Driven Out: The Forgotten War Against Chinese Americans by Jean Pfaelzer

Swallowing Clouds: Two Millennia of Chinese Tradition, Folklore, and History Hidden in the Language of Food by A. Zee

Boxers & Saints by Gene Luen Yang

Samfow: The San Joaquin Chinese Legacy by Sylvia Sun Minnick

Hatchet Men: The Story of the Tong Wars in San Francisco's Chinatown by Richard H. Dillon

Handbook of Chinese Mythology by Lihui Yang and Deming An with Jessica Anderson Turner

Sweet Cakes, Long Journey: The Chinatowns of Portland, Oregon by Marie Rose Wong

In Manchuria: A Village Called Wasteland and the Transformation of Rural China by Michael Meyer

The Devil Soldier: The American Soldier of Fortune Who Became a God in China by Caleb Carr

The Art of War by Sun Tzu

Japan and Its Mythology

The Fox and the Jewel: Shared and Private Meanings in Contemporary Japanese Inari Worship by Karen A. Smyers

Sources of Japanese Tradition, Volume II, compiled by Ryusaku Tsunoda, William Theodore de Bary, and Donald Keene

India

Children of Kali: Through India in Search of Bandits, the Thug Cult, and the British Raj by Kevin Rushby

Theodore Roosevelt

Mornings on Horseback: The Story of an Extraordinary Family, a Vanished Way of Life, and the Unique Child Who Became Theodore Roosevelt by David McCullough

Mark Twain and the Colonel: Samuel L. Clemens, Theodore Roosevelt, and the Arrival of a New Century by Philip McFarland

The Rise of Theodore Roosevelt by Edmund Morris

Fun with Poison

The Poisoner's Handbook: Murder and the Birth of Forensic Medicine in Jazz Age New York by Deborah Blum

A is for Arsenic: The Poisons of Agatha Christie by Kathryn Harkup

For a current reference bibliography, please visit www.BethCato.com.

Acknowledgments

Breath of Earth required intense research into early-twentieth-century California and the hardships suffered by Chinese immigrants. I am grateful for the assistance of folks on Codex Writers who provided information, conversation, and book recommendations that resulted in a novel more grounded in historical accuracy. Any remaining errors are my responsibility, and I beg forgiveness for my ignorance.

After I completed my initial draft of *Breath of Earth,* I was delighted that the Phoenix Art Museum had an exhibit and lecture on namazu-e. This artwork is very rare since the propaganda prints were actively sought out and destroyed in the 1850s. Phoenix Art Museum, thank you for such impeccable timing for this exhibition.

Many thanks to my first readers and initial cheerleaders for the book, Anaea Lay and Rebecca Roland. This project was daunting from the very start and they provided me with a positive boost to keep on going.

This book is dedicated to my literary agent, Rebecca Strauss, but she deserves a bonus mention here, too. She's awesome like that. Much gratitude to the whole crew at DeFiore & Co.

Hugs and cookies to the wonderful folks at Harper Voyager. You made my dreams come true by releasing *The Clockwork Dagger* and *The Clockwork Crown,* and I'm thrilled that we're together for my new series. Huge thanks to my editor, Kelly O'Connor; my magical publicist, Caroline Perny; and so many others there. Sloth power!

Of course, there is my family to thank. My parents, who encouraged me to delve deeper into California history on my own after I kept pestering them with questions that couldn't be answered by my elementary school textbooks. My husband, Jason, who copes with my madness during drafts and revisions. Then there is my son, Nicholas, who has been fascinated by the laminated-and-scribbled-on 1896 San Francisco map on my office wall these past few years. See, dude? I told you it would help me write a book.

About the Author

Beth Cato is the author of the Clockwork Dagger fantasy duology, which includes *The Clockwork Dagger,* nominated for the Locus Award for Best First Novel, and *The Clockwork Crown,* as well as two short stories and a novella in the Clockwork realm. Her novella *Wings of Sorrow and Bone* has been nominated for a Nebula Award. She writes and bakes cookies in a lair outside of Phoenix, Arizona, which she shares with a hockey-loving husband, a numbers-obsessed son, and a cat the size of a canned ham.